THE COLOR OF MURDER

I pulled the old Volvo to the side of the road at the bottom of the hill.

So, he has time to play with the girls.

I climbed from the car into ankle-deep mud. Rain smacked into my face.

And the girls have time to play.

I left the car with the driver's-side door ajar, engine running, interior light glowing, and hiked up the hill through the muck. As I approached the house, I left the road and moved among the trees.

Music and laughter drifted from the house.

Did you ever have dreams that sang to you? Mine are blue.

Death dreams.

"The girl that keeps touching his arm dies," I whispered, staring through the window and wondering if I could get off a decent shot.

Everyone dies sometime.

I pushed myself up from the muck, wiped the rain from my eyes, and struggled through the scrub growth. I found the road, and hiked the hundred yards downhill to the car.

If you would like to draw a picture, I have finished with the blue.

I will be using the red now.

DREAMS
IN THE
KEY
OF
BLUE

John Philpin

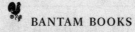 BANTAM BOOKS

New York Toronto London Sydney Auckland

DREAMS IN THE KEY OF BLUE
A Bantam Book / August 2000

ISBN 0-553-58006-x

Published simultaneously in the United States and Canada

Bantam Books are published by Bantam Books, a division of Random
House, Inc. Its trademark, consisting of the words "Bantam Books" and
the portrayal of a rooster, is Registered in U.S. Patent and Trademark
Office and in other countries. Marca Registrada. Bantam Books, 1540
Broadway, New York, New York 10036.

PRINTED IN THE UNITED STATES OF AMERICA

OPM   10 9 8 7 6 5 4 3 2 1

For Elizabeth Frost Knappman

the vacant wide October sky
was my only friend in the end
when I sleepwalked from the stage
and spoke my final line:
my dreams are in the key of blue

PROLOGUE

I STARED AT THE WALL, THE SOURCE OF AN INSISTENT scraping and scratching.

"Mice," the cop said.

I resisted the impulse to smash through the ancient plaster that remained in place only through the grace of generations of wallpaper and artlessly applied paint.

The metallic stink of blood stung my throat and fused with the acrid scent of decay, and the fragrance of citrus fruit.

When cops work a crime scene, they dust with black fingerprint powder, spray magical mists, shine high-tech blue and black lights into sinks and shower stalls in search of blood traces, hairs, skin cells, semen.

They do not spray orange-scented air freshener.

Someone patiently peeled and ate an orange.

I looked from the wall to the floor, where a dark stain stretched like a four-foot, crimson-black Rorschach blot waiting for a subject's response.

A single word nailed itself behind my eyes: slaughter.

My hands were cold, but I sweated in the overheated space. I grew dizzy with the smells and mind-clouds, and the grating racket concealed behind plaster and lath.

Citrus consumed, seeds placed neatly on rind, traces of blood.

The crime scene photographs I was looking through showed a once-attractive brunette, nude, splayed in the middle of the glistening stain. Her throat was sliced—three deep, yawning wounds. Her torso was riddled with punctures.

Then there was the coup de grâce.

"Looks like he tried to cut off her head," the cop said.

I clenched my teeth and swallowed hard.

"This one's name was—"

"I know who she is," I interrupted.

I tossed the glossy eight-by-tens onto the coffee table, crouched, and touched the carmine blemish with my fingertips.

When life ends, some of us pack ourselves in burnished copper cases for a short descent into the earth, others choose to go quickly to ashes, and some are denied choice—abandoned as waste for cleaning crews to eradicate.

"I knew her," I said.

CHAPTER 1

I DROVE INTO RAGGED HARBOR, MAINE, AND FELT AN immediate sense of déjà vu.

The freedom that seemed so illusory to me as a street kid in Boston's Roxbury section, I discovered south of the city on Nantasket Beach in my teens. I prowled the bay side of my seven-mile peninsula, explored each inlet and cove, examined skate eggs, horseshoe crabs, and sand-shark cadavers. Then I shifted my attention to the ocean's infinite rhythms, and probed seaweed and driftwood, new treasures that arrived with each tide change. I met the resident scavengers and predators; I knew the wildly shifting ocean currents, the indifference of an immense and surging sea.

I drove Ragged Harbor's mile-long causeway between mudflats and seawalls, and into the village. The inner harbor on my right was a bay, a haven for water craft. Beyond a cove and a breakwater on the left, the dark Atlantic—my familiar friend—throbbed.

The smell of dead fish billowed from stacks of crab pots. Great black-backed gulls bombed the rocks along the breakwater with mussels and clams, then dropped from the sky to pick at the shattered shells with their orange beaks. A dory rested upside down on a stony beach.

Gulls screamed; sandpipers minced ahead of low tide's bantam waves; terns dove at the cracked shells left behind by the gulls; a cormorant's head and long neck slipped through the harbor's placid surface.

I felt as if I had rediscovered a private paradise, a place where I could continue my lifelong love affair with the sea.

"Why move to Michigan?" my daughter Lane asked when, years ago, I had announced my imminent departure from Boston. "That's nearly midway between the two oceans. You said you couldn't stand the thought of being landlocked."

"Well, that guarantees that I'll be back."

Seven years after that conversation, I drove into Ragged Harbor's village.

The town lived a divided life. A leaning white church behind an erect white picket fence, the general store, a hardware store with gas pump in front, the post office and police station housed in the municipal building—all indicated an old New England community. "Willy's Twice-Daily Whale Cruises," guaranteeing sightings, and "Ragged Ts," each shirt sporting a jagged neck seam, lured summer tourists.

I consulted my map, turned left at the second of the two stoplights, and drove into the community's third identity, the college town.

Harbor College was small, four hundred women on a hilltop with views of the Atlantic Ocean and the cove that served as safe harbor for dumpy lobster and crab boats, fishing trawlers, and sleek cruisers. The fieldstone and wood college buildings, originally a seminary, dated from the nineteenth century. With religious fervor fading in the 1940s, the seminary closed its doors. Progressive educators approached the board of directors and proposed the creation of a small, student-centered liberal arts college. In 1955, the board ceded the campus to the college.

Stuart Gilman, my contact at the college, occupied an office in the administration building, but lacked a title. The short, paunchy, balding man was power-attired in reds and browns, and deceptively satin-tongued. Had it not been for his extensive repertoire of nervous gestures, he would have made a well-oiled public relations drone.

"I've heard that Dr. Lucas Frank is a recluse," Gilman said, bobbing his head. "I was surprised that you agreed to come out here."

"The timing of the invitation was right," I said, feeling not the slightest need to tell him anything more.

During my years as a practicing psychiatrist, I ministered to the ills of the neurotic and psychotic, the personality disordered, and those who were just plain confused. I quickly tired of the "same stories, different faces" routine. Then, when the faces suddenly looked the same, I felt like I was drowning in a mad scientist's genetic sink. It did not help when managed-care companies insisted that they would set my fees and grab quick peeks at my files whenever the spirit moved them.

My work was never interesting or challenging enough, so, on the side, I developed personality profiles of killers, rapists, and any other purveyors of mayhem who drifted my way. Charming, no?

Police detectives became my best customers, as they sought new insights into the crimes and criminals they were charged to investigate. Their municipalities did not pay well, but the work was far more satisfying. Unlike HMOs, cops did not demand monthly reports in triplicate, written in a jargon that sounded like glossolalia emanating from one hell of a Pentecostal bingo night.

But even that work was not enough. I felt compelled to chase the bastards down. Whenever I grew impatient with law enforcement's investigative or interrogative techniques, I developed my own. Most of the time I operated within the law. Sometimes I considered it necessary to . . . improvise. A serial killer doesn't recite a Miranda warning before slitting your throat and disposing of you in six counties. Why should I bother with the law?

There was never any slowing down for me, not until I said goodbye to craziness and said hello to my retreat at Lake Albert in upstate Michigan. I quit the business, took up bass fishing, listened to music cranked loud enough to crack plaster. I confined my communication with the world to a fax machine that my daughter, Lane, a homicide detective in New York City, gave me and insisted I plug in.

In the past few months, I had begun to feel as if my half dozen years of retirement were years spent on the run. Before I agreed to teach a course on gender and serial violence in the women's studies program at Harbor College, I was bogged down in a slough of depression. I had turned my back on the demons that haunted my professional life, and in retaliation they crept up on me, nipped at my backside, invaded my dreams. I was restless, not sleeping well, and suffering from a world-class case of anhedonia—a total loss of interest in the pursuits that I most enjoyed. Translation? I was bored to the brink of a vegetative state. The time had come to declare myself unretired.

"Are you on the faculty, Mr. Gilman?"

"It's Stu. I'm the liaison between MI and the college. Harbor is the primary recipient of the educational grants that MI awards each year. I don't think it's exaggerating to say that this place would fold without our financial support. In addition to the cash we provide, we also own several buildings in town, including the house where you'll be staying. MI is paying your stipend and expenses, of course."

Gilman was not gloating. His tone and attitude suggested that he disapproved of the arrangement. I doubted, however, that he objected to his office, a virtual showplace of the finest leathers and woods, albeit dusty and appearing unused.

"I'm afraid you're way ahead of me, Stu," I said. "What is MI?"

"You've never heard of Martin International?"

I shook my head.

"Huh," he grunted. "It was Melanie's idea to invite you."

"You may as well tell me who Melanie is while you're at it."

Gilman's head wobbled and his shoulders jerked. "Melanie Martin *is* Martin International. She's the company's founder, principal owner, and CEO. We're a small firm, but easily one of the most successful and powerful enterprises of its kind in the world. Melanie insists on serving as a board member here. She monitors the meetings by phone."

Five years ago, Gilman continued, Martin International was nothing more than a $200-per-hour consulting firm specializing in organizational development for a dozen American companies. Melanie Martin was fresh out of Harvard Business School and possessed by a single obsession: to build the most powerful consulting network in the world. The company's operations in Mexico and Canada were natural moves after GATT and NAFTA. Europe always made financial sense. Countries in the Far East, the Pacific Rim, transformed Martin International into a multibillion-dollar power broker for the politicians who regulated the moves and mergers of Martin's former corporate clients.

My quick read was that the company had done the sideways slither from business to politics.

"Our clients don't close deals on anything without MI's . . . input," Gilman concluded.

I was not sure, but I had the feeling that he had wanted to say MI's "approval," then yielded to a late surge of restraint.

Without any effort, I had managed to never hear of a company with the kind of money and influence usually reserved for a Nike or a Disney. I knew what GM and Wal-Mart were, but Martin International was a mysterious Goliath.

I had also never heard of Melanie Martin. She obviously knew who I was. I decided that was unfair and would have to be rectified.

GILMAN INTRODUCED ME TO JAYCIE WAYLON, A MEMber of my seminar, who escorted me to Bailey's Silo, the building that housed my classroom. The red, barnlike structure loomed at the north end of the oval drive.

"It really was a barn," Waylon said. "When this was a seminary, they kept horses there."

"Why did the seminarians need horses?" I asked.

We walked in silence for a moment, then Jaycie looked up at me. "I don't know," she said. "Maybe they just liked to ride. Nobody ever asked me that."

"They should've been reading their Bibles," I muttered.

Jaycie laughed. "You have an unusual way of looking at things."

She was a senior, an attractive young woman whose brown eyes laughed when she did.

We wandered on oiled hardwood floors through the hallways and found the room that Gilman had assigned me. Faculty members stopped and introduced themselves—Ted in tweed and English Lit, shaggy-haired Molly in history, Steve Weld in tie-dye and communications. Most of them struck me as psychologically institutionalized, wondering how students simply drifted through on their way somewhere else, somewhere in the real world.

The students smiled, nodded as we passed each other in the hall, but were not driven by the same compulsion to share names, shake hands, and tell me how many years they had been "on the hill."

My classroom featured fifteen-foot ceilings, dangling light fixtures, radiators that clanked and hissed, a black slate chalkboard, and a wall of windows that offered a view of the harbor islands. The desk-chair combinations were vintage 1950s, branded with the carved initials of subsequent generations.

As we entered the room, Jaycie whispered, "I'll find out why they kept horses."

I was impressed with the students in my seminar. Dawn Kramer, who resembled Sinead O'Connor in her bald period, came to class armed with a copy of June Stephenson's *Men Are Not Cost-Effective.* Like many of her peers, she dressed in jeans, T-shirt, and fleece vest.

"Why should I pay taxes and fees to fund jails and courts and police departments at the same rate you pay?" Kramer asked. "Women are responsible for only four percent of corrections department expenses."

Kramer got no argument from me. The human male's evolution clearly has lagged from when the first Neanderthal stood outside his cave, picked up a rock, gestured in a menacing manner toward his captive spouse, and said, "Cook."

In addition, the male-dominated criminal justice system has developed a lexicon of excuses for women who do engage in aggressive behavior. Even if the courts were to hold women accountable for behavior typically excused as premenstrual, menstrual, post-partum, or menopausal medleys of hormones and emotions, I doubted that women would achieve criminal parity.

Jaycie Waylon, my guide and equestrian researcher, was a tall, slender brunette, a business major who intended to pursue a graduate degree in organizational psychology. "Aggression fascinates me," she said. "I've read about the things that people do to each other and I don't understand them. I've read Konrad Lorenz and some of the other ethologists, but I don't see how we can generalize from instinctual animal behavior to human atrocities. There has to be some other explanation."

"Tigers might get into an occasional territorial tiff," I agreed, "but they don't prey on one another. With the exception of some fish, we're unique in that regard. Hell of a claim to fame, isn't it?"

Amanda Squires was raven-haired and dressed in jeans and a red flannel shirt, the latter unbuttoned to reveal a Patti Smith T-shirt. "I read your last book," she said. "Harry Tower, Stanley Markham, George West. Except for the victims, there weren't any women in it. Aside from references to male sexual pathology, there was very little about gender."

"It's an issue that I've thought about over the years," I said. "I haven't done much with it. I have a few ideas that I'd like to explore with this class, but I hope that the group generates some ideas of its own. Did you want some background on the subject?"

A few heads nodded.

"Researchers have found evidence of varieties of abuse, often sadistic, in the histories of men who behave violently," I began. "They estimate that as many as seventy-five percent of all violent offenders were maltreated during childhood. The theory is that these men experience their pain, then inflict suffering on others."

"Vengeance," Waylon said.

"Or, they've learned violence as a way of dealing with the world. There are many more men who experience trauma and don't become aggressors. We don't know why. Each clinical discipline seems to have its own theory. The general belief about women who kill is that they have turned their trauma inward, and that childhood incidents in which they were trapped, helpless, and repeatedly preyed upon, especially by someone they trusted, caused a fragmenting of personality. Men *and* women dissociate, or split off, feelings and experience. With the predatory male, the splitting seems to assist him in his violence. Women are perceived as candidates for multiple personality disorder, which *DSM-IV*, the psychiatric bible that metamorphoses nearly as fast as the phone book, has relabeled dissociative identity disorder."

"The man takes his pain and lashes out," Waylon said, smiling at my editorial comment, "but the woman collapses inwardly. Both are coping, but managing to survive only in ways that are destructive."

I nodded. "That's a succinct and effective way to put it. I want to add that this gender distinction is a popular view, but I don't necessarily subscribe to the theory."

Kramer cocked her bald head to one side. "Explain, please."

I shrugged. "Most of us experience spontaneous hypnoid states. We continue to function. We don't break into pieces. The best example is 'highway hypnosis.' The mind wanders to pleasant, distant, sensory-rich places, and the mind continues to correctly operate two tons of machinery hurtling through space. We have a wonderful head trip, we don't crash or take a wrong exit, and when we snap back, we've painlessly gobbled up thirty miles of the journey."

"What about the exceptions to the theories?" Squires asked.

"Do you mean someone like Billy Milligan?" I asked,

referring to the famous Ohio case from the seventies, the first verdict in U.S. legal history that validated a defendant's insanity claim based on a diagnosis of multiple personality disorder.

"Milligan suffered from MPD and was also a human predator," Kramer said.

"Aileen Wuornos," Squires added. "She's on Florida's death row, a serial killer who certainly didn't seem like her mind wandered from the task at hand."

"Good examples," I agreed. "Most female serial killers have been caretakers . . . nurses, that kind of thing. Or they've killed relatives. Some have participated, along with predatory males or other females, in what amounts to a symbiotic, or mutually interdependent, relationship. I hasten to add that I don't consider someone like Wuornos an exception. She's a variation on a theme."

"No woman on her own has done it all," Squires observed. "Killed people she knows or is related to, *and* killed strangers, only because she loves to kill."

I hesitated, unsure where Squires was headed. She, like the others, brought eagerness and intensity to a subject that was both frightening and strangely titillating.

"I don't know of a case," I said, nagged by the feeling that I did know of a case but could not recall it. "That doesn't mean it hasn't happened."

Carol Bundy grew to enjoy the sexually sadistic murders of Sunset Strip prostitutes. Tapes of Carla Homolka's Canadian killing spree revealed her pleasure at exercising homicidal power. In Texas, Karla Faye Tucker claimed to have experienced orgasm while wielding a pickax at her one victim. All of these women participated with males in their carnage.

Squires sat up in her seat and leaned forward. "What I'm talking about is a hybrid."

"Yeah," Kramer agreed, "someone so far outside the labels and theories that she defies classification."

"What if I were a serial killer?" Squires hypothesized. "What if I killed people I knew, and also killed strangers?"

"Would that make her unique?" Waylon asked.

"Say that it's lots of people that she does away with," Kramer added.

Squires nodded. "A father who abandoned me. An abusive stepfather, maybe. The people I don't know, don't forget about them. The strangers. I kill them, too."

"Why?"

"Why not? I mean, isn't that how she would think?" Waylon said. "I mean, it's not like she would have a conscience."

"She, my hybrid, is a woman who kills repeatedly over time because she enjoys it," Squires continued. "She knows some of the people she kills, like Marie Hilley did, or Velma Barfield, that woman they executed in North Carolina in 1984, but she also kills strangers, and she's not about to stop until somebody stops her."

Barfield murdered five times, administering arsenic to her victims, including her mother. Until Texas lethally injected Karla Faye Tucker, Barfield held the distinction of being the last woman executed in the United States. Audrey Marie Hilley also preferred the cumulative effects of arsenic and nearly succeeded in killing her daughter. Hilley died of a heart attack before the state of Alabama could complete a final tally of her victims and exact its retribution.

"Off the top of my head, I don't know," I said weakly. "You may drive me back to the books." I was still wrestling with the notion that their hypothetical hybrid existed.

I ended the day pleased at the promise of an excellent seminar. These young people thought for themselves, and would challenge traditional notions about human behavior and motivation.

"HOW DID IT GO?" STEVE WELD ASKED AS WE WALKED together to the parking lot.

"Communications, right?"

He smiled. "An essential field in a civilized society. If only we were civilized."

Weld was a slender man of average height. He was in his early forties, and sported a long gray ponytail and a prematurely white beard. His tie-dye was a Grateful Dead artifact that looked as if he had worn it through a few road trips.

"The seminar went very well," I said. "An intelligent group."

"The kids here are bright. The setting is beautiful."

I followed Weld's gaze at the Atlantic. With clouds billowing across the sky, and the sea surging in swells, the view was worthy of a *Yankee* magazine cover. In the foreground, students crossed the oval from one vintage New England building to another.

"Seems like it should be the perfect place to teach," Weld said.

"You have reservations?"

"Not with the students," he said, returning his gaze to me. "You just got here. Give it time."

"I don't understand."

He climbed into an old Subaru. "You will."

As Steve Weld drove off, Stuart Gilman stumbled from the administration building and walked over. "One of our more disgruntled faculty members," he said.

"Oh?"

"I suppose he was entertaining you with stories."

I did not intend to dive or be shoved into the swamp of

college politics and personal squabbles. "Actually, we were discussing how bright the students at Harbor are."

He shrugged. "Weld can be a negative influence," he said. "Your day went well?"

"Yes," I told him. "I have an excellent group of students."

"Anything you need, let me know," Gilman said indifferently, slipping into his silver Jaguar.

Stuart Gilman and his wheels did not fit on the Harbor College campus. I wondered if he had twitched his way out of the corporate boardroom's good graces and into the make-work position of liaison to the college.

It was after six P.M. when I left the campus and drove into the village. I planned to do a complete shopping, but for the first few days I could survive on my stops at Downtown Grocery.

The small general store was dark and dusty, and reeked of dill pickles and fish. Dead flies and wasps decorated the plate glass window's sill. However, a half-hour drive across the flats and back was out of the question. The village market had the only game in town.

A plump, middle-aged woman whose name tag identified her as Angie stood behind the counter trimming steaks. When I gathered what I wanted and placed the items at the checkout, she turned, wiping her hands on an already bloody apron.

"What time do you close?" I asked, intending to make small talk as she tallied my purchases on an adding machine.

"Twenty minutes ago," she said.

There was nothing subtle about the woman's demeanor. She wanted no part of conversation, and she did not look at me. She completed the transaction, pushed my change across the counter, then grabbed a cleaver and turned to whack at a bloody slab of beef.

I was only days away from the safety, sanctity, and relative sanity of my retreat at Lake Albert, and already I was remembering why I didn't like to venture among people in their natural environment, people who were not in leg irons or otherwise restrained behind electrically charged, steel-barred sliding doors. Humans in the wild were ill-humored and uncivil for no apparent reason.

Shit, they were too damn much like me.

CHAPTER 2

AS I STEPPED OUT OF DOWNTOWN GROCERY, JAYCIE Waylon greeted me. "I thought I was going to have to rescue you," she said.

"From?"

"Angie. She doesn't like people from the college."

"How would she know I had anything to do with the college?"

"This time of year we're the only strangers in town."

Jaycie walked with me to the municipal parking lot. "I can usually get her to crack a smile," she said. "I vowed that before I graduate I'll get a real belly laugh out of her."

"You may have set yourself up to be disappointed," I said.

"I can be very determined."

"Are you originally from this area?" I asked.

"Augusta. Well, I moved there to live with my aunt when I was eight. My parents were killed in an automobile accident. We had a little farm in Canterbury, New Hampshire."

"I'm sorry," I said.

"So am I. My parents had great plans for the farm. They saved their money and paid cash for it. I haven't been back. At first it was because people didn't think I should. Now it's just so long ago. You're originally from Boston, right?"

"I was a permanent, if not proper, Bostonian, until about seven years ago."

"Then you dropped out."

"Then I dropped out," I agreed.

"How come you don't talk like Ted Kennedy?" she asked, doing her best imitation of a Boston accent.

"Both my parents were from Scotland. Until I was in my twenties, I had a wee bit of a brogue."

She laughed. "I think you still do."

We arrived at my Jeep.

"MI gave you the house on the hill, right?"

"My directions tell me to turn left on Atlantic Hill Road."

"Make sure you check out the view of the ocean from the bluff."

I DROVE UP THE DIRT ROAD TO MY TEMPORARY GIFT—A modest, light blue Cape Cod overlooking Ragged Harbor—from, as Stu Gilman had informed me, and Jaycie had confirmed, Martin International.

I unlocked the house, inspected the interior briefly, then sat in a rocker on the front porch and sipped a bottle of Shipyard Goat Island light ale. Whoever had equipped the place for me was familiar with my personal tastes. I had found a dozen bottles of the brewed treasure waiting for me in the refrigerator.

I hoisted my legs onto the porch rail, leaned back, and stared into the scrub growth across the road. A battered gray car passed, headed up the hill. The driver, with his ball cap turned backward on his head, waved. I returned the gesture, wondering where he was going. Mine was the only house on the dead-end road.

At home on Lake Albert, traffic had limited itself to an occasional passing boat, or a four-legged guest on my fenced ten acres. When I quit the business and left Boston, I had retreated into isolation. Only now had I reluctantly reentered the crazy world that I watched grow around me.

"The kid probably likes scenery," I muttered, remembering Jaycie's promise of a panoramic view of the ocean and the outer islands.

I had been sitting on the porch for fifteen minutes when the light breeze that blew off the water threatened to become a bone-chilling squall. Dark clouds tumbled inland, and a hard rain pelted the maple trees and showered down a scattering of leaves in the shades of late autumn's dead and dying colors. It was a frigid rain, and the offshore wind gained force.

"God, that came up fast," I said as I slammed the door behind me.

I stacked pieces of beech and maple on the fireplace grate, over the newspaper and kindling that someone from the college maintenance department had thoughtfully left for me. I put a match to the paper and watched it flare, then settle into a crackling collage of colors and warmth.

The sound of the car returning down the hill distracted me. I turned and saw the old Volvo slow in front of the house, then accelerate and disappear from view.

"Guess the storm drove you away, too," I said.

I popped the cap off another Shipyard, switched on the radio and found a station playing the New England jamming band Bruce, and sat on the edge of the raised hearth. I felt the fire's heat on my back, sipped my cold brew, and listened to "Dennis the Wolfman," accompanied by the clatter of rain against the house. I could have remained like that for a long time, but a car pulled into the driveway, followed by a pounding on my door.

"Might as well live in Manhattan," I muttered as I opened the door to four guests.

"We ran from the driveway," Jaycie Waylon said. "We still got soaked."

She handed me a shopping bag.

"That's Sara Brenner," she said, pointing at a smiling young woman whose black hair was as bedraggled as her wool shawl. "She sits behind her hair in class."

Sara waved.

"Kai Lin is nearly dry," Jaycie said, indicating her second friend, "because she remembers things, like bringing an umbrella when it's raining. If you examine her closely, you'll see that she's also wearing waterproof shoes. Kai Lin had a schedule conflict so she couldn't sign up for the seminar. And you know Amanda Squires. She's our thinker and provocateur."

"Drag some chairs near the fire," I said. "I'll find a few towels."

"We're the unofficial Harbor College welcoming committee," Sara called.

Jaycie traipsed after me to the hall closet. "I hope you don't mind us inviting ourselves over."

I glanced at her, thinking how much she reminded me of my daughter Lane as a college student.

Jaycie held up her hands. "I know. If you minded, you'd say so."

"Right," I agreed. "Besides, after our conversation this afternoon I half expected a home intrusion."

We returned to a semicircle of chairs near the fire. The students decorated the hearth with two pairs of saturated tennis shoes, one soggy shawl, and a damp windbreaker.

Sara pointed at the shopping bag. "Jaycie read some-where that you liked microbrewed ale, so that's what we got. The corn chips are just corn chips, but the salsa is amazing."

"Why do I sense heartburn in my immediate future?" I asked.

Kai Lin reached into the bag. "Hot," she said, holding up one jar, then lifting a second. "Mild."

"I'm relieved."

"There are some Tums in there, too," Sara added. "Amanda bought them, but I'm sure she'll share."

"Thinkers are prone to acid indigestion," Kai Lin said.

"This is for you," Amanda said, handing me a narrow white box. "From the unofficial welcoming committee."

"This is very kind," I said, opening the box to reveal a carved ivory letter opener.

"Oh, it's scrimshaw," Jaycie said, peering over my shoulder. "Good choice. Can you explain the etching?"

I glanced at the shipwreck scene that decorated the bone blade.

"The story's a downer," Amanda said. "I'll tell you some other time."

I examined the delicately etched whalebone. Its fine lines depicted the drama of a whaling ship yawing in wind-blown seas, its harpooned catch, a sperm whale, harnessed precariously on the starboard. A giant sea serpent, jaws wide, fangs bared, loomed behind the tableau, ready to devour the ship, whale, and crew.

"This is magnificent work," I said. "I will want to hear that story sometime."

Kai Lin opened chips and salsa, Sara used her pocket-knife's bottle opener to snap the caps off four ales, and Jaycie rubbed her wet hair with a bath towel.

"Doesn't the college frown on this sort of fraternizing among faculty and students?" I asked.

"Harbor College is a liberal institution," Sara said with a smile.

"Which means," Kai Lin added, "they don't care what anybody does so long as they pay their tuition."

"We wanted a different course offering," Sara said. "We also wanted somebody from outside the college to teach it."

"We nearly got wrecked driving up here," Jaycie said. "Some idiot coming down the hill wanted the whole road."

I thought of the young man with the backward ball cap in the small gray car.

"Townies don't like Harbor girls," Sara said.

"Let's not get into that," Kai Lin said. "Whose idea was the seminar?"

" 'Gender and Violence' seems pretty radical even for Harbor," Sara agreed, and added, "Dr. Frank's beer has the smiley face."

"The board member from MI who gives all that money to the college," Amanda said. "What's her name? She like owns the company or something."

"Melanie Martin," Jaycie said.

"Didn't you have an internship there?" Kai Lin asked.

"Still do, but I've never met Ms. Martin."

I added a log to the fire, then returned to the circle, where my ale grinned an orange grin at me. I grimaced.

"I know he likes the ale," Jaycie said. "Must be he doesn't like smiley faces."

"You've got it," I said. "They're from the soporific seventies, symptomatic of the entire decade."

I peeled off the minimalist design and stuck it on the hearth.

"What interests you besides murder?" Jaycie asked.

"Well, I'm a fishing fanatic," I said, sipping ale. "I enjoy reading a good mystery."

"I love mysteries," Sara said. "Who do you think writes the best mysteries today?"

"No one," I said with a laugh. "My favorites are the Nero Wolfe stories by Rex Stout."

"Wolfe's the one who weighs a seventh of a ton and wears yellow silk pajamas," Sara said. "I read some of those."

"That's nearly three hundred pounds," Kai Lin offered.

"Good math," Jaycie said. "What else do you like, Dr. Frank?"

"Music."

"Classical?" Sara asked.

"He was listening to Bruce when we came in," Jaycie said.

For an hour the conversation bounced from their questions about my interests, to their interests, to life, politics, and the universe. Sara was firm in her belief that President Clinton did not suffer from a sexual compulsion. "He's like any other guy," she said.

Kai Lin found Newt Gingrich far more psychologically interesting than Bill Clinton. "He's a totally different species," she insisted. "He says he resigned for the good of the nation and the good of his party. Don't get me started or you'll have to wash out my mouth with soap."

Jaycie lamented what technology was doing to the business world. "All the old sci-fi is coming true," she said. "Watch the drones file into the office building and march to their cubicles. I'd rather work on an assembly line. At least then I could shout to my neighbor."

Amanda Squires, the group's thinker, had little to say. She sipped ale, dipped chips, and observed.

"What about the serial killer in Washington State, Dr. Frank?" Kai Lin asked. "He's killed mostly in Spokane, but also across the state in Tacoma."

"I doubt that Dr. Frank wants to talk business," Jaycie said.

"You get to ask him in class. I don't."

I shrugged. "I'm not familiar with the case."

"His victims are women . . . drug addicts, prostitutes, street people. The police haven't said much about what he does to them, except that he shoots them execution-style. That's unusual for a serial killer, isn't it?"

I hesitated, and carefully chose my words. "A gun is not a common choice of weapon for a serial murderer, but I think that how this killer's choices are statistically different is less important than what the manner of killing means to him."

"A gun is noisy," Kai Lin said. "It can be traced."

"Which suggests something about the killings," I said, "and raises a question about the killer. The women were most likely killed in isolated areas, and the shooter isn't concerned about the gun being traced."

"What does it mean to him?" Sara asked.

"We could state generalizations about weapon choice, but without knowing much more, we can't be at all specific."

"Police experts say the killer has some legitimate reason to be traveling from one end of the state to another."

"They know more than we do," I said, "but killing might be reason enough."

"The article I read also said that killers who target prostitutes are street people. They don't look out of place. They fit in with the scene, so nobody suspects them."

"That's one possibility," I agreed.

"What's another one?" Kai Lin asked.

I thought of my experiences in Boston's "Combat Zone." "Cops, military personnel, college kids out for a night on the town."

"They think he spends time with his victims before he

kills them," Sara said. "I know. They know more than we do. The same expert said that criminal profiling is a science that's based on comparing the patterns of known serial killers with a particular case."

"Which explains why no profile ever caught a killer," I said.

"Do we have to talk about this now?" Jaycie asked.

"Just this one thing," Amanda interjected. "You've caught killers. How do you do it?"

"Short answer," I said. "I don't want to spoil the party."

Amanda agreed.

"Everything we do reveals something about us. Regardless of whether we want it to, our behavior always communicates. Archeologists learn the history of past cultures from their remnants. I examine behavioral traces at a crime scene and learn the history of a personality."

"But that's so insubstantial," Sara protested. "How do you make the jump from personality to a person?"

"It has to do with the way Dr. Frank looks at things," Jaycie told Sara, "and the questions he asks."

Then she shifted her attention to me. "When our seminarians weren't reading their Bibles, they bred and boarded horses to help pay for their education. I told you I'd find out. Now can we talk about something else?"

Jaycie Waylon was a bright, clever young woman whose sense of humor, and the accompanying sparkle in her eyes, delighted me. One of the reasons I had snapped up the offer of a temporary teaching position was to be among young, inquisitive minds. Jaycie epitomized the type of student I had imagined.

Our party wound down shortly after ten, and my guests departed, leaving me with a smile and a good feeling about abandoning my Michigan sanctuary.

CHAPTER 3

I PULLED THE OLD VOLVO TO THE SIDE OF THE ROAD at the bottom of the hill.

So, he has time to play with the girls.

I climbed from the car into ankle-deep mud. Rain smacked into my face.

And the girls have time to play.

I stared at a chain-link fence across the road.

In the place where they forced me to live, the walls were brick and tall. Gargoyles crouched on cornices, their concrete shoulders hunched, teeth bared, fingers splayed, as if they were about to pounce. Steel screens covered the windows. Circles of razor wire topped the chain-link fences, row after row.

"There's no way out," the attendant had said when he found me with my face pressed to the screen.

I believed that if people could get in there, they could certainly get out.

No one sees the same world that anyone else sees. What is inside must sometimes be outside.

I made myself small, nearly invisible. No one noticed me. I vanished, sometimes even from myself.

Now, I checked the clip on my .22 semiautomatic and slapped it into place.

I left the car with the driver's-side door ajar, engine running, interior light glowing, and hiked up the hill through the muck. As I approached the house, I left the road and moved among the trees.

Music and laughter drifted from the house.

Time, fucking time to play, all the time in the world.

Did you ever have dreams that sang to you? Mine are blue. Spilled blood surges through them like raging red cascades.

Death dreams.

Scenes from a slaughterhouse set on indigo.

These screaming mind-scrawlings and their flutish, stringy, percussive soundtrack are my concerto of reciprocation. If you wound me, you die.

He fucking wounded me. She pisses me off.

"The girl that keeps touching his arm dies," I whispered, staring through the window and wondering if I could get off a decent shot.

"Off with their heads," a voice crackled behind me.

I spun around and saw nothing but spruce and white pine and barren beech. The trees crowded me like ghostly guardians. The fall of rain hissed and snapped through the trees.

Then, as if an echo, or a distant voice in the forest, or a whisper, the voice came again.

"Off with their heads."

I ran through the woods, sliding and falling into the mud. "I'll kill all of you," I screamed into the night.

I stayed down, feeling the mire soak through my clothes and soil me. Today, tonight, the blackness, the rain—I have waited all days for someday.

No one answered my scream. There was no echo.

I had learned to never expect an answer. Voices arrive only when they are unsolicited. They make me angry.

I see slash-and-burn images in colors that do not exist. I hear echoes of sounds that I never sent into the world.

Coming back to me.

I saw him. He's so fucking old.

I wanted to live on Pleasant Street, but it's much too late for that.

Instead, I spawned an appetite for murder. Then I nurtured it, like you nourish a complicated thought sequence as you struggle to bring it to fruition.

Closure.

Everyone dies sometime.

When you fail to touch me, and I want—need—to be touched you have given me the only license that I need.

When I was a child, my stepfather punched my mother so hard that she heard echoes inside her head. She felt nothing after the first blow, and if she saw the first one coming, she didn't feel that, either. She never struggled. She knew there was nothing she could do.

He used his knife to let her know what would happen if she told anyone. He always drew blood—nicked her on the arm or the leg. She has scars all over her body.

So do I.

I pushed myself up from the muck, wiped the rain from my eyes, and struggled through the scrub growth. I found the road, and hiked the hundred yards downhill to the car.

If you would like to draw a picture, I have finished with the blue.

I will be using the red now.

CHAPTER 4

I SPENT SATURDAY MORNING ARRANGING MY TEMPO-rary living quarters to my liking. A seascape that looked as if it had been sold out of the back of a van parked on the side of a highway, had to be closeted. I trashed the bath-room night-light, a hollow plastic rendition of a dashboard deity, then tossed the blossom-scented soap and placed a bar of Ivory in the soap tray.

The study also required attention. The last visiting professor to occupy the house must have been a writer, or at least a teacher of writing. At eye level beyond the desk was an entire shelf of how-to books—everything from character and plot to selling that first novel—volumes dedicated to homogenized expression.

"Wonder if Anne Sexton read this shit," I muttered as I swept the paperbacks into a carton.

When I finished with the shelf, it held a small stone carving of an African lowlands gorilla that was a gift from my daughter, a photograph of Lane and her mother taken on Lane's recent trip to Congo, a stack of CDs, and three books: Reid Meloy's *The Psychopathic Mind*, volume four of *The Collected Papers of Milton H. Erickson on Hypnosis*, and Mary Beth Rogers's *Barbara Jordan: American Hero*.

At noon, Jaycie Waylon stopped by and invited me to lunch. "There's this great little Portuguese restaurant on the flats," she said. "They make the most incredible fish sandwiches."

"I'm sold," I said, and grabbed a jacket.

"My motives are not entirely honorable," Jaycie said as she drove north on the causeway. "I have some questions."

"Quest away," I said, enjoying the view. "I assumed you had an agenda."

"Did you work on other kinds of cases besides murder?"

"A few. What do you have in mind?"

"White-collar crime."

I glanced at her. "One case," I said.

"You don't sound like it was the high point of your career."

"A bank retained me through an intermediary. My job was to examine several death threats sent through interoffice mail to a bank officer, to provide a personality assessment, probable motive, and assist them with focusing their investigation. When I realized that I hadn't received all the information, I called my contact. Some of the threatening notes had been withheld because they alleged sexual involvements by the officer, dalliances which the bank deemed irrelevant to the case."

"That should have been up to you to determine," Jaycie said.

"I returned their materials and quit."

"Do you think it was blackmail?"

I shrugged. "Never gave it another thought. I also never worked for a private corporation or a federal agency after that. It's too much like trying to work a jigsaw puzzle that the cat's been using for a sandbox."

Jaycie laughed. "What an image."

"Why do you ask about white-collar crime?"

"I'll explain over lunch," she said, pulling into a gravel parking lot in front of what appeared to be a shack on stilts leaning precariously over the mudflats.

A small, paint-flaked sign said only "Nuñez Fish."

"What it may lack in aesthetics, it more than makes up for with its food."

"I was thinking of architectural soundness. Let's find a table on this side of the building. I don't want to share my dessert with the clams."

The ambience was fishnet and buoys—seafaring in cramped quarters. My haddock sandwich on a homemade roll was everything Jaycie had promised.

"Told you so," she said.

"What's the salad dressing?"

"Olive oil, tarragon. Oh, that's right. You're a food freak."

I laughed. "I think I might phrase it differently. How do you know so much about me?"

"When I heard you were coming to Harbor, I did some research, mostly on the Internet."

"You mean that my love of food is floating around in the electronic ether?"

"That and a lot more."

"My life is an open byte," I said. "You wanted to ask me about corporate crime."

She wiped her mouth with her napkin and shot glances around the crowded restaurant. "When I was a sophomore, before I got my internship with Martin International . . ."

At that moment, Stu Gilman walked into the restaurant. He spotted us immediately and made his jerky way to our table.

"God, I don't believe his timing," Jaycie said.

"Lucas, Jaycie," Gilman said, with head bobs that might have been greetings or minor seizures. "Beautiful day. Enjoying lunch?"

"Excellent food," I said.

Jaycie said nothing.

"Showing Dr. Frank our eateries?" he asked.

Her face reddened. She smiled, nodded, and re-arranged the few remaining home fries on her plate.

"Well," Gilman rumbled in a lower register, "gotta get my lobster roll. Enjoy the day."

Jaycie watched Gilman waddle to the counter. "Let's go," she said.

She was silent as we drove to the village.

"Gilman rubs you the wrong way," I said.

She hesitated. "Yeah."

"Anything you want to talk about?" I asked, leaving the option entirely to Jaycie.

After a moment she said, "I guess not."

"What about sophomore year?"

"Not that either, I guess."

I nodded. I liked Jaycie Waylon. That may sound like an odd statement, but I don't like many people.

Gilman's arrival at the restaurant had startled and si-lenced Jaycie. Whatever distressed her would eventually surface, I thought. She had assumed the role of my per-sonal guide to the school and the village. We would have other opportunities to discuss white-collar crime.

Jaycie dropped me at the house, then headed to her Saturday class.

I completed my reclamation project on the house, and curled onto the sofa with pen and pad. The class had al-ready suggested directions for itself: aggression, the male propensity for aggression, male sexual pathology, the poli-tics of gender, theories of serial violence, and exceptions to the theories.

All I had to do, I thought, was put a little meat on the bare bones, and I had the next five months knocked.

CHAPTER 5

I HATE SUNDAYS.

When I was young, church was mandatory. The minister was a gentle, wise Frenchman who seemed to know something about everything. The building was an architectural dream, a stone mini-cathedral perched on the bank of a river. That my attendance there on Sundays was required was an abomination.

My mother issued the order; my sister enforced it.

"Why do I have to?" I whined.

"Ma says," my sister said.

"That's not a reason."

"Change your pants."

"If Ma said, 'Chop off your brother's head,' would you do it?"

"Where's that blue sweater I like?"

Even the light was different on Sunday. It flooded the living room—yellow, dull, dusty.

"It's holy light," my sister said.

"The air is putrid," I muttered.

My sister took my hand. "We'll be late for the bus."

Now, years later but with the same Sunday angst, I yanked on my jeans, grabbed a flannel shirt, and shuffled in my moccasins to the kitchen to make coffee. I gazed through the window at the overcast day and watched as an unmarked police cruiser pulled into the driveway.

Herb Jaworski was a short, two-hundred-pound man whose curly hair remained black, despite his sixty-five years. He arrived at my door attired in coveralls and a red wool jacket. During my few days in Maine, it had become clear to me that this was "the Maine uniform." It was also the uniform of the Ragged Harbor Police Department. Jaworski had been chief of the small-town police force for thirty-two years.

That morning, he stood on my porch, hat in hand, and said, "I've heard of you, Dr. Frank. In fact, I read one of your books, *Crime Reconstruction and Personality Profiling*."

I assumed it was a social call. "Come in. We can talk over coffee."

The chief shook his head. "We don't get too many murders here," he said as he stood on my porch, fidgeted with his navy watch cap, and shifted his ample weight from one lug-soled boot to another. "When we do, we get good support from our state people. This situation has stretched all of us pretty much to the max. We don't know what the hell we're dealing with."

I raised an eyebrow and waited for him to latch on to a coherent thought. He didn't.

"Chief, I'm afraid I'm not following you," I told him.

"It's been all over the TV."

Jaworski's tone and facial expression communicated pure astonishment. How could I not know something that had been defined as reality by the tube? If Tom Brokaw says it is, *it is*.

"I don't watch much TV," I told him. "There isn't one here."

"Well, I talked it over with some folks in Augusta.

They checked you out, said there wouldn't be any harm done if I could get you to take a look at this."

The chief's circumlocution amused me, but I figured it was time to put him out of his misery and get to the point.

"Just what have you got?"

I never should have asked.

I DRAGGED OVER A CHAIR, SAT, AND STARED IN HORROR at two bloodstained beds.

In every other way, the room resembled any room occupied by college students. The twin beds were separated by a scarred oak desk. A second desk, with bureaus on both sides of it, squatted against the opposite wall. Both desks held computers, stacks of books, papers, and spiral-bound notebooks.

But this room wore rust-colored smears on its walls, and there were coagulated pools of black blood in the bedding. The students, now and forever to be known as victims, had departed in zippered bags.

They left as packaged people, I thought.

Technicians carried vials and plastic Baggies in and out of the apartment. Uniformed cops measured and sketched.

"Give me the photographs," I said, reaching behind me, never allowing my eyes to move from the evidence of the carnage that someone committed there.

"Susan Hamilton, twenty years old," Herb Jaworski said, placing a folder in my hand.

I sat surrounded by the trace evidence of homicide, and examined the crime scene photos.

"The medical examiner says seven perimortem and postmortem stab wounds," Jaworski said.

"While she was dying and after her death," I mused. "The gunshot killed her."

"Twenty-two caliber, copper jacket."

I looked at the photo of the small hole in the young woman's temple, then studied each of the remaining photographs in the series. Even gray and dead, Susan Hamilton appeared younger than her twenty years. Her face wore the expression of someone at rest. There was no paroxysm of pain. There was the small black hole, probably an immediate absence of consciousness, then death.

"He pulled back the blanket and the sheet, then did his cutting," I said.

"That's the way we figure it. No holes in the bedclothes."

"Then he pulled up the blankets, threw them over her."

"Even covered her face."

Was the killer ashamed? I wondered. Did he attempt to conceal the evidence of his havoc? If he could not see the dead girl, maybe she was not there. Perhaps he did not want Susan staring up at him.

"What about the blood on the wall?" I asked.

"Don't make any sense."

I stared at the wall on my left, at the streaks of dingy red that originated three feet above where Susan's head would have been and descended downward at a sixty-degree angle.

"No prints apparent in the smear," I said. "Probably wore latex gloves."

Like somebody playing with watercolors. Picasso gone wild with the sweep of a single-hued rainbow.

"The bed wasn't moved?"

"Not that we could determine."

I reached across the bed to the wall and touched the Sheetrock a foot above the blood trail. Then I looked again at the smear.

"There's a break here," I said. "It's as if his hand

twisted or slipped. There's an imprint that looks like knuckles. Do you have a tape measure?"

Jaworski handed me a six-foot cloth measuring tape.

"It's an inch and a quarter between the two points," I said, then measured the distance between the first two joints on the index finger of my left hand. Two inches.

"Probably should photograph these impressions with a crime scene measure," I suggested.

Jaworski made a note. I looked again at the photos of the dead student and asked if the police had determined what she was doing earlier on the night of her death.

"Susan had a paper due in the morning," he said. "She logged off her computer a few minutes after midnight. That was late for her."

Jaworski made a clacking noise with the cinnamon gum he was mawing as he handed me another set of photos. "Kelly Paquette, nineteen," he said.

I turned to my right and made a cursory examination of the bed and the wall. It was a mirror image of Susan's side of the room.

There is no interruption in the streak of crimson on the wall.

"Window dressing," I muttered, staring at the bands of red. "Dead kids don't smear their own blood."

"We know she got back from a date around two. The towel on the floor was damp. She showered, then went to bed. Blood alcohol concentration was point-one-three. She was blitzed. The bullet entered behind her right ear. Seven stab wounds."

Kelly faced the wall, but the intruder covered her anyway. Was this a pathological need to conceal?

I examined the remainder of the photographs, then returned them to Jaworski. "Show me number three."

I suspected that the murders were Jaworski's most painful professional experience in all the years that he had been a cop. He struggled to maintain his poise, and he did a decent job of it, but he hurt.

"I heard somewhere that you guys prefer to go through a crime scene alone, that you need to be able to concentrate or something."

"You've been reading too much bad fiction," I said, following Jaworski into the living room.

A shelf stereo sat on the fireplace mantel, surrounded by stacks of CDs, everything from the Butthole Surfers to Beethoven. I crouched at the coffee table to examine a rental video's opaque plastic container.

"Who rented the movie?" I asked.

The chief consulted his notes. "I don't think we checked that."

"It's *Kiss the Girls,*" I said, "an unlikely story about a pair of killers who work in tandem on the two coasts. I'm a Morgan Freeman fan."

"You watch that stuff?"

"I enjoy catching Hollywood's psychological inaccuracies," I said as I glanced at unopened mail, a five-day-old copy of the *Ragged Harbor Review,* and a pile of orange peels. "Films like this one are today's morality tales. Who ate the orange?"

Again, Jaworski flipped through his notepad. "I don't have that, either. State folks figured the kids watched the movie, one of them ate an orange."

"Any of the victims have finger cuts?"

"No," he said, pleased to give me a definitive answer.

"There's blood on the orange peels."

Jaworski was quick. "After he killed these kids, he sat there and ate a fucking orange?"

"Have the blood checked."

I walked into the kitchen and opened the refrigerator. "No oranges," I said, distracted by the scent of citrus and a vague notion that it held some significance.

"He brought it with him?"

"That's one possibility," I told him, still trying to get a handle on an elusive association to oranges.

I followed Jaworski through the living room and stood at the second bedroom's doorway. He handed me another stack of photos. The top one showed a once-attractive brunette, nude, splayed on the floor outside her bedroom. I stared at her face, her eyes, the startled expression.

I clenched my teeth and swallowed hard.

"This one's name was—"

"I know who she is," I interrupted, tossing the glossy eight-by-tens onto the coffee table, crouching, and touching the carmine blemish with my fingertips.

"I knew her," I said.

CHAPTER 6

I SAT WITH MY FACE BURIED IN MY HANDS.

"One of your students?" Jaworski asked.

"And a friend," I said, pushing myself up and pacing the room.

I stared at the neat stack of orange peels.

I had met Jaycie Waylon only days ago. She had wanted me to feel at ease in my new surroundings, introduced me to her friends, invited me to lunch. Now she was dead.

The heat in the apartment was oppressive. I pulled off my jacket and slung it over my shoulder. A persistent scratching noise cracked the room's silence and yanked my attention from the orange peels to the old plaster wall.

"Mice," the chief said.

Intruders, I thought, concealed behind a wall creased with fissures from every shift in the old building's frame.

"I had lunch with Jaycie yesterday," I said.

"We figure she was his primary target," the chief said. "State investigators say they think she was in bed when he shot her. Then he dragged her out here. The cutting came after."

Jaworski's breathing sounded labored. Sweat beaded

on his forehead. Each time he spoke, he took a half-step back, wiped his forehead with a red bandanna, then stuffed it in his pocket and stepped forward.

"Sexual assault?" I asked him.

"The preliminary report says no."

"Why is she the suspected target?"

Jaworski shrugged. "He did more cutting. Looks like he wanted to cut off her head. He didn't cover her."

"You okay?" I asked, watching what looked to me like a pre-coronary two-step.

"Just quit smokin'."

I nodded. "Herb, do you think he stalked Jaycie, picked her out ahead of time, followed her?"

"Then waited until the lights were off, let himself in through one of the living room windows. None of them were locked. State folks say he probably went out the same way. Closed the window behind him."

The display makes this one different. He concealed Susan and Kelly, then hacked at Jaycie and posed her corpse in grotesque sexual mimicry to assault the eyes of anyone who walked through the door.

Jaycie Waylon was the target, but he could have killed her without killing the other two. "This guy has a taste for it," I said. "What about Jaycie's movements earlier in the evening?"

"She was here, studying, listening to music. We've got four different kids at four different times telling us that."

"She dropped me off at one-fifteen in the afternoon. She had a one-thirty class."

Jaworski flipped through a small notebook. "The class ended at three. She and a friend walked to the village. Jaycie bought a lamp and a hairbrush at Cash Mart at three-forty. The time was printed on the sales slip. They ate at Pizza Garden, then Jaycie walked home. She was here from just after five."

"The friend didn't notice anyone watching them, following them?" I asked.

Jaworski shook his head. "They ran into a few girls from the college. Waved, said hi, kept on going. Nothing. We checked it out."

I walked to the living room's trio of windows. The first one clattered when I opened it, wobbling in its tracks. The second refused to stay up. The third was painted shut. It didn't seem likely that the killer had made his entry through any of the windows.

Under most other circumstances I would not have shared my thoughts with the chief. Over the years, I learned the hard way to never contradict a seasoned cop, at least not until she or he recognized that even as a civilian, I might have something worthwhile to contribute. This case was different. Jaworski came after me because he and his people were stymied. There was no time to waste on politic niceties.

"Anybody actually open these?" I asked.

"Guess they just looked at the window locks," he said sheepishly.

I walked back to Susan and Kelly's room. "I'll want a set of the photos," I said. "What about the preliminary reports?"

"I've got copies for you of what we have so far. Still a lot of tests to be done, more interviewing. Whenever we get that stuff, I'll see that you get copies."

I returned to the two beds and looked again from one side to the other. "This room is balanced," I said. "See the way the kids set it up? A desk with a bed on either side at this end of the room, and directly opposite, a desk braced by two bureaus. The posters, one on the east wall, one on the west wall, directly opposite each other. I think the killer responded to the balance of the room. Shoot once, pull down the blankets, stab seven times, spread the blood from the same height, at the same angle, on both sides of the room. Balance."

"What does it mean?"

The killer arrived with gloves, a gun, a knife—the homicidal predator's kit. The room's equilibrium dictated his behavior. Except for Jaycie. Her walls aren't painted. Her death isn't balanced. The space around her did not determine any of her killer's behavior. He was head-tripping, flying through a set of associations that were uniquely his.

"I don't know what it means, Chief. Something."

The scene was both simple and complex. The staging in the double room was obvious, and probably reactive. He arrived with his kit and a rudimentary plan, then allowed stimuli in the room to dictate discrete behavior.

I looked at the poster to my left, a movie placard. *The Seven-Per-Cent Solution.* Freud meets Sherlock Holmes. The one on the right advertised *The Seven Samurai.*

"How many times did he stab Jaycie?"

"It's a guess right now. Eighteen to twenty puncture wounds, three deep cuts across the throat."

The influence of balance is transient. He leaves this room and the behavior changes.

"No sexual mutilation," I said.

Jaworski was silent.

The homicidal psychopath thrives on control, possession of his victims, humiliation, then destruction. All three of these young women were executed, then stabbed.

"What are you estimating for time?"

"A friend of Susan's found the bodies at six this morning," Jaworski said. "They were supposed to go hiking. We're figuring a possible maximum range of about three hours. The medical examiner's best guess is between three-thirty and five-thirty A.M."

"No one heard the shots?"

"No one heard anything. No one saw anything. There

was a bridge game going on at the house across the street until after two. Kids in the upstairs unit got home from a rock concert around three. Nothing. Parking lot's on the west side of the building. Folks who own the house on the east side winter in Florida."

I wandered through the apartment. Jaworski followed at a distance.

"I'll also want a set of the autopsy photographs," I said.

The pool of dried blood remained where Jaycie had been found. A trail of blood drops led into her room, and two stains were visible on her pillow. There was no pooling anywhere on the bed, as there was with her roommates. Nor were there any drag marks, only drops.

"Stippling around Susan's and Kelly's gunshot wounds is apparent," I said, referring to the pinpoint gunpowder impressions surrounding the wounds. "I didn't notice it with Jaycie."

Jaworski shrugged. "We figure the shooter was more than three feet away from her."

Jaworski was right about that, of course, but Jaycie was not in bed when the killer shot her. The pillow stains and the blood drops on the floor were more window dressing.

Jaycie heard something, probably the shots. She got up, didn't bother with her bathrobe, walked into the living room. The shooter stepped into the doorway and fired. About twenty feet. A single shot from a .22, through the young woman's forehead, from across the room. Not an easy shot.

"After I review the material, I'll have questions," I told Jaworski.

"That's it?"

"For now."

He nodded. "My numbers are on the folder. Appreciate anything you can do to help."

As we stepped onto the porch, I gazed at the row of houses across the street, each one with a brightly painted door—reds, greens, blues. Beyond the houses, as if it were drifting through their backyards, an incoming lobster boat churned the placid waters of Ragged Harbor. A man and a woman walked red door to green door along Crescent Street.

"You know Karen Jasper?" Jaworski asked.

I shook my head.

"That's her doing door-to-door. She's a state police detective. Karen went to that FBI profiling school in Virginia. Helps out with cases around the state. I thought you might've run into her."

Uh-oh. Quantico's self-styled wizards and their clones had even less time for me than I had for them. Probably derivative of my very open contempt for their half-wit, paint-by-number methods of crime solving. "Not likely," I said.

As I glanced up the street at the wooden barriers that blocked all but local traffic, Jaworski followed my gaze. "Those are to keep the media sharks out," he said. "They're still arriving. One guy with a bunch of cameras tried to sneak back here by boat."

"News is entertainment. Reporters compete for ratings like any other performer. Violence and sex are the big sellers, and it's a weightier story when there's a celebrity involved. The networks abandoned the Pope in Cuba for Monica Lewinsky in Washington."

I glanced behind me at the crime scene sign and the yellow tape stretched across the lawn from the porch railing to an old maple tree.

"There must not be much happening in the news capitals this week," I said.

I wondered how many times I had done this, yanked myself alert to the nuances of a murder scene, and how many of those times the victims had been new and fresh to whatever lives they might have chosen to live. For these three, all choice was gone, snapped away in the night by person or persons unknown.

Experience had taught me to maintain an emotional distance from victims, their families, their friends. As psychically wrenched as I might be, I could not allow surges of feeling to interfere with my task. The only way I knew to catch a human predator was to create a mental space for him, to invite him into my life, and to gaze at the world with his eyes. When I achieved the mind-set, there was no room for sympathy, sadness, tears.

Never having learned to grieve well was an asset. I wanted only to bring down a killer.

Herb Jaworski did not have the luxury of dispassionate inquiry. "Folks in town pretty shaken?" I asked.

"Doors locked and guns loaded," he said, removing his cap and running his hand through his hair. "We ain't had a murder in Ragged Harbor in nine years. Last one was Joe Pinelou. He got himself tanked at the cafe, went home and shot his wife, then turned the gun on himself. That upset a few people, but when they thought about it, most folks decided they could see it coming. Joe and Shirley had been going at each other for fifteen years. If he hadn't done it, she would have. Maybe Joe Pinelou was crazy, but what we got here goes off the scale."

I nodded. "No one ever sees this coming. We don't know what happened in there, Chief. Even at the end, when you've got the bastard locked up, we still won't know. Not all of it."

CHAPTER 7

JAWORSKI DROVE ME BACK TO THE HOUSE. I TOLD HIM that I would stop at his office later with questions, and walked inside.

I stood at the fireplace and surveyed the small area where I'd sat with Jaycie Waylon and her three friends.

"I know he likes the ale," Jaycie said. *"Must be he doesn't like smiley faces."*

I glanced at the slate hearth where I had discarded the sticker. The orange circle leered back at me.

"Shit," I muttered, and moved to the kitchen, where I spread the crime scene photos on the table, glanced at them, and scanned the preliminary reports.

Rain again began its tap dance on the roof.

The first step in understanding a mind that designs and delivers butchery is to reconstruct the discrete events of the crime, to discard the least likely scenarios, and retain all probable choreographs.

I had eliminated the living room windows as a point of entry. Also, two sliding bolts coated with undisturbed dust secured the back, solid-core door. That left a single small window in Jaycie's room, and the front door.

If the shooter had climbed through Jaycie's window,

the entire scene would be different. If she was the killer's only target, his activity might have been confined to that room. Susan and Kelly would still be alive. If she had awakened, there would be evidence of a disturbance in the small area—which there was not.

The scene suggested a linear progression. He arrived knowing that he would kill them all, and moved methodically from one task to another. He was patient, comfortable with his surroundings, unconcerned with the passage of time.

Jaworski had told me that the young women were meticulous about locking the front door. Friends who visited the apartment teased them about it. They tried the door, then waited while one of the roommates unlocked the apartment.

No forced entry. You had a key.

You knew what you were doing. You let yourself in through the front door, then moved to the left, toward the double bedroom, away from Jaycie's room.

Why?

I found the apartment's floor plan in the case file and imagined walking through the door in darkness. The double bedroom was immediately to the left. Jaycie's single was to the right, at the far end of the living room. A sofa and chair were also on the right, effectively dividing the room and creating a natural traffic flow from the front door to the left toward the bedroom.

If I stalked Jaycie, knew who I wanted and where she was, I would move to the right. But this killer did not.

Did you react totally to the space?

It was possible. It was just as possible that he visited earlier and knew the layout, but chose to begin by eliminating the human obstacles who might awaken and come between him and his target.

The stippling that surrounded Susan's and Kelly's

wounds indicated that the shooter had held the gun approximately six inches from his target each time. I stood and extended my arms as if I were holding a weapon, turned to my left, *bang*, then turned to my right.

Why turn to the left first? Why not the right, then the left? More reactivity—merely responding to the room's stimuli?

The medical examiner could not determine which of the two victims in the double room was killed first. I favored Susan Hamilton, on the left, with my havoc, and I would have to trust that for now.

Jaycie emerged from her room.

I prepared a list of questions for Jaworski. Who has access to apartment keys? Who owns the building? What about previous tenants?

I stepped backward, pictured myself in the doorway of the double bedroom, then turned to look across the living room. I estimated the distance. Jaycie would have stood near my fireplace. Hell of a shot. If the room was dark, the shot was even more amazing.

Someone familiar with weapons. A practiced shot.

I skimmed through the case file, and when I did not find the information I wanted, I added to my list: Lights on or off when bodies discovered?

Three down. I know that Susan and Kelly are dead. I walk out to where Jaycie dropped. She is dead.

"This doesn't make any fucking sense," I muttered, glancing through the window at windblown sheets of rain.

I grabbed the photograph of Jaycie's head surrounded by an aura of deep red, and examined the blood with a magnifying glass. There was a disturbance at the outer edge of the pooling on the left side. Ah, yes, the window dressing.

What do I use? What have I brought for this task? A cloth? Too absorbent and retentive. A sponge. Absorb the blood, then squeeze it out in a trail of drops, and a final draining over the pillow.

The executions were flawless, performed by someone who, I was convinced, had killed before. The postmortem behavior, however, still confused me.

He savaged Jaycie's body, then lingered and created performance art.

He cut Jaycie's flannel nightgown along the seam, then removed it and placed it over the arm of a chair.

Not torn. Cut. A neat cut. Not cast aside. Placed.

Why not just rip the damn thing off? You carved into her throat like a fucking butcher gone wild with a bone saw.

I found the photograph of the nightgown and examined it with my lens. There was no fraying along the seam where it was cut. I saw a few short, loose fibers.

"That wasn't cut with a knife," I said. "He used scissors."

There is no passion here. He is efficient, relaxed, loving what he's doing, but he is not driven. His anger is spent.

He anticipates community reaction, prepares Jaycie's body as a twisted greeting to those who enter the apartment.

I made a note to have my discovery checked microscopically, and added scissors to the list of contents of the killer's kit. It made no sense that he would prowl through the apartment to find them, and there was no indication at the scene that he had.

You attended to detail, and you anticipated every contingency. You planned well, but you were not flawless in your performance.

None of them are.

The scene suggested fear of the victims.

Three well-placed shots.

A gun is an unusual weapon for a serial killer. I thought of Kai Lin's question about a Washington case and remembered my response. What does weapon selection mean to the killer?

Death is the absolute controller.

He could not tolerate the thought that his victims might rise up and strike back.

He stabbed Jaycie repeatedly, slit her throat, and attempted to cut off her head.

Brutal. Gruesome.

"No sexual mutilation," I said.

You were too deliberate. You created a display, a horrifying tableau of savage sexual predation, but you had no carnal intent. Rage, yes, but with a rapid recovery.

"These are executions," I muttered. "The only rage is directed at Jaycie."

He enjoys the killing, the game with the cops, horrifying his audience.

I leaned back in my chair, breathed deeply, allowed my eyes to close, and listened as rain rattled on the metal roof, the refrigerator hummed a bass accompaniment, and the kitchen faucet's staccato drip clicked like a metronome.

My breathing slowed.

Whether from the knife, or from his artwork with the sponge, there should be some contamination. If events played out as I imagined, traces of blood from the double room will show up on Jaycie's pillow.

He has a design in mind.

I returned in my reverie to the double bedroom. Again, I sensed movement to the left. The determinants of his behavior are mixed, conscious and unconscious, deliberate and reactive.

Susan.

Pull back the blankets, push up her nightgown, stab seven times to the middle abdomen. No sexual mutilation. No slicing.

Seven.

Per-Cent Solution. Seven. Samurai.

I can't react to what I can't see.

The light is on. I see the room's balance.

He dipped his sponge in blood, smeared the wall to create his display, but his hand slipped. A frontal stroke by a right-handed person would not cause a problem like that, just as a left-handed person would have no difficulty reaching across Kelly's bed to the wall and sweeping the sponge downward.

The smears must be identical, beginning and ending at similar locations on their respective walls.

It was a stretch for him to reach that section of the wall. The desk and bed are in the way. My hand extended effortlessly above the smear.

Short reach. Short span between the knuckle impressions. Short killer.

He pulled down Susan's nightgown and replaced the blankets. Covered her. No display.

Display and no display.

He turned to the right and duplicated his actions. His hand did not slip.

He's left-handed.

It was a beginning.

He sat on the sofa, held his orange in his right hand, and peeled it with his left. A leisurely set of kills, a frenzy of butchery, an unhurried repast.

As usual, I had more questions than answers.

I opened my eyes and scribbled another note to Jaworski: Did the crime scene technicians find any trace of Susan's or Kelly's blood with Jaycie's blood?

Then I stared again at the rain. "Why a fucking orange?" I muttered.

The narrow white box that contained my students' gift of scrimshaw rested on the table beside me. As I reached for the piece of whalebone, the telephone rang. I glared at it. I have no tolerance for being summoned by an insistent whine that intrudes in my space whenever somebody has a whim and nothing better to do.

I grabbed the insidious blue plastic device. "What?"

Stu Gilman was my electronic interloper. It figured.

"This whole thing is so unbelievable," he said. "Just terrible. I came back from Portland Friday night to help with calls from parents and the media. This is just like that business in Gainesville, Florida, several years ago. We've got national TV camped at the bottom of the drive. We're not allowing them on campus. Listen, I called for a couple of reasons. I know you're working with the police on this. The chief called the college to find out where you're staying. You probably can't discuss the murders in any detail, but are you making progress?"

"I can't discuss the case at all, Stu," I said, imagining Gilman's head nodding, his eye twitching. "If you're concerned about a press release, just say the usual for now: You have confidence in the local and state police."

"That's what I've written here," he said. "We're working closely with the authorities. It doesn't seem adequate. Is it okay if I say that you're working on the case?"

"No," I told him.

"I thought that might reassure people."

What was this guy thinking? I have never known of anyone who found it encouraging when cops turn for help to the sort of shrink that people view as a 900 phone call away at the psychic hotline.

"It would hurt more than help, Stu," I said. "Keep it general for now. What else did you want?"

"Oh, right. Yeah, you're probably busy. We're having a memorial service for the three girls Tuesday morning. It'll be in the old chapel. We're going to have the regular afternoon schedule. I considered clearing the day, but decided to try and get things back to normal as soon as possible."

Gilman hesitated, cleared his throat, and said, "Jaworski told me that he'd have officers stationed around the chapel. He said it was routine. Is that true?"

"Standard procedure, Stu."

"Huh. The college hasn't had police on campus since the sixties. I'm not comfortable with that."

I hung up and wondered again about Stuart Gilman. What were the president and her four deans doing while Gilman managed the college? His were administrative concerns. Why did it bother him to have police on campus? They were investigating a triple murder, not infringing on anyone's civil rights.

AFTER THE PHONE CALL FROM GILMAN, I DROVE INTO town and dropped off my list of preliminary questions and suggestions with Herb Jaworski's dispatcher. I came back home and heated a can of soup for dinner—something I often resort to on Sundays. I had just finished eating and was washing my few dishes when the chief arrived.

"Sorry to drip all over your floor," he said.

I eyed him and grinned. "You look like you crawled out of the surf. Where's your Mrs. Paul's logo?"

"Rainin' like hell out there."

He slipped out of his raincoat, settled his bulk into a chair, and popped a stick of cinnamon gum into his mouth. "Chewin' gum hurts my jaw," he said, "but it keeps me from smoking. Listen, you've already got some of our people rethinking this thing. A couple of us went back to Crescent Street. I think I know what you're getting at. The rear door wasn't disturbed. The windows don't work for a quiet entry. Too noisy and too difficult to manage. We went over every inch of the front door, removed the lock and examined it, and found nothing. So the killer used a key and let himself in."

Jaworski consulted his notes. "Let's see. Martin International owns the building. College maintenance has three copies of the key on campus. They keep all keys to all buildings in a locked cabinet. None are missing. The head of maintenance, Nelson Kiner, has his own set that he keeps at his house in the village. His cabinet isn't locked, but we've accounted for all of those."

"You might want to check on previous tenants, find out when the locks were changed last."

Jaworski smiled for the first time since I met him. "We're doing that. I told you, I read your book. Now, when we first got to the scene, no lights were on. When we were down there an hour ago, we took a closer look at the switchplates. I think we've got a smudge, blood, on the plate in the double room. Like he had the light on, then switched it off on his way out."

You shot from light into darkness, from what you could see, into the forehead of a moving shadow.

"He's a crack shot," I said.

"Looks that way," Jaworski agreed. "But lots of folks around here hunt, target shoot. His skill doesn't make the pool much smaller. Your question about blood mixture will take a while. I have to get the lab people to come back and take more samples. We should have an answer on the fabric sometime tomorrow. So, what else have you got?"

"Nothing right now," I said.

"I know you do this stuff kind of step-wise. Put the crime together first, then figure out the sort of killer who fits it. I just wondered if you had any notions that I could work with."

I understood Jaworski's impatience. "I have some

vague ideas," I told him, "but I don't want to set you running in the wrong direction. Two physical details suggested by the scene are that he's between five-six and five-nine, and left-handed."

The chief nodded. "I watched you work those smears and measure your hand."

"As far as what goes on in his head, I need more time."

"I remember you had a piece in your book about Stanley Markham. You worked that case."

Stanley Markham was a slice of violence from the past. Markham took his early victims to clearings in remote, wooded areas. Each time, eleven that we knew of, a young woman walked with him to the place where he ended her life.

Then he escalated.

"I worked Markham," I said warily. "Why?"

"That's right. I forgot. You definitely need to get a TV in this place. Markham escaped."

The fucking orange.

I felt like I'd been punched in the gut.

"He's been on the run for ten days. The U.S. Marshals said he'd head back to the Boston area. That ain't far from us."

Stanley Markham was not as bright as some of his brothers in carnage, but he was every bit as destructive, maybe more. After his eleventh victim, Markham killed weekly, and cruised more frequently than that. Risk was irrelevant to him. He exploded into homes, waltzed into schools at noon, breezed through malls at any hour seeking his prey.

And he always signed in at his kills. As he studied his work, he peeled and ate a piece of fruit and neatly piled the rind and seeds.

Now he was free.

According to Jaworski, Markham used a ploy that

must have come out of a 1940s James Cagney movie. Assigned to sort laundry, he hid in one of the huge dirty-linen hampers. The laundry service wheeled him from the medium-security institution for the criminally insane.

Medium security. It boggles the mind.

"The last I knew, Markham's sister lived on Boston's North Shore," I said. "The two of them were close. People change, but he always needed a home base."

"He's a little guy, right? Like what you're describing."

Markham certainly had the time to get to Ragged Harbor and kill. "The orange," I began.

"That came through on the bulletin we got," Jaworski said. "The way I hear it, he killed in Massachusetts, Connecticut, Rhode Island, New Hampshire, and Vermont. Dumped his fruit leavings in all the New England states but this one. That may not mean anything to him, but I ain't comfortable with it."

Jaworski dropped a package on the table. "More reports and photos," he said, preparing to leave. "We can talk tomorrow, but I've got one more question, Lucas."

I looked at the worried expression on the cop's face and knew what was coming.

"Markham or not, we could have more victims, couldn't we? We're talkin' about somebody who'll go on killing until he's caught."

"Yes," I told him.

CHAPTER 8

AS I SIPPED MY MORNING COFFEE, I SPREAD THE NEW crime scene photographs on the kitchen table, then walked around the table and gazed at them from different angles. I stopped walking long enough to thumb through the most recent reports, then I started pacing again, looking at the graphic portraiture of death.

Something was wrong with the gestalt. The parts remained just fragments; the crimes lacked a sense of completeness.

A murder scene informs. The killer's droppings wait to be analyzed for hints at thought patterns, pathways into twisted fantasy, descriptors of personality.

I was refusing to see these three women as anything other than vibrant young people with their lives in front of them. Jaycie was a new friend. I was not allowing myself to view her and her roommates as prey, which is what I would have to do if I expected to experience the savagery that intruded in their night.

The education and training that I bring to the analysis of a homicide is less important than the flexibility of mind, the willingness to visit the beast in the wild and to liberate the one inside. If I approached a crime scene with a plan,

I'd already conceded defeat. Savagery has its own logic, conforming to no rules but its own.

I could not force the mind-set.

I had other matters to attend to, so I set aside my work and drove into the village.

I APPROACHED THE TURN FOR THE COLLEGE AND SAW the media camp that Jaworski had blocked from Crescent Street and that Stu Gilman had locked off campus. Half a dozen trailers and four large flatbeds decorated with satellite dishes reduced Main Street to two congested lanes. A virtual truck rodeo surrounded the college entrance, directly across from the locked gate to the Screamin' Demon, Ragged Harbor's small amusement park and roller coaster.

I sat in traffic and gazed at the park entrance, the mouth of a giant aluminum monster. I imagined an army of kids in summer, trooping gleefully beneath the demon's silver fangs, then running for the 1950s-era wooden coaster.

A cop waved me through the traffic snarl.

As they prepared to broadcast from Ragged Harbor to the world, TV reporters and technicians sipped coffee or brushed their teeth over Styrofoam cups. Print reporters tapped at laptop computers. Their TV counterparts wore microphones that resembled wasps clinging to lapels; these were connected to battery packs clipped to the backs of their belts.

A college security guard checked my identification and allowed me to pass, prompting glares from two media people standing near the barrier. I was familiar with news reporters' sense of entitlement from my Boston years. More recently, they'd given us O.J. with a cast of thousands, instant experts, and Dolby Surround sound, then milked the presidency as if it were a prurient soap opera, frequently reminding us of their obligation to report the news. TV producers and newspaper editors spent more time checking audience share and distribution than verifying the accuracy of their stories.

The campus resembled a ghost town. Many students had gone home. Others probably slept after remaining awake, terrified, all night. A few with vacant expressions stood at the crest of the hill and watched the attack of the minicams.

A light glowed in Stu Gilman's office at the end of the corridor, but I walked only as far as the room labeled "Student Records." I had no interest in being twitched at.

The information packet that I received from the dean of studies required that I verify my students' enrollment status and determine that they had paid all fees due the college. After a half century of often virulent attacks on bureaucracy of any stripe, I was now an instant bureaucrat. At least the mundane chore relieved me of trying to do the impossible: force awareness of a killer's mind-set.

The records room door was locked, but was easily persuaded to open when I slid back the bolt with my pocketknife's screwdriver blade. As a lifetime member of the Oscar Wilde fan club, I never apologize for my excesses. I did not want to deal with Gilman, and had no reason to assume that he would have a key to the records room.

"Shit," I muttered, gazing at the roomful of computers.

My daughter Lane considers me a technophobe. I prefer to think of myself as a neo-Luddite, a Ted Kaczynski without bombs.

I've never been clear about whether there actually was a Ned Ludd who knew that rebellious workers in early-nineteenth-century England invoked his name. Gangs of textile workers from Nottingham to Yorkshire smashed machinery to protest low wages and widespread unemployment caused by the introduction of labor-saving equipment. These "Luddites" also claimed that the quality of the material produced by the machines was inferior to the products they made. I suspect that they were right, but in the not-so-merry old England of 1813, it was a no-brainer. A dozen or more Luddites were hanged, and within three years, the movement had been squashed like morning cockroaches in the kitchen sink.

"If we allow it to, progress will kill us all in the end," I said, staring at rows of plastic and silicon obelisks.

It is not that computers send me into fits of short breath and eruptions of bumpy red sores. I use them. I just don't like the fucking things, and I especially don't like the impact they occasionally have on my life. My feelings for IBM and Microsoft are akin to the Hatfields' toward the McCoys.

I expected a nice, little oak box filled with five-by-eight cards and holding all the information I could possibly want. Instead, I stared at rows of machines. Why did a college the size of Harbor need ten computers to manage the data generated by a couple of hundred students?

"What are you doing in here?" the voice behind me demanded.

I turned and saw Stu Gilman standing in the doorway.

"Rethinking the Industrial Revolution, and checking on my students," I said.

His head was in high-vibration mode. "How did you get in?"

Gilman's wide-eyed glare held indignation, shock, confusion, fear, and loathing. His mouth had its own affliction, an involuntary snapping of muscle and nerve that left him somewhere between a sneer and a snarl.

"I opened the door and walked in. Is there some problem?"

He hesitated, then quickly recovered. "No. No problem," he said, walking to one of the computers and switching it on. "This one has the records you want. Is this something to do with the murders?"

"This is for my seminar, Stu," I said, sitting at the console and selecting "Students Enrolled" from the computer menu. "Verification of student status."

"That door is supposed to be locked."

Gilman's voice was a pastiche of conflicted feeling—self-conscious distress and raw anger. I tried to find his eyes, but they were doing their best imitation of pinballs popping off a bonus bumper.

"MI paid for these computers," he said.

"Should've invested in something useful like electric guitars," I said, typing my search criteria. "Les Paul and Leo Fender have done more for humanity than Bill Gates."

He finally looked in my direction. "I don't know what the hell you're talking about."

"Electric guitars. I'll be sure to tell you when I'm done. You can frisk me and relock the door."

The nettled and bewildered little man turned and strode from the office.

I breezed through my list of names until I got to Dawn Kramer. Her tuition payment was overdue. The computer also insisted that Amanda Squires did not exist. I wondered how she felt about that.

I switched off the machine, walked to Gilman's office, and tapped on the open door.

"Sorry I was so short with you," he said, patting his few remaining strands of hair. "This place is like a zoo. There are media people all over the village, trying to sneak onto the campus, calling me at all hours."

"I'm finished wi;th the computer," I told him. "I shut it down and covered it. You'll want to lock that door, I guess."

Gilman's hands trembled. "How long until you have this murder thing wrapped up?"

Murder thing? Jesus. The man had the sensitivity of a granite slab.

"No idea," I said.

He turned and gazed out his window at the Atlantic.

"Stu, what does it mean if a student isn't listed in the records?"

"I wouldn't know anything about that," he said distractedly.

I wondered, but did not ask, why Gilman would have a key to the room and know which computer contained the registration files, but know nothing about student data.

"I guess you've got your hands full," I said.

"What?" he asked, snapping his attention back to me.

"This whole business."

"What business?"

"The murder thing."

"Oh. Right. Yeah. The phone's been ringing off the hook. You can't blame people."

His phone was silent.

Stu Gilman was wired, but I did not think that it was only the murders that had him cranked.

CARRYING MY COMPUTER PRINTOUTS, I WANDERED INTO Bailey's Silo.

I was headed to my classroom when I heard someone playing the piano in an adjacent music room. I hoped it was "someone." I pictured reels of tape unwinding or, worse yet, a computer regurgitating programmed sound samples.

I was relieved when the nonexistent Amanda Squires looked up from a Steinway baby grand.

"I heard you from down the hall," I said.

"I enjoy playing."

She pushed back her shirtsleeves and continued to play the adagio from Brahms's First Piano Concerto.

"I think that Brahms was infatuated with Robert Schumann's wife," Squires said. "He wrote the adagio for her. Schumann attempted suicide around that time. Makes you wonder if he caught the two of them . . . at something. A friend of mine describes this piece as music written in the key of blue. I like that. There is so much sadness, so much muted rage."

I considered introducing the subject of the murders, acknowledging Squires's loss of her friends and the horror that had gripped the campus. Before I could speak, she abruptly stopped playing, turned, and lowered and buttoned her sleeves.

"I think I'm going to enjoy being in your seminar," Squires said. "Violence isn't a pleasant subject to study, but some people believe it's the only choice they have."

She stood and prepared to leave.

"Oh, I was checking student records," I said, fumbling with my batch of papers.

"I'm probably not in there yet. I'm a transfer."

I nodded. "I wondered."

"Did you want to know about prior course work?"

"There are no prerequisites for the seminar. I have to initial a form that verifies student status."

"I have my photo ID. I'll bring it with me tomorrow."

Squires walked to the door, then hesitated. "I think we've all met the only possible prerequisite," she said. "Experience."

Before I could react, she left the room and walked down the hall.

• • • ▬

I SPENT AN HOUR SORTING THROUGH BOOKS AND ARTI-
cles to determine what preliminary materials I would copy
and offer my students. I wanted a sample of the varieties
of ways to view and consider violence and its contexts.
When I had that task under control, I headed for the police department to find out if the autopsy photos had arrived.

As I left Bailey's Silo, Steve Weld waved to me and
trotted across the oval. "I just got through with the police,"
he said. "I had to verify my alibi. Jesus. I was in Bangor."

Weld's tie-dye for the day promoted Ben & Jerry's ice
cream.

"In a situation like this, Steve, everyone's a suspect."

Weld shook his head. "You're every bit the crusty cynic
I heard you were. When you started working with Jaworski
and his crew, did they ask you for an alibi?"

"No. Good thing they didn't. I don't have one."

Weld laughed. "Any ideas?"

"About?"

"The murders."

I shrugged. "What about you?"

"I thought you solved them before they happened."

It was my turn to laugh.

"No," Weld said. "I don't have any ideas about the
murders, but if I were a cop, I'd jump all over Stu Gilman."

"Gilman? Why?"

Weld hesitated. "He knows everything that goes on
here, but he never says shit. He lies. Drives a car worth
more than I make in a year. Wears a diamond pinkie ring.
You're the crime shrink. You figure it out."

I was no more interested in getting into personal
squabbles with Weld than I was with Gilman.

"He probably told you guys that he was at home in
Portland, right?"

Weld did not wait for a response. "If he did, that's

bullshit. He was at the Clear Skies, the airport motel and restaurant. I saw his silver Jag parked there when I headed out of town Friday night. I told the police."

He held up his hand. "Don't try to tell me he had a drink at the bar and went home after I drove through."

"You seem certain that he didn't."

The teacher gazed at the administration building. "He's used the Clear Skies for meeting MI clients ever since the incident two years ago," he said, still looking away, his voice softer. "I'm not accusing Gilman of killing anyone. The man is an encyclopedia. That's all. He has to be. He works for Melanie Martin."

"What incident?" I asked.

Weld shook his head. "Talk to Jaworski."

"Steve, we've had two brief conversations, and both times you've left me with the feeling that all the closets around here are filled with skeletons."

Weld turned to face me. "Doc, you may just be as smart as they say you are," he said, and walked off.

I DROVE DOWN THE HILL, MUTTERING ANGRILY TO MY-self about people who talk in riddles.

I wound my way through the media encampment to the rear of the ancient brick municipal building that housed the police department. Reporters who were not huddled at the college entrance or the end of Crescent Street lurked on the sidewalk in front of the town offices. I had been out of the camera's eye for years and wanted to keep it that way.

Soot-coated black-and-yellow civil defense signs led me through the basement. I climbed the front stairs and arrived in a small waiting area, where the department dispatcher checked my ID. He punched buttons on his console, mumbled into a telephone receiver, then directed me to the chief's office.

Jaworski met me in the corridor. "Got somebody in here I'd like you to meet, Lucas," he said, leading me into his oversized room with a view of Main Street.

A red-haired woman in her middle thirties stood near a table to my left and talked into a cell phone. She had parked her charcoal jacket over the back of a chair, revealing a pager clipped to one hip and a Walther nine-millimeter semiautomatic handgun on the other. Her briefcase, laptop, and plastic bottle of designer water—not Maine's own Poland Spring—rested on the table. She sat, and scribbled in a narrow notebook.

"She'll be off the phone in a minute. I told you about Karen Jasper. She's in investigations with the state, went to that FBI school. Sort of stuff you do, I guess."

"I doubt it," I muttered.

"What's that?"

"Like to meet her," I said, gazing beyond Jaworski at a silent TV that offered a view of the media crews loitering at the building's front door.

"Wish I'd been here to see me drive by," I said.

Jaworski glanced at the screen, then back at me. "Our mirror on the world is aimed at us."

"We'd best be careful. Those autopsy photos come in yet, Herb?"

Jaworski handed me a manila envelope. "Came in an hour ago. I haven't had a chance to look at them. We've got two sets, so you can take your time getting that package back. They'll probably tell you more than they will me anyhow. You've got another set of reports in there, too. Don't ask me which ones. I copied them and stuck them in the envelope."

Karen Jasper put down her phone, swung around in her swivel chair, and said, "I've checked NCIC, VICAP, and our own computers. Our focus is Stanley Markham. This is the work of a traveling pro, and we have no other pros on the road in the Northeast right now. We had a hit in southern California, but that guy is taking kids under twelve. Who the hell are you?"

She directed her rapid-fire report at Jaworski. The final remark was for me.

"Karen Jasper, I'd like you to meet Dr. Lucas Frank," Jaworski sputtered.

Jasper glared at me.

I had showered, and had changed my socks and underwear, so I could not imagine why she was firing such a pissy expression my way. Perhaps she had heard of my disdain for all bureaucratic hacks.

Trying to make nice, I stuck out my hand. She ignored my gesture.

"I'm recommending that you request federal assistance," Jasper said to the chief.

See what I mean? I never enjoy my meetings with people like Karen Jasper. I usually go away feeling that I've met someone who has missed her or his calling—you know, inventory management, or maybe even pyramid sales.

Jasper planned to fill her plate: a main course of Markham, with a side order of pale people in suits wandering around with copies of *The Wall Street Journal* tucked under their arms looking for a private place to take a shit. Not that they're not perfectly nice people.

"Karen, I mentioned Lucas to you. He's the one—"

"I'm familiar with your work," she said through her continuing glare. "We spent an entire class on the early contributors to the field. All that history is interesting, but has little contemporary relevance."

Ouch. If I were sensitive about my age, "early contributors," however accurate, would have stung.

In the late sixties and early seventies, the few people in the U.S. who examined crime scenes for the leavings of a personality were trained and educated broadly in criminology, psychology, and sociology. They probed their own minds, then plunged into the streets with the cops. They knew they had to acquire a feel for the setting of slaughter and for the mind of the veteran homicide detective whose intuitive leaps were the inspiration for investigative shrinks.

Too many from my generation remained in university offices and played with statistics. Some wrote scholarly, theoretical treatises. Others had established lucrative private practices consulting on issues related to violence that they read about in their brothers' and sisters' articles. Most of their advice was common sense, but they saw it as a chance to turn a profit on fear. They also shaped a national belief that pure science could explain the vagaries of human violence.

Art and intuition were out; math and science were in. The new generation, of which Karen Jasper was surely a member, followed their household gods to the FBI Academy in Quantico, Virginia. A few independent thinkers ventured to Europe and found that even more quantifiable work was under way. The governments and universities that funded research wanted cleanly calculated accountability. They loved bar graphs and pie charts.

Jasper was crisp, pure business. All she needed was an infomercial and a bar code to slap on her product, whatever it was.

I thought of James Brussel, the New York psychiatrist who was responsible for the existence of "the field." "Surely Dr. Brussel merited—"

"Same class," she snapped, cutting me off. "Brussel was an urban myth. He wrote his own book, then the folk tales took over. I don't have time for this."

She swung back to the table and flipped open her laptop.

Jaworski glanced at me with an expression of helplessness.

I grinned at him. Maybe this was going to get fun. "Ms. Jasper, if Brussel's analysis of George Metesky, New York's 'Mad Bomber,' was a myth, why did your federal colleagues rely on it when they did their profile of the Unabomber?"

"I don't believe that's so, Dr. Frank," she answered, slapping her palm on the table. "Look, we have three dead women here, and—"

"I have doubts about Stanley Markham," I said.

She swiveled around. "I see. You have some *psychic* insight about Markham."

"He worked the Markham case," Herb said with a look of desperation that told me he did not have a clue about what was happening in his office. "He knows Markham."

"I also know that Quantico won't work a case if you recruit your own 'mind hunter,' Herb," I said. "Why don't I bow out? You'll have the pros coming, and I have a class to teach."

The pros. Shit.

Through two decades, I had watched the pros grow increasingly political. They learned and applied the marketing techniques necessary to justify and sustain funding. They knew their target audience and quickly reacted to the public's perception of crime. A de facto hierarchy of atrocity evolved. Serial murder topped the list, but included its own gradations of outrageousness. Multiple killings of prostitutes or the homeless did not approach the monstrousness of child murders. The slaughter of three female college students was near the top of the list.

Jaworski followed me through the station to the parking lot. "What the hell was that all about?" he asked.

"I guess we old farts don't know much."

"I'm sorry, Lucas. I had no idea she was going to be so, well . . . hostile. This is my case, and I need your help with it. When I want the feds around, I'll ask them."

I stopped at the door, turned, and faced the veteran cop. "I meant what I said. If the FBI Support Services people know you have someone private working the case, they won't come in."

"We'll manage."

I hesitated only a moment, then nodded my agreement. "I ran into Steve Weld this morning," I said.

"He tell you about seeing Gilman's car at the motel?"

I nodded. "He's got no use for Gilman."

"Weld is a funny guy. Dresses like a hippie, but he's sharp. I called the motel after I talked to him. Gilman was there with two guests. All of them checked out Sunday morning."

"Why is he lying?"

"I don't know, but I'm keeping that information to myself for now."

I asked Jaworski what two-year-old "incident" Weld had referred to.

"We didn't have much to do with that," the chief said. "One of MI's foreign visitors got drunk and disappeared from the campus. Gilman filed the missing-persons report the next morning. The fear took over after that. The body . . . well, what was left of it . . . washed up on the beach two weeks later. Fish did a thorough job on him. The medical examiner never determined a cause of death. Why do you ask?"

I shrugged. "Weld implied that there was something to it. I don't know."

"I'm gonna go have a talk with Karen. You take a look at the autopsy material."

I watched the chief disappear into the building.

A murder investigation usually reveals unrelated misdeeds and the myriad foibles of the cast of characters.

Two years earlier, an intoxicated foreign visitor had become a meal for the fish.

Steve Weld hinted that Stu Gilman was a fountain of knowledge. The head-bobbing Gilman was wired like an inner spring and lied about his whereabouts on the night of the murders.

A human killing machine disguised himself as dirty laundry, broke out of his cage, and had ample time to play fall tourist in Maine.

The state investigator assigned to the murders behaved like a snappish stockbroker unable to see beyond Markham & Markham, her favorite NASDAQ big mover.

Karen Jasper was right about the bottom line. We had three dead students. We also shared the single objective of removing a killer from the streets.

CHAPTER 9

TEN MINUTES AFTER LEAVING JAWORSKI TO DEAL WITH Karen Jasper, I walked into my borrowed Cape, slammed the door, and dropped the most recent package of photos and reports on the sofa. I had been away from the nuts and bolts of criminal investigation for nearly seven years. Maybe Jasper was right, and I was nothing more than a curiosity from a bygone era.

"Bullshit," I muttered. "I refuse to go quietly into the investigative night."

The crime scene photo display remained on my kitchen table. I popped the cap off a bottle of Shipyard and stared at the top photo, a kid barely out of her teens who could be sleeping. A cop's latex-gloved hand pointed at a small black circle on her right temple. Susan Hamilton was in college, learning and having a good time, until someone walked in and put a bullet through her head.

I looked down at my clenched fists, whitened knuckles. Tumult churned inside, a rumbling flood of anger that was essential if I were to absorb a killer's mental circuitry into my own and prowl the world like a methodical hunter of humans.

"Stanley Markham couldn't find his way to Maine," I

snarled at no one, shoving myself from the table and pacing the room. "She's barking up the wrong tree."

Markham was a short, slender man, wiry, pale-complexioned, with soft-skinned hands that he babied. He washed his hands often, treated himself to an occasional manicure, and always wore leather gloves when he killed. My first impression of the man had been one of softness, gentleness. I wondered how he would cope with the sexual politics of prison.

I remembered a cop's comment after one of Markham's preliminary court hearings: "Slap a wig and some lipstick on that guy and you've got a handsome woman. He's bound for hard time."

As Jaworski observed, Markham was the right size for this crime. The height of the blood streaks on the wall beside the two beds, and the distance between the impressions left by two knuckles when the killer's hand slipped, suggested a small man.

When he had terrorized New England, Markham had required a strict set of stimuli before going into action. His behavior before, during, and after his excursions into the wild was well documented.

The initial, discrete behavior was what his wife called "restlessness." He would come home from his job as a desk clerk at a local motel and not be able to sit still. Markham said he was depressed.

He always drank a couple of beers when he got home, and when he grew restless, he drank more. Sometimes he passed out. Other times he sat up all night staring at TV. When his wife asked about his behavior, he pleaded trouble at work or said he was annoyed with one of their neighbors.

"We always had money problems," Markham told me.

Their money was tight, as it was for most young couples, even with both partners working, but the Markhams were not headed for bankruptcy.

Dorothy Markham would tolerate her husband's behavior for two or three days, then announce that she was going to her sister's for the weekend. Stanley Markham would drop her there, but he never went inside. He hated Dorothy's sister.

"I'd take Dorothy over there on a Saturday morning," Markham told me, "pick her up late Sunday. That gave me all the time I needed. No questions asked. I look back on it now, I got so calm, so relaxed. I'd bring Dorothy flowers when I went to get her. I even played with the baby."

Markham described what went on in his head; like most of his ilk, he never told all of it. He made a stab at a plea of not guilty by reason of insanity. His lawyer eventually talked him out of the NGRI, a nearly unwinnable defense in Massachusetts, but our early conversations were dominated by talk of noises in his head, blackouts, tales of how one victim resembled an old girlfriend who had rejected him. As he drifted toward trial time, Markham claimed that he needed help, treatment. The act was transparent. On the morning that jury selection was to begin, Markham folded his bluff hand, entered a guilty plea, and walked away with life without parole. After a brief stint in a penitentiary, the corrections department moved him to a mental health facility for the criminally insane, proving yet again that state systems are vulnerable to the psychopath's machinations.

"To be the most powerful man in the world," Stanley Markham told me, "is more important than anything else."

He always knew what was coming, he said. He never tried to stop it.

"I wanted it to hurry up and happen. I wandered through the house, thinking. I took inventory. I kept the knife and clothesline behind the seat in my van. I had plenty of rags, a change of clothes, a gallon of water, cleaning solvent for the van. After I dropped Dorothy at her sister's, I drove around."

Markham covered more miles than most truckers. He cruised through Springfield, Amherst, and Northampton in western Massachusetts, zipped up the highway to Brattleboro, Vermont, then over state roads to Keene, New Hampshire. He prowled neighborhoods where girls raked lawns and rode bicycles and young women jogged.

Markham also traveled in his head. "If she's on the next block and she's wearing red," he told himself, "she's waiting for me."

Perhaps he would see a flash of red and feel an instant erection. The woman would be too old or too fat or too tall or with somebody else, but the moment's excitement, the proximity of a "possible," kept him wet with sweat, his jeans tight through the crotch.

It was magical thinking. "She" was not waiting, so he continued driving east from Keene through Peterborough and Nashua, and by late afternoon he prowled the outskirts of Portsmouth. He did not see the saltwater marshes and mudflats as he guided his van through a long, slow curve and changed the color in his mind.

"If she's wearing white . . ."

"You always knew what you were going to do," I told Markham.

"There were some things I didn't know. I always knew that I'd recognize her. I never saw any of them before in my life, but I recognized every one of them."

"You remember each one."

"Not as people. Everyone who comes here needs me to say I feel bad, that I'm sorry for what I did to them. Taking them away from their families. Taking away their lives. I could say the words they want to hear, but I won't. They wouldn't be true. I felt great after each one. Really pumped. I'd get flowers or candy for Dorothy, something for the kid. I felt like a million bucks. It never lasted. Couple of weeks, a month, then it started all over again. When Dorothy moved out, I went on the road more often. I didn't wait for the girls to come out and play. I went in after them. There are only two things that I regret, Dr. Frank. I wanted each one to last longer, and I don't want to live the rest of my life in prison."

Markham stabbed most of his victims, although bludgeoning and strangulation were occasional methods of choice for him. He never shot a victim, never owned a gun. Guns were too noisy, he said, too messy, too easy to trace. Besides, he loved the intimacy—the scent, the soft feel, the taste, the heat—of a close kill.

Now Stanley Markham was free, trying to find his way home. Had he somehow found his way to Ragged Harbor instead? I didn't think so. But what if I was wrong?

I HAD WORKED OTHER CASES IN WHICH THE MIND-SET was slow to come. I learned early to leave them alone, to allow my attention to go elsewhere. This time I headed for my worn copy of Wes "Scoop" Nisker's *Crazy Wisdom*. Over the years, my cat Max had chewed numerous page corners, as if marking them for my attention. He never bothered with other books, probably because they were not as readily available, but I enjoyed believing that Max and I shared a love of the nonlinear. I always opened to one of Max's selections.

I pulled the book from my duffel bag and switched on the radio to find some decent music. The host of a local show read the weather, the tides, and a fishing forecast, then launched into a report on the murders, followed by an editorial.

"Herb Jaworski has served this town during four decades of growth, increased tourism, and rising crime rates," he said. "He has kept up with most law enforcement advances. His achievements are many. However, all of us reach the time in our careers when we need to hand over the reins to the younger folks coming along. That time has come for the chief."

What blither. I snapped off the radio and wandered into the small study at the back of the house. "Aging is bad enough," I muttered. "We don't need a fucking Greek chorus."

I settled into the chair, found what looked like Max's most recent chomp, and flipped open to Chapter Four, "Crazy Western Wisdom."

"Appropriate," I muttered, thinking again how we had been trained to value thought, intellect, and reasoning, to the nearly total exclusion of an empty and receptive mind.

As I considered whether I could read by the light from the window, I sensed movement to my right.

I continued to read, but struggled with the words because I was distracted by motion where there should be none. Finally I turned my head, and immediately wished that I'd found somewhere else to sit.

I stared into the broad face of a four-foot timber rattlesnake coiled on the shelf at eye level. Its tail segments were silent as it slowly raised up. The snake sensed the presence of warm-blooded prey. I watched its tongue flick in and out as the rattler completed its coil, then arched backward, prepared to strike.

Sweat poured down my neck. My fingers trembled as I allowed the book to fold into my lap, then moved my hands to the ends of the chair's arms. When I had a decent grip, I propelled myself from the chair onto the floor in the middle of the room.

The snake lurched at my vacated space and landed on the leather chair.

Now the rattler buzzed its alarm and looked mighty pissed.

I pushed myself to my feet, silently cursing my stupidity for not bringing a weapon with me from Lake Albert. I thought I would be teaching school, not defending myself against vipers.

I ran to the living room, grabbed the fireplace poker, and returned to the study. The rattler remained on the chair, its head tucked low in its coil, its tail vibrating. I glanced at the poker in my hand and decided that a full retreat was in order.

I jogged to the front of the house, grabbed the phone without a second's hesitation, and called Jaworski.

MINUTES LATER, I WATCHED AS THE CHIEF STOOD IN the study doorway, aimed a .22 caliber rifle, and fired. The gun's crack echoed through the small house.

Jaworski's shot shattered the snake's head. A spattering of skin and blood decorated the chair.

"That's a timber rattler," he said. "We don't get them around here. Way up north you hear about a few, maybe near Rangeley or on Mount Katahdin. They like heat and big, flat rocks. You got a first for Ragged Harbor."

Herb sounded like a little boy at the ballpark for the first time.

"I could do without the distinction," I said, wondering how a snake that was not indigenous to the area had made its way into my study. "Is there any possible way that thing just wandered in here?"

Jaworski reached behind the chair, then turned. He held a burlap sack.

"One bite won't kill you, but it will take you out of

commission for a while. Doubt he'd bring his own burlap bag. Like I said, there aren't any rattlers within fifty miles of here."

Jaworski used his rifle to nudge the dead snake into the sack.

I glanced at my still-trembling hands and felt my heart thudding like a poorly tuned engine.

"You must have been hard at work to piss off someone in the four or five days you've been here."

"The only obvious hostility I've noticed was in your office a few hours ago, from the lovely Detective Jasper, and from the clerk at Downtown Grocery every time I go in there."

Jaworski nodded. "I don't understand Karen. She's a damn fine detective, but she sure doesn't have much use for you. She'll have to live with it. I made that clear to her. Angie Duvall down at the store is like most folks in town. They don't like anyone who's connected to the college. This time of year, the only strangers in town are on the hill."

"I don't get it."

"It's the college and its fat endowment from Martin International. The kids raise hell, piss away more money on beer and pizza in one night than some folks earn in a week. Then there's MI. If you believe the rumors, they wash and move money."

"Have you had any specific complaints about MI?"

Jaworski thought for a moment. "One or two. Mostly it's rumors. I tried talking to Gilman about it, just to let him know he had a public relations problem. He showed me the door. Attitude like that irritates the local folks. This isn't the richest town in the world, and Martin's flak catcher drives around in a silver Jaguar. Two years ago, when their visitor washed up on the beach, Angie Duvall for one was convinced that somebody murdered him. I pulled the file on that case after you asked me about it. He was Hispanic. So were the two Gilman was with Friday night. When I tried to do a little background on the dead guy, I got shut out. The feds handled it."

Jaworski walked to the door. "What about this?" he asked, holding up the burlap sack.

After I called Jaworski, I had examined the doors and windows and found no signs of forced entry. Somebody besides Karen Jasper did not think kind thoughts about me. My gut told me that whoever it was had a key to my house.

"I'll be more careful," I said, walking the chief to the door.

"You have a weapon?"

"Didn't think I'd need one to teach school."

Jaworski stopped on the porch. "Might be a good idea if you got one."

The chief gazed at the sky, then looked at me with a flicker of a smile. "Lot of violence these days," he said. "More than when we were kids."

I GLARED AT THE PHONE. WHEN I HAD USED IT TO report my intruder, I had been under duress. The next call was elective, so I had time to think about it.

I don't have a phone in my home in Michigan. My concession to electronic communication is the fax machine. My daughter Lane insists that my refusal to "reach out and touch someone" is symptomatic of my technophobia. I tell her that when she quits Homicide and enrolls in medical school, I will pay more attention to her diagnostic efforts.

After a moment of loathing, I overcame my aversion to using the damn thing and called my oldest friend, Ray Bolton, a detective with the Boston Police Department.

I knew exactly where to find him. He quit work at three, napped, and ate an early dinner. Then, each evening for the twenty-five years that he had worked in Homicide, he rode the subway back to his office. As the city watched sitcoms, Bolton studied murder and listened to classical music. He was a methodical investigator who refused to retire until he cleared all his unsolved cases. Last I knew, he had three remaining.

He answered on the first ring and chided me for not keeping in touch.

I mumbled my customary apology: "Guess I lost track of time."

"Your little town of Ragged Harbor made the national news this morning," he said. "How did they get you to work this thing?"

"The local police chief knew that I was teaching at the college."

"Lucas, when you closed your office and left Boston, you couldn't get out of here fast enough. What changed your mind?"

"I think I might have been premature in declaring myself retired."

Bolton's long pause communicated his disapproval. "We'll have to talk about that when we get together," he said. "Have the local police run a ballistics comparison?"

"They've run a VICAP check. They'll probably do ballistics through one of the national databases, FBI or ATF. Chief Jaworski seems like a knowledgeable guy."

"We received a fax about Stanley Markham stealing a white Chevy pickup in Pennsylvania three days before your murders. We're getting updates twice a day. Sounds to me like he's headed home. Maybe our boy Stanley made a wrong turn and ended up on the Maine Turnpike."

I told him about the orange. Bolton and I had worked the Markham case.

"Ray, it doesn't feel right. This crime scene has as many elements of reactivity as it does of well-planned choreography. Markham operated from a strict script in his head, magical cues, a repeating tape loop."

"Are you dealing with a traveler or a local?" he asked.

"I don't know," I told him.

"You used to give me that much in the first five minutes."

"I think the killer wants us to interpret the murders as sexually motivated. I'm having trouble wading through the misdirection."

"A certain forensic psychiatrist once told me that when the obvious doesn't work, dump it and make room, because something's coming out of left field for a landing in your lap."

"Must be the rattlesnake," I said.

Bolton waited, then finally said, "Lucas, what rattlesnake?"

I explained.

"I want to get a handle on this now, Ray, before any more guests come calling."

"You know, I don't run to the hot ones anymore. I let the young officers do that, and I catch up later. You and I aren't young."

"I'm tired of hearing that."

Again he paused. "What about home intrusions in the area? Not burglaries necessarily, but the creepy stuff that usually doesn't make it into the computers. Rearranged panties and half-eaten pork chops."

Checking break-ins that included confrontation or stank of strangeness was routine procedure. I felt certain that Jaworski had sent out inquiries.

"This isn't your killer's first time out," Bolton said.

"Not by a long shot," I agreed, "but I don't think his

priors include rummaging through the indigenous underwear. Check the databases and find out what you can
about a management-consulting outfit, Martin International. I'd like to know how they make their millions.
They're heavily invested in Harbor College. I want to know
why. A guy named Stuart Gilman calls himself MI's liaison
to the school. Who is he, and what does he do for the
company? The founder and CEO is Melanie Martin.
Might as well check her while you're at it."

Bolton whispered to himself as he took notes.

"When things settle down, I'll visit for a weekend," I
promised.

"What does this Martin outfit have to do with the
murders?"

Maybe nothing, I thought. They owned the house that
the three students rented. Whoever killed them used a key
and walked through the front door. Jaycie had been an
intern at the company. Martin also owned my house, and I
was convinced that my visitor used a key. I have always
rejected coincidence as a convenient conceptual excuse
for those who were unwilling to see the interconnected-
ness of all things.

"Humor me, Ray," I said.

I gave him my number and hung up.

Local or traveler, Bolton wanted to know. "Local," I
said now, thinking that I'd slipped from five-minute analy-
ses for Bolton because I was sliding down the
goose-shit-greased slope to senility.

"Fuck it," I grumbled. "You've been a little senile since
you were twelve years old."

CHAPTER 10

LATE THAT AFTERNOON I DROVE BACK THROUGH MEDIA central. More reporters had arrived, adding to the bottle-neck.

Perhaps they were interviewing each other.

I parked at the administration building. Gilman's Jag-uar was gone, which I interpreted as an invitation. I would not risk the little fat man's rage.

I went directly to the records room, performed an in-stant replay of my earlier forced entry, and ensconced my-self at the computer. I selected the index of current students and ran the names of the three victims. I wanted some sense of who the young women were.

Susan Hamilton was a senior from Massachusetts, an A and B biology major who was considering a medical ca-reer. She was also a member of the student senate. The college sent its bills to her father, a freelance photogra-pher. Her mother was an elementary school principal, and her younger brother was a freshman at the University of Massachusetts.

The information was sterile, meaningless.

Kelly Paquette was a junior from a small Maine town, a mediocre student in history who listed "None" under career interests. Her mother was a "Housewife." Her father worked at a paper mill.

Jaycie Waylon, a junior from Augusta, was a stellar performer in business and psychology who listed "Organizational development" as her career interest. She also served as president of her class and as a member of the Student Discipline Committee. As she had told me outside Downtown Grocery, her parents were deceased.

Her status as a Martin International intern was also listed; Stuart Gilman was her supervisor.

Strike three on Gilman, I thought.

The paunchy bag of nerves had never mentioned Jaycie's affiliation with MI, and certainly not his relationship with her.

I secured the records room and walked down the hall to Gilman's office. His door, too, was locked, but not for long. I quietly let myself in. Sometimes, consorting with a criminal element has its advantages.

Glass-enclosed bookcases lined the walls. They were crammed with dusty volumes of educational law and grant directories from the 1970s. The room confirmed my first impression of a stark, unused space, appointed with the finest leather, mahogany, polished brass, maple. The desk drawers were unlocked and empty, except for a well-chewed pencil and a fingernail clipper.

"If this guy's an encyclopedia," I muttered, thinking of Steve Weld's remark, "he's a walking one."

The only area that appeared vaguely used was the corner of the desk occupied by the telephone. There were notes to return calls from media representatives; none from parents, as Gilman had claimed. There was also a fax from the home office in Portland advising Gilman and the deans that, courtesy of MI, four mental health counselors would arrive in the morning to assist students and staff with their grieving.

We had institutionalized every other aspect of our lives. Why not sorrow? These shrinks were slow. The mind mechanics usually arrive at disaster locations ahead of the media. It would not be long until they got there before the catastrophe happened. They had a lock on business. If I chose to mourn privately, I was "in denial" and obviously in need of intensive therapeutic work.

I slipped out of the office thinking that I was no closer to answers than I was on day one, but I continued to formulate questions.

WHEN I GOT BACK TO THE HOUSE, THE PHONE WAS ringing.

"I expected to get a machine," Ray Bolton said. "When did you start answering the phone?"

"Well, I managed to avoid most of the twentieth century," I told him, "but nobody's perfect."

When my daughter Lane was ten, she shared a concern with her godfather Ray: "I think Pop's deaf. The phone rings, but he doesn't answer it. He can't hear it, Raymond."

Then Bolton educated her about phobias. The prick.

"I just walked in. Hang on while I check the house for cold-blooded creatures."

The dried spatter of skin and blood on the study chair was the only evidence of snakes. The house was as I had left it.

"What have you got?" I asked him.

"A possible sighting of Stanley Markham in Connecticut, the day after he was in Pennsylvania."

"The little shit's going home. Is his sister still in the area?"

"Winthrop Beach. We have her place under surveillance."

"That's where he's headed," I concluded.

"The question remains, Lucas. Was he in Ragged Harbor?"

As much as I wanted one, I had no answer. Maybe yes, maybe no.

"Your Martin International is a major player in global trading," Bolton said. "They forge deals between unlikely partners, and they broker currency exchanges. I couldn't get into the national database that we use for this kind of inquiry. It's classified. I don't know what that's about, but I left my agency code and my personal code, so I'll hear from someone federal."

"The feds have their own investigation going?"

"I don't know," Bolton said. "Could be. I've never run into that kind of roadblock before."

Two years ago, federal agents had handled MI's dead guest. Interesting.

"What about Gilman?"

"Stuart Gilman is a creep."

"I didn't need you to tell me that."

"He lives in Portland. Thirty-eight years old, married, two kids. He's been with Martin for three years. Before that, he worked in human resources for an insurance company here in Boston. He has two priors, both misdemeanor trespassing. Care to guess?"

An uncommon charge, I thought, usually the result of a plea bargain. "Slithering through backyards and peeping in bedroom windows."

"He wasn't fussy. Bathroom windows, too. His only felony is that he worked for an insurance company."

I laughed. Bolton and I shared a belief in the immorality of insurance.

"Targets?"

"Young women."

"Hmmm . . . a liar with relevant priors," I said.

"His name surfaced during the Markham investigation. We pulled the sheets on anyone who came close to a sex offense. You have to look at him. Gilman's boss, on the other hand, is a mystery."

"Melanie Martin?"

"She got her MBA at Harvard, top ten percent of her class, and immediately established the Martin Corporation, which became Martin International a year later. They're based in Portland. I couldn't find a home address for Martin. Before grad school, it's as if she didn't exist. No records of any kind. I can't even find a date of birth."

"What about a driver's license?"

"I'm telling you, Lucas. Nothing. I don't know how people manage to erase their tracks in the world, but they do. I suppose if you have the money, you can buy whatever privacy you want."

"What about the company's interest in the college?"

"I can't give you figures, but I can tell you that it's substantial, and that it started the second year Martin was in business. They donate money elsewhere, but Harbor College is the top recipient."

"Fat lot of help you are," I chided.

Bolton laughed and said that he would keep digging, wait to hear from whatever feds might have an interest in MI, and keep me posted on Markham.

"So, Sherlock, who killed the three kids?" he asked.

"Call me in an hour and I'll tell you," I said, and hung up.

I CURLED UP ON THE SOFA, YANKED A BLANKET OVER me, and allowed my eyes to close. Self-hypnosis was integral to my work, and to maintaining my sanity. If I was getting in my own way or flirting with emotional disaster, my unconscious informed me. When I missed something obvious, it usually bubbled from the deep.

With a suddenness that startled me, a killer transformed the blackness of my mind into cinematic splashes of color.

The killer, Stanley Markham, drove his red Ford Econoline van. There was no traffic in front, none behind.

"The color is yellow," Markham said.

The young woman, Darcy Smith, walked beside the rural road west of Portsmouth, New Hampshire, shrouded in overhanging maples. Reds. Split-leafs. Sugars.

No one knew how many victims Markham claimed. Darcy was number eleven of the twenty-three that Bolton and I identified. She was also Markham's transition kill: he changed M.O., moved indoors after Darcy Smith.

She turned her head, glanced over her shoulder at the sound of the approaching vehicle, and stuck out her thumb.

They were alone, isolated in early summer.

Clumps of orange day lilies bloomed at the edge of the field. Darcy wore white shorts and a yellow T-shirt, and held strings that restrained a bouquet of balloons in shades of blue.

The colors crashed, mutated into a cacophony of cymbals, horns, and dissonant plucked strings. The phenomenon is called synesthesia, or cross-sensing. The stimulus received by one sensory channel triggers a perceptual response in another. A fragrance can stimulate a feeling of warmth and comfort. A tune from the sixties might evoke the image of a woman's face. Or, music becomes a multihued assault, and color an explosion of sound.

Markham slowed the van, pulled to the side of the road, and watched the door open.

Darcy's face was scrubbed innocence. Creamy skin. Blue eyes. Blond ponytail. Lips painted a frenzied red.

She was a young woman who engaged in a transaction with the mighty.

Darcy glanced at the slender man, at his stringy brown hair and bad teeth.

He didn't ask her where she was going, and she didn't tell him. The van pointed in the right direction for both of them. It drove itself to the crest of the hill, then onto an unmarked dirt road.

There was no tone of urgency when she finally asked about their destination. It was matter-of-fact. Curiosity.

"To the end of all roads," he said, and that seemed to make sense to both of them.

Years ago when Markham told me his story, I imagined that I heard piano notes—a tinkle at first, a soft and simple melody, then a crash, as if someone sat on the keys. Once associated only with LSD and other hallucinogenic drugs, synesthesia is a common occurrence in any altered state of consciousness. Colors often became dissonant sounds when I slipped into a hypnoid state.

Darcy Smith was seventeen years old. She accepted a ride with a stranger. There was a dynamic at work, face validity, the appearance of legitimacy. As this transaction began, a service was offered and accepted. She wanted a ride; he provided it.

She believed. She trusted.

Markham said there was conversation. I have imagined the two of them talking, neither of them eager to string together long chains of words. He was excited. She struggled to avoid the notion that things were not as they seemed.

I know that Markham had removed the inside handle on the van's passenger door. When she climbed into the van, Darcy was trapped.

She stood in the clearing, looked at a wall of beech and birch and thick undergrowth. She wore a placid expression,

*but her balloons were gone. Idly, she scratched a mosquito
bite high on her thigh, pulling the hem of her shorts up
unselfconsciously.*

Darcy never felt intimidated by the world.

*The afternoon sun was hot in the clearing. Sweat slith-
ered in beads from the back of Markham's neck, across his
shoulder blades. The scent of wild roses drifted on the lan-
guid summer air.*

*Darcy's arms remained at her sides. She made no at-
tempt to flee. Her face registered the presence of the knife in
Markham's hand. Her nose wrinkled. Her eyes widened as
he walked toward her and raised the knife.*

I knew what came next. I knew all of it. Short of re-
writing history, there was nothing that I or anyone else
could do to stop it.

I remember that I looked around at the cramped hallway where we sat outside Markham's holding cell.

*Rolled mattresses; a thirteen-inch black-and-white TV
that his sister had brought him; a lunch tray with leftover
beans, a partially eaten hot dog, hardening in the stale, dry
air; the smell of three hundred inmates' shit and dirty laundry.*

Steel doors crashed shut.

Markham said, "I could see the hand move. It held a
knife. I knew what would happen, but I couldn't change
that. It wasn't my hand. It was there in the space between
us."

I fragmented, split into more pieces than I could keep
track of, accompanied by the chattering of English sparrows beyond the barred and screened window.

"What happened to the balloons?" I asked.

He shrugged, his forehead creased.

I knew the answer. Markham took them home to his
kid. A surprise gift from a dead girl.

"What balloons?"

Then I saw the hand plunge the knife into Darcy Smith's chest.

Markham sat cross-legged on the ground and, with his bloody knife, peeled and ate an orange.

I opened my eyes and listened to the sea throb in swells. Rage surged through me like currents churning from the ocean's floor.

The mind-set for murder was mine.

"Stanley Markham never did any postmortem cutting," I said. "When his victim was dead, and he had snacked, he was done."

I sat up on the couch and pushed aside the blanket.

Even at the end, when Markham tipped totally out of control, he stabbed, throttled, or bludgeoned, sated his desire for a piece of fruit, and then he fled. Period.

"You know," Markham told me, "fear never came into it while they were alive. A few girls freaked out and I had to calm them down, or kill them sooner than I planned. After they were dead, though . . . God. Dead people scare me. I watched them while I ate. I expected them to sit bolt upright, undead, and lurch after me. I didn't get close to them after they went down."

Death did not frighten the killer who cracked the silent night on Crescent Street.

It was conceivable that Markham had changed his M.O., that he would use a gun now because it was expedient, because he knew that police would catch him or kill him anyway. But he could not alter his fear of the dead; it was a characterological fixture.

As I pushed myself from the sofa, I realized that my mind was not working only Markham and the murders. Karen Jasper had sliced her way under my skin.

Subconsciously, I sought an incontrovertible argument against Stanley Markham having any status as a suspect. I was inclined to label my need to prove her wrong as "professional competitiveness."

That was not all that nipped at nerves. Jasper had dismissed me as an artifact.

"Face it," I told myself. "Growing old pisses you off."

I sipped coffee and examined one of the new reports that Jaworski had given me—lists of vehicles seen on or near Crescent Street on the night of the killings. Investigators had identified most of the cars, interviewed the owners, and appended their statements to the reports.

As I leafed through the sheets, a corner light in the living room switched on, startling me. My first night in the house, I thought the bulb had blown when it extinguished itself at eleven P.M. I glanced at the clock. It was eight-thirty P.M. More technology of dubious value, I thought, and returned to my reports.

Jaworski had placed a red check at the top of one field-interview form. Luther Peterson, a local resident, had observed an old, dented, light-colored Volvo with Maine license plates parked across from his house when he got up at three A.M. to stoke his woodstove. The reason he paid any attention at all, he said, was that his neighbor, Brenda Noddy, worked eleven P.M. to seven A.M. at the regional hospital and always parked in the space occupied by the Volvo. She was usually tired when she got home, and he worried that she would have trouble finding another place to leave her car.

As Brenda's friend returned to bed thirty minutes later—"That's how long it takes me to do the stove"—he saw a slightly built young man, a "student-type" wearing a flannel shirt, jeans, and backward ball cap, and carrying a knapsack. He walked to the Volvo "from the vicinity of 42 Crescent," made a U-turn, and drove downtown.

Why did that sound so familiar?

Then I remembered—the car that had passed the house as I sat on the porch.

Gray, battered, and a Volvo.

"Wonder if he makes snake deliveries," I muttered.

CHAPTER 11

MONDAY MORNING I STOOD OUTSIDE THE OLD CHAPEL as students and a few local residents filed to the memorial service for the slain young women. I estimated the crowd at two hundred inside, another fifty outside.

Stu Gilman, doing a Richard Nixon imitation, lurked near the end of the queue. He wore an expression intended to convey sorrow. It looked more like a scowl with a five-o'clock shadow. The man was facially challenged, and doomed to live life looking like a presidential crook.

Steve Weld nodded as he walked past. I watched him avoid Gilman.

I recognized most of my students. Dawn Kramer and Amy Clay walked together. Sara Brenner stood behind Gilman. Amanda Squires held a young man's arm.

Jaworski's officers videotaped faces and license plates. Other cops, armed with Stanley Markham's mug shots, surveyed the crowd.

The ceremony inside the chapel was for the living, in remembrance of the dead. The photographs viewed by those in attendance were of three smiling young adults. They were the focus of the memories, the sad thoughts, the prayers.

The women in the photographs that I studied wore no smiles.

Jaworski spotted me and approached from the parking area. "I was looking for you," he said.

"You getting it on tape?"

"Not that it will do much good."

He felt no guilt. When he had exhausted his rage, he felt nothing.

"He's here," I said, watching the faces move slowly by.

Some internal conflict . . . what was it? It was not a startling experience to feel nothing.

"What the hell are you talking about?"

You created a design for murder, prepared the kit, slipped into the apartment. You controlled the scene, but you reacted to it.

"He's here because he knows we can't see him. We can capture his image on tape, but we can't know him."

"It ain't one of these things where he's here to get himself absolved, is it?"

"He doesn't need absolution. He feels justified in what he's done."

Jaworski stared at me. "Don't imagine he'd stand out in that crowd."

Stragglers shuffled into the chapel. "He belongs here. He fits right in."

I looked at Jaworski. "You have his picture now."

He had not left much of himself at Crescent Street, but he had left enough. The crime scene's nuances, the killer's behaviors, even some of his thoughts, had sunk their roots in my mind. I did not know how many times I had invited a killer in, but I knew the torrent of images and dreams and dialogue that was coming.

You want me to believe that you're Stanley Markham.

"This why you quit?" Jaworski asked, nodding at the chapel.

"No."

In twenty years as a crime shrink, I had worked nearly two hundred homicides. I remembered victims' names, faces, funerals, family members, and their horror. They did not haunt me. With few exceptions, I maintained the clinical distance necessary to complete my work and move on. I quit because tossing out a red carpet for killers, welcoming them into my mind and looking at their worlds through their eyes, drove me to the precipice too often.

"I reached a space where there was no room for me," I told Jaworski. "I didn't like that feeling. Anything new at your end?"

He removed his cap and ran his hand through his hair. "Jesus. I nearly forgot. We got a ballistics match on the gun."

"Oh?"

"Looks like our boy used the same twenty-two to kill a man in Portland. The P.D. down there ran a comparison check same time we did. Pure luck they matched up, but they did."

"What have you got on the case?"

Jaworski shrugged. "He was killed in his apartment, like our three. That's all I know. I figured I'd drive down there in the morning. You want to make the trip?"

"Definitely," I said.

CHAPTER 12

I STOOD ON THE HILL, A GUN IN MY HAND. I WATCHED mourners march to their chapel and debated whether to use the gun.

The experience was like bad TV reception—black and white with multiple shadows, static, no focus, little contrast. The principal players did not help the reception. They wore baggy faces filled with sadness, masks donned for the occasion, and they walked like images on a screen just before the film snaps.

To kill now would be satisfying but self-defeating.

Sensation must lift us higher, then divide—shatter into sonic distortions, screams of color, superheated flares of foul odors—experiences so intense they define madness.

Then the identical phenomena might become one, suddenly narrow to a laserlike intensity with a single focal point.

Did you know that? These experiences are not overwhelming. They are intensely pleasant.

In Portland, I forget how many nights ago, I soared from my body in an ecstasy that exists only with murder.

Imagine a single, long crescendo—Ravel's Bolero—tedious at first, always familiar, repetitive, harmonic. Then thin horns and bent strings, hints of cacophony, then a bit louder with variations in the theme.

Ravel's work is not a long fuck; it is the anticipation of a kill.

I heard *Bolero* inside my head, despite the crushing roar of sounds crashing among the apartment building's halls.

When I reached the basement, I slipped my key into the lock, kicked open the door, and stepped into the darkened room.

The old man, slumped over a stinking cot, mumbled about sitting in his mother's house. He sat at her cherry table, and gnats suddenly flew and landed everywhere. I watched him swat his hallucinated bugs.

A small white dog sat politely in a corner, its head cocked to one side.

The room reeked of his nightmares, his whiskey, his sweat. I walked to the bed and stood beside him.

"The gnats," he said.

Then his visions became mine.

Swarms of nearly invisible flying insects filled the room. I couldn't squash them fast enough. More kept rising from the floor. I sniffed my fingertips where I had pressed the little buggers to death. My hands reeked of damp earth.

I mashed gnats, but more kept coming, and the smell grew stronger—the odd, musty stench of dirt dug from a grave.

Each time I pushed against a gnat, I heard its dying shriek, I heard the earth shift, I heard the old man groan— "*Mama, Mama, Mama*"—and then I heard the gun fire eight times and the metallic clicks when it was empty and I did not want it to be.

Bolero thundered to its ending inside my head, and there was silence.

No gnats. No rancid stink of the earth, no solvent smell of the old man's bottle.

Nothing.

I pocketed the gun and slipped a hunting knife from its sheath, pruning shears from my pocket.

It was time to go to work.

Now I left the marchers to their prayers and descended the hill to Main Street.

A woman carrying a microphone approached me. "Did you attend the service?" she asked.

I shoved her aside and walked away.

CHAPTER 13

THE STUDENTS IN MY SEMINAR HAD JUST ATTENDED A service for three murdered friends. Now they sat in a classroom where the topic was the predatory aggression that had taken their classmates. A note in my mailbox that morning informed me that two of my class members had gone home and would not return to campus until police arrested the killer.

A radiator clanked at random intervals. Two students engaged in short bursts of whispered conversation. Otherwise, the room was silent. One young woman gazed at the ocean.

"We're going to spend the next several months investigating gender and serial violence," I said, handing out copies of a few papers and a bibliography of recommended reading. "Perhaps the best use of our time today is to decide how to conduct our inquiry."

Someone muttered. A few heads shook. One pale student stared at the ceiling and dabbed at tears with a tissue. Sara Brenner sat behind her hair, just as Jaycie Waylon had described on the night they visited my house.

Finally, Dawn Kramer spoke up. "Dr. Frank, nobody

seems to know what's going on. The police don't say anything. The deans can't answer our questions. The TV news
reported that the murders were sex crimes. There hasn't
been any kind of murder in this town for nearly ten years.
Now three women have been raped and cut down by a
man."

The rumor mill was working overtime, much as it had
in Gainesville, Florida, in 1990 when the media reported
erroneous crime scene information. The reality was repug-
nant enough and did not require distortion or embellish-
ment.

"Reporters keep saying that crimes like these are serial," Kramer continued. "None of the women in this
room, on this campus, or in this town can feel safe. Not
even in our own homes. Not if we have roommates."

A few class members murmured their agreement.

"This kind of violence . . . no one understands it,"
Kramer said. "We need answers."

"Anyone else?" I asked.

Amanda Squires arrived late. "Is this about the
murders?" she asked as she walked to her seat. "Are we
talking about what happened to Susan, Kelly, and Jaycie?"

"We don't know," Kramer said. "We need a focus,
someplace to start, but . . . we're too close to this."

The young woman who had been softly weeping
grabbed her books. "I can't stay," she said, and left the
room.

At the University of Florida in 1990, a teacher had
assigned Pete Dexter's *Paris Trout*, a well-crafted, terrifying
tale of a man whose smoldering rage explodes in multiple
murder. The instructor withdrew the book from her reading list following Danny Rolling's Gainesville rampage. I
was not dealing with the issue of a single book, rather an
entire class devoted to homicidal violence.

Betsy Travis sat away from the group, reading the *Ragged Harbor Review*. Travis was the youngest member of the seminar, a sophomore from Long Island who had not yet chosen a field of concentration. She wore black, her usual attire, and her ears were festooned with a gaggle of silver earrings.

"They shouldn't have lived off campus," Travis said, folding her newspaper. "Something like this could happen in a dorm at a city university, but not here on the hill."

"Campus security checks the dorms twenty-four hours a day," Jen Neilson agreed. Neilson planned a career in criminal justice. "The town cops write parking tickets. On weeknights there's one officer on duty from one-thirty to five-thirty A.M., and he doesn't leave the station unless one of the locals drives a pickup into the mudflats."

"There are guys living upstairs in that apartment building," Kramer said. "The killer didn't bother them."

"Still," Travis said, "it wouldn't have happened if they were up here."

Travis was distancing herself from the victims. She was safe, she believed, because she lived on campus. Her thought process was a variation on the blame-the-victim theme: if the three young women had been good, if they had done the right thing, if they had lived where everyone else lived, they would be alive.

Neilson sought a scapegoat. If she could assign responsibility, she had no need to understand murder. The local police had fucked up; case closed.

Kramer's agenda covered the murders and a myriad of other sins; all men were assholes. "You can pick up any newspaper," she said, "whether it's New York City or some little town in Nebraska, and read about abductions and rapes and murders. These are crimes committed by men against women."

"Age is a factor, too," Neilson said. "I read an FBI

publication about how killers choose victims. They go after children because it's easy to control them. Same with elderly people."

"The FBI looks at behavior," Kramer said. "What did the killer do before, during, and after the crime? They don't pay any attention to human development. No man was born a killer. How did he get that way?"

In my experience, federal agencies were little more than incestuous, bureaucratic impediments to inquiry. I hoped that I would not feel provoked to share that opinion.

"I think it's also important to know how people perceive events in their lives," I said. "Each of us writes our life story with a heavy editorial hand."

"There are genetic factors, too," Amy Clay, a student in biology and physiology, contributed. "Also, most human predators are men, but an increasing number are women."

"If you mean that woman in Florida," Kramer said, "the experts agreed that she was unusual."

"As long as we're gonna do this, why don't we compare male and female killers?" Neilson asked.

"Can we include method as one of the concepts?" Kramer asked. "According to most of the studies I've read, women prefer to kill with poison. To administer something like arsenic, especially in small doses over time, you have to be close to your victims. *Poisoned Blood*, Philip Ginsburg's book about Marie Hilley, is a good example of that."

"Arsenic is easily detected," Amy Clay said.

Clay was a tall young woman with long auburn hair who planned to attend medical school.

"How many doctors consider symptoms like high fever, intense pain, and vomiting and conclude arsenic poisoning?" Neilson asked. "I think appendicitis is a more common diagnosis."

"After the fact," Clay persisted.

"Meaning death?" Squires asked rhetorically. "Why

subject the deceased's family to the ordeal of an autopsy
when there's no reason to suspect foul play? In the Hilley
case, prosecutors exhumed victims. You are right, though,
Amy. I'd use something like succinylcholine. It's much
harder to detect. The body doesn't retain it the way it does
arsenic. Killers who were nurses preferred it because it has
a legitimate medical use as an anesthetic."

"One mistake that I don't want to make," Kramer said,
"is subscribing to a history of women written by men.
Women who behave violently have been treated as biological oddities, victims of menstrual syndromes or hormones
run amok."

So it went.

At Kramer's request, Jen Neilson agreed to include
Stanley Markham as one of her topics for study.

"He's all over TV now," Kramer said. "It's scary to
think that they catch these people, convict them, lock
them away, but they can't hold them. The police think
Markham was here. He's their main suspect."

"Dorothea Puente, the woman in Sacramento who
killed her boarders, she vanished while police were digging
up bodies in her yard," Travis said. "They found her in a
restaurant. Women are just as lethal and elusive as men."

The room sounded as if it were filled with kids swapping baseball cards, but the names were not Ken Griffey,
Jr., Sammy Sosa, or Mark McGwire. My students were
trading the likes of Albert DeSalvo, Velma Barfield, Ted
Bundy, Gary Lee Schaefer, Marie Hilley, Aileen Wuornos,
Stanley Markham, and others in their select and dubious
set.

Most of the students were standing, ready to move on
to their next class, when Sara Brenner, still seated,
brushed her hair from her face and said, "Dr. Frank, what
are you going to do?"

I knew what she meant. "Whatever I can," I said.

"Did Stanley Markham kill Jaycie and her room-mates?"

"I don't know, Sara."

"Are you working with the police? I mean, you're here. You catch killers. You should be helping the police."

That night at my house, Sara had wanted to know how I made the leap from a theory of personality to a specific person. Jaycie had answered her.

It has to do with the way he looks at things, and the questions he asks, Jaycie had said.

"I intend to help," I said lamely, wanting to avoid discussion of my role in the investigation.

"Jaycie was my friend," Sara said. "She was your friend, too."

WHEN I LEFT THE SILO, I EXPECTED TO ENCOUNTER Steve Weld ready to piss and moan, or Stu Gilman prepared to slip into his Batmobile. One rendezvous or another seemed routine.

The hilltop was deserted. I heard students behind me, and listened to the wind rustle through the fallen leaves as I gazed into the graying afternoon.

I stopped at Downtown Grocery, gathered the ingredients of a meal, and fenced briefly with Angie Duvall. When I stepped onto Main Street, a sense of loss enveloped me like a coastal fog. Jaycie was not there, waiting.

I drove to my house. The moment I stepped inside, I reflexively reached for a weapon that was not there, and nearly dropped my bag of groceries.

Someone had impaled an orange on my kitchen counter with a hunting knife.

I walked to the counter, dropped my parcel, then grabbed a thick piece of limb wood from the carrier near

the fireplace. I prowled through the house expecting someone or something to leap out at me.

The place was empty. Nothing was disturbed.

I returned to the kitchen and stared at the
bone-handled knife that had sliced through the orange,
then penetrated an inch through the Formica and pressed
board. To create the display had required great force.

"Someone is stalking me," I muttered, gazing uneasily
around the room.

CHAPTER 14

HERB JAWORSKI ARRIVED PROMPTLY AT SEVEN A.M., and we drove south on I-95 to Portland. I intended to make small talk, pass the time, gab about something other than the murders.

"What do you do when you're not managing the police department?" I asked.

The question proved to be a mistake.

Jaworski collected Portlands, and he seemed about to dump them on me. He knew the population of Portland, Iowa, and the latitude and longitude of Portland, Ohio. He owned police department patches from all the Portlands big enough to have a full-time force, and he had visited most of them.

"New York's got two Portlands," he said. "There's a little bit of a place not far from Ithaca. Then there's a more normal-sized place southwest of Buffalo."

"Normal-sized?"

"For a Portland. The one in Indiana is normal-sized, but it isn't a port. A lot of them aren't. Kentucky's got three. One of them's a port on a river, one sits near a creek, and the other is the only stop you'll find on Highway 467 before Knoxville, Kentucky. I think my favorite, though, other than this one right ahead, is Portland, North Dakota. It's a small town north of Fargo. Biggest body of water around there is what they call the Goose River, so it sure as hell isn't a port. I had the best damn meal there. Ever have frittered rabbit?"

"I hope not," I muttered.

"I stayed an extra day so I could go back to that restaurant."

I thought I'd weathered the storm as we left the interstate and picked up Forest Avenue. "You're from Michigan," Jaworski said.

I knew what he was getting at.

"You got one, too," he continued.

"One what?" I inquired, just to be contrary.

"A Portland. Not far from Lansing, on the Looking Glass River. I've never been there."

"Neither have I."

WE DROVE DOWN MELLEN STREET AND PARKED.

"Dorman had the basement apartment," Jaworski said, leading me up the front steps and through the door. "All the way to the back, turn left, then down. The lead detective, Norma Jacobs, should be waiting for us."

The building fit in with its neighborhood. It was a turn-of-the-century brownstone, originally a single-family home, that had been renovated and subdivided in the 1970s. I walked through the open basement apartment door and saw a solidly built, fortyish woman on her knees beside a cot. She wore jeans and a Boston Red Sox warm-up jacket.

"Norma?" Jaworski inquired.

"Hey, Chief," the cop said, turning and pushing herself up from the floor.

If the Portland P.D. had a height requirement, Jacobs

barely passed. She was a shade over five feet in her flat shoes. "Got a triple in Ragged Harbor, huh?" she said. "Husband and I used to drive up there now and then because it's such a pretty, peaceful town. He likes to take pictures of the ocean. Don't imagine it's peaceful today. Hear you got more satellite dishes than lobster pots."

The two friends shook hands.

"This is Lucas Frank. He's helping me on this one."

Jacobs nodded. "You were in Boston for a lot of years. Used to see you on TV from time to time."

"I live in Michigan now."

"Go Tigers," she said. "Guy's name was Harper Dorman. Lived alone here with his dog. He'd been through chemo and radiation for cancer. He was sixty, pretty much waiting to die. The dog was supposed to be therapy for him. Must've run off."

Jacobs hitched up her jeans and pointed at the cot. "That's where we found most of Dorman. Eight copper-jacketed slugs to the head."

"Stingers," Jaworski said, referring to the ammunition. "Same as our three."

"Probably an eight-shot clip," Jacobs added. "No spent shells. Shooter cleaned up after himself. Well, more or less."

Jacobs handed Jaworski a set of crime scene photos. I glanced over the chief's shoulder as he skimmed through them.

"Looks like the other went down on the floor in front of the bed," she said.

"The other" was the worst carnage that I had seen in years.

"This probably got started with him fully clothed in gray chinos and work shirt," Jacobs continued. "Drank all evening. Point-two-three blood alcohol concentration. We figure he flopped against the cot, grabbed a blanket to cover his lower legs. Passed out, like. You see the back of his head there?"

Jacobs tapped the photo with a pencil. I had missed two holes at the man's hairline. Reflexively, I looked around the apartment for something that suggested the number eight. I found nothing and thought that Jacobs was probably right. The shooter had emptied a clip.

"Looked like a wildcat tore into him. Castrated him. We haven't found the sex organs. You tell me this, Doc. What kind of strength does it take to rip open a man's chest? We found his heart on the coffee table next to his bottle of Jim Beam."

"Jesus Christ," Jaworski said, continuing to scan the photos. "I didn't know you had a slaughter here. Lucas, you ever hear of anything like this?"

I examined the thirty-five-millimeter photographs of what was left of Harper Dorman. Eight shots to the head, then Dorman's killer had hacked at his face and throat like Angie Duvall wielding her cleaver on a slab of meat in Downtown Grocery. Dorman's chest looked as if it had exploded. A mass of blood and stringy flesh covered his groin.

"Ed Gein, one of Alfred Hitchcock's inspirations for *Psycho,* gutted some of his victims and hung them up to bleed out like deer," I mumbled in rote response to Jaworski. "He also stripped the skin from some of them. Made lampshades out of it."

"Jeffrey Dahmer," Jacobs said.

I nodded, still staring at the photograph. "Dahmer lunched on some of his. Richard Chase drank human blood and carried body parts around with him."

I was aghast. How could this be our killer?

I pulled my attention from the photos, glanced around the studio apartment, then looked at Jaworski. "I don't know of any flailing, over-the-edge type who graduated to the kind of control and precision that we have in Ragged Harbor. We have evidence of rage. We don't have this. The scenes look like the work of two different people."

But as soon as I said that, I had doubts. There was a case years ago, before Quantico gave the words "organized" and "disorganized" new meaning. A killer who was both, but I could not recall the case. Yet another indication of aging, I decided.

"Gun changed hands maybe?" Jacobs asked.

She hoisted her jeans, then answered her own question. "That ain't too likely. Not in thirty-six hours. That's the time spread, right?"

Jaworski nodded, still examining the crime scene photos. "This is out of one of those videos the kids rent to scare themselves into the shits."

"He was the building super," Jacobs said. "We found the door open. Maybe one of the tenants was pissed he didn't dust the banister."

Jacobs had the razor-edged humor shared by many seasoned homicide detectives. She was talkative, rattling on as if she were enumerating the ways her Red Sox lost baseball games.

"He walks in," Jacobs continued, "stands about where you are, blasts away. You've got a mess of pumped blood on the bed from the shooting, leakage on the floor from the cutting. You got some on the other side of the coffee table, where we found the heart. If you step into the hall and turn right, there's a smaller pool just inside the furnace room. No drag marks. *You* figure."

"Fruit," I muttered, thinking of Stanley Markham's signature and the gift impaled on my kitchen counter.

"What?" Jacobs said.

"We had orange peels at ours," Jaworski explained.

"Nothing like that here."

"I received the whole orange last night," I said, and described my montage.

"I'll want to take a look at that," the chief said.

"Ain't too likely you'll get prints off a bone handle," Jacobs said. "You a target, Doc?"

"I'm beginning to feel that way."

I looked at the bottle that held two inches of bourbon. There was a single empty glass beside it. I crossed the room, glanced at photos, and examined the small apartment. The cops' voices behind me settled into a soft drone as I stepped into the hall and followed Jacobs's directions to the furnace room.

I pushed open the unlatched door. The blood pool was immediately inside the small room, two feet from a nightmare-sized boiler that dominated the confined space. The pool appeared larger than it did in the photograph.

No blood trail. No drag marks.

"What the hell," I muttered, slowly gazing up at a large dark stain on the ceiling.

I looked for a light switch and found a string with a cardboard pine tree attached, just inside the door. When I yanked the string, what could not be more than a twenty-watt bulb flickered on and off, intermittently illuminating shelves of empty pint and quart bottles.

"Dorman minded his Ps and Qs," I said.

Six feet from the ceiling stain, a trapdoor hung open.

What I assumed was the superintendent's winter coat lay across a backless chair. His work boots, wool socks stuffed inside, squatted side by side on the floor. I grabbed what remained of the chair, placed it beneath the trap, and pulled myself into the crawl space.

Jaworski and Jacobs entered the room below. "You got something?" Jacobs called.

The furnace room light continued its stuttering performance, creating pockets of dark shadow that seemed to move.

"I can't see worth shit," I yelled. "Got a flashlight?"

"What the hell are you doing up there?" Jaworski asked through the trapdoor as he handed me his three-cell.

Estimating the distance to the ceiling stain, I crawled forward, pausing to shine the light ahead of me.

Copper heat pipes, metal-encased wiring, a pile of loose insulation and . . .

I balanced on a joist, the edge of the two-by-six digging at my knees. A sharp pain knifed from my right knee to my shin. I fell forward. The flashlight slipped from my hand, indirectly illuminating what I had thought was a mound of pink fiberglass.

I shoved backward violently and smacked my head on a pipe. "Jesus Christ," I yelled, struggling to understand what I stared at.

"Lucas? You okay?"

A small white dog with its neck snapped, the head nearly torn from the body.

"It's the dog," I said.

Disemboweled, with bits and pieces of entrails flung about like confetti.

"What's left of it," I added.

I stuggled to the trapdoor and lowered myself through the opening. Jaworski reached up and gave me a hand.

"We always look down," Jacobs said, squinting at the ceiling, "check surfaces. When do we look up?"

I rubbed the back of my head tenderly.

"Jacobs, we need to interview the tenants," Jaworski said.

She climbed onto the chair, pulled herself up, and peered into the dark space. "They've been talked to, but go right ahead. I'll get the crime scene techs started again. How'd they miss the fuckin' dog? Shit."

She pulled her head back through the hole. "Come down when you're finished and we'll go to Big Mama's for lunch."

Cops know good restaurants. The thought of lunch filled me with the willingness to carry on, despite my headache.

JAWORSKI SAID THAT HE WOULD HANDLE THE TWO apartments on the first floor. I climbed the stairs, taking time to admire the ornate, original wood moldings while I tried to make the ringing in my head go away. I wanted someone to tell me why I left the comforts of forest dwelling. Anyone. Probably I should have banged my head a lot earlier and a lot harder. As I climbed the second flight, I realized that I was out of shape. Knowing that I was lying, I promised myself that I would get back to my morning walking routine. I read somewhere that graceful aging involves acceptance of "our increasing limitations." Must have been some of that conservative AARP crap sandwiched between ads for walkers and electric carts in *Modern Maturity*. I was still in my fifties, for chrissake.

From the time I was forty in Boston and visited Doc London for an annual medical checkup, he always smiled and said, "So, you can't pee over the tops of cars anymore."

Obviously I had blown my youth, never having tried to pee over a car. I missed an exercise in twisted virility, and my prostate would not let me return to the days of yesteryear. I was not about to go gracefully, but I would be damned if I got suckered into soaking my Jeep. Maybe I *would* restart my walking routine.

Apartment three found me. A thrumming electric bass

resonated inside, shook two hallway pinup lamps, and threatened plaster walls. I recognized the tune, Leonard Cohen's "Waiting for the Miracle."

"I'm watching the miracle," I muttered, expecting an instant replay of Joshua in Jericho.

When the song faded, I pounded on the door.

Wendell Beckerman was young, probably a student, and most likely specializing in something vaguely artsy, with a minor concentration in a decidedly aromatic field. He wore glasses with thick lenses and fat plastic frames, and had a sparse goatee and a fluff of black curly hair.

Beckerman opened the door on its chain. "You got a search warrant?"

Huh?

"I'm not a police officer, Mr. Beckerman. I have no interest in what you smoke. I want to ask you about Mr. Dorman."

Shit, I was beginning to sound like a reporter for *The New York Times*.

He glanced over his shoulder into the apartment. "What about my brew?"

"Why don't you step into the hall," I suggested. "That way there won't be any problem."

He considered my proposal. Then he looked into his apartment again, nodded, unfastened the chain, set the catch on his lock, and slipped into the hall. Beckerman was barefoot, dressed in black pants and shirt, and he sported one black onyx earring. He also looked vaguely familiar.

"Harper Dorman," I said.

"Let me see the badge."

The kid glanced at his hands, his feet, the ceiling, never at me. He was pissing me off.

"Mr. Beckerman, don't push your luck. There are two police officers in the building. The way we're going to do this is I ask questions, you answer. If I get annoyed, then I call the cops and you get a paid vacation to a place that isn't at all like Club Med. Based on the aromas that blew into the hall, my guess is that you were enjoying a joint while cooking up a batch of lysergic acid diethylamide."

Beckerman's jaw dropped into slack position.

"My second guess is that you have enough shit stewing in there to be charged with intent to distribute. Mandatory-sentencing laws suck, but some judges get their giggles slapping kids with ten years to take it in the ass. We together on this?"

"Dorman's the landlord," he said. "He drinks. I didn't know he was into dope."

I resisted the urge to shake the little prick.

"He's dead," I patiently reminded Beckerman.

"No shit? Wow. Somebody said he had cancer or something."

"The police talked to you a few days ago. Dorman was murdered, Mr. Beckerman."

"Oh. So that's why the cops . . . I get it now. Murdered?"

I nodded, bemused.

"Like, with a gun or something?"

"Did you see anyone, or hear anything unusual in the building last Thursday night?"

He considered the question. "Everything I hear is unusual."

I was certain of that. "When did you last see Mr. Dorman?"

Beckerman furrowed his brow, attempting a thought, no doubt. "Yesterday," he finally said. "He was coming in. I was going out. It was late afternoon."

"Mr. Beckerman, he'd been dead for five days yesterday."

Beckerman shrugged. "I don't own any clocks or

watches or calendars or anything. My shrink says I'm field-dependent. Like, I have to rely on my environment for information like that. I told her I—"

I interrupted what threatened to become painfully taxing. On my part.

"Were you here the middle of last week?"

"If I was, I wasn't," he said, with a perfectly straight face.

I understood. "You live alone?"

He looked pained. "Not always, I don't think. Friends stay here sometimes. I hear their voices. I don't remember."

We stood in silence for a moment, then I asked, "Where have I seen you before?"

Beckerman established eye contact for the first time. "Shit, man, that's your problem."

He was right. It was my problem.

I thanked Beckerman, who slipped back through his door and locked it.

I climbed another flight, found apartment four, and knocked. A tall, blond young woman with brilliant blue eyes, dressed in jeans and a Bowdoin College sweatshirt, answered my knock. I explained who I was and why I was there. She said her name was Gretchen Nash and invited me in.

The place was a loft, an area with a kitchenette in one corner, a metal closet in the opposite corner. She had five windows, a partial view of the harbor, no curtains, and a bed in front of the windows. A small red, green, and gold octagonal mirror hung at the foot of the bed between two of the windows.

"It's feng shui," Nash said, following my gaze. "It's not a paranoid thing. I like to wake with the sun on my face, but I should be able to see the door behind me."

She pointed at the mirror. "That's an important eighth

of the room . . . fame and reputation. I placed all the mirrors to help with the chi flow."

Mr. Beckerman and Ms. Nash were quickly making me appreciate not being able to pee over my Jeep. I had forgotten how strange youth could be. Was I ever *this* young? Doubtful.

Nash had hung half a dozen mirrors in the rectangular room, probably creating a chi flow like a pinball game.

The morning sun illuminated a large easel and canvas.

"The light is perfect until early afternoon," she said. "After that . . ." Nash shrugged, allowing the sentence to dangle.

"I usually work until noon. I might eat something then, but I'm not an eating fan. It's such a face thing."

She'd covered one wall with her artwork. Most of her paintings and sketches were of people, in various states of dress and undress, alone or involved as couples or trios locked in physical postures that appeared vaguely sexual.

None of them had heads.

"Heads are the least attractive part of the anatomy," Nash said, seeing me stare.

Despite the tangles of limbs, the breasts that emerged between elbows and buttocks, Nash's work possessed a symmetry. She consistently set her chaotic collisions of people at center and contained their silent groping, reaching, or flailing within perfect squares or circles. The technique paradoxically added to the sense of tumult, while it controlled the disorder.

One of her headless people was a slender male, dressed in gray chinos and work shirt. "Harper Dorman?" I asked.

"I heard what happened," she said. "I mean, I heard *about* it. I didn't, like, hear the shots or anything. The cops were here. I don't know who'd want to kill him. He could be hard to get along with, but he was dying anyway. Cancer. Nobody had to kill him. He figured he had six months. That's what he said two months ago. It's strange. Nothing like this ever happened to me before . . . knowing someone who got murdered. I nearly moved out. I mean, there was a killer right in this building. Then—I know this sounds callous—but fear fades."

She gazed at the drawing. "I sketched him when he first moved into the building."

"How was he hard to get along with?" I asked.

"Tea? I was just gonna fix some."

"Please."

She filled a kettle and set it on the small electric range. "Mr. Dorman has a nasty temper," she said. "*Had,* I guess. He'd blow up over nothing. A burnt-out lightbulb in the stairwell. A doorbell that didn't work. He drank all the time. That was most of it. He didn't pose for me or anything. I remember people. Their bodies. You can't see it in the painting, but the reason he's on his toes is that he was standing on a stepladder, reaching up."

She demonstrated. I got the idea.

"I've got most of the Zingers and Cranberry Cove," Nash said. "Celestial Seasonings. I don't like caffeine. There's enough stimulation going around. No. Wait a minute. I've got some Earl Grey decaf, too."

"Earl Grey sounds good," I said. "When was the last time you saw Mr. Dorman?"

She placed two mugs and two tea bags on the table, then sat across from me. "Let's see. I came in late that Wednesday night," she said. "A friend of mine who's a sculptor had an installation here in the city. His show is called 'The Surge to the Electric Dot.' He called the final piece 'The Electric Dot,' so all the other stuff surges toward it."

She extended her arms and stood on one foot, leaning.

122 *John Philpin*

"Well, he thought it did. It's a black-and-gold Styrofoam ball with an extension cord hanging out of it. There was supposed to be a straight section of coat hanger stuck in it, too, but that kept falling out. He nearly called it 'Bad Sex' because of that, but he didn't. One guy wanted to plug it into a wall socket to see what it would do. Jesus. He could've shorted out the room, or worse. We went to the Old Port afterwards, drank champagne. Mr. Dorman was sitting on the steps outside when I got back. I was tipsy, maybe. He was wobbly. Seemed like he always was. He didn't say anything. He never talked to the tenants unless he had to. I said hi, but . . ."

Again she shrugged, and left the sentence hanging.

"Did he have his dog with him?"

She raised an eyebrow. "I didn't know he had a dog. I wouldn't think he'd want to take care of an animal. I mean, I'm sorry he's dead, but he wasn't a very nice person."

"Did you ever see him with anyone?"

"Just the rental agent, Mr. Crandall. He came twice a month or so. They talked. Mr. Crandall took the rent checks, paid Mr. Dorman. I saw them a couple of times in the downstairs hall. That's Mr. Crandall over there."

The kettle whistled. On her way to the stove, Gretchen Nash pointed to one of the sketches. Again I was struck by a sense of recognition; the short, stocky, headless figure looked vaguely familiar.

"That one's a caricature," she said, pouring hot water into the mugs. "He isn't really that obese. I felt like he should be, or maybe would be one of these days."

"Crandall?"

She nodded. "Twitchy guy in his early forties maybe. All tics and fidgets."

Aha. Finally. Gretchen Nash had drawn and described a bloated version of Stu Gilman.

"You're not from Maine, are you?" she asked.

"I live in Michigan."

"Really? That's one of those places . . . like Iowa. I'm pretty sure it's there, but it's hard to believe. I'd believe in a caring god a lot sooner than I'd believe in Iowa or Michigan or . . . *cyberspace*."

She shuddered. "I can get a handle on the god concept, but miles of flat nowhere and electronic wizardry leave me barren."

What is going on with America's youth?

"Do you have any idea who owns this building?"

She shook her head. "It's a company, not a person. That's all I know. Mr. Dorman was murdered, huh? Like I said, I didn't hear anything that night. Not shots or anything. It's usually pretty quiet around here. The guy downstairs, Wendell Beckerman, cranks his stereo sometimes, but you get used to it. He's into grumbly music. Tom Waits. Beck. Randy Newman. Steady diet of that bums you out. It does him, anyway. So, you're not interested in the woman, huh?"

"Woman?" I asked, sipping my Earl Grey.

"Maybe you already investigated about her. The one who was in the building a month ago. She said she was looking for Mr. Dorman,"

I looked up. "I don't know about her."

"Money," Nash said. "She was dressed like she'd just left a Paris fashion show. She wore dark wraparounds, a kerchief over her head. It was as if she didn't want to be recognized, like a Jackie Onassis thing. Slender. Pale skin. Stretch limo parked at the curb. It was weird. I was going out. She was standing there in the hall looking lost. I asked if I could help her, you know? She said she was looking for Harper Dorman. No way she was after an apartment to rent. That's her up there."

I walked over and stared at the painting of a headless

woman dressed in a black sheath, a strand of pearls across the neckline. She wore black spike heels and a ring on her left hand.

"Hair color?"

Nash shrugged. "Like I said, her head was covered. That was nice of her. With the sunglasses, too, I couldn't see much of her face except the shape of it. I told her that Mr. Dorman had the basement apartment. Then she turned and walked out. Her driver opened the limo door for her, and off they went."

"Did you say anything to Dorman about her?"

"It was bad enough wading through his fumes to tell him when the stove shit the bed, then listening to him rant about how I must've left the burner on for ten days like Beckerman does. I figured if she wanted him bad enough, she'd find him."

"Can you describe her driver?"

"African-American," Nash said. "Big, like a football player. No. Basketball is the tall guys, right? He was more tall than big. Shaved head. Lots of neck. White shirt, black pants. Maybe thirty-five."

"He's not up here," I said, surveying the paintings and sketches.

"I don't do everybody I see. He wasn't that interesting. Watch TV. You see guys like that all the time selling sneakers."

Another of her paintings was populated only by a headless, waifish child—a girl, I thought—reflected in a cracked mirror at the center of what appeared to be an amusement park. A chaotic arrangement of lines and arcs and circles created the sense of Whips and Roundups, Coasters and Flying Scooters, that wound wildly toward space with no hope of return.

I asked Nash if she had any objection to my having

photographs taken of her paintings of Dorman, Crandall, and the woman.

"You can borrow them," she said. "You have an honest body."

I gave her a quizzical look.

"I know. People always say 'honest face.' I don't read faces. I read bodies and their movement. You're a Leo, aren't you?"

I nodded.

"See?"

I CARRIED GRETCHEN NASH'S PENCIL SKETCHES OF Dorman and Crandall, and her acrylic painting of the mystery woman, and headed down a flight.

Jaworski stood in the hall. "You make a purchase?" he asked, cracking a grin.

"They're on loan from the artist, Gretchen Nash, on the third floor. I'll explain later."

"First floor rear is a Vietnamese family," Jaworski said. "The kid's the only one who speaks English, and not real well. They don't know anything. Thought I was there to collect rent. Kept trying to force money on me. Front apartment is an old guy, pretty close to deaf. He hadn't seen Dorman since he paid his rent last month."

"Does the name Wendell Beckerman ring any bells with you?"

He shook his head.

"Beckerman has the apartment on the second floor. I've seen him somewhere, but I can't place him."

Jaworski and I caught up with Norma Jacobs on the front steps.

"We found some court papers with Dorman's stuff," Jacobs said. "He was married. Lived with the woman in South Portland for sixteen years. Fifteen years ago, the woman filed a child abuse complaint against Dorman, then got a permanent restraining order. Prosecutor dropped the charges against him. Doesn't say why."

"You got names?" Jaworski asked.

"Names are blacked out. Court records should have them. Social Services would. You guys came down here because of the ballistics match. You want connections to your murders, and I want to clear this one. Think I've got something here. Five years ago, Dorman worked in maintenance at Harbor College."

CHAPTER 15

HERB JAWORSKI TOLD ME ABOUT HIS FAVORITE PORTLAND.

An enlightened city government and an active citizens' group had reclaimed and gradually restored the city's Old Port district, he said. *Utne Reader* had named the city one of the top ten most enlightened cities in the U.S.

"I was born on Sheridan Street, over by Standpine Park," Jaworski said. "Lived there with my folks and my little brother Henry until I went into the service. I was an M.P., spent a year in Korea. When I came home, Portland P.D. didn't have any openings, but Ragged Harbor needed somebody to wear a uniform and walk up and down Main Street. Been there ever since."

We parked on Commercial, at the bottom of Dana Street, then hiked over the cobblestones to Big Mama's. I'd heard of the restaurant, christened when its pregnant owner bought the place. The small eatery was famous for its breakfast special: any style eggs and chorizo, a Mexican sausage.

"Took the select board a few years to realize that crime was drifting up from Portland and down from Augusta," Jaworski said, breathing heavily from our walk up the slight grade. "Then we had the sixties. We seized drugs and couldn't identify them. Had to drop a whole lot of cases because we didn't know what the stuff was."

Big Mama's offered old wooden tables in odd shapes and sizes. There were equally varied help-yourself chairs all over the crowded room. We walked across the scuffed linoleum floors to a vacant table, consulted our menus, and ordered.

Over lunch, we attempted to puzzle through what little we knew.

Someone had fired eight shots into Harper Dorman's head, then torn at him with a frenzy usually reserved for lions ripping apart wildebeests on the African plains. Thirty-six hours later, the same gun was used in the triple murder on Crescent Street in Ragged Harbor.

But that scene was controlled. There was evidence of rage, not of frenzy. The killer patiently designed a stage set, then ate an orange.

Five years earlier, Dorman had worked at the college.

"I don't remember the guy," Jaworski said. "Must be we didn't have any dealings with him."

"Why did he leave his job at Harbor?" I asked.

"Dismissed," Jacobs said. "He grieved it through his union. Didn't do any good. Administration had a paper trail of reprimands on his alcohol abuse."

"Who owns the building on Mellen Street?"

"Rental agent is Paul Crandall. He handles Mellen and eighteen other properties in the city for Martin International. They've got a big spread out by the highway, but they ain't exactly in real estate."

Martin International again. Curiouser and curiouser.

"Have you met Paul Crandall?" I asked.

She shook her head.

"Herb, maybe we should stop at MI on our way out of town."

"Doubt you'll find Crandall there," Jacobs said

through a mouthful of burger. "He collects rent. MI is millions of dirty dollars. Crandall's a percentage gofer on a bunch of rentals."

"You know about the company," I said.

"They smell worse than low tide, but nobody can touch them. Couple of months ago an informant called, young gal who works out there. She saw a TV news thing about money laundering in South Florida and thought maybe that's what she was doing here. She handles deposits and withdrawals for a dozen MI client corporations. We checked a couple of names she gave us and they were dummies, bank accounts and post office boxes. Last time she called was ten days ago to set up a meeting for this week. She didn't show, and we haven't heard from her."

"Think she got spooked?" Jaworski asked.

Jacobs nodded. "Martin is major league. We've had undercover people at the airport when some of their guests came through. First I thought it was drugs. Then I thought it was guns. Now I figure it's the money from all of the above. Colombians, Dominicans, Libyans, Mexicans . . . we even saw a few Iraqis last year. Papers were always in order. A honcho at MI, guy named Weatherly, complained to politicians in Augusta and Washington. We can't check papers anymore. Have to stay a hundred feet away from the pricks and prickettes. All that diplomatic shit."

"What about Stuart Gilman?" I asked.

"Never met him. I know the name, though. He's MI's all-purpose 'hands-on' man."

"What does that mean?"

"He does everything but plunge the toilets. Maybe he does that, too."

"The owner and CEO seems to be something of a mystery," I said.

"Melanie Martin," Jacobs nodded. "Never laid eyes on her. She has to be smart. She was in business only a year when they broke ground on that fortress they call corporate headquarters. She's done a lot for the city, restoring old buildings, funding a women's health center, writing big checks for the arts. I can't say anything critical of her, except that her company sucks."

Jacobs stabbed french fries with her fork and soaked them with ketchup. "You getting the Markham updates, Herb?"

"Last I knew was the sighting in Connecticut."

"Plenty of time to get up this way."

"Karen Jasper's convinced."

Jacobs nearly choked and then burst into laughter. "You got the frustrated feebie on it, huh? Jesus, Herb. You got more trouble than I thought."

"She seems smart enough," Jaworski protested. "She doesn't care for Lucas working the case, but she's helped on a lot of tough ones around the state."

"All she knows how to do is play computer games, organize her file folders, and call in the feds. She's suckin' up because she wants to graduate from here to there. No fuckin' help from that one, pardon my French. Oughta spend more time on her red hair and less on red herrings. Had her down here twice last year. She types shit into that laptop and says the butler did it. Trouble is, there ain't no butler."

Oh, yes. I imagine I was looking quite smug.

Jacobs inhaled the last of her fries and yelled for the check.

"The select board on your back?"

Jaworski snorted. "Nothing new there. They wanted me to retire five years ago. Hubble Saymes chairs the board. He says that new crimes require new cops."

"Hubble's full of shit. Couple of years ago, I popped his kid on a possession charge. Hubble called in every chit he had. His pothead kid still got court diversion, same as all the others."

"You follow up on Dorman at this end," Jaworski said. "We'll take a look at his history up our way."

She nodded, then looked at me. "So, Doc, when do you do your magic?"

I laughed. "Wish I could."

"Bullshit," she snapped as she stood and yanked up her jeans. "I read your profile on the Markham murders first time around. You wrote it a long time before the bastard got nailed. I still think murder profiling's a little shit and a lot of hocus-pocus, but you had him pegged. You think it's him again?"

"I have my doubts."

"So do I. Somebody should shoot the bastard anyway."

The waitress brought the check and Jacobs grabbed it. "You want to know what I think?"

"Sure," I said, wondering what was coming next.

"Karen Jasper did it," she said, and erupted in choking laughter.

"SWING BY MARTIN INTERNATIONAL," I SAID TO JA-worski as we drove out of the city.

"Plan to. I've never seen the place."

"What's with this Saymes character?"

"It's like I told Jacobs," he said. "Hubble Saymes thinks I'm too old."

"Is he responsible for the 'dump Jaworski' radio editorial?"

"His wife owns the station. Saymes says the public sector should be run with the same businesslike efficiency as his insurance agency. He wants a forty-year-old chief with experience and degrees in criminology and public administration. The rest of the board didn't pay any attention to Saymes until these murders."

"I've seen young hotshots hobbled by serial murder cases," I said. "Education, experience, age . . . none of it matters when you're dealing with a psychopath. They don't operate according to our logic. That's why they're always a step ahead. We follow a few threads and hope they lead us in the right direction."

"Tell that to Saymes."

"He wouldn't listen to me, either," I said.

"We had a woman come in who said she had information about the murders. Turned out she's an astrologer, and Mercury's screwing around with Pluto. A guy came in this morning after driving all the way from Newport, Rhode Island. Says he got hit on the head when he was a kid and now he has visions. I was staring out the window at the ocean while he was telling Jasper that our killer lives near a body of water. Maybe it ain't efficient, but we don't know what someone's going to say unless we take the time to listen."

Five minutes later we sat in the crowded parking lot in front of a fenced-in, low brick building.

"There's no sign," Jaworski said. "How's anybody supposed to know what it is?"

"Maybe we're not supposed to know."

I gazed at the gated fortress and watched as two German shepherds approached the razor-wire-topped fence. "What's the need for that kind of security?" I muttered.

"Keeps out people like us. You think there's a direct connection between MI and the murders?"

"I don't know," I said. "I've never been a fan of coincidence. This outfit keeps coming up."

I opened the car door. "I'll be right back."

As I walked to the gate, the dogs followed silently on

their side of the fence. I pressed the buzzer beneath a small plastic sign that read INFORMATION. A woman's metallic voice blatted from a shielded speaker. "Do you have an appointment, sir?"

"My name is Lucas Frank. I'd like to see Melanie Martin."

"Do you have an appointment?"

She was not a recording, but the experience was unsettling—a crisp, disembodied voice similar to a tape you would expect to hear when dialing the IRS. "Yes," I lied. "I have an appointment."

"I have no record of any appointment in your name, sir."

"Then no. Ms. Martin is not expecting me."

"This is a secure facility, and I must ask you to leave the grounds immediately. The Portland police will be notified of the name you have given and the license number of the automobile in which you arrived."

In my best, post-ironic, clipped British accent I asked, "Are you doing anything for dinner, love?"

I walked back to the car and felt like pissing over the top of it. "Let's head north," I said to Jaworski.

"This the right place?"

"It's either Martin International or the Department of Motor Vehicles."

Jaworski looked at me. "Bastards, are they?"

"They just called in your plate to the Portland P.D."

"Must be we don't look Iraqi," he grumbled as he opened a stick of cinnamon gum, popped it into his mouth, and guided the cruiser out of the parking lot.

WE DROVE IN SILENCE AS WE APPROACHED THE TURN onto the straightaway to Ragged Harbor. Gift shops and food stands lined the road, offering everything from wine-colored murgatroyds—lawn ornaments consisting of glass balls on plaster pedestals—to neon-red hot dogs.

The commercial area gave way to mudflats and eelgrass marshes on both sides of the two-lane road.

"Did you know that Jaycie Waylon was an MI intern?" I asked.

"I saw that in one of the reports."

"Didn't you have an internship there?" Kai Lin asked.

"Still do, but I've never met Ms. Martin."

"Why doesn't anyone ever meet Melanie Martin?" I asked.

"Guess she doesn't want to be met."

"From the unofficial welcoming committee."

"Jaycie Waylon and three of her friends came by the house the first night I was there. They brought me a gift, a carved whalebone letter opener."

"Scrimshaw? Sounds pricey even for the kids on the hill."

"There's a shipwreck scene on the blade."

"There's stories behind all that stuff. I don't know 'em. Never had much interest. If you get time to play tourist, that little shack ahead on the left is Ben Loudermilk's. Ben's a silversmith, but he sells scrimshaw. He knows all the folk tales."

Loudermilk's one-room shop squatted at the edge of the tidal flats. His weathered sign offered works in silver, pewter, and scrimshaw.

Delicately etched whalebone. A whaling ship yawing in windblown seas. A sperm whale harnessed on the side of the ship. A giant serpent prepared to swallow it all.

"Why you thinking about that now?"

"I'm not. I've moved on."

"What?"

I imagined the students' apartment and retraced my

movements when I'd walked through the crime scene. "Let's stop at the house," I said.

"I swear I can't follow your head."

"I'm ready to spend more time there," I said. "Not in my head. In the apartment."

"Lucas, in maybe thirty seconds you went from MI, to whalebone, to murder."

"It's not asking why that allows me to speed-think," I teased.

"I ain't sayin' it's a talent," he shot back.

Jaworski made the left turn onto Crescent Street and skirted the roadblock where one of his officers talked with two reporters. He stopped the car in front of 42 Crescent, and sorted keys as we walked to the porch.

Jaworski remained by the apartment door. I crossed the living room to my left, stood between the two beds, and reenacted the shooting as I had done at my house.

Squeeze off a single round to my left, another to my right. Take two steps back, aim at Jaycie across the living room.

You were confident of your shot. You knew that she went down dead, and you were not concerned about time.

I wandered into the bathroom. Black fingerprint powder coated the bathtub, sink, counter, toilet, walls, and towel racks. The counter held the usual array of toothpaste, brushes, shampoo, mouthwash. Nothing caught my attention, so I moved to Jaycie's room.

You methodically cut away the nightgown and placed it over the chair's arm. You arranged the body, and you did not cover Jaycie.

"What time did the guys in the upstairs unit return from the concert?"

"They estimated three A.M."

"The neighbor, Luther Peterson, saw the young man with the knapsack walk to his Volvo at three-thirty."

You heard the guys returning from the concert, didn't you? You listened, but you were not concerned.

"An earthquake wouldn't have distracted Dorman's killer," I said.

It didn't matter if someone came to the door. You would have killed them all.

"Who rented the video?" I asked.

Jaworski flipped open his notebook. "*Kiss the Girls,*" he muttered. "Jaycie did."

"When?"

"Saturday at eight-fifty P.M."

"She was here, studying and listening to music," I reminded him. "Someone used her card."

"The killer?"

You curled up on the sofa, ate your orange, and watched a good movie. Was it your selection?

"Possibly."

I had a decent reconstruction of the triple murder and could begin to consider what the criminology types call "offender characteristics."

You completed your chores, patiently attended to the decorative details, then relaxed.

"This stinks of Stanley Markham," Jaworski said.

"It does and it doesn't," I said with a sigh.

As Jaworski and I stepped onto the porch, a shout from farther out Crescent Street near the lobster pound snapped my head around. A man in a police uniform ran toward us, waving his arms. His hat blew off his head.

"That's young Dickie Stevens," Jaworski said. "I just made him corporal. What the hell's he doing?"

We stepped into the street.

Stevens stopped running, bent at the waist, vomited, then resumed an awkward jog. He was forty yards away, still yelling as he staggered along the road.

Finally, I understood what he was saying.

"His face," Stevens bawled, his arms raised in the air as if he were pleading with the heavens. "Somebody shot him in the face."

Jaworski and I converged on Stevens as the corporal's knees buckled and he fell to the pavement.

"Oh my God," the young cop moaned. "What is happening here?"

Two news reporters standing behind the Crescent Street barricade stiffened to alert status. One of them raised a camera, the other a cell phone.

Jaworski's face glowed an unhealthy purple. "Dickie," the chief began.

"He's still in there," Stevens gasped. "I heard noise at the back of the house. Last place on the right before the lobster pound."

Jaworski grabbed Stevens's portable and called for backup, and medical attention for his corporal. "Sounds like we got one dead in there that we know of," he growled into the radio. "Shooter possibly on the scene."

He handed me his nine-millimeter semiautomatic pistol. "You know how to operate one of these?"

I nodded.

Jaworski spit out his cinnamon gum, grabbed a double-barreled shotgun from the trunk of his cruiser, rammed two slugs into it, and led the way down Crescent.

The house was a white Cape Cod, its red door standing open.

"You go in the front the way Dickie did," Jaworski said. "I'll come in along the seawall out back."

I watched as Jaworski made his unsteady trek through a yard of sea-thrown rocks. His eyes moved from window to window along the side of the house. He held the shotgun like someone prepared to blast clay pigeons from the sky. Anything that moved back there ran the risk of getting cut in half.

I released the nine's safety, engaged its action, and stepped through the open door into a narrow hall with a flight of stairs on the right and an archway ahead on the left. I slid along the wall to the arch and peered around the corner at a man lying on the living room floor, his face blood-covered and unrecognizable.

The dead man's multicolored T-shirt bore the logo of the Grateful Dead and the words "Highgate, Vermont, Keep On Truckin'."

Steve Weld.

I stepped into the room in time to see Jaworski slip through the back door into the kitchen. He signaled that he was headed upstairs.

I knelt beside Weld and made the futile gesture of feeling his throat for a pulse. The body was warm with no rigor, but the soul had made its exit.

I sighed deeply. What a waste.

Things were beginning to get very complicated. Tests on the bullets that had slammed into Weld's face would take a couple of days, but I was already certain that we were dealing with a busy killer.

"What set you in motion?" I whispered to no one in particular.

Jaworski moved slowly across the plank flooring above as backup arrived: two Ragged Harbor auxiliary officers and Karen Jasper, all with guns drawn. The four of us waited in silence until Jaworski descended the stairs.

"Everybody out on the porch," he said. "I don't want this place tramped over. The crime scene techs and the medical examiner get first crack at it. You get Dickie tended to?"

One of the temporary cops said that paramedics were with Stevens.

"Lucas?"

"It's Steve Weld," I said. "He hasn't been dead long."

Jaworski nodded his head once, then ushered all of us onto the porch.

Karen Jasper snapped on latex gloves.

"What are you doing?" Jaworski asked her.

"I'm going to take a look at the body," she said.

"No you aren't. You help secure this scene and make sure nobody goes in there."

The color disappeared from Jasper's face. She placed her hands firmly on her hips and said nothing.

"Who's at the barricade?" Jaworski asked.

"I was," the temp said. "Dispatch said you needed me down here."

More reporters gathered at the end of Crescent. Three of them advanced forty yards onto the street.

"Cooper, get your ass back to that fuckin' roadblock and herd those assholes off this street."

The young man ran toward Crescent's intersection with the village's main street.

"Jesus," Jaworski grumbled.

He turned his attention to the second temp. "Batson, get the roll of crime scene tape out of the trunk of my cruiser. You and Jasper tie off this place."

Jaworski walked toward the seawall. "Maybe the son-ofabitch didn't get off the peninsula yet. If he went out the back, he might be down in the rocks near the lobster pound. I'm going to walk out that way."

I was ready to follow the chief when the squeal of tires distracted me. I turned and saw Jasper and Batson run to the side of the road and draw their weapons as a gray Volvo roared by, picking up speed. The three reporters propelled themselves over a roadside barrier. Both cops yelled after the car's driver, who paid no attention. The car was hitting fifty when it crashed through the roadblock, slamming Cooper against the side of the Tradewind restaurant on the corner.

The battered gray car was the same one that I had seen pass my house and, I was willing to wager, the same one spotted on Crescent Street the night of the murders.

Jaworski ran back across the rocks behind me yelling, "Jasper, radio for a roadblock at the end of the flats. Tell them what we've got here. Lucas, you get a look at that bastard?"

"It was quick," I told him. "Dark-colored baseball cap. Blue vest. The car has a Maine plate. I didn't get the number."

Jaworski breathed heavily. "Look like anyone you saw at the memorial service?"

"I couldn't tell."

"That's got to be the same car Luther Peterson told us about."

"It's also been on my hill," I said. "First day I was at the house. He had the cap on backward, and he waved to me. Nearly forced Jaycie and her friends off the road."

"Wonder if he likes snakes," Jaworski muttered.

I returned the chief's nine-millimeter; there was no point bothering with the lobster pound. "You'll have your hands full here for a while. I can hike to my place."

Jaworski took the gun, then pointed a finger at Batson. "We ain't had shit for evidence. Put somebody out back and don't let air get in that fuckin' house until Jasper gets the mobile crime lab down here."

AS I WALKED TO MAIN STREET, I PICTURED STEVE Weld sprawled in a pool of blood. I inched through the press contingent standing in the debris that had been a barricade. Their eyes were fixed to the action on Crescent Street. Two reporters glanced at me, then turned away.

There were five dead and, I believed, one fast-moving killer with more than a passing interest in me.

Why the hell did I ever come out of retirement?

CHAPTER 16

I WALKED THROUGH THE HOUSE, ALERT FOR SNAKES OR other uninvited guests. When I felt confident that I was alone, I turned my attention to the phone.

The answering machine blinked at me, its rhythmic succession of three red winks hinting that three messages awaited me. I was well on my way to mastering the technological age.

I put on my reading glasses and studied the buttons, pondering which to push first.

I pushed the one labeled Save in case I screwed up anything when I pressed another button. The flat, tan box beeped four times; the light continued to blink.

When I pushed Play, nothing happened.

I poked one button marked <<<, heard a whirring noise, then a click, then nothing. Shit.

I hit Play again.

The first message was from my daughter Lane in New York. "Hi, Pop. If you can figure out how to operate your answering gizmo, then you can punch the numbered buttons on the phone and give me a call. Talk to you soon."

I chuckled.

The second was from Ray Bolton. "Lucas, this is Ray. Call me as soon as possible."

Bolton was gone from his office for the day, so I called his home number and left a message on his answering gizmo.

I propped Gretchen Nash's sketches of Dorman and Crandall, and her painting of the headless woman, against the dining room wall. Then I wandered back to the photos and files, grabbed a legal pad and a felt-tipped pen, and doodled when I didn't have a thought, scribbled notes when I did.

The caricature of the over-chubby Mr. Crandall squatted like a headless troll against the wall. Put a head on that full-figured dude, I thought, and you have a Gilman ready to prowl backyards and peer in windows.

I was not about to lose sleep over MI's failure to file IRS Form blah-blah-blah. The feds had an army of raincoat-clad cops who packed adding machines and specialized in tracking numbers. Let them get the glory.

Gilman bothered me because he lied, his face and most of his body were in permanent jitterbug mode, he had had an early career in voyeurism, his name had surfaced in the Markham investigation, and Steve Weld had pointed a finger at Gilman as an information source.

There was nothing remarkable about the Dorman sketch. The drawing was well done, but it was a man in work clothes. Period.

The woman in black fascinated me. I studied the pearls, her slender shape in the clinging dress, the ring, her hands, her long, narrow fingers, the black shawl, her arms.

"Who are you?" I asked the picture, and wondered what she had wanted with Dorman.

I gazed at the photo array on my kitchen table.

When I examine a crime scene, the more evidence of

excitability that I find, the more encouraged I feel. Impulsive killers leave more evidence than their methodical kin. Norma Jacobs and her technical people should discover trace evidence left by a frenzied killer.

The most difficult cases are ones in which everything is planned and rehearsed in fantasy, then acted out against strangers. Even the intrusion of an unwanted moment of rage does little to disrupt the performance. A decision has been made, a script opened at act one, and one person knows the stage directions.

Harper Dorman was savaged, his dog killed and concealed. Dorman was not concealed.

After the fact, you were conflicted about killing the dog, but not about killing Dorman.

The building superintendent was a walking dead man with perhaps six months to live. He was very likely inebriated and probably oblivious when the shooter stood beside the cot and blasted away.

Another unconscious victim.

Vulnerable, as my students noted in class discussion.

He represented no threat. Why rain bullets through his head?

Rage.

Fear of the victim.

A single, well-placed shot does the trick. A second might be considered insurance. Without an external cue for the number eight, the possibility of an idiosyncratic association, something inside the killer's head, remained. If that were the case, I would expect to see greater consistency in the murders.

It was not there.

Rage, and the eight-shot capacity of the clip.

Killing Dorman was personal.

I imagined myself standing over the building superintendent and firing eight times into his head. There's no way that he's coming back to life. He is not a threat.

How did Dorman hurt you?

Killing him was not enough.

Norma Jacobs said that years ago Dorman had lived with a woman, and that police had charged him with abusing the woman's daughter. Men have been killed for that, but not typically fifteen years after the fact.

You castrated him, ripped open his chest.

It is no easy task to tear into the human body.

You placed his heart on the coffee table near his bottle of bourbon.

Personal. Debt paid.

Thirty-six hours after the Portland slaughter . . .

. . . how did you graduate to such meticulous attention to detail?

You had an orange to eat, a movie to watch.

I grabbed the most recent case reports. As I suspected, microscopic analysis of Jaycie's flannel nightgown showed that her killer had cut it with scissors.

So prepared. You folded the garment over the chair.

I scanned Luther Peterson's statement. The young man he saw leaving 42 Crescent carried a knapsack.

The knapsack held the killing kit.

Years earlier, Harper Dorman had worked at Harbor College. The three young women were Harbor College students. Dorman managed an apartment building owned by Martin International. Jaycie Waylon was an intern at the company. Steve Weld made no secret of his antipathy to Stu Gilman and MI.

There was no way to know whether Weld's killer had had postmortem plans for him. Corporal Dickie Stevens had arrived minutes after the shooting.

Norma Jacobs had raised the question of two killers,

one gun, then immediately dismissed it. Now, as unreasonable as it seemed, that possibility nagged at me.

"I don't fucking get it," I said, and slammed my hand on the table.

WHEN BOLTON CALLED, HIS VOICE HAD DROPPED AN octave and his customary laid-back demeanor had been replaced with a distinct edginess. "Lucas, this is sensitive," he began.

I could remember only a time or two when Bolton felt it necessary to caution me. One notable occasion involved a foreign diplomat and his son's proclivity for the international transport of regulated substances.

"I understand," I told Bolton, thinking that, like the diplomat's son, whatever he was about to tell me would show up in the *New York Post* before I had a chance to repeat it.

"My inquiries about Martin International were red-flagged by a combined federal task force."

I shuddered. My experiences with task forces were not good. Combined task forces were worse, and whenever you tossed federal into the mix, it was time for the Three Stooges.

"FBI and DEA are involved," Bolton continued.

"Alphabet soup," I muttered. "What about NBC and CBS?"

Political pressure creates task forces, which usually accomplish two ends: they provide the public with the illusion that something is being done about a problem, and they demonstrate the inability of law enforcement agencies to work together.

Yes, things were certainly getting complicated.

"They've got somebody undercover up there," Bolton continued.

"At Martin International?"

"At the college."

"Drugs?"

"Money," Bolton said. "The agent who called me was not happy to find my tracks in the computer."

"Fuck 'em," I said, happy to play even a tangential role in pissing off the feds.

He ignored me. "The essence of it is that MI could be the largest broker of illegal cash transactions in the country. The feds have their agent in place. They see no relationship between their investigation and the murders."

"Who are their suspects?"

"When they complete their investigation, we might know that."

I would not hold my breath.

"The ballistics comparison turned up another victim," I told him, and briefly described the scene at Dorman's.

"This guy is an animal, Lucas."

"I'm not finished. We got back into town about the time that our shooter took out an instructor at the college. It isn't official that he's connected to the others, but only because no testing has been done yet."

"What other serial killer ever did five in one week?" Bolton asked.

"Danny Rolling in Gainesville, Florida," I reminded him.

"Rolling was easy to read compared to your guy."

When I hung up the phone, I turned to stare at my dagger and orange. In my analysis of the connections among the homicides and some of the players, I had ignored the most obvious.

My letter of invitation to teach at Harbor had come from the college's academic dean. Her note explained that the suggestion to invite me had originated with a board member familiar with my work. I'd glanced at the list of names printed down the left side of the stationery and recognized none of them. I had considered the offer for a day, then faxed my acceptance, thinking that my benefactor would remain anonymous for the moment, and that I owed this person a thank-you for hauling my ass out of Lake Albert when I hit bottom with boredom.

Now I reconsidered the debt of thanks. What promised to be a pleasant sojourn by the sea had immersed me to the teeth in murder.

"Am I a target," I muttered, "or an audience of one?"

CHAPTER 17

LATE-NIGHT RADIO OFFERED MAHLER, GARTH BROOKS, and Madonna. I opted for silence on the short drive to the police station.

I made the mistake of entering through the front door. Reporters talked on cell phones, ate lobster rolls, or stood in small groups comparing rumors about the murders. They filled the small waiting area and spilled over onto the stairwell. As I waded through the media trap to the dispatcher's window, a young man shoved himself from the wall and blocked my way.

"Dr. Frank, I'm Bailey Lee with the *Ragged Harbor Review*," he said.

"Tide charts, fishing forecasts, and the seafood specials at Downtown Grocery," I said, sensing the loss of my anonymity.

A TV reporter shoved her microphone at me as a cohort aimed his camera. "What links these murders, Dr. Frank?" she demanded.

I doubted that Jaworski had said anything about connections among the killings.

"Is it true that the FBI has entered the case?" Bailey Lee asked.

"Direct your questions to the chief," I said as I waved to the dispatcher and caught her attention.

I grabbed the handle on the security door and waited for the signal that would allow me to enter.

"Steve Weld was shot with the same gun that killed the students, wasn't he?" another reporter shouted, jostling his way through the crowd.

"What about Stanley Markham?" someone yelled as the steel door clicked and I stepped inside, temporarily rescued.

I found Jaworski in his office preparing for a press conference. "Late for that, isn't it?" I asked.

"I had told them I'd hold a briefing this afternoon. Then our shooter hit Weld. Same gun. Looks like two shots to the face. I put the media folks off. They want something for morning."

The chief pushed away from his desk and paced the room, tension evident in the lines below his tired eyes. "I have to say something. This town's coming apart at the seams. Hubble Saymes wants the National Guard down here. Jesus Christ."

Karen Jasper stood at one side of the room with her arms folded tightly across her chest.

"I'm beat," Jaworski said.

"Anything more on Weld or Dorman?"

"Not much. Too soon on Weld. They're still working at the scene. No fruit, though. We got the name of the woman Dorman lived with in South Portland. Katrina Martin."

I stared at Jaworski. "In her fifties."

"I didn't do the math. You look like you've seen a ghost. You know the woman?"

For part of one summer in Provincetown on Cape Cod, I knew a Katrina Martin. It was the mid-sixties.

How many Katrina Martins could there be? I wondered.

I worked as a short-order cook in an oceanfront restaurant. Katrina bounced from one relationship to another, always where the drug scene was happening, smoking and swallowing anything available on the beach. She was from Maine. I hadn't thought about her or that summer in years.

"Maybe," I answered.

I remembered one of the first afternoons I worked the grill that summer. I was preparing to leave for the day when Katrina arrived with the rest of the crew that waited tables during dinner. The others were in uniform; Katrina wore a bikini.

She looked at me. "You won't mind," she said, slipping off the bathing suit.

I leaned against the dish shelf and watched her perform.

"Haven't you ever seen a naked girl?" she asked.

"Not like you."

She dressed. I observed.

Finally, she looked at me again. "I get off at nine. Come back and we'll go for a swim."

I did go back, but Katrina was gone. I found her on the beach an hour later, stoned and cold and doubled over with peyote cramps. That night established the pattern for many nights to follow.

Through those few weeks, she told me that her mother was crazy, a frequent flyer at a state psychiatric hospital. I wondered if Katrina was soaring in the same direction. I held her hand and talked her through drug-induced hallucinations, assured her that they were caused by the chemicals and would pass when the drugs ran their course.

I remembered that her craziness frightened me. For a while, I avoided her.

She smothered me with notes, greeting cards decorated with pictures of kittens, bunches of wildflowers. She said that she loved me. Then she changed her mind and said that she loved the idea of being in love. I am no longer certain whether Katrina was irresistible or unavoidable.

"It's been more than thirty years," I said to Jaworski. "It is unlikely she's the Katrina Martin I knew."

In July, Katrina had gone home to have a breakdown in the same hospital that her mother favored. She wrote me a disjointed letter about not knowing whether her dreams were dreams or bizarre slices of reality. She'd met a young man, she said. He worked at the hospital, and they were dating.

"This Katrina Martin has a place in Bayberry Trailer Park in South Portland," Jaworski said. "Norma Jacobs went out there, tried to talk to her. Martin wouldn't open the door. A neighbor told Jacobs that Martin's mentally ill. She sits in her trailer, watches TV, and talks to herself when she isn't talking to Vanna White."

Jaworski handed me a file folder. "Jacobs sent that. She thought you'd be interested. It's a psychological report on Martin's kid that was appended to Martin's petition for a permanent restraining order against Harper Dorman."

"I'll take a look at this," I said, yanking myself back to the moment.

"Why the hell would any of this matter?" Jasper demanded shrilly. "I'm sure that some mental case holed up in a trailer, who may or may not be a blast from your past, is just totally fascinating. But let me remind you that we are looking for a killer."

Jaworski covered his weary face with his hands, rubbing his eyes. "The weapon connects these cases," he said. "To some extent, so does Martin International. Dorman was an MI employee, and he was married to a woman named Martin. Lucas doesn't believe in coincidences. I'm getting pretty skeptical of them, too."

"Stanley Markham is our suspect," Jasper said. "He connects these cases, and he's at the top of an extremely short list."

I looked at Jaworski, then at Jasper. "How the hell does Markham connect the cases? We've got a pile of bloody orange peels on Crescent Street. Nothing at Dorman's; nothing at Weld's."

I did not mention my skewered orange. I had no intention of reinforcing Jasper's Markham obsession. Jaworski noted my omission by turning away.

"Probability alone is enough to require that we eliminate him before we start flying off in all directions," she said.

"Probability also dictated that Sonny Liston hammer the daylights out of Muhammad Ali. Twice. Once right here in Maine. My memory does get a little furry at times, but I don't think that's what happened. Numbers offer only an illusory comfort."

"We know that Markham headed this way," Jasper said.

"I think he's going home," I told her.

"You can't know that."

I shrugged. "Okay. I don't know it."

"We have to be concerned with Markham's movements," she continued. "His most likely destination is Canada. Based on sightings so far, that increases the likelihood that he will travel through this area. We've intensified patrols on all the primary routes. New York, Vermont, and New Hampshire are cooperating. We're saturating the border towns with Markham's picture."

Jaworski looked at me. I breathed deeply, briefly debating whether to respond to Jasper's steel-fortified rigidity or to keep my thoughts to myself. Never the diplomat, I crashed ahead.

"I'm not certain of anything," I said, "but Markham is a creature of habit. When he was killing, he drove during high-traffic times. His was one of thousands of cars on the road. If he needed rest, he pulled off at vacant hunting and fishing camps, ski chalets, or lake cottages, concealed his vehicle, broke in, and slept. He doesn't like to drive at night. He's afraid of the dark."

"He could be driving north on the interstate right now."

"He could be," I conceded.

Jasper's intensity radiated from her darkening eyes. She was angry, unaccustomed to having her judgment questioned.

"I don't think he is," I said.

"Jesus. You're insufferable."

"Look, Jasper, let's put our personal differences aside," I began, but before I could offer the terms of a truce, the detective stormed out the door and slammed it.

Jaworski leaned back in his chair and sighed. "Hell of a team I've got here."

"She's right," I said. "I am insufferable."

Jaworski made a snorting noise, unwrapped a second stick of cinnamon gum, and said, "What now?"

"We'll wait for Detective Jasper. She just needed an excuse to go outside for a smoke. Considerate of her, really. She knows that you recently quit."

The chief held his piece of gum poised at his open mouth and stared at me. "You being insufferable again?"

"Nicotine stains on the index and middle fingers of her left hand. Distinctive odor despite the breath mints she prefers. I smoked off and on for twenty years."

He nodded slowly and slipped the gum into his mouth. "I'd appreciate it if you didn't share all that with her."

I smiled. "No problem."

"She says you're as bad as her father. Maybe worse. Guess they don't get along."

"Why me? Why not you?"

"I'm not the insufferable one."

"Huh," I grunted, wondering if I really *was* insufferable. Cranky, yes. But insufferable? Surely not.

"Well," I said, "when we don't confront the demons in our emotional closets, we do go blindly through life re-creating the past in the present. Jasper needs to work through her anger."

That didn't sound insufferable, did it?

I wandered to the window and gazed at Main Street, illuminated by intersecting beacons from the competing networks' klieg lights. The street's soundtrack was a collage of voices, the hum of diesel generators on grumbling flatbed trucks, and a simmering, black ocean's hiss in the background. A group of students participated in the college beer-drinking rite and waited to be interviewed about their take on the town's horror.

"You know what brings people into psychotherapy?"

I watched Jaworski's reflection in the window. He shrugged.

"If therapists probe deep enough, they will invariably find conflicts related to sex or anger. We've been culturally conditioned to not deal well with either."

When I was completing my psychiatric residency in Boston, my supervisor remarked that he considered me the angriest person he'd ever met. He wanted to know about my family, so I told him. His facial expressions ranged from contortions of horror to open-mouthed disbelief.

"You understand rage because you contain so much of your own," he said.

He intended his observation as a penetrating insight for me. It was not. I never denied my anger. I struggled with my closet ghouls and achieved a working relationship with fury.

Later, when I opened my practice on Beacon Street, a friend gave me an urban renewal map of the Roxbury section of Boston. The map was detailed, and a small square represented the tenement where, for a decade, my family had occupied the third floor. I framed the map and hung it on my office wall. It was my reminder of a past that I could too easily have left behind.

Dear Lucas.

Katrina Martin's last letter arrived in the spring of 1967. I remember wondering why she wrote. I told myself that on a few rough occasions the previous summer, I was kind to her. That was all.

She had sensed the turbulence that was my life. She knew that I was not yet comfortable with the person I was becoming.

Feeling so much better. Married. Baby. Do you remember Steampot Pond?

I don't know if I would have answered the letter. It didn't matter. I lost it, and could not remember the return address, although I was nearly certain it was somewhere in Maine.

One Sunday that summer, we carried a picnic lunch to a pond that had no name. It was near a low railroad bridge where a steam train stopped to take on water for its boilers. Perhaps she derived Steampot from that, but what did it have to do with getting married and having a child?

Now I turned from the window and told Jaworski, "If we refuse to know and feel the early wars in our lives, we end up reliving those conflicts in our relationships with others. We hurl all of our shitty baggage at our friends and lovers and wives and children and colleagues."

"You've got Jasper diagnosed, do you?"

"Herb, I don't have myself diagnosed. When it comes

to human behavior, it's the biggest toss-up there is. Heads, I'm sane; tails, I'm starkers."

In five minutes, Jasper was back.

"I apologize," I said to the detective.

Arms folded, she glared at me.

"Scan the highways for Markham," I said to Jaworski. "I'll chase after the Martin angle."

The three of us marched upstairs to the select board's conference room. I wandered in through the rear door behind two dozen newspaper and TV reporters, sharks crowding the shark pool.

Jaworski and Jasper entered at the front. The detective stood to one side; the chief stood behind the podium and eight microphones. Before he could speak, hands shot up, accompanied by a howl of shouted questions. The chief called for quiet.

"It's late," Jaworski said. "We're all tired. I'll answer as many of your questions as I can. There are some things that we can't talk about, and I'll ask you to respect that."

Stanley Markham topped every agenda.

"The state police have established additional patrols on all the main roads," Jaworski said. "The next step is roadblocks. We're flooding the area with his photograph, and we ask your help in giving it maximum exposure. We don't know that Markham had anything to do with these killings, but he's got to be found. The United States Marshals are directing the search."

I was impressed with Jaworski's handling of the media. He was waiting for forensic test results in the Weld case, he said, and refused all comment.

Only Bailey Lee, the local reporter, asked about Harper Dorman. Lee's big-city colleagues paid no attention.

"You'll have to talk to Portland P.D. on that," Jaworski said.

Yes, the chief was aware that folks in the village were frightened. "We all got a little panicky during the big storm and the flooding we had last winter, and we survived that. We'll get by this, too."

He also knew that some students had opted to leave Harbor College. "That's their choice. We've got a state fella who'll be on the campus tomorrow to talk about safety measures for those who choose to stay."

"Has the department retained Lucas Frank to do a profile?" Bailey Lee asked. "If so, will you release it?"

"Dr. Frank is teaching at the college, and he's been kind enough to give us some of his time."

"On a profile, or on the Markham angle?" Lee persisted.

I left after twenty minutes or so, as the questioning remained fixed on Stanley Markham, and I was unable to evict Katrina Martin from my thoughts.

CHAPTER 18

MORNING CRASHED INTO MY ROOM.

Brilliant sheets of sunlight reflected from the ocean's rolling swells and cascaded onto the walls. I showered, trimmed the shag from my beard, yanked on jeans, a sweatshirt, and hiking boots, started Mr. Coffee, then headed uphill to the bluff overlooking the Atlantic.

Visions of Katrina Martin danced in my head.

Three decades earlier, she sat across from me in Provincetown's Pilgrim Restaurant eating clam chowder and gazing at the framed caricatures of celebrities that lined the walls.

"Why now," I wondered, "and why here?"

In the roadside pullout near the dead end, a battered gray Volvo on four flat tires, its two doors open, listed over the embankment. I walked to the passenger door and gazed inside. A blue plastic tag dangled from the ignition key. I leaned forward and read the tag's stamped, gold message: "Your name and address printed here."

"Big fuckin' help," I muttered as I turned and walked down the hill to call Jaworski.

The chief arrived at the house in minutes, and we returned to the bluff. Jasper drove in behind us.

"We'll need a flatbed," Jaworski said as he approached the Volvo.

Jasper circled the car. "He sliced the tires," she announced as she scribbled in her notebook.

Jaworski followed the detective. "Somebody seems to be sitting on your doorstep," he said to me.

"It's my magnetic personality."

Jasper's head snapped up, her expression setting new records on the Richter glare scale.

"Occasionally magnetic," I amended.

"Sure likes your neighborhood."

"Chief, who do I call about the flatbed?" Jasper asked.

"Call Sue's Sunoco. Tell her to leave the car inside the town garage."

"The mobile crime lab should finish at Weld's this morning. Then they can tear this apart."

Jasper walked to her car.

"So far, they've pulled twenty different hair samples in Weld's living room," Jaworski said. "More fibers. Turns out he held one of his classes in that room. Maybe we'll get lucky with the car."

Jaworski stood beside me, gazing at the Volvo. "You know, I can understand Jasper putting all her time into the Markham angle. He's a known quantity, something she can get her teeth into. He's predictable."

He nodded at the Volvo. "This guy's unreal."

EARLY THAT AFTERNOON I NEGOTIATED MY WAY through the traffic snare on Main Street and drove onto the hill. I had an obligation to my students to discuss killers. I had another obligation to track a killer. Gender and violence—what difference did it make? Male killers, female killers—they took lives, period.

The classroom was quiet.

Jen Neilson doodled on her notebook cover. Dawn Kramer rubbed her tired eyes as she prepared to forge ahead. Betsy Travis read her *Ragged Harbor Review*. Sara Brenner was absent.

"Aileen Wuornos kept me up all night," Kramer began, rubbing her bald head as she consulted her notes. "Wuornos's parents were teenagers who split up before she was born. She lived with her mother until she was four. Her grandparents raised her. She got pregnant when she was fourteen and gave up the baby for adoption. Her grandmother died around that time, so losses keep coming up in her life. She quit school and worked the streets as a prostitute."

Kramer possessed the rare ability to bring a clinical curiosity to questions of the killer's personality while retaining a sense of horror over the act of murder.

"What about her facial scarring?" our future doctor, Amy Clay, asked. "I noticed it right away in the photographs. She had to be self-conscious about it."

"That happened when she was younger," Kramer said, "kids playing with matches. Maybe she felt that life had dealt her a bad hand, that she'd paid for the right to do whatever she wanted. She carried a gun when she was in her teens."

"There are many other women and men who experienced similar or worse events in their childhoods," I said, "and they did not become serial killers. Some never experience anything remotely traumatic, but they kill."

"I read that paper you gave us," Kramer said, "the one on dissociation. I read a bunch of stuff that Wuornos said, but I didn't see anything that suggested dissociation."

"In her confession to police," I said, "if she had consistently used a passive voice—'He was shot,' or 'Then he was killed'—she would have been presenting herself as someone who observed events unfold without any direct participation. That descriptive style distances the killer from the act and from any responsibility for the act. When Wuornos uses the passive voice, within a sentence or two she says, 'So I shot him,' or 'That's when I shot him.' She claimed that she was defending herself, that the men who picked her up hitchhiking hurt her, or threatened to hurt her, or took advantage of her. She seems to have a porous denial system, accompanied by the desire to place blame elsewhere. I think Wuornos was very much in the moment when she killed."

Kramer nodded. "It's like she was saying, 'If I didn't have the gun, none of the murders would have happened.' It was the gun's fault."

"She emptied the gun into one of her victims, reloaded, and shot him again," I said with a shrug.

Amy Clay's research took her to Springfield, Vermont, and fundamentalist church member Gary Lee Schaefer. The slightly built, bespectacled Schaefer confessed to the abduction-murders of two young girls. Police suspected him in other killings.

"What he described," Clay said, "sounded like what you called 'splitting.' One psychologist who examined him thought he was dissociative."

Schaefer claimed to have been the victim of a sexual assault by an older sister and her friend in a cemetery. He said he was just a boy at the time. The family history included a repressive religious atmosphere, a hostile-dependent relationship with his sister, a sense of betrayal when his sister announced that she was pregnant and leaving home to marry. Each of Schaefer's victims bore a striking physical resemblance to this sister.

"He cruised around in his car," Clay said, "listened to music, usually Styx or Led Zeppelin, and then, it's like he snapped. He drove past this girl standing at the side of the road, looked into his rearview mirror, and clicked out."

"Bogus," Travis said. "Even that 'Hillside Strangler,' Bianchi, had it more together. He watched *Sybil* on late-night TV, wrote a script for himself, faked a multiple personality, and suckered psychologists into believing his act."

In the late seventies, Kenneth Bianchi and his cousin, Angelo Buono, claimed ten victims in a five-month killing spree in Los Angeles. The pair dumped their victims' bodies on hillsides around the city.

"What went on in those sessions with the psychologists," I said, "became classic lore on how not to conduct an evaluation, especially using hypnosis. The clinicians approached Bianchi harboring a diagnostic expectation, MPD, then proceeded to ask leading questions which reinforced their own suppositions. They were duped. The gentleman who exposed Bianchi's fraud was Dr. Martin Orne from the University of Pennsylvania."

"I'd rack up Bianchi as another psychopath," Travis said.

"What about Danny Rolling?" Kramer asked, referring to the killer of five in Gainesville, Florida. "Didn't he claim multiple personalities?"

"He's the worst of them all," Travis said. "Talk about gaining inspiration from the movies. He saw *The Exorcist III,* called his evil self Gemini, then spelled his own name backward . . . Ynnad . . . and that became another entity. Totally spurious. Life does another poor imitation of art. That bastard sold his autograph and his drawings. I've always been against the death penalty, but I'd make an exception for him."

"What about this observation?" I said. "The men we're talking about possess stereotypical female qualities. Rolling fussed about cleanliness, his hands, his fingernails.

The women are more masculine than the men. Aileen
Wuornos was the toughest guy in Daytona Beach. Do they
embrace those characteristics? Do they hate themselves
for them?"

"What about Sydny Clanton?" Amanda Squires asked.

"I'd forgotten about her," I said.

It was the Clanton case that I had tried to recall while
examining the photographs of Harper Dorman's remains.
In 1967, at age nineteen and wearing flowers in her hair,
Sydny Clanton set out from her hometown near Moscow,
Idaho. Behind her, in their three-bedroom ranch home, lay
the bodies of her parents. She had hacked her father beyond recognition.

Clanton's destination was San Francisco and the
"summer of love." She was ready for the Bay Area's party
in the park before she crossed the Idaho state line, wildly
tripping on two hundred micrograms of LSD.

She made her way to a crash pad on Waller Street in
San Francisco, and within days met a man who told her he
would crawl inside her mind, change her middle-class
thinking, and broaden her to new experiences. He said
that he was just like God.

Sydny Clanton told the five-foot-two-inch Charlie
Manson that he was full of shit.

When one of Manson's omnipresent girl-gofers inter-
ceded, Clanton grabbed her by the hair, slapped a knife
against her throat, and glared at Manson. "You know what
decides whether she bleeds, Charlie?"

Manson glanced at his silent audience. One witness
said it was the first time that the little con lacked a snappy
retort.

"How I fuckin' feel," Clanton said, and shoved the
young woman at Manson.

The rumor in Haight-Ashbury was that Manson left
town and hung out on the north coast because he feared

Sydny Clanton. Manson did not know it, but Clanton's run-in with the self-styled guru meant nothing to her.

She moved on to the posh environs of Walnut Creek, where she broke into a house. She found eighty dollars in a sock drawer, ate a peanut-butter-and-clover-honey sandwich, and watched TV until the family—Herbert Gleid, his wife Emily, their two sons Bill and Kevin—returned. Clanton killed them all.

"Something happened in the Gleids' house," Squires said. "Clanton couldn't leave. She had plenty of time to get out of there, but she didn't."

"The FBI doesn't include her as a true serial killer," Travis said. "She killed because she wanted the eighty bucks. Or she killed to steal a car. She gained something from the murders. There's a word for that, but I don't remember it."

"Instrumental," I said.

"They always go hunting for a sexual motivation," Dawn Kramer said. "If you aren't aroused, you don't get to be called a serial killer. With Wuornos, supposedly it was okay because she was a prostitute. I don't understand what that has to do with anything besides how she found her victims."

Squires clasped her hands and leaned forward. "I think there's a confusion about what *Lustmord* means," she said. "It is the pure joy of killing, the excitement that is unlike any other. Some of us love to fuck. Some of us love to kill. Karla Faye Tucker learned that when she sat on her victim and hammered him with a pickax. Sydny Clanton knew that to be passionate about murder is certainly not the exclusive province of men."

"Clanton was a predator," I agreed.

"God, she was so beautiful," Travis said. "She could've been a model."

"It was like the Gleids became her family," Kramer

said. "A court-appointed psychiatrist said she was delusional."

"One of the psychologists blamed the LSD," Squires said. "None of them considered the possibility of a peak emotional experience. To quote a friend of mine, 'Sydny Clanton was dreaming the blue dream that never ends.' "

"She was watching TV when the Gleids arrived home," Travis said.

"Does anybody know what she was watching?" Kramer asked.

I believed that TV triggered Clanton's dissociative episode in the Gleids' home, and that LSD caused the synesthesia she experienced. "I could smell what that girl was saying," Clanton said of the newscaster she watched. "She had an aura of fresh-cut pine. The screen turned blue. It made me sad, and I don't like to feel sad. So I got mad."

The capacity to translate depressed feelings into rage was a phenomenon I'd frequently encountered in my practice. When a patient presented depression, I probed for unexpressed anger.

After killing her parents and eviscerating her father, Sydny Clanton hitchhiked I-80 west. Everyone who picked her up—two men, a woman, a young couple—died.

In Walnut Creek, California, Clanton watched an in-depth TV account of her parents' murder. Carl Clanton, the respected realtor and Rotarian, received most of the coverage. The broadcast included Mrs. Clanton only as one of the two found dead in their mountain home.

Later, when they considered Sydny Clanton's account of her parents' murders and the physical evidence at the scene, investigators speculated that the rebellious daughter returned home drunk and stoned late one night, became embroiled in a heated confrontation with her father, and killed him. When her mother walked out to see what all the noise was, Clanton killed her, too, then gutted her father.

It was a sixties wrap: rebellion, drugs, and violence. Case closed. The town buried its dead, and America banished the case to its great, silent subconscious.

When Clanton later told a tale of sexual abuse by her father while her mother pretended to be unaware, it was a one-day story on the inside pages of mainstream newspapers on the West Coast. The tabloids gave it page two at the grocery checkout.

Clanton's prison psychiatrist, Susan Paynter, sent me a tape and transcript of a session with her client and asked for my opinion. The convicted killer described sadistic sexual abuse from the ages of eight to thirteen and offered the kind of detail that was verifiable.

I had sent Ray Bolton a wish list: any available police photographs of Carl Clanton's basement office and workshop; copies of inventory sheets listing materials removed from the Clanton residence. Bolton did not disappoint me, and I wrote to Dr. Paynter.

"Police photos taken of the two basement rooms while the bodies were *in situ*," I wrote, "show none of the items that Clanton describes. The police inventory log of items removed from the residence lists no bondage magazines, no photos of children in sexually provocative poses, and no leather straps or other bondage paraphernalia."

I listened to Paynter's taped therapy session. The lack of emotion in Sydny Clanton's voice struck me immediately. "I enjoyed the killing," Clanton told Paynter. "There was this rush, a high that was better than any drug."

She recited dates and facts, recounted atrocities, and discussed her favorite music, all in the same flat tone of voice. She could have been reading a grocery list.

Dissociated rage, I thought, a fury so overwhelming that Clanton split it off to its own compartment and self-medicated with any mind-altering substance she could find.

"She killed eleven times," Squires said. "She carried a leather pouch, and every time she killed, she placed a small stone in the pouch. She was keeping score. When a killer runs up those numbers, and loves what she's doing, she can't be dismissed as a thief."

At the end of class, Dawn Kramer approached me. "I heard about Mr. Weld," she said. "I never took any of his classes, but I knew who he was. Sara Brenner went home. My parents want me to come home. I've been stalling them. Are the police close to arresting someone?"

"Investigations take time," I told her, wishing that I could say something reassuring.

"People keep dying," she said, shaking her head as she walked from the room.

CHAPTER 19

AS I GUIDED MY JEEP SOUTH ON I-95 THAT AFTER-
noon, I felt like a Ragged Harbor–to–Portland commuter.

My gut told me that I was driving in the right direction. I was also nearly certain that I was about to visit what
Jasper had erroneously called a blast from my past.

In the mid-sixties, sitting beside me in the sand at
Race Point, Katrina Martin announced that she wanted to
be a dancer. "Not ballet," she said. "Cabaret."

She pushed herself up, twirled her way to the water's
edge, and stared at the dark, early-morning sky as waves
washed over her feet. Suddenly she turned and ran back to
where I sat.

"I want to be an actress," she said. "I want to be Cle-
opatra and Cordelia, Arthur Miller's Katie in *A View from
the Bridge,* and Shaw's Saint Joan, and all those Ibsen
women."

I patted the sand and asked her to sit.

"Shit," she said, dropping to her knees. "The acid's
wearing off. I was going to play the Palladium next. There's
no point in praying to an empty sky."

She curled into fetal position, wrapped her arms
around my waist, and said, "When I get married and have

babies, one of them will be a girl. She'll grow up to be just like Joanne Woodward or Bette Davis. New York and London theaters will chase after her."

Her voice faded to a whisper, and she slept.

With the aid of Herb Jaworski's directions, I had no trouble finding Bayberry Trailer Park. A single nail held a bullet-riddled, rusted Nehi sign dangling on a vegetable stand's burned-out shell. Below the sign was a scrawled invitation to Bayberry Court.

The "courtyard" consisted of hard-packed dirt and broken glass, and reeked of dog shit. Clumps of grass grew at the corners of a dozen trailers that appeared to have settled at odd angles into the earth.

No one answered my knock at number three. I stepped away from the door, gazed through the louvered window and saw a TV's blue glow in a darkened room. I was about to pound louder when a woman stepped from between trailers two and three and said, "She don't answer when her soaps is on."

She was short, nearly toothless, and poverty-thin with sunken eyes. Her voice was husky and ragged from too many cigarettes over too many years. She pulled a frayed, knitted shawl around her shoulders. "Soaps is like going to church for her. You don't want the Lord's house to be a shithole like the one you live in. Some days Katrina don't answer the door at all. Freaks me out 'cause I gotta use my key, go inside, and make sure she's alive. Stinks in there. She don't keep the place clean."

Wind whipped through the trailer park, stirred fallen leaves, and threatened with storm clouds rolling in from the east.

"Who are you?" she asked.

"A friend," I said.

She cocked her head to one side. Her expression said disbelief.

"It was a long time ago," I added.

"Musta been."

"If she's going to open the door . . ."

"Cartoons come on at four. Like I said, even then she mightn't open that door. Katrina don't remember too good. Lot that she don't want to remember. I don't blame her."

"My name is Lucas Frank."

"I'm Ellie. You want coffee and talk while you wait? Or are you gonna bother waiting?"

I imagined a dusty aluminum box with low ceilings and the odor of refuse, but Ellie's trailer was clean and comfortable, complete with plastic-lace placemats. With the exception of a proliferation of crucifixes and religious statuary, the place was not at all foreboding. Ellie had maintained the sheen of her dark, paneled walls and the polished metal molding's luster.

We sat at a small, laminated kitchen table and drank a respectable coffee. A radio played softly in another room.

"I don't watch the soaps. I listen to Imus when I wake up, maybe watch Oprah in the afternoon."

"I'm trying to learn what I can about Harper Dorman," I said.

"I'm glad the bastard's dead," Ellie snapped, staring hard into my eyes. "I seen on TV where somebody shot him. Should've done it a long time ago."

"What can you tell me about him?"

"I thought you were Katrina's friend."

I nodded. "We were young."

"You with that cop that was here?"

"Detective Jacobs. I know who she is."

She sipped her coffee and looked away. "I guess I don't mind talking. Harper fixed outboards at a boatyard. Most Fridays he got a check, picked up his Jim Beam at the port, and was halfway through the bottle by the time he got home. He beat Katrina something awful. Around here, we don't call the cops. More trouble than they're worth. Besides, Katrina said not to. Couple of times I did anyway. Never told her, but I did. Just made matters worse. I feel bad about doing that."

Ellie wanted to talk. Bayberry Park was a relic, a decaying scrap heap of low- or no-rent hovels sinking into the back-filled tidal marsh where a developer dumped them in the 1950s. These days, young families mired in poverty sought subsidized housing in the city where they could walk to the make-work jobs the law required of the disenfranchised. The park's last "new" tenant had arrived in 1986 and died in 1991.

"Katrina and Harper had a child," I said.

"You mind if I smoke?"

I shook my head.

"So many people do these days," she said, lighting an unfiltered, generic cigarette. "The state took Lily. Put her in an institution. She ran away when she was fifteen."

Ellie took a deep drag from her cigarette, then exhaled. "Harper beat on Lily, too," she said, looking down at the table.

That summer day at Steampot Pond, Katrina decided that the most amazing flower in the world sprouted from the earth beneath six feet of water, then surged its way to the surface with flamboyant white blossoms and broad green leaves. A water lily.

"I think he did more than beat on that child, but Katrina never said. Whatever happened, he got away with it for years. The cops arrested him, but nothing came of it. She finally threw him out. Got a court order, not that it did much good. He still came around. That was a long time ago, mister. Katrina should've killed him back then. She didn't kill him now, if that's why you came here. She ain't been out of the park in months."

I assured Ellie that Katrina-as-suspect had not entered my mind.

She dragged on her cigarette and tapped the ash onto her saucer. "I remember when Harper killed the dog," Ellie said. "The cops came that time, too. Some days he came home, and he had cookies and chocolate milk for Lily. That day, he came home and killed her dog. What's a child supposed to make of that? He smeared the dog's blood on the living room walls."

I pictured the sweeping arcs of blood on the walls above the two dead students' beds. Before I could make sense of the image or formulate a question, Ellie spoke.

"Harper always quoted Scripture. He grabbed his King James and banged on that Bible and banged on his chest, and told every woman within hearing that her duty was to God and her man. 'God is first,' he yelled, 'but I ain't far behind. Fix my supper.' Somebody shoulda fed him that blessed dog."

"What exactly did he do to the dog, Ellie?"

She looked at me as if I were a dunce. "He shot it. Is that what you mean?"

Ellie stubbed out her cigarette. "Then he cut it open to get at the blood. Got his hands all covered with it and wiped the walls red. The place looked like a war went on. Lily spent that night with me. It was stay here or go to foster care, and I couldn't let that child go through another nightmare on top of what she already saw. She sat at this table and drew pictures. I kept paper and colored pencils in the cabinet for when she visited. Lily was good at drawing. She was left-handed, and she kind of wrapped her arm around her pictures while she worked on them, like she was protecting them."

Left-handed arcs of blood—shit. My stomach threatened to erupt. Was this tortured kid our killer?

Ellie demonstrated. "I couldn't see what she made until she showed me. She drew people. When she finished each one, she took the red pencil and made slash marks across it. I asked her what she was doing. 'I'm making them bleed,' she said."

"Did Lily ever come back here?" I asked.

"I don't know. Last year there was a woman came around who'd be about the right age. She was tall and just so beautiful. If that was Lily, she turned herself into something special. Rich, too. That woman that was here, she was a princess."

"Did Katrina say it was her daughter?" I asked.

"When she ain't taking her pills, you can't put stock in what comes out of her mouth."

I had a hundred questions, but could not organize my thoughts. I imagined Katrina and Lily in their separate struggles against an abusive drunk.

"What was Lily like as a child?" I asked.

"Strange," Ellie said, sipping her coffee. "Lily was a smart kid, did real good in school, helped her mother. She cooked the meals, cleaned house, did the laundry. When she got time to herself, she did her homework, wrote in her diary, or she prowled the swamp behind the park. She'd come out of that swamp talking to herself. 'Vanessa Stripe needs help taking care of the babies,' she'd say. Or, 'Billy Brown-spot is overweight.' Don't ask me. She walked by my kitchen window gabbin' away to herself. There were times she'd come press her face against that window and stare in here, like it was someplace she'd rather be. The swamp's where she buried Spike. That was her dog. She dragged him down there in a burlap sack, dug the hole all by herself. Maybe Spike's who she was talking to."

Ellie paused, examined my face, then continued. "Times after Harper . . . did whatever it was he did to her, she'd come out and sit on the stoop. He'd passed out from his drinking by then. More than once I saw specks of blood on Lily's arms. Her shirt stuck to her when the blood dried. She yanked on the sleeve and started the bleeding all over again. Harper carried a skinny, black-handled knife with a long blade. Those times she cut herself, Lily had that knife. She poked at her arms with it. I always cleaned her up and asked her if I could help her. She couldn't hear me. Her eyes clouded, but she didn't cry. I expected her to bust out sobbing. She never did."

Ellie cleared her throat and lit another cigarette. "Katrina's a sick person. You got to work at it, but you can talk to her. She don't always make sense, but you can get her to. With Lily, it was different. She was empty. Like there'd be an echo inside if you tapped on her. She was little then. As she got older, she got hard, real cold. They came to get her that time and found out fast that they didn't bring enough people. Took five men to get her into that state van."

"How old was she?"

"Maybe fourteen. She looked younger. She didn't weigh but ninety pounds."

A kid, I thought. Five adults wrestled her down and slapped her into restraints.

"What was it about the woman who arrived in the limo that made you think it was Lily?"

"A lot of things," Ellie said. "She visited Katrina, and that would be reason enough. Katrina don't get visitors. None of us do. She had Lily's bright yellow hair. When the sun hit her hair just right, it was like she glowed. She was the right age. Mostly it was her eyes. The one time I saw her without the sunglasses, those eyes weren't Lily's soft hazel eyes. They were Lily's ice blue eyes."

"I don't understand."

She flicked ash into the saucer. "At the end, back when I knew her, it was like there were different Lilys. She waved to me and smiled in the morning when she went by on her way to the school bus. I might go over in the evening to visit Katrina, and Lily looked at me like she didn't know who I was. I wasn't sure who *she* was. Her face was different. I swear her eyes weren't the same color as morning. Probably the worst was when they were taking her out of here. She yelled. She didn't want to go. She was going to kill everybody, she said. Not just the people who came to get her. Everybody. She meant it, mister."

Ellie shook her head. "That wasn't Lily."

"Why did they take her?"

She took a deep drag on her cigarette, sighed smoke into the air, and tapped her fingers on the table. "Harper fell asleep on the couch. Katrina was in the kitchen heating vegetable oil to make french fries. She turned her head for a second, and Lily had that pot of oil over Harper's face, ready to pour. Katrina couldn't get there in time. If you seen Harper's picture in the paper, you seen the scars. More coffee?"

"Please."

She poured. "The cops said Lily was out of control. They said she was crazy, so they put her away."

Ellie leaned back in her chair. "Lily sat rocking in a corner. Two guys came for her. She had Harper's knife and she cut one of them. The boss cop called in the troops and they put Lily in a hospital. At first, she wrote to her mother a lot. After a few months, she didn't write so much. No one notified Katrina when Lily escaped. The kid turned up at her door. Katrina was bad off. She didn't know what to do, so she called the cops. Right after that, Lily Dorman disappeared."

THERE WAS LITTLE DOUBT IN MY MIND THAT THIS KA-trina Martin was the woman I'd known in Provincetown thirty years earlier. Katrina the cabaret dancer. Katrina the actress.

I delayed my visit. I did not want to drop into her life after three decades and complicate her already distorted world with questions about her marriage and vague suspicions that her daughter figured in five murders. I would have to talk to her, but I wanted to know more than I did, and to be able to answer her questions while asking mine.

I walked to the rear of the trailer park and found a path into a wetlands area crowded with cattails and sumac. It was the swamp that Lily had prowled as a child. An earthen dike veered away from the path and led into the middle of the bog.

I didn't expect to find anything. I wanted only to be in the place where Lily Dorman had spent time alone. It was a private place, peaceful in a strange way, and haunting. A small, weathered, wooden cross, held together with roofing nails and pounded into the earth, marked Spike's resting place.

A red-tailed hawk circled in the slate-colored sky. Wind whispered through the cattails. A water snake slid from a branch, revealing telltale brownish spots on its belly. The snake wound its way across the water's surface.

I wondered if I had just met a descendant of Lily Dorman's Billy Brown-spot.

CHAPTER 20

THE JEEP'S DIGITAL CLOCK READ 8:25 WHEN I PULLED
into my driveway.

I prowled through the house, grabbed a bottle of Shipyard, tuned the radio to a station that promised to play
Eric Clapton's "Rainbow Concert" without interruption,
and curled onto the sofa with the copy of Lily Dorman's
psychological report that Norma Jacobs had sent via Jaworski.

The timered light in the living room switched on.
"Okay, so it's eight-thirty," I said.

Hubert Penniweather, Ph.D., had evaluated Dorman
when the state sought a custodial placement for her. Penniweather's report was appended to Katrina Martin
Dorman's application for a permanent restraining order
against her husband. The court document was a standard
form. Someone had typed the relevant names, dates, and
places; Katrina had written two sentences to justify her
petition for relief from abuse.

The psychologist's summary included a brief history of
Harper Dorman's drinking and explosive behavior, and Katrina's psychotic episodes and hospitalizations. The report
also included excerpts from a police incident form:

Minor subject (LD) poured hot cooking oil on her father. Subject refused to talk to officers; Mental Health Services notified. Subject attacked the two responding attendants, cutting both men with a stiletto-type knife. Subject stated homicidal intentions. Back-up officers and attendants (5) subdued subject, placed her in restraints, and transported her to in-patient.

Ellie did not exaggerate. There were five adults on one kid.

Penniweather reported that Lily had tested in the superior range of intelligence, next door to genius. Her achievement levels smacked the top of the chart; she read and comprehended at the college level. Not bad for a fourteen-year-old. Penniweather described her as a "bright, highly verbal child."

Lily's responses on the Thematic Apperception Test (TAT), a series of pictures that the client is asked to make up stories about, were of concern to the psychologist.

When Henry Murray introduced the TAT at Harvard in the 1930s, he described Card 6GF as a young woman gazing backward at an older man. During my years of practice, I supervised many psychologists recently out of graduate school and eager to embark on a curing spree. They were ill equipped to succeed, having spent years studying statistics, research design, rats, and rhesus monkeys. They knew all that could be quantified, but lacked the ability to listen to a human.

A few of the more sophisticated clinicians administered the TAT, and often read a client's responses during case presentations in our sessions. It was common for a woman to attribute surprise, annoyance, or a startle reaction to the female in Card 6GF, as if the old guy intruded, crept up silently behind her, or said something shocking.

Lily Dorman responded: "She sees him. He lives in her closet. He comes out when he wants to play. The game makes blood. It's different this time because she's older. She has a gun in her hand. She shoots him. If Lilith comes out of the shadows, she chops him up."

She saw the old man as a predator, a bogeyman. Like most of the monsters of childhood that specialize in victimizing children alone at night, he resided in the depths of her dark closet.

When Harper Dorman wanted to "play," blood flowed. He smeared the trailer's walls; his daughter punctured her arms.

Lily was fourteen when Penniweather administered the TAT. She was not "older." In Card 6GF, only the woman's right hand is visible, and she does not hold a gun. The child infused her story with her wishes and fantasies.

If Lilith comes . . .

Despite recent attempts to rewrite her story, Lilith was best known as a mythical tempest demon found in deserted shadows, abandoned haunts. Would a child of fourteen know this? Lily was bright, a reader, an abused child probably in desperate need of an avenging spirit.

. . . she chops him up.

Penniweather noted the child's flat affect. Lily exhibited no feeling as she offered her interpretation of the picture. The psychologist prompted, "How is she feeling in that picture?"

Lily was stumped. She had no idea.

She split away all emotion in order to survive.

"What about the man?" Penniweather persisted. "How is he feeling in the picture?"

"Hungry," Lily said.

Penniweather cited another response, on Card 9GF: one woman ran along a beach, another watched the first from behind a tree. Lily stared at the picture and slowly moved her fingers over the tree trunk, a diagonal black band.

"She's swapping," Lily said. "When she goes through the dark place, she's this other girl."

The psychologist emphasized the response's dissociative nature. Again, he probed for feelings and found none. Following the test administration, Penniweather asked Lily if she ever "swapped," ever felt that she was some "other girl." She did not respond.

Penniweather's recommendations included psychiatric assessment to rule out a dissociative disorder. His suspicions were justified, but tainted by clinical and cultural stereotypes of women who behave violently. Implicit in the diagnostic impressions was the assumption that when Lily Dorman scalded her father, she was "not herself."

The phone interrupted my reading. I glared at it, then thought that my caller might be Bolton or Jaworski, so I pushed myself up and grabbed the receiver.

"There's a package waiting for you," a young woman said, her voice cold and hard.

"Who is this?"

She ignored my question. "You'll find it on a concrete barrier in the municipal parking area behind the grocery store."

Whoever she was, I figured that she had a short agenda: deliver her instructions and hang up. I did not expect her to remain on the line, so I gambled.

"I just returned from Bayberry Court," I said.

There was silence, then, "I know that. You had coffee with Ellie. Two cups. Leave now. You don't have much time."

"Lily . . ."

The line went dead.

• • •

I DROVE INTO THE VILLAGE.

Lily, if that was who had called, had concealed herself directly outside a window or the door while I sat, drank coffee, and listened to Ellie. She had probably followed me into the swamp behind the trailer park.

As I turned the corner at Downtown Grocery and parked, Stu Gilman's silver Jaguar streaked past on its way out of town. The car's engine noise faded, and the downtown night slipped into silence. I watched Gilman's taillights disappear in the distance. I walked through the dark alley between the grocery store and Wooly's Ice Cream Castle and stepped into the municipal parking lot. As I surveyed what looked and felt like a scene from a 1950s horror film, a cold wind off the water churned through the corridor behind me.

Black and white and gray.

All that was missing was Lon Chaney or Boris Karloff, and eerie background music. I heard no sound but the wind, and felt as if I should be looking at a grainy picture flickering on a giant screen.

No, not horror.

This film was intended for Humphrey Bogart as Sam Spade. The trouble was that I felt more like Bob Dylan's Mr. Jones. Something was happening here, but I could make no more sense of the moment than I could of the last several days.

A film shown in the outdoor theater that was the parking lot behind Downtown Grocery.

A thin spiral of smoke coiled from a cigarette on the pavement. I could not smell the burning tobacco, but I could smell cordite. Someone had recently fired a gun back here.

A small brown paper bag sat on the last concrete parking barrier. I picked it up and gazed in at a silver .22 caliber semiautomatic.

"Money says it's the murder weapon," I muttered.

A man sat in a compact car ten yards to my left. He leaned away from the open window on the driver's side, his hand pressed against his face.

As I stepped closer, I saw that he had tried to ward off what could not be stopped. There was a hole through his left hand. Black blood dripped from his ear and the corner of his mouth. There was another small, neat hole above his left eye.

My hands dropped to my side as I stared at Wendell Beckerman, the drugged-out kid from Mellen Street.

"Jesus Christ," I muttered, scanning the lot.

When I had stood in the hall outside Beckerman's apartment and questioned him about Harper Dorman's murder, he had looked familiar, but I could not place him. I could now. I saw him walk into the Old Chapel with Amanda Squires to attend the memorial service for the three slain students.

Headlights suddenly approached through the alley to my right. More lights arrived at the entrance to the municipal lot on the other side of Beckerman's Toyota.

Blue strobes throbbed on the roofs of both vehicles.

Sounds and colors filled my film with a roar—engines, sirens, a man in uniform held a gun and yelled, blue pulses of light collided with the black corners of night.

The cop crouched behind his patrol car door.

This is a dream. This can't be real. It is not happening.

"Drop the gun and clasp your hands behind your neck," the cop shouted.

What gun?

"Drop it now."

Then I remembered. The harmless-looking .22 in the brown paper bag. The gun I was convinced would link six homicides.

How does he know that I have a gun?

I dropped the bag and placed my hands behind my neck.

Karen Jasper emerged from the shadows, lowered and cuffed my right wrist, then my left.

"You've got some explaining to do," she said.

CHAPTER 21

DARKNESS CONCEALED AND PROTECTED ME. I LOVE TO wrap myself in shadows.

I stood in the Tradewind Cafe's doorway and gazed across Main Street into the alley beside Downtown Grocery. I heard voices—real voices, radio voices—but I could not identify words. Streaks of blue light banged against the buildings' walls, careened silently across the damp pavement, and illuminated the night for brief, repeating fragments of time.

He stood in the mercury-vapor glow, pushed his hand through his steel-gray hair. I knew what he was thinking. Someone had set him up, and he wondered where and how to begin unraveling the mystery.

He did not have a prayer.

When a mind has eyes, it does not rely on appealing to an empty sky.

I stepped into Crescent Street and walked to the opposite corner. I watched a woman snap handcuffs on his wrists. Two uniformed men flashed their lights into the small car that contained a dead man.

I watched with ebbing interest.

   *Eliminating humans removes nothing of any signifi-
cance from the world. Predators are vital to ecological balance. Farmers protest the resurgence of the timber wolf, but
the wolves will return.*

   *People are unnecessary. They are excess baggage on a
dying planet's trip through a crowded universe.*

   *Extraneous people consume valuable oxygen, clutter the
landscape, crack the sky with their foul emissions, while
they commit atrocities on the bodies and souls of their off-
spring.*

   Murder has purpose.

   A paring of the herd is essential.

CHAPTER 22

HERB JAWORSKI PUSHED A CUP OF COFFEE ACROSS THE table. "Black, right?"

"Thanks, Herb."

State technicians had fingerprinted me, drawn blood, taken hair samples, and coated my hands with paraffin to determine whether I'd recently fired a gun.

"Jasper says I should arrest you."

I glanced at Jaworski. He clenched his jaw, and his eyes bore back at me.

"How about if you start at the beginning?" he said as he sat opposite me.

I sipped the hot brew. "I'm not sure where that is."

"Then start at the end. How'd you manage to be standing in the municipal lot next to a homicide victim, with a bag of murder weapon in your hand?"

"Why did your people get there when they did?"

"Anonymous call. Jasper took it on my phone. Female, refused to give her name. She said we'd find a victim, a weapon, and a killer behind Downtown Grocery. We got it on the tape log. Jasper's making copies."

"Sounds like my call. She directed me to the gun. I

figured she was going to hang up, so I told her that I'd been at Bayberry Trailer Park this afternoon."

"You think it was Dorman's kid?"

"Whoever it was, she knew that I'd been at Bayberry. She was there, too. Watching me."

Jaworski chewed his cinnamon gum and listened as I told him the story of Lily Dorman. I recounted my conversation with Ellie and described the abuse that Lily and her mother had suffered.

"I think I'm being set up," I concluded.

"By this kid?"

"She'd be in her early thirties now," I said.

"The victim's driver's license says he lived in the Mellen Street apartment building in Portland."

"Wendell Beckerman. I talked with him about Harper Dorman. The kid was stoned. He didn't make a whole lot of sense. I told you I thought I recognized him. I saw him enter the memorial service with a student from my seminar, Amanda Squires."

"Did you talk to Katrina Martin?"

"She wouldn't answer the door."

"Did the same thing to Norma Jacobs," Jaworski said.

At that instant, Jasper barged through the door.

"Dr. Frank, your official involvement in this investigation is over. As far as I'm concerned, you are a suspect until cleared. At the very least, I will see that you are charged with obstruction."

Jaworski's face reddened and he spun around in his chair. "We still believe in civility around here, Detective Jasper," he growled. "And manners. We knock before we go charging through closed doors."

Jasper assumed a now familiar pose: her arms folded tightly across her chest. Her glare flew off the scale for withering power. I suspected that Jaworski had just joined the ranks of the insufferable.

The chief returned his attention to me. "Who wants to set you up, and why?"

"I don't know. This young woman, Lily Dorman, but I don't know why."

"She got any connection to MI?"

I looked up, surprised, at Jaworski. "I don't know."

"Chief," Jasper said, with a cautionary edge to her voice.

Jaworski waved his hand in dismissal. "Did you know that the feds were having a look at MI?"

I had no idea what he was getting at. "They have an undercover operative in place at the college."

"Had," Jaworski said. "Steve Weld."

I leaned back and absorbed Jaworski's words.

If I were a cop, Weld said, *"I'd jump all over Stu Gilman."*

Weld was a cop.

Gilman lies; he uses the Clear Skies for meetings with MI clients.

Two years earlier, Gilman's guest had vanished from the campus and washed up on the beach.

He has to be an encyclopedia because he works for Melanie Martin.

"Steve, we've had two brief conversations, and both times you've left me with the feeling that all the closets around here are filled with skeletons."

Gilman had streaked out of town as I entered the alley.

"You just may be as smart as they say you are," Weld said.

Jasper snorted her disgust with Jaworski's egregious breach of law enforcement confidentiality and turned to stare out the window.

"There's a combined task force," I said.

Jaworski nodded. "Weld was DEA."

"You'll have an army of feds on the way."

"They arrive tomorrow."

"Before Weld's death, the feds didn't see any connection between the murders and whatever they're looking at."

"Guess they do now," he said.

Jasper whirled away from the window. "How the hell do you know all this?" she demanded.

She was like a Florida mockingbird, pissed off because someone is mowing the lawn too near her nest. The black-and-white bird drops from the sky like a jet fighter and dives at the intruder's head. If you want to mow that lawn, you find a football helmet.

I glanced at Jasper, then focused my attention on Jaworski.

"Melanie Martin wanted you out here," he said. "She was familiar with your work, wanted you to teach a class, so the college issued an invitation, and MI picked up the tab. All of that makes sense. Within days of your arrival, three young women were murdered. One of them, Jaycie Waylon, was an MI intern."

I stood and walked to the windows on Main Street. My mind drifted as I stared down at a uniformed cop directing reporters and their battery packs, and kids with six-packs performing their nightly sidewalk ballet.

"A left-handed person, between five-feet-six and five-feet-ten, killed the students," I said. "Stanley Markham is both. I had doubts along the way, and now I don't buy Markham as the killer."

I sat with Stanley Markham outside his jail cell.

"Did you ever watch mothers and their kids at a playground?" he asked, lighting a cigarette. "It's the most amazing thing. The moms talk to each other, have a regular conversation. They react to their kids at the same time, and

they continue to talk without losing the thread of their conversation."

Markham was genuinely impressed. "It isn't a learned behavior, Dr. Frank. Fathers can't do it. They have to stop talking about the Celtics game, deal with the kid, then they've forgotten what they were talking about."

"Mothers spend more time with young children," I said.

"It doesn't have anything to do with the kids," Markham insisted. "It's a difference in brain circuits. Men and women are wired differently."

I dismissed Markham's amateur neuropsychology and did not think about it again until several years later when I read an article on gender-based parenting practices. The author believed that parental, social, and cultural conditioning tended to produce boys who acted on their environment in "single-task" mode, and girls who both acted and reacted in "multi-task" mode. Few of the boys in the study "accommodated themselves to environmental change." The girls reacted to change and incorporated the environment into their strategies for task completion.

I returned to my chair and sat. "I'm not comfortable even assigning gender to this killer," I said.

As soon as I spoke, I knew that I'd nailed what bothered me about the case from the first day.

The crime scene reflected method, deliberate linear activity. It also reflected reactivity.

"What are you talking about?" Jasper snapped.

Again, I ignored Jasper.

"You think we've got a woman serial killer?" Jaworski asked.

"In the first few days, I thought that I was looking at the work of a conflicted killer, someone determined to murder but not entirely congruent with the act. The mix of rage and organization confused me. Then I saw the photos of Harper Dorman's mutilated remains. Jacobs suggested and dismissed the two-killer scenario. I considered that, but we don't need two, Herb."

"You've gone over the edge," Jasper said, and paced the room. "We are looking for a white male."

"We're looking for a woman who enjoys killing," I said. "She is deliberate, and she is reactive."

You were not conflicted. You wanted to experience the pleasure of disposing of them, and the added delight of misleading the cops.

"How do you explain what he did to Jaycie Waylon? If that sexual display wasn't the product of a sadistic male fantasy, I don't know what is."

"Explosive anger, rapid remission, then misdirection," I said.

"You've got an answer for everything. What about Harper Dorman?"

"That was personal."

Jasper strode to the table and pushed her face close to mine. "I can't think of a better way to obstruct an investigation," she hissed.

"Serial killers are rare animals," Jaworski said. "A woman?"

"I put my trust in accepted facts," Jasper snapped, and slammed her palm on the table.

I stared at the detective and swallowed an urge to slug her. "Do you remember your Lombroso from criminology classes?" I asked.

Jasper's eyes shifted as she made the cognitive adjustment. "The bumps-on-the-head guy," she said as she backed away from the table and continued to glare.

Cesare Lombroso was a nineteenth-century Italian criminologist who postulated that the criminal population could be identified by their unique physical characteristics, including their skull terrain.

"Lombroso believed that biology was at the root of all

female criminal behavior," I said. "He thought women to
be about as morally sophisticated as two-year-olds, and not
terribly intelligent. He figured that if they weren't kept
pregnant and in the kitchen, they should damn well be in
church or there'd be unholy hell to pay."

Jasper turned away. "This is crap."

"Lombroso believed that a woman was a born criminal. When she acted, she became an absolute fiend. Nature was everything. Nurture didn't figure into it. You're
right. It *is* crap. Women commit violent crimes, and we
know that their histories are similar to their male counterparts'. We insist that the primary gender difference is the
manner in which males and females process life events,
how defensively equipped they happen to be. Men explode. Women implode. Bullshit. We need a new theory.
Wuornos shot and killed six men. Homolka helped to kill
her own sister. Tucker took a pickax to her victim and
experienced orgasm while she hammered him full of
holes."

Jaworski raised his arms in the air. "Enough. What the
hell are we dealing with here?"

"Fiction," Jasper shouted. "Pure fabrication."

"We all have a bit of the beast in us, Jasper," I said,
fixing my eyes on hers. "You too."

She was silent. I considered her lack of response an
acknowledgment that she would never speak.

"I have to go back to Portland," I told Jaworski. "Then
I should be able to tell you what we're dealing with."

"You're not letting him go, Chief," Jasper said.

"You don't have enough to hold me," I told her, eerily
certain that she would soon have exactly what she wanted.

"Technically he's a suspect. He had the weapon. He
was standing where the caller said he'd be. Chief, he
hasn't explained a damn thing. He's obstructing."

I watched the standoff. Jasper looked at Jaworski; the chief studied me.

"I want to know what you're doing," Jaworski finally said, and Jasper turned away and grunted in disgust and frustration. The chief continued, "You call me and tell me what you find. I want to know where you are."

"Agreed," I said.

CHAPTER 23

I TOSSED IN BED MOST OF THE NIGHT. KAREN JASPER, Amanda Squires, Stanley Markham, and Lily Dorman waged war for control of my sleep.

They won.

Markham was male, a savage killer whose most remarkable traits were feminine. Dorman was female, possibly a killer whose mimicry of male murderers was nearly perfect. Squires knew Beckerman and had initiated classroom speculation about a hybrid killer eerily similar to the one I now imagined. Karen Jasper was an unbridled pain in the ass whose theory of the crimes fingered Markham, ignored Dorman, and sought to suck me in as an obstructionist and, therefore, a co-conspirator. And she bugged me.

I sipped coffee and spaced out while staring at crime scene photos.

There is no evidence of compulsion.

The previous Sunday morning, I had stood between two beds on Crescent Street and noted the balance of the room, the symmetry of the killer's actions. Jaworski had asked me what it meant.

"I don't know what it means, Chief," I told him. "Something."

You arrive prepared to kill and to leave no evidence. You have a linear agenda for the women in the double room: eliminate them.

Two shots.

Jaycie stumbles groggily from her room. One shot.

You proceed with your script, and you remain receptive to environmental influence. You also remain in tune with your rage.

You have all the time in the world.

Jaycie Waylon was the primary target, I thought, but not of a sexual predator. There were no defensive wounds, none of the bruising or tearing that results when a victim is confronted by the type of killer who prefers to attack with a knife, a length of rope, a club, his hands.

You seethed with the desire to cut off her head.

I grabbed a crime scene photograph and examined the blood pool adjacent to Jaycie's head, the light blood flow across her abdomen, and the smaller stains beside her right hip.

You yank yourself back, contain your fury.

Cut off and fold the nightgown. Position the body, then do your artwork with the knife and sponge.

Why target Jaycie Waylon?

I remembered Norma Jacobs's words over lunch in Portland. Her Martin International informant had been "a young gal" who made deposits and withdrawals for dummy client corporations.

"She was set to meet with us, but we never heard from her."

"Not enough," I muttered. And no connection if our killer was Lily Dorman.

Jaycie wanted to discuss something over lunch. Gilman's presence stopped her.

As I pondered possible connections, someone pounded on my door.

Herb Jaworski stood on the porch in the morning sun. He gripped his knit cap and shifted his weight from one foot to the other. The chief displayed the same tentative quality, like a man contrite about having intruded, that I had observed the day we met. It was a safe bet that he was not there to arrest me.

"Just in time for coffee," I said.

He stepped inside. "I've got a thermos. Been drinking the same brand since 1947."

I poured a cup of the steaming black brew that I favored.

"I thought some last night," Jaworski said, as if reporting an unusual occurrence. "I brought you into this case. Keeping me up to date on what you're doing ain't your strong suit, but I expected that from when I checked on your background. I decided that we'd best work this one more closely together."

I prefer to work alone, but my respect for the veteran cop had grown steadily. If frequent reporting to Jaworski was to be the price of my freedom to pursue the case, I was ready to yank out my wallet.

"You plan to keep an eye on me?" I asked.

He watched his fingers explore the dark cap, then his eyes snapped up and met mine. "The rattler convinced me."

"I could have arranged that."

"Not with the expression you had on your face when I showed up with my rifle. Besides. I read your book."

The crack about the book was Jaworski's dry sense of humor. He was not smiling. He had a state police detective who wanted my ass in a cell on any technicality she could conjure, and nearly enough to justify putting me there.

He pulled a small tape recorder from his pocket and

switched it on. I listened to a young woman give Jasper instructions similar to those the caller had given me. There were two differences. In addition to the bag of evidence, the cops would find a new victim, and their killer.

"It's the same voice," I said, "but I can't tell you who she is."

"What about this Amanda Squires, the one you saw with Beckerman?"

I shrugged. "It could be."

Jaworski lowered himself into a chair. "Where do we go from here?"

"You've got Jasper's federal friends on the way," I said.

"Just make life more cluttered for a couple of weeks. Whoever that is on the tape, we want her. She led us to the gun, and she led us to Beckerman. She also put your ass in a sling. Angie Duvall worked late at the store last night. She heard the shots, went to the back window, and saw you."

I sat opposite Jaworski. "Of course she saw me. I was there, for the same reason that most of your department was there. That woman called me, Herb."

"Angie didn't mention the bag. She said you had a gun in your hand and there was smoke."

"The smoke was from a discarded cigarette."

"We got that. The lab is running tests on it. Won't amount to anything. Beckerman had a pack of the same brand in his pocket."

Jaworski sighed. "How do you figure a woman for the killer? You didn't talk about that in your book."

"We've ignored the female serial killer. We've made her a footnote, an obscure subcategory of crime. Our chauvinism or chivalry, depending on how we define the male privilege of granting the presumption of innocence to females, might kill us all in the end. When a woman forms a homicidal duo with a male psychopath, he is the aggressor, she is labeled one of his victims. With a female pair, we look for the dominant or 'masculine' partner. If she operates alone, we look for duress."

I shrugged. "We haven't given credit where credit is due."

"Is it possible that we've got more than one person involved here?"

Images of Harper Dorman's savaged body flashed through my mind. "That was one of my thoughts when we visited Mellen Street in Portland. There was a case I was trying to remember. Amanda Squires reminded me of it. Sydny Clanton."

"I don't know that one," Jaworski said.

"Charlie Manson and his family held the headlines that year. The media put a drug spin on the Clanton case . . . the wages of teenage rebellion, defiance of authority, that kind of thing. Drugs figured in the case, but no substance creates complex chains of behavior. Clanton killed both her parents and did a carving job on her father. Her next five murders were clean executions. With each one, she was careful, left very little for investigators who were convinced they were looking for a man."

"I can understand why."

"Outside San Francisco, she encountered the Gleid family. She killed all four of them, but mutilated only Mr. Gleid."

"How do you account for it?"

"Part of the picture is developmental. She claimed to be a victim of sexual abuse at her father's hands. No one could determine whether her claims were true. We know that she was dissociative."

"I know the term," Jaworski said, unwrapping a stick of cinnamon gum. "She left her body, went somewhere else in her head."

I nodded. "One effect of the hallucinogenic drugs she was taking was cross-sensing, or synesthesia. Anything was enough to trigger murder. Clanton enjoyed killing. Add a father or father figure to the mix and suddenly she was smelling the voices on TV, hearing the colors, tasting the pain that she claimed her father inflicted on her."

"She was crazy."

"Not according to the law. Clanton knew that what she was doing was wrong. She had the capacity to conform her conduct to the requirements of the law. She was scheduled to be executed, then the state commuted the sentence when the Supreme Court knocked down capital punishment."

"Same thing happened with Manson," Jaworski said.

"Clanton's prison psychiatrist determined that for Clanton, each color had a specific, fixed, auditory association. Rare, but not unheard of. Her father's nickname was Red. Dr. Paynter reconstructed what happened at the Gleids' home. Clanton broke in, found some money, ate something, then watched a newscast about her parents' deaths. There was some broadcast glitch and the screen went completely blue for a matter of seconds. She couldn't pull herself away from the TV. When the telecast resumed, there were pictures of a California wildfire—red trucks, streaks of red in the flames—just as Mr. Gleid walked into the house with his family. But she didn't 'see' the red. She heard it—her father's name."

"You think we've got someone like her running around here?"

"More likely that scenario than Stanley Markham."

"Jasper insists that it's Markham."

"I don't see it."

"The Markham sightings stopped. We haven't heard a thing for the last couple of days. It's like he went underground."

"He's probably holed up," I agreed. "When he thinks he can make it, he'll go to his sister's."

"No male killer ever switched back and forth like Clanton did?"

"There's always variation in the kills," I said. "The concept of a rigid, repeating M.O. is more a law enforcement wish than a reality. Ted Bundy is the best example. He killed during home intrusions. He wore a fake cast on his arm and acted as if he needed help. He impersonated a cop. At different times he beat his victims to death, stabbed them, strangled them. This may sound like a fine distinction, but his variations weren't extreme, nothing like what we have here. It's not a radical stretch to look at the orange and see Markham's touch at the Crescent Street scene, but on close examination, it doesn't hold up. The scene is mixed . . . methodical execution, and reactivity to stimuli in the apartment. Harper Dorman was savaged, Beckerman and Weld executed."

"What about your orange?"

"Stanley Markham would remember my name, and perhaps that I had something to do with the police arresting him. Beyond that, he couldn't care less. He had his fantasies; he wanted his freedom."

"You're convinced that we're dealing with a woman," Jaworski said, skepticism evident in his tone.

"That's the angle I want to pursue."

He pushed himself from the chair. "How do we do it?"

"Each of us grabs a thread and follows it. You talk to Amanda Squires here in Ragged Harbor, pursue the Beckerman angle. I'll head for Portland."

"Katrina Martin?"

"That's where I'll start."

"Norma Jacobs will give you a hand with anything you need down that way," Jaworski said as he prepared to leave. "Call me after you see the Martin woman."

"Herb, you're walking proof that Yankee independence is alive and well."

He stopped at the door. "Jasper's meeting with Hubble Saymes," he said. "I ain't ready to retire. We're both climbing out on a limb, Lucas. If it snaps off, we'll welcome a visit from a rattler."

I watched Jaworski amble across the grass and climb into his car. As he backed out and drove down the hill, I remembered watching Amanda Squires play the piano in the Silo's music room.

"A friend of mine describes this piece as music written in the key of blue," she said. *"There is so much muted rage."*

"Maybe not so muted," I said.

CHAPTER 24

AS I DROVE UP THE HILL TO THE COLLEGE, A RADIO newscaster droned about the murder epidemic without mentioning my name. I wondered how much longer my luck would hold.

Amanda Squires sat alone in the classroom. "I hoped you'd come in," she said.

"We have a class scheduled. Where is everyone?"

"The academic dean canceled the seminar."

"I didn't stop at my mailbox," I said, thinking that the dean's action made sense.

"They may close the college until this is over. The hill is nearly empty. Dawn Kramer left this morning. I think Amy Clay is still here."

"Have the police talked with you?"

"Wendell was a friend. I knew they'd want to ask me questions, so I went to see Detective Jasper this morning."

"Do you mind if I ask you a few questions?"

"I wanted to talk to you. That's why I waited."

"Your friend Wendell lived in the same building where another man was murdered."

"Mr. Dorman. The detective asked me about him. I

saw him a few times when I visited Wendell, but I didn't know him."

"Does the name Lily Dorman mean anything to you?"

She shrugged. "Ms. Jasper asked me where I was last night, how well I knew Wendell and Mr. Dorman. She didn't ask me about other people."

Squires sat comfortably in her chair, her legs crossed, her hands folded in front of her. She stared at her hands as she spoke, and I could not see her eyes. There were no overt indications that she was lying or withholding information, but I could not assess the patterns of her involuntary eye muscle movements. I consider these subtle shifts more accurate than a polygraph at detecting deception.

After a moment I said, "Did you have something you wanted to ask me?"

"I figured if you were going to be here anyway . . ."

I waited.

"When I get angry," she said, "and I yell, or throw something, I feel like I've lost control. I feel guilty about it. I think most women do."

"You were here for the discussion about Aileen Wuornos," I said. "She didn't feel any guilt. She felt justified in what she did."

"Don't you think that women want to avoid situations that might end in violence? I mean, *their* violence. Or, do they just explode and feel bad afterward?"

Amanda Squires seemed to be looking for reassurance that women remained the gentler and more reasonable gender. "A woman can be just as predatory as any man," I said. "Have you heard of Carolyn Warmus?"

She furrowed her brow and shook her head.

"She was a predator," I said. "Warmus was having an affair with a colleague. She pushed for a more permanent arrangement, and he didn't want it. Warmus obtained a gun equipped with a silencer, went to the man's home on a night when she knew he wasn't there, hit his wife over the head with a blunt instrument, and shot her nine times. That's predatory. She passed a polygraph and managed to deflect suspicion from herself to the victim's husband. That's calculating. It took two trials to convict her. The newspapers called it the '*Fatal Attraction* murder.' The violence was planned, and it had a purpose. She didn't lose control, and she certainly didn't express anything remotely close to remorse."

"She was obsessed," Squires said.

"Obsessed with having her own way," I qualified. "So was Pamela Smart."

"That was the New Hampshire murder," she said. "I know about that one. She seduced a fifteen-year-old high school student, manipulated him, and convinced him to kill her husband. It was just one step removed from the woman you described."

"The question is whether these two would have killed or arranged murder again if they had not been caught. Warmus had earlier relationships where she quickly became obsessed with the men, possessive. When they backed off, or dated other women, she went ballistic. Pardon the pun."

She smiled.

"She wrote letters to these boyfriends, called them repeatedly, threatened them. She focused most of her attention on any other women in the picture. One guy had to get an injunction to keep her away from his wedding. Past behavior is the best single predictor of future behavior."

"For her to do it again," Squires interjected, "I think she'd have to be involved in a nearly identical situation, an impossible relationship."

"We don't have any reason to believe that she would suddenly, spontaneously change."

"What about feelings?" she asked. "Warmus and Smart must have felt something."

"Smart's nickname was the Ice Princess. She had appetites, wants. I doubt that she felt much of anything unless someone ignored her demands or got in the way of what she wanted. An affront or snub that you or I might disregard elicits rage because it is seen as an attack, a threat to the entire structure of the personality."

"That sounds like what the experts speculated about during the O.J. Simpson murder trial," she said. "Nicole was pulling away from him. Her family snubbed him at the dance recital. The model he was dating, Paula Barbieri, broke up with him. I remember commentators saying that he'd always controlled his world and suddenly it was coming apart."

As Squires prepared to leave she said, "I wonder if I sat and talked with Pam Smart before, or even after, she'd arranged her husband's death, would there be any way to know?"

"You have a keen interest in the subject," I observed, "and you've obviously read extensively."

Again, Squires shrugged. "I'm trying to understand," she said. "There doesn't seem to be any place for conscience."

I watched as she walked away, unsettled by the feeling that Squires was not examining a hypothetical situation. She struggled with something far more personal.

I DROVE NORTH TO THE FLATS, THINKING ABOUT A fourteen-year-old child strong enough or panicked enough to wage war with a roomful of adults hell-bent on wrapping her in canvas restraints. Harper Dorman—her father, someone she trusted to protect her and comfort her—had dragged his daughter into horror. I empathized with Lily's suffering, understood her rage. Now I was beginning to have a sense of what she had become.

When I saw the small, shingled building with its weathered sign, I slowed the car and pulled off the road. Loudermilk's.

I pushed open the door and a bell jingled.

Ben Loudermilk was a short, wiry man in his late forties. He wore a trimmed goatee, and his steel-gray hair appeared to have been shocked into a Beethoven mop. He sat behind a drawing table, where a gooseneck lamp illuminated an ink sketch that held his attention. Loudermilk gazed down through rimless eyeglasses.

"This is the time of year when I do most of my design work," he said. "Business is slow. After we get the first snow, I don't bother opening the shop during the week. Tourists don't want any part of Maine winters unless they're over in ski country or running snowmobiles. You don't look like a tourist."

"No," I agreed.

Loudermilk sketched a necklace of interlocking fish. His attention to detail was impressive.

"Local kids come in," the garrulous silversmith continued. "They want single earrings. Loops for their pierced navels, studs for their tongues, chains for their nipples. One kid whipped off her shirt and attached three different pieces while I was making change."

He shrugged. "Used to be that everyone wanted tattoos. It's a fad. It'll pass. Although I guess their parents get pretty upset. Is there something I can help you with?"

"I hope so," I said, and handed him the scrimshaw letter opener.

"I sold this piece," Loudermilk said.

He riffled through the contents of a shoe box and produced a Polaroid photo. "That's it right there."

In the snapshot, the scrimshaw rested on a bed of blue velvet.

"The date's on the photo. What was it, two years ago?"

I nodded, studying the photo. "Who was the customer?"

He held his hands in the air. "Why?"

I showed him my identification. "I'm working as a consultant to the Ragged Harbor police. I'll be happy to wait while you verify that with Chief Jaworski."

"Hang on," he said, opening a wooden box of five-by-eight cards.

I sensed a fellow neo-Luddite.

"This may not be real quick," Loudermilk said. "When I go through these cards, I see names, sketches of pieces I've made. I like to remember. I do remember her, but not the name."

He continued sorting through the file, occasionally examining one of his sketches. "Here it is."

He handed me the card.

"When the tourists leave, a sale like that is completely unexpected. She paid in cash."

I looked at the name: Melanie Martin. There was an innocent, even innocuous, explanation. MI funded nearly everything related to the college. Expensive gifts for visiting instructors could be a routine line item. Jaycie was an MI intern, so her informal welcoming committee made the delivery.

I didn't buy it. Martin had personally attended to the purchase two years earlier. When I opened the package, Jaycie expressed pleasure and surprise. Only Amanda Squires knew the box's contents.

"You said you remembered her," I prompted.

Loudermilk's eyes shifted down as he considered. "She was tall. Dressed . . . fashionably, I'd call it, in a blue suit. Blond hair. She wore eyeglasses, tinted, the kind that adjust to the light. Late twenties, early thirties."

"She was in only one time, two years ago," I said. "What made her so memorable?"

"She was in twice," he corrected. "She wanted the sketch embellished."

I looked again at the card. "Is that what these notations are?"

Loudermilk emerged from his work area and pointed at the card. "That was enjoyable work. I studied photographs and drawings of snakes, then did my own sketches. I consider myself an artist, not a merchant. I could never forget a customer like that. She arrived in a limo."

"No address? No phone number?"

He shrugged. "She was quiet, private. It was a cash transaction."

Again, I looked at Loudermilk's notes: timber rattler. "This was your choice?"

"I narrowed it to five. Ms. Martin chose that one."

Loudermilk crossed the room and pointed to a display case that contained dozens of delicate whalebone and walrus-tusk etchings. "This is a popular depiction of a folk tale from the 1840s. She didn't want one of the old renditions. She wanted her serpent to be real."

Again, he shrugged. "People have their quirks. The oceans have their monsters."

"What about her driver?"

"He waited outside. Big, African-American, bald."

I thanked Loudermilk, pocketed the whalebone, and turned to leave.

"There's a song about that one," he continued. " 'The Wreck of the *Lily D.*' "

I froze. "The what?"

"She was a Maine whaler. No one knows what happened to her. She sailed on what was supposed to be a three-year voyage. That was common in those days. The *Lily D.* never returned to port, which wasn't uncommon, either."

I stood, riveted.

"When a ship went down in a storm, wreckage washed up, or word of the tragedy drifted back to the crew's home port. Sometimes it was years before families learned what happened to their sons and fathers and brothers. The *Lily D.* vanished without a trace. The ship had a remarkable record. The captain knew the best whaling waters in the North Atlantic and always sailed his ship into port laden with whale oil. Every sailor heard and retold stories of monsters . . . giant squid, whale sharks, sea serpents. The folk tale about the *Lily D.* grew around the notion that a serpent took the ship, its crew, and its cargo, in payment for their years of pillaging the sea's treasures."

"Vengeance," I said.

Loudermilk nodded. "We don't always know our sins, but we pay for them."

CHAPTER 25

ON THE DRIVE SOUTH, I ALLOWED MY PUZZLE PIECES to grab whatever random assembly they wished.

The woman in the limo visited Mellen Street and asked for Harper Dorman. A similar woman visited Katrina Martin. Two years ago, Melanie Martin arrived in a limo and supervised Loudermilk's design modifications to the scrimshaw. She selected the timber rattler as her serpent.

Were Lily Dorman and Melanie Martin the same person?

Always, there were questions.

Amanda Squires presented the gift of etched whalebone that depicted a tale of vengeance.

Was Squires connected to Martin?

Days later, someone crept into my house and deposited a timber rattler in the study. After that, a knife impaled an orange on my kitchen counter.

Why focus on me?

Someone prowled my road, raced away from the Weld crime scene, then dumped the suspect Volvo at the bluff, a hundred yards from my front door.

Coincidence is for fools.

A woman invited me to find Wendell Beckerman's

body, and planted the notion that I killed the young man. The weapon connected six homicides and left the question of my complicity hung on the line like putrid socks after a rugby match.

Whalers were hunters. They captured their prey, lashed it to the side of the ship. A larger predator rose out of the sea and devoured whalers, ship, and whale.

Payment received for damage done.

Vengeance.

Harper Dorman's murder made sense if Lily Dorman had destroyed and shredded the agent of her horror.

"Wonder if she arrived in a fucking limo," I muttered.

Why target the three students?

Why kill Steve Weld and Wendell Beckerman?

Why stalk me?

Always, there were more questions than answers.

Martin International connected Jaycie Waylon and Steve Weld, albeit tenuously. Melanie Martin and Amanda Squires also shared a possible connection. Stuart Gilman lurked somewhere in the mix.

The kid with a fondness for LSD was Squires's friend, but had no MI connection that I knew of.

Where does Beckerman fit?

The hybrid kills people she knows, and she kills strangers.

"Fuck it," I muttered. "Strip away the horseshit and all you've got is another murderer."

ELLIE MCLEAN STEPPED OUT OF HER TRAILER AS I walked through the courtyard.

"Her soaps are over," I said.

"I knew you'd be back. I've been getting her to take her pills. She showered, cleaned the place. I told you you'd been here. She remembered you, hoped you'd come back."

"Thanks, Ellie."

"She said you were a doctor."

I nodded.

"Why does a doctor wear jeans and not get a haircut?"

"Neckties get in the way when I'm fishing," I said, walking to number three. "The hair keeps the bugs off my neck."

The TV glow had disappeared from Katrina's trailer. I knocked, thinking about the woman I had known briefly thirty years earlier.

Late one night, near closing time, she had walked into the restaurant and ordered an ice cream cone. She sat at the counter, held the cone, and stared at it as it melted. When business slowed, I cleaned her mess.

"Time vanishes," she said. "It melts away. Everything dies."

The trailer door swung open. Katrina Martin looked as if she had shrunk. I remembered her as a tall, dazzling blond. Her long, lush, flaxen hair was gone, replaced by a thin fall of brittle white strands. She wore faded jeans and a tan cardigan buttoned wrong.

She looked at me and tried to focus her eyes. Remembering seemed to be a strain for her.

"Lucas," she said, with a strength in her voice that I had not expected. "Please come in."

I stepped into the low-ceilinged kitchen. The place was the same vintage as Ellie's, and we sat at a similar, but damaged, laminated kitchen table.

"I thought this would feel strange, but it doesn't," she said. "We were friends one summer. I remember the beach. You look different."

I stared at her, trying unsuccessfully to see the woman I had known for a few short weeks so long ago.

"Age," I said.

"Not just that."

I prodded Katrina to talk about her life, about experiences that I knew were painful. She dropped into silence and stared at the table.

Memory is selective and often unreliable. When she spoke, she erased segments of her life, remembered some events in a rewritten or revised form, and described others with nearly eidetic recall.

"When I left Provincetown, I came home to Portland," she said. "I went to the hospital where my mother used to go."

"That's where you met your husband," I said.

She nodded, still staring down, and rubbing the back of her left hand with her right. "Harper worked there. He was young, handsome, an electrician's apprentice. He didn't drink then. When I was eligible for off-grounds privileges, we started dating. I got pregnant right away."

Katrina selected a hard candy from a dish, unwrapped it, and popped it into her mouth. She was coping with one of her medications' dry-mouth side effect.

"The first place we lived was an apartment on Danforth Street," she continued. "It was beautiful there. I could see the harbor from the kitchen window. Then the hospital fired Harper because of me, so he couldn't get his license as an electrician. He worked at the port, did different kinds of jobs. We always seemed to have enough to get by, but then he started to drink. He moved us here when Lily was two."

Katrina broke off her narrative and stared into a corner of the room. A slight smile creased her narrow lips before her eyes rediscovered me. I'd seen the behavior in schizophrenic patients numerous times over the years. Katrina listened to noises only she could hear.

"Katrina?"

"He drank most of the time," she said, the smile gone, her eyes fixed on mine, as if she had never paused. "I was having problems again, but I didn't know it. That's not true. I knew it, but I didn't want to go back to the hospital."

She clasped her hands tightly in front of her. "Did you return to Boston after Provincetown?"

I nodded. "I went back to school."

She pushed her hair out of her eyes. "I never finished school. Is your wife a doctor, too?"

"Savannah is a veterinarian," I said, seeing no point in explaining that Savvy and I had been separated for years, and that she lived in Africa.

"Lily always loved animals. We had a dog once." Katrina's eyes clouded. "The dog . . . died. Lily kept snakes after that. She didn't keep them in the house. They lived in the swamp. She wrote everything about them in a notebook. Even gave them names. The notebook's here. She asked me to send it to her in the hospital. Then she left it here. I don't want to talk. I'm tired. You came here for a reason. Tell me what you want."

"I want to meet Lily," I said.

Katrina turned away. "She was here. Not too long ago, I don't think. She and Edgar, her driver, took me to the waterfront in Portland. There's a little park with benches on Eastern Promenade. I fed the pigeons. We sat on a bench, and Lily sent Edgar to get cracked corn. I watched the ships go by, and I saw the islands. Lily held my hand."

Again, she hesitated. Then, as if finding a bookmark in her thoughts, she said, "Edgar brought the corn. I fed the birds. Lily was so thoughtful. She said she'd come back and take me out. She hasn't yet, but I know how busy she must be. I never knew a black person before I met Edgar. He's a large man, but he's very gentle, and he protects Lily."

I was losing her, and there was so much more that I

needed to know. I was uncomfortable probing her pain, but I had to. "Harper killed the dog," I said.

She stared at me, her eyes narrowed. "Who told you that?"

"A police report."

"They shouldn't have come here."

"Lily stayed with your friend Ellie."

"They took Harper away. He screamed in pain. It's hard to think of him dead. Whatever else . . . we were together all those years."

Her gaze shifted to a corner of the room, and tears rolled from her eyes. I saw no semblance of a smile this time.

"I betrayed Lily. I didn't know the right thing to do. She left the hospital. She came here, and I was confused. I called Mental Health and told them she was here. Lily ran. This last time when she visited, she said she forgave me for that."

Katrina's eyes locked on mine. "I have her back now, and I'm not going to lose her again."

I was reluctant to push her, but I had no choice. "Katrina, I would like to meet Lily," I said again.

"Lily is a successful woman," she said.

I nodded.

"You can't hate her," she said, with the first real emotion in her voice. "You don't know her."

"I want to know her," I said, wondering why Katrina would assume that I hated her daughter.

"You're going to hurt her."

She pushed away from the table and walked to the window.

"I have no wish to hurt her," I said to Katrina's back.

She turned, her eyes darting from one corner to another. "Edgar helps her when things get really bad. I can't help her."

"How do things get bad for her, Katrina?"

She stared into the living room. "Harper smeared blood on the walls."

"The dog's blood," I said.

"He hurt her," Katrina said as she returned to her chair, sat, and rocked back and forth. "He held her by the neck. She couldn't breathe. He made her . . ."

She stopped talking and spread her palms across her face.

"Katrina," I said, reaching across the table to touch her hand.

She was gone, wandering among the many realities that her world comprised. When she looked back at me, her eyes cleared, and she nodded her head. Something had clicked for her, but I did not know what.

"I'll tell you," she said.

Lily Dorman was born on May 1, 1967, in Portland, Maine. "We couldn't afford to send announcements. We called a few relatives."

Harper Dorman provided a sporadic, ever-shrinking income; Katrina cared for the child, the house, the meals, her husband, and the noises—the bits of static that beckoned to her from her mind's dark corridors.

She inhabited multiple realities, wormwood worlds replete with holes and contradictions. Sometimes, when Katrina could not disregard her summons from the kaleidoscoping corners of her soul, she "rested" at Maine Central Mental Hospital.

"Lily always said her first memory was of the move from Danforth Street to Bayberry. She hated it here, and she cried for the old place."

Katrina, confused and confusing, told her two-year-old daughter that the child was too young to have feelings. Later, she told Lily that she had been too young to have any memory of the move.

Harper called Bayberry "a step up." Katrina's smoky eyes saw nothing of her new home's prefabricated horror, nothing of the trailer park's rancid poverty, and nothing of her husband's incipient violence.

"I think now that Lily felt everything," Katrina said. "She had feelings that I couldn't know about."

I imagined the little girl tasting and smelling the sweaty fear and rage that roiled the air within and beyond the trailer's walls. The next day always arrived in a bottle with a smooth white label, one she could run her fingers over until Harper yelled or smacked her hand.

"I always said he had a love affair with Mr. James Beam. He called the bottle Jim. It smelled like cleaning solvent. He stared with those blood-streaked eyes. 'Keep your fuckin' hands offa Jim,' he'd yell at Lily, after he stung her wrist or the back of her hand with a hard slap."

He glared. He swallowed. He roared.

"When Lily was six years old, I asked Harper to break off his affair with Mr. Beam. Lily was watching TV, but she turned to see how he moved, how he held his shoulders, whether his hands were open or closed. That's how she knew what was coming. She read his body."

Dorman pushed himself from the sofa, swayed, stumbled into the dining area where Katrina sat crocheting, wrapped his hands around her throat, and squeezed. Neither one said a word. He grunted once with anger or exertion; she uttered a single squeal like the soft peep of a kitten. The only other sound crackled from the TV.

"Lily said she had a terrible headache, like something grew inside her skull and clawed to get out."

Lily watched Katrina's chair tip backward and the two of them crash to the floor. Harper passed out. Katrina stared at the ceiling.

"Lily said, 'He's out like a fucking light.' I looked at her, and I asked her where she'd heard a word like that. I didn't have to ask. Harper said it all the time. But it wasn't like her to talk that way. I told her he didn't mean it. I told her that he would bring flowers."

Katrina stood and walked to the rear of the trailer. She returned with a blue notebook, opened it, and slid it across to me.

"She left this here when she ran away from the hospital."

I looked at the neat handwriting.

"I read some of it," Katrina said. "Part of it's about her snakes. The rest . . . I had to put it down."

The Story of Lily
Part One
(for Dr. Westlake)

Am I to sleep forever, silently, somewhere in black shadows?

My mother is one person struggling with many worlds. I am many people at war with one world.

Will the others always shove me aside?

On Lilith's first night, we looked down at Harper where he lay across our mother. We listened to him snore and cough and nearly choke. Lilith wished him dead.

Our mother was motionless, her eyes wide, her face without expression. She looked as if she did not dare to move.

For three years, Harper brought flowers on the days after pain. He brought tulips or roses or miniature carnations, whatever the florist threw into the compost.

I was seven when Harper invited me to sit on his lap.

"Please don't read it here," Katrina said.

I closed the notebook. "I'll return it," I said.

"Give it to Lily when you see her. I don't want to look at it again."

"How do I find her?"

"I have a phone number. Lily said I could call anytime I wanted to. I haven't. I don't want to pester her."

Katrina found a slip of paper in her pocket. I copied the number and returned it to her.

"Please leave, Lucas. I want to sleep."

"I'd like to come back," I told her.

"No. I don't think so."

I stepped out of the trailer and walked slowly across the courtyard. A chill crept up my spine and radiated through my neck and shoulders. Sadness and helplessness washed over me. I gazed back at Katrina's narrow metal home.

"It isn't my problem," I muttered.

But it was.

CHAPTER 26

I WALKED UP THE RUTTED ROAD THAT WOUND AMONG trees that had tentacles for branches—slender, gnarled limbs that creaked in the soft, chilling breeze. A one-room cabin appeared in a clearing at the top of the hill.

I crept onto the porch and peered through a sooty window at the single room, dimly lit by a low-burning kerosene lantern. I watched as a man slept on the floor with a rug pulled over him. I walked to the door and knocked. When I heard rustling noises inside, I shouted that I needed directions.

I don't know what I expected, or if I even thought about it, but he was a slightly built man, not quite as tall as I am. He opened the door and squinted out. He had no weapon. His hair was dark, dirty, in disarray. He needed a shave, and he stank of kerosene and sweat.

He asked me if I was lost. Then I said his name.

He groped behind him, staggered backward.

I raised my gun.

He studied my face.

I aimed at his face.

"Who are you?" he asked.

I told him the story of his recent adventures, and how I made them possible.

Then I killed him.

The gun's sharp crack was surprisingly loud and satisfying in the small cabin. He fell, his expression that of a man who finally remembered something that he desperately wanted to know.

Perhaps he learned that there was reason to fear the victim in his mind's eye.

I kneeled to examine the hole in his forehead, above the midpoint of his eyebrows. A trickle of blood followed the slope of his face and the angle of his head. The slender red stream looked like a fat piece of yarn.

I was mildly disappointed.

I expected more blood.

CHAPTER 27

FALL TOURISTS WANDERED THE OLD PORT'S COBBLED
hills gazing in shop windows. I parked on Commercial
Street and wound my way through the gang of gawkers
pinching a final few days before New England winter fell
like a sodden white blanket.

I sat at the counter in Big Mama's and ordered coffee.
Lily Dorman's blue notebook seemed insubstantial—a
kid's seventy-page, wide-ruled theme book—for the narrative it contained. She had illustrated "The Story of Lily"
with pencil sketches and ink drawings, some stark, many
cryptic, most marred with slashing streaks of red.

Harper told me that I could feel Jim's label, but only
while he gripped the bottle. He said nice things to
me—what a good girl I was, how smart I was—while
he rubbed my shoulders and moved me around on
his lap. He said he wanted to be comfortable.

He flattered me, told me that I was a big girl and
would have to sit just right. He slipped his rough
hand beneath my shirt and rubbed my back. If we got
along, he said, Mom wouldn't have to go back to the
hospital.

I didn't want my mother to be sick, but I didn't want to sit on his lap, either. Harper's movements were jerky. His face sweated. His eyes closed. He held me with a firm grip, and I felt pressure against my leg.

Each time he let me go, I found red marks on my arms and shoulders, the imprints of his hands and fingers. I rubbed my arms to make the marks go away.

Harper took his black-handled knife from his pocket. The blade appeared with a loud click, as if from nowhere. He cut into an orange and slowly peeled it, leaving a pile of rind on the table. I thought I would choke on the tart scent of oranges. Harper stuck the blade into each piece of orange, bit it from the end of the knife, slowly chewed, and stared at me every second.

Images from a child's tortured past informed the scene on Crescent Street. Take care of business, and enjoy a piece of fresh citrus fruit. For me, she plunged the knife through an orange and deep into the wooden counter. Why?

One night, Harper came home after eight o'clock, his Jim nearly empty. He wanted to know what was for supper. Mom told him that I'd made ravioli, and he asked if it was from a can.

My mother wrinkled her forehead and tugged at her hair. Canned ravioli was the only kind she knew, what we always ate. Chef Somebody in the pretty can.

Harper said he hated it. He walked to the stove, glared into the saucepan, and complained that the ravioli was cold and stuck together.

Mom reminded him how late it was.

Harper lunged at her. He caught her by the shirt, spun her around and punched her. She slammed against the sink and the wall before she crashed in a heap on the floor.

I scrambled under the table where I sat with my arms over my head, my head tucked down. I heard my father's footsteps, saw his legs as he staggered past me, heard the click when he switched on the TV, and the smash when he fell across the coffee table and cracked his head on the sofa's arm.

I crept from my hiding place and crawled to my mother. Her eyes were open. Blood trickled from the corner of her mouth, and my stomach threatened to empty. I smelled the blood, heard it slide across my mother's skin.

I went to the sink, moistened a dishcloth, then crouched beside my mother. As I wiped away the blood, I swallowed to keep down my stomach.

"I want a different father," I told my mother.

She nodded and closed her eyes.

When I heard Harper snoring, I walked into the living room and stared at him. He looked peaceful, indifferent. His black-handled knife lay nestled in the carpet. I picked up the knife and carried it outside to the stoop. I tried to re-create the snapping noise, to make the blade magically appear like I saw him do. I twisted it, pulled at it, pushed the silver buttons on its side. The blade shot out, sliced my right palm, and sent a stream of blood coursing through the spaces between my fingers.

I sent a different stream, a torrent of partially digested ravioli, spewing onto the steps.

My mother heard me and dragged herself from the kitchen floor. She saw the cut, wrapped it with a piece of torn bedsheet, and said that we were going to out-patient. I didn't want to go. I don't like the smells, or the nurses' swishing sounds when they walk, or muffled voices, or hallways where some noises echo and others do not.

She wiped the knife clean, placed it by Harper's side, then got our coats. We walked through the damp, cold night to the bus stop and waited.

Then Mom told me that Harper wasn't my real father.

My real father was Lucas Frank.

"Jesus Christ," I muttered.

"You need anything?" the waitress asked.

I shook my head and read the paragraph a second time. Now I understood my role in Dorman's life, why she considered our lives entwined.

Lily Dorman's world was a nightmare, a twisted, agonizing dreamscape populated by a father who betrayed and tortured her, and a mother who redefined the child's reality by providing her with a new father.

You were alone with your snakes and nightmares, wandering from the swamp, pressing your face against Ellie's window.

I resisted the impulse to drive back to the trailer. To challenge Katrina would waste time that I did not have.

When I sat with Ellie, you watched.

"Coffee. Two cups," my caller had said.

Lily, as Melanie Martin, would have the money and the power to bring her father home. Still, he ignored her— and gave his attention to Jaycie Waylon.

You stood in the rain and watched through my window, didn't you?

He was a doctor. I imagined him as a nice man, gentle, one who loved children. Mom told me that he loved me, but he was too busy to be any one person's father.

I wanted to see his picture. Mom had one photograph, she said, her voice soft in the darkness. She promised to show it to me the next day. I sensed that my mother was smiling.

"Why doesn't he visit me?" I asked.

"He doesn't have time, Lily."

"Maybe someday?"

My mother agreed. Someday.

The next morning, before she showed me the photo, she swore me to secrecy. Harper must never know that he was not my father.

My mother opened her special wood-and-leather box that she kept hidden in the closet. A tiny pillow of pine needles made the box smell like the evergreens across the road from the trailer park. She studied the photograph and gently touched it before she handed it to me.

I stared at the picture. My mother, much younger in the photo, stood on a beach beside a tall, slender man. Both grinned at the camera.

They were in Provincetown, at the tip of Cape Cod, and met in a restaurant where my father was a cook and Mom a waitress.

He had a mustache, and I wondered if it tickled when he kissed her.

My mother's eyes glistened, and she smiled and told me about a special coffee cup she bought him. He loved coffee, but when he drank it, his mustache got soaked. The cup was made with an extra piece across the top so that wouldn't happen.

I liked him.

I couldn't wait for someday.

I remembered the coffee cup. I thought it was a shaving mug because it had a picture of a barber with a handlebar mustache. Katrina explained, and we laughed at my misunderstanding.

In the summer when I was nine, while I waited for someday, I discovered the swamp behind the trailer park. At first I was afraid to walk on the dike, so I sat in my favorite dry spot, listened to the breeze creep through the bayberry bushes, and wondered why my father—a doctor, after all—did not arrive, fix my mother, and send Harper away.

I couldn't ask my mother. Questions like that might upset her, and I would never do that. If she got too upset, she might have to go away. Then what would happen to me?

In July, when the high water receded from the marsh, I walked onto the dike and discovered new friends, the snakes that lived in the bog.

I went to the school library and read articles about snakes and their habits. I studied the varieties that like to live in saltwater bogs and marshlands.

One day in August, I sat on the dike and called to Billy Brown-spot, Suzi Stripe, and Lenny Lemon-color. I advised them about their health, about shedding their skins, about the cold weather to come. I picked up Suzi Stripe. The small snake slithered and squirmed from my hand, but I always had my other hand ready to catch her so that she did not fall.

Then I heard Harper slam his pickup door and yell, "Where's the fucking dog?"

It was early. What was he doing home? What did he want with the dog? He always stayed away from Spike.

I ran across the dike and up the path. When I got to the courtyard, the truck was there, but Harper had disappeared. I ran into the trailer.

My mother lay in a familiar heap on the kitchen floor. Before I could say anything to her, I heard a loud crack, then Harper's voice: "Fucking piece-of-shit dog."

There was a second loud noise.

Mom did not move. She didn't seem to know that I was there.

Harper crashed through the door, his shoulders hunched forward, elbows jutted out, and feet wide apart. His hands and gun glistened red, coated with gore. He told me to take off my pants and get my ass on the sofa.

I slipped out of my jeans as I hobbled to the living room.

Harper told Mom to get off the floor and go to Ellie's.

I heard her moan and cry softly. I peeked over the back of the sofa as she stumbled down the front steps.

Harper slammed the door behind her, blood flying like spittle from his left hand, the gun gripped in his right. I lay unmoving on the couch, my fists pressed to my mouth, my bare legs cold, my eyes shut tight.

When Harper stepped around the sofa into the living room, he held something in his left hand and stared at whatever it was. He placed the gun and the other object on the coffee table, then wiped his hands in broad red strokes across the trailer's walls.

He stared at his work, then slowly turned and pointed at the bloody mess on the table.

"Fucking dog's heart," he said.

"The man deserved to die," I growled.

"You reading a mystery?" the waitress asked.

"It's no mystery anymore," I said.

You ripped him apart, then dropped his heart on the table.

I tucked the notebook under my arm and walked to the phone, a black-and-silver box decorated with coin slots and fine print. When I got to the part about calling cards, I had no idea what they were talking about. I popped in a quarter, punched numbers, then listened to beeps and hums followed by a digitized voice lecturing me about placing calls outside my local dialing area.

"Phone company needs more humans," I muttered, as I made a second attempt.

This time I listened to a crackling noise, then another virtual voice informing me that the number I had dialed was no longer in service. "I'm calling a damn police department," I shouted into the phone.

"Need help?" the waitress asked.

"Stay out of this," I grumbled. "It's between me and this machine."

I reread the instructions. Calling collect seemed the easiest of the options, so I did.

"A fucking miracle," I muttered when I heard Jaworski's voice.

"What's that?" he asked.

"Nothing. You get anywhere with Squires?" I asked.

"Motor Vehicles has nothing on her. If she has a phone anywhere in the state, it's unlisted. We may have to get a subpoena for that."

"She talked to Jasper this morning."

"Jasper ain't been around. If Squires told you that, she's pulling your chain."

"There's a connection between Martin and Squires. Ben Loudermilk sold Martin the scrimshaw letter opener two years ago. She arrived in a limo. Loudermilk's description of her sounds like the woman in the painting. He also told me the story of the *Lily D.* That's what's depicted on the scrimshaw."

"I ain't following all this, but that's nothing new," Jaworski said. "Did you see Katrina Martin?"

"It's worse than I thought."

"She the one you knew?"

"For a couple of weeks one summer, thirty years ago," I said. "Herb, Dorman abused his daughter. Lily told her mother that she didn't want him for a father, that she wanted someone different. Katrina told her that I was her father. Lily grew up believing that I would come for her. She thinks that I should have rescued her and cured her mother."

"Jesus. That's more than enough reason to hate you. I've run into craziness over the years, but nothing like this."

"I don't understand why she's playing games. She could have killed me. She's had plenty of opportunity."

"You said there's a logic to murders like these," Jaworski said. "Killing Dorman makes sense. What about the others?"

"I had time for Jaycie Waylon. I didn't have time for Lily. I don't know. All the connections are tenuous. I feel like I need a playbill."

"Lucas, when are you coming back?"

"Feds all over the place?"

"They are, but it ain't that. I had a call from a detective in Portsmouth, New Hampshire. They found Stanley Markham."

"That's the first good news I've heard in days," I said, feeling relief wash through me. "Maybe they'll keep him locked up this time."

"No need," Jaworski said, breathing heavily into the phone. "He's dead. One shot through the forehead from the twenty-two I've got sitting here on my desk."

"What the hell?"

Seven dead from the same gun, and one of them the killer, Stanley Markham.

"Jasper and her friends from Washington want you to get your ass back up here."

"No," I said, as I struggled to understand what Jaworski was saying.

Lily Dorman went after Markham, found him, and blew him away.

"Herb, come to Portland tonight. Stay at the Holiday Inn by the highway. I'll get there when I can."

"Lucas, that limb we're on is cracking. Jasper had her talk with Saymes. The board is meeting tomorrow night."

"What the hell is she thinking?"

"You pegged Markham the last time. You could have sent invitations to his arrest. Jasper figures you found him again. You had the gun. She knows you don't play by the rules."

"I found him and capped him. Sure, I could have. I didn't. We don't have time to waste on this shit, Herb. You got a phone book there that covers Maine Central Mental Hospital?"

"You planning a vacation?"

I laughed. "Yeah. I need the number to make my reservation."

As soon as I hung up, I called the hospital and asked for Dr. Westlake. After a pause, the receptionist said, "We don't have a Dr. Westlake."

"She or he was a psychiatrist or psychologist there seventeen or eighteen years ago."

"God. I was five then. Hang on."

While I waited, too many violins ruined Beatles tunes.

"The woman who runs the gift shop remembered," she said. "She's been here forever. Dr. Julia Westlake is the one you want. She has an office in Portland."

I thanked her and checked the Yellow Pages. Julia Westlake, M.D., maintained an office in the heart of the business district. I called, explained to Westlake's secretary that I was a psychiatrist who needed to consult with the doctor about one of her former patients. I assured her that it was an urgent matter, and she penciled me in for five-thirty that afternoon, when Westlake would have finished seeing patients for the day.

I returned to Big Mama's counter and to my reading.

I sat on the dike and talked to my snakes. Lilith insisted that there be no laws. She promised to learn about my world, but said she would draw her own conclusions and decide whether the rule of one eye for one eye applied.

I lived the life, but I held no power.

Others arrived then. They were not particularly smart, but they were responsible. They did errands, cleaned up after Lilith's messes, and helped Mom.

Lilith learned how to make headaches go away. Whenever she could arrange events so that Harper suffered inconvenience or pain, the throbbing faded. Those who knew of the headaches loved her for that magical ability. She controlled one agony.

Whenever we most needed Lilith, she reminded us that she would not stay unless she had her own way about things. We always agreed. She also told us that she was not happy with our father, Lucas Frank.

He failed us, she said. Some of us grumbled about that, but we were afraid to make a serious fuss.

What each of us knows is fragmentary, bits and pieces of the whole story. No one knows the complete life.

In my twenty-five years of practice, I encountered one case of multiple personality disorder. Now, sitting at Big Mama's counter with Lily's diary, I had trouble breathing, my hands trembled. MPD is rare. It is also difficult to treat, devastating to endure.

Many years ago, a colleague referred Chastity Bancroft to me for assessment. On the half dozen occasions that I saw her, if she became frustrated in her attempt to express herself, she curled into fetal position in her chair and went mute. I considered her histrionic.

When I described Bancroft's behavior to my mentor, Dr. Herman, he asked if I had considered MPD. "It is rare," he said, "but certainly possible."

Using the primitive techniques suggested by the literature then, I began an exploration of Bancroft's sense of time, her memory for remote and recent events, the ways in which she handled the unpleasantness in her life. When it was apparent to me that Bancroft spontaneously dissociated, I inquired about her treatment sessions with her regular therapist.

"She asks to talk to parts of me," Bancroft said. "The angry part. The sad part. The part that has the nickname Chas. She says that one's a boy."

I concluded that Bancroft suffered from depression, that she was indeed dissociative, and that she adjusted her illness to accommodate her therapist's expectations. Bancroft's depression was a disabling illness; her MPD was iatrogenic, or therapist-induced.

When I submitted my report, a gender war engulfed

me. The MPD epidemic was in its early stages, but already boasted an advance guard of vocal and politically connected advocates. The women's movement embraced this mutation of hysteria as evidence of man's oppression and abuse. Experts stridently informed the public that sexual diddling and sadism by adult males against female children ran rampant in the land. Any attempt at objective analysis of this pastiche of disease and folk myth was akin to treason.

"The furor will pass," I told Dr. Herman.

Twenty years later, the debate raged. MPD had spawned post-traumatic stress disorder, repressed-memory syndrome, and claims of satanic ritual abuse. Daytime TV offered victims who switched personality or told tales of subversive alters and sacrificial altars, abreacting in agonizing throes for the audience.

A cottage industry was built on a foundation of anecdotes. No one found evidence to support the true believers' extravagant claims.

The nineties saw MPD downgraded to dissociative identity disorder (DID) in the American Psychiatric Association's diagnostic bible. The few real casualties of shattered personality suffered in silence.

I continued to read Lily Dorman's diary, convinced that what the spiral-bound notebook contained was genuine.

I'm pretty sure that there are eleven of us, but I have not met everyone. Lilith is scary.

One night, I watched as Lilith stood beside our mother in the kitchen. Mom promised to make french fries and was heating the corn oil.

Harper was drunk, curled on the couch, his breathing a ragged rumbling.

Lilith waited until Mom was distracted with another task, then grabbed the pot of hot oil, walked to the back of the sofa, and dumped it on Harper. Then she laughed.

Harper screamed that he was blind. Mom was hysterical, barely able to give directions over the phone. I wondered who she called, but with the arrival of the ambulance and the police, I understood.

Paramedics took Harper to the emergency room. Then Mom and the police and Lilith were supposed to talk. Lilith refused. As far as she was concerned, everything was over, and she wanted to go to bed. Then I saw the two men in starched white pants walk through the door.

That's when Lilith shoved me aside.

I have heard the stories. Men were knifed and bleeding. More men arrived. Lilith held them off and screamed that she would kill the whole fucking world. It took five men to restrain her.

I understand that whenever I am threatened, Lilith will emerge from her cave deep inside and take control. Some of us will die then.

When Lilith controls, her logic is simple: she kills, therefore she exists.

I glanced at the wall clock. It was nearly five P.M., time to call on Dr. Westlake. I reluctantly closed the notebook, and promised myself that I would continue reading later.

CHAPTER 28

TWO GRANITE BANKS SANDWICHED JULIA WESTLAKE'S wood-frame building. I climbed to her top-floor office overlooking a small city park that offered the requisite benches, pigeons, and placard-bearing protesters, but no grass.

"A concrete park," I muttered as I turned away from the commuter hour's traffic and human congestion.

Westlake's secretary was gone for the day. I stood in the empty waiting room and flipped through a copy of *The Sun*, a small, polished magazine published in Chapel Hill, North Carolina. The issue contained an excerpt from *Finding Freedom: Writings from Death Row*, by Jarvis Jay Masters, a practicing Buddhist awaiting execution at San Quentin.

"Sad case," Westlake said, walking from her office and nodding at the magazine. "The street animal got humanized too late. The state will kill Masters. You mind if I smoke?"

She lit a cigarette and inhaled deeply. "When I get rid of that last patient at the end of the day, I have my cigarette. I used to smoke two packs a day. I was one of the lucky ones—it wasn't that hard to quit. Except for this one. I'm Julia Westlake."

"Lucas Frank."

Westlake wore jeans and a blue wool sweater. Her graying black hair was brush-cut and served as a parking space for her eyeglasses. "The real pisser about the Masters case," she continued, "is that three inmates were involved in killing a guard. Masters was convicted of sharpening the shank. Another inmate committed the murder. Only Masters got the death penalty. Doesn't sound much like equal justice."

" 'Equal justice' is an oxymoron," I said. "The quality of your day in court depends on what you can afford."

Westlake smiled. "So, which of my former patients brings you so urgently to my door?"

"Lily Dorman."

She hesitated for only a moment. "Maine Central," she said. "That was years ago."

"You remember her."

She took a final drag on her cigarette. "I don't want to get all formal on you," she began, "but do you have a release?"

"If I have to get authorization, it would not be a release," I said gently. "It would be a court order."

It was a bluff. I doubted that any judge would authorize a fishing expedition into confidential records, but I did not have the time or patience to muck around in the quixotic world of professional ethics.

"Give me some idea of just how urgent this is," Westlake said.

"I'm working as a consultant to the Ragged Harbor police."

"The three murdered students."

"There are seven connected murders."

"Jesus. You think Lily Dorman had something to do with them?"

"Her father is one of the victims."

Westlake sat in her secretary's chair. "Harper Dorman. When I read about the murder in the newspaper, I didn't make the connection. Lily was terrified of him. She hated him. He sexually abused her for years. Lily was a disturbed kid, but when I knew her she was not nearly homicidal."

"Will you tell me about her?"

"What I can remember. I don't have her file. That would be at Maine Central, if they still have it. Lily was my first MPD case. She'd been there six months before I understood what was going on."

I sat on the sofa opposite Westlake and listened as she recalled her early sessions with Lily Dorman. What began as straightforward psychotherapy with an adolescent soon became the complex, demanding tasks required with an MPD patient.

"I like to encourage journal work," Westlake said. "Lily was young, but she was bright, and she was already writing in a notebook. At first, we talked about her adjustment to the ward, her schoolwork, other kids on her unit. I felt as if I was building trust, slowly developing a relationship with her. I saw her two or three evenings a week. I'll never forget the session when she revealed that she was a multiple. She looked different, the way she talked changed, everything about her altered. I swear that her eyes were a different color. She told me to call her . . . oh, what the hell was it?"

"Lilith?" I prompted.

"That's it. Lilith was tough, angry, sort of a protector. She was sarcastic, didn't trust anyone, but Lily convinced her that I could be trusted. She was the one who told me there were others. I was so blown away, I couldn't believe it. Angel was one of the alters. She was younger, always needing to be hugged. Molly was older. There was a fussy one, too, kind of a caretaker. I don't know how much help this is."

"Anything you remember is enormously helpful," I told her.

"It's so long ago. I blamed myself when she took off. I should have known it was coming. She had only one close friend on the ward, a girl a few years younger than Lily who was a smart, tough, street kid. None of us had any success with her. She was there for in-patient evaluation because of an accumulation of the usual juvenile offenses. They used to call kids like that 'unmanageable.' Lily asked me if I would see the girl because she was talking about leaving the hospital. I had to say no."

Westlake lit another cigarette. "Maybe I'll take up smoking again," she said. "Lily left with her friend. We heard later that Lily showed up at her mom's, then took off again."

"The incidents that led to her hospitalization confuse me," I said. "She dumped hot oil on her father. That was an act of vengeance and rage . . . maybe impulsive, maybe calculated. She fought with the police, stabbed a couple of them. A few months later, you saw no potential for violence."

"I didn't say that," Westlake interrupted. "I said she wasn't homicidal. Lily Dorman was the genuine article. Each personality was discrete. Lilith had a nasty streak. Myra was the prissy one. A year after she ran off, Lily sent me a postcard from San Francisco. I remember thinking how troubled she was, and wondering whether she could survive in a real city."

Westlake crushed out her cigarette. "The newspaper said the police were looking for a serial killer."

"Stanley Markham. He's dead, one of the seven victims."

She stared at me. "Someone killed the killer. That's poetic, if nothing else. How can you be certain that all these murders are related?"

"The same gun was used for all seven. Julia, is there anything more that you remember about Lily?"

"Let me get this straight. You think Lily Dorman tracked down and murdered a serial killer. Markham killed women, didn't he? How the hell could she get near him?"

"I don't know."

"Why do you think Lily Dorman killed any of these people?"

I outlined the case for her and described my involvement.

"That's why your name was familiar," she said. "Lily insisted that Harper Dorman was not her biological father. At first, she refused to tell me who was, but then she brought a magazine article to one of our sessions. The article was about you, and how you developed personality profiles that led police to killers."

The Markham case had broken then, and media attention was nonstop. Only Boston's "Strangler," Albert DeSalvo, claimed more Boston headlines than Stanley Markham. A good friend, investigative reporter Anthony Michaels, wrote an in-depth story about my work.

Again, the scourge of coincidence blistered my mind. Markham's escape was too convenient.

"She told you that I was her father."

Westlake nodded. "Lily said that she had your 'fine mind.' Does she?"

"I'm not Lily Dorman's father," I said.

HERB JAWORSKI WAS NOT REGISTERED AT THE HOLIDAY Inn. I checked in, found my room, and thumbed through Lily's journal until I discovered the relevant entry.

I have my father's good mind.

Mom told me that. She gave me an article that said Lucas Frank has an instinctive grasp of the criminal mind. The story was about how he made images of killers in his mind and helped the police catch them.

I studied his photograph. My father had a neat beard and trimmed dark hair. He also had a serious expression, intense.

I read the article, but I did not understand it.

Mom said that I would understand it soon because I have my father's good mind.

She allowed me to keep the magazine. She liked that I stared at my father's photograph. I reread the article dozens of times and studied the words until they made sense.

First, I learned how the killers thought, how they reasoned about the world, and how they made decisions. A few months later, I knew how my father could retreat from his own habits of thought and make room for another person's way of looking at life.

Father was like daughter; he created mind boxes.

He did not describe the people he hunted only at the moments that they committed their murders. He absorbed everything—every habit, every quirk, every belief. He told the police that one man they wanted was afraid of the dark. He did not drive at night.

I was mystified. How could he identify someone else's fear?

Lily knew about Stanley Markham from the time Katrina told her that I was her father.

You arranged Markham's escape, didn't you? You set him free, then you went after him.

I remembered the Michaels article and my reconstruction of Markham's crimes. After three failed, late-afternoon abduction attempts, each one a two-hour drive from Boston, there were victims in those same areas the next day. Markham killed within nine, eleven, and seventeen miles of each failed abduction, after police had swarmed into those towns and surrounding communities.

The pairings of those attempts and kills were so close, so risky, and so far from where I believed he lived, I decided that the killer feared something more than being apprehended. He was afraid of the dark.

Following an attempted abduction in western Massachusetts, police there had a good description of the suspect. They knew he drove a red Econoline van. Maybe he was sleeping in it, maybe he was sitting in a movie theater but, after dusk, he was not driving it.

They caught Markham sitting in his van at the Holyoke Mall, reading *Shadow of Death*.

Lily Dorman's attention to detail was remarkable. She was disturbed, as Dr. Westlake said, intelligent, as Dr. Penniweather reported, and emotionally starved for a father's attention. Harper Dorman was a sadist, so Katrina indulged her own fantasies and gave her daughter a new father. Lily devoured every scrap of information that she could get her hands on.

> When he was fifteen, Markham's school sent him for psychological testing. I don't remember all the words, but the article said he was aggressive, and that he had no interest in having relationships. What I didn't understand, I looked up in my dictionary, then found books about personality disorders in the school library. Now I wonder if he had to take the same tests that I did.

When he was sixteen, Markham quit school and lived with his sister. Police arrested him for burglary. A psychiatrist told the court that the most remarkable aspect of the B&Es was Markham's choice of loot: a can of dog food, a used Gillette razor, an identification bracelet imprinted with the name Henrietta.

My father said that the doctor missed the most important fact: all the victims were women who lived alone.

When he was eighteen, Markham approached a woman walking alone on a dark Boston street. He held up a knife, but didn't say anything. The woman thought she was being robbed, so she gave Markham her money. He stood there looking confused, so the woman ran.

Markham said, "I saw everything in my mind's eye."

He said he always knew what would happen ahead of time, and insisted that the women never gave him money.

Much later, my father said that the words "in my mind's eye" were the most important to understand Markham. He was able to split away from the moment while continuing to be in the moment.

I wanted to know what I was doing when my head thought its thoughts and my body did something entirely different. Dad gave an excellent example: A man mows a lawn. Afterward he knows he cut the grass, but he has no memory of it, no proof except that he can see the cut grass, and he's gripping the lawn mower. He did a good job on the yard, didn't destroy any flowers or shrubs, trimmed neatly around the bushes, but he can't tell you about it. He has been "in his mind's eye."

I can't decide whether I am more like my father or the people he chases. I have a mind's eye. What I see and hear there are my blue dreams. Sometimes the dreams are sad. They are always violent. Perhaps if I were evil, Dad would have to find me.

"I always think of this piece as music written in the key of blue."

Amanda Squires played the piano. In the seminar, she discussed murder.

"Sydny Clanton dreamed the blue dream that never ends," Squires said, attributing the remark to *"a friend."*

Shit. Something was wrong. I left the notebook on the desk and walked the length of the room.

"I think there's a confusion about what Lustmord *means,"* she said.

I stood at the door and read about room rates, occupancy rules, and emergency exits.

"Every time Clanton killed, she placed a small stone in the pouch. She was keeping score."

Clanton's psychiatrist had told me that. There had been nothing in the media about the pouch, or the fact that her pocket had contained 31 small stones awaiting transfer to the pouch. It was 1967; stranger-stranger killings had yet to become a national plague. Little more than a year had passed since Albert DeSalvo had introduced himself to the American public. Besides, Sydny Clanton was a woman.

How would Amanda Squires know about the pouch and the pebbles?

Squires had presented me with a gift purchased two years earlier by Melanie Martin.

"The Wreck of the Lily D."

"And the lady in the limo," I muttered, returning to the desk.

Something whole emerged from the fragments of Lily Dorman's shattered personality. An entity, a complete and lethal being, evolved from her primal storm.

Every day, my father saw people in his office. He talked with them, studied them, absorbed everything he could about them. He knew what went on in their minds, why they did the strange or hurtful things they did, and he helped them to understand and to change. He knew what debris lay behind them because his patients told him.

When the police asked for his help to track Stanley Markham, there was no patient to study. He could only sit in his office and stare at an empty chair. All he had was the litter left in a killer's wake.

It was nearly ten P.M. when Jaworski rapped on my door.

"You look like you've been through the wringer," I said.

"That and more."

Jaworski sighed. "Jasper knew I'd be seeing you, said I should bring you in. She's got the feds pretty worked up."

"Markham's dead. Whatever assistance I might have offered is no longer needed."

"She's convinced you know more than you're saying. I know your reputation. I'm inclined to agree with her."

"Herb, I don't *know* anything. I have some ideas, possibilities. Shall I fax Jasper a list? It'll give her something to file."

Jaworski ignored my sarcasm. "This business about a woman killing all these people . . . it doesn't make any sense."

I dropped Lily's notebook in his lap. "It's the scenario that makes the most sense to me," I told him. "Squires connects to Dorman, and Dorman is probably our limo lady."

"Lucas . . ."

"What else can you tell me about Markham's escape?"

Jaworski looked from the notebook to me. "You know, I have a hell of a time following your train of thought."

"My daughter Lane says the same thing. That's Lily Dorman's journal. What about Markham?"

Jaworski's eyes darted from Lily's notebook to his own, then back to me. "Markham had a twenty-minute jump on the guards. As soon as they realized he was gone, they put out an APB. The state police stopped everything moving, including the laundry truck. No Markham. Also, no stolen vehicles, no home intrusions. They figure he had help outside, but they don't know who."

"Where did police find him?"

"It was like you said. He was holed up in a fishing camp outside Portsmouth. Couple of kids found him. Investigators are still working the scene."

"I have a couple of stops to make. Check with the U.S. Marshals. Ask them about Markham's correspondence, any phone calls, visitors."

I walked to the door. "Anything from the Volvo?"

"Nothing. Wiped clean."

"What about Weld's house, Beckerman's car?"

Jaworski shook his head. "What do I tell Jasper?"

"The truth. I blindsided you with a train of thought that doesn't slow down at crossings. Herb, read the diary. I'll be back in a couple of hours."

CHAPTER 29

IT WAS NEARLY MIDNIGHT WHEN I SLIPPED THROUGH
the door into the Mellen Street apartment building.

Amanda Squires had attended the memorial service
with Wendell Beckerman. Gretchen Nash knew Beckerman. I wondered if Nash knew Squires.

As I climbed the stairs, the door squealed and clicked
shut behind me, and the old wood groaned beneath my
feet. I was gambling. Gretchen Nash could be out or
asleep. I tapped softly on her door.

The scream from inside the apartment startled me.
"You open that door and I'll blow your fucking head off."

I stepped back and to the side and leaned against the
railing. "Ms. Nash, it's Lucas Frank. We talked a few days
ago."

"You're changing your voice," she shrieked, her voice
vibrating with terror and rage.

As I considered what to say next, a large-caliber gun
exploded in the apartment. An entire door panel shattered
into the hall and showered me with wood slivers. I dove to
the floor as the gun discharged a second time and demol-
ished the molding.

"Gretchen, for chrissake," I yelled.

"Prove who you are or I'll keep shooting."

"How can I do that?"

I lay still in the silence, surrounded by rodent droppings and two fat, gray barn spiders.

"What kind of tea did you drink when you were here?"

"Oh shit," I muttered.

She had offered me several herbal teas, and something else . . . what was it? It was in a yellowish package. Twinings? "Earl Grey," I called.

This pause was shorter. "Stand in front of the door and open it."

"Gretchen, I don't want to get blown away."

"If you're who you say you are, I won't shoot."

"Who the hell else would I be?"

"Amanda," she screamed.

The hallway went silent again.

"Just do what I told you," Nash said, with meanness and determination in her voice.

I pushed myself up. "Gretchen, I'm trusting that you won't shoot me," I said as I walked to the door, twisted the knob, and shoved.

Gretchen Nash stood in the center of her studio-room. Both hands gripped a .44 Magnum aimed at my chest.

"It's you," she gasped, lowering the weapon. "That woman was my friend. She slept here, for chrissake."

"Amanda Squires," I said, but Nash paid no attention.

"Nights that she was afraid to be home alone, she curled up on the floor in my sleeping bag. Then she shows up and goes fucking postal. I've got a bullet in my shoulder."

"Let me take a look at that," I said, examining the wound high on her right shoulder.

A burn that had to be painful surrounded a narrow flesh wound. The bullet had grazed her arm. The bleeding had slowed, almost stopped. I found a box of gauze in her bathroom cabinet, formed a compress, and applied pressure to the small crease.

"We should get you to a hospital. That has to be cleaned."

"You made it hurt. It didn't hurt until you did that."

"Sorry," I said, relieving her of the gun. "When did you last get a tetanus shot?"

She sighed deeply, shuddered, and sat on the edge of her bed. "Hospital smells make me sick," she said.

Nash seemed to be in a mild state of shock. She was not in medical danger, so I decided to wait until she was ready to seek treatment for the wound.

"She killed Mr. Dorman," Nash said.

"Amanda?"

I'd been nearly convinced that Martin was Dorman. Squires as Dorman? What the hell was going on?

"Beckerman was stoned that night, but he thought he heard her voice, or thought he was talking to her, something. It was late, he said. I didn't pay any attention to him because he's always so fucking out of it. Now he's dead, too."

Nash sobbed quietly to herself. "She was here that afternoon. We hugged, sipped tea, drank wine, had dinner, listened to music, talked. Jesus."

I tried again to get confirmation. "Amanda Squires?"

"We were friends for . . . a long time. That night, I told her I was going to Barry's installation. She always called Barry's sculpting 'soup cans in sexy poses.' We joked about the show giving Jesse Helms shit fits. Amanda looked at my sketches. She asked me about the limo lady."

Nash gazed at the space vacated by her headless woman. "Amanda was here a couple of times after I put that up. She never noticed it. I told her I had to rush, just to leave the dishes in the sink and lock up when she left. I trusted her. I never had any reason not to trust her."

Nash turned to look at the shattered remains of her feng shui mirror. "The bullet must have hit there," she said. "My chi flow is screwed up."

"When I talked to Wendell Beckerman, he thought he might have heard a woman's voice in his room the night of the murder."

"He had his Bose really cranked," she said. "I figured he was tripping. He usually is. Was. When I talked to him the next day, he asked me if I'd been in his apartment. Every time he hears a woman's voice like that, when he's taken acid, he thinks it's his mother. She died a few months ago. I told him I was out, and he said it must have been Amanda. I called her after I talked to him. I was freaked. The cops had just gone. Somebody was murdered here in the building. I wanted to move out. So I called my friend. Makes sense, right? I called the fucking murderer. Woke her up. I told her what happened and asked her what time she'd gone home. She said, 'I haven't been home in years.' Crazy. I told her to make some coffee."

She winced and gazed at the wound on her arm. "This stings."

ON THE SHORT DRIVE TO THE HOSPITAL, NASH SAT huddled in silence.

I signed the register in the emergency room and joined her on a row of orange and green fiberglass chairs. We were alone in the waiting area.

"There isn't any hospital smell," she said.

I detected a faint odor of isopropyl alcohol. Otherwise, Nash was right.

The E.R. receptionist walked in carrying a cup of coffee, glanced at the register, then sat at her desk. "Nash?" she inquired.

We joined her as she fired up her computer and prepared to record the admissions information. Her name tag identified her as Mrs. Hackett. The brusque, permed, fifty-ish woman wearing a laundered pink smock was a model of impatient efficiency. I looked behind me to make sure that the ill and injured were not arriving in droves and tripping over their crutches.

"I don't have insurance," Nash said.

Mrs. Hackett pushed herself away from the computer console.

"Visa okay?" I asked.

She accepted the card and rolled her chair into keyboarding position. "Are you the father?"

"Friend," I said.

When she reached the section that required a description of the illness or injury, I explained, and suggested that she call Detective Norma Jacobs.

Hackett whipped the forms from her printer and ushered us into a curtained area. "Dr. Kent will be with you," she said, and bustled out.

I stood, and Nash sat on a gurney.

"When I talked to Amanda the day after Mr. Dorman's murder, she said she left the building right after I did. She was just so cool about it. Like, 'Don't worry. The cops will figure it out.' Then she said, 'People die,' as if it was no big deal. Jesus. I don't think Mr. Dorman planned to do it so soon. I asked her if she was coming over. She said she didn't have time. She had some errands to do."

Her errands probably took her to Ragged Harbor, I thought.

WHEN DR. KENT HAD TENDED TO THE WOUND, HE SAID that Detective Jacobs was on her way.

Nash wanted to wait outside. "Guess I don't like hospitals," she said. "It isn't just the smells. Sound is so muted. I feel like I say something and the walls suck it up."

We stepped into the chill night air. "What happened tonight?" I asked.

She sighed and said, "I wish I had a cigarette. I feel like I'm acting in a horror movie. They always smoke when they're talking about what the monster did."

Nash took a deep breath. "Amanda came by late," she said. "I was cleaning my work area, putting away tools. I figured it was one of those nights when she was afraid to stay at her place. She was jumpy. Amanda has nightmares. She never said much about them, just that they were scary, and that she didn't want to be alone. Anyway, she was staring at my painting. Out of the blue she said, 'I killed Harper Dorman.' I looked at her, but she wasn't looking at me."

As if she were reciting something that she had memorized, Amanda Squires had told Nash that she had waited in Beckerman's apartment, then walked downstairs after two A.M. Dorman's door had been open. She had looked in and seen him asleep, sprawled half on his cot and half on the floor.

Nash paced the E.R. ramp, sliding her hand over the rail as if for guidance, not stability. "Dorman had a bottle of Jim Beam. That's what he always drank. Amanda called it 'Mr. James Beam.' She said, 'Mr. Jim smells like blood and beatings.' I didn't know what to say. She said she wanted Lily Dorman to see her tormentor sprawled and stinking, but that she always puked at the sight of blood."

I pictured Squires-as-Dorman in an abreactive state, all the horror from her past erupting with its original intensity in the present. Then I dismissed the image.

You can't have it both ways.

You can't be fragile and fragmented, and weave elaborate schemes that span years.

"It took me a while to figure out that she didn't have somebody else with her," Nash said. "She was talking about herself. She's two fucking people. Or more. She stood over Mr. Dorman with a gun and said, 'My dreams are in the key of blue.' What the fuck does that mean? That's crazy. Then she shot him."

I listened to Nash's words and imagined Dorman shudder—a quick, jerking motion, like one of his many spasms when he pleased himself under his daughter's backside.

"She kept shooting until the gun was empty."

Squires told Nash that she remembered Lily Dorman screaming, the metallic stink of blood, the illusion of faces in red rainbows, and the roar of blue rage.

"Maniac talk," Nash said. "She told me that she used Beckerman's phone to page her driver, Edgar, then waited on the street. I didn't know she had a fucking driver."

Squires was with the other students when the Volvo nearly drove them off the road. She had not peered through my windows; she was in my house. Nothing made sense.

Nash spun from the rail. "She said that she killed another man . . . Stanley."

"Markham?"

"I don't know. I listened to her, but I was scared shitless. I told her that she couldn't have killed Mr. Dorman. Today's paper had that article about what the killer did to him."

"I didn't see it," I said.

"One of those 'unnamed sources' called the murder a ritual killing. I know what that means. He was mutilated. Parts of him weren't even there. God. I gave Amanda the newspaper, like I was going to prove to her that she couldn't have done something like that. She kept saying, 'Oh no,' and holding her head. She said she didn't remember any cutting, that she certainly hadn't done anything like that. Then I thought she was saying 'Lily' again. She wasn't. She was saying 'Lilith.' She staggered around the room muttering about Lilith. That's when she pulled the gun. I dove across the bed and grabbed my Magnum. I don't know how many times she shot at me. I fired once, and she ran out."

NORMA JACOBS PARKED HER UNMARKED CRUISER IN the E.R. lot. I made the introduction and gave Jacobs a brief description of what Nash had told me.

"I'll need a formal statement from you about what happened tonight, Ms. Nash. We can do that at my office. Then I want to have a look at your apartment. Have a seat in the car. I'll be right with you."

Nash touched my arm. "Thanks for everything, Dr. Frank."

I nodded and watched her walk to the cruiser.

Jacobs turned her attention to me. "I interviewed Amanda Squires a couple of days ago. She has a place on Danforth Street."

The address was the same building where Katrina, Harper, and Lily had lived for the first two years of Lily's life.

"Hers is the only apartment that's occupied in that building, which is strange with all the students around here. The art school and the museum are right up the hill. Same outfit manages her place. Paul Crandall for MI. Still haven't caught up with Crandall."

"What did Squires tell you?"

"Said she was in Nash's apartment the day that Dorman got it," Jacobs said, pulling at her jeans.

"Average height, slender, black hair, usually jeans and a flannel shirt."

"That's her. She couldn't remember times. Said she got there early and left early. She said she knew who Dorman was, but never spoke to him, and didn't see him that night. Now she's telling Nash she did it?"

"Nash will tell you the whole story, but that's the essence of it."

"Squires is a strange duck. I asked her if it worried her to think that she might've been in the building at the same time as the killer. She said no."

Jacobs agreed to call Jaworski at the Holiday Inn for me. "Tell him it counts as me checking in."

"He's got you on a short leash, does he?"

"Jasper is certain that I'm guilty of being insufferable, and possibly guilty of obstruction."

Jacobs laughed.

"Tell Herb I'll be another hour."

She nodded. "My case is Dorman," Jacobs said. "How does Squires connect to him?"

"What Gretchen Nash observed suggests that Squires is Lily Dorman."

"I read that psychologist's report before I sent it to you. She's probably wished Dorman dead since she was a kid. Can't say I blame her, but why is she taking out half the population?"

"Squires was in my seminar at the college. She talked about a killer hybrid, a woman who doesn't fit any of the stereotypes. That idea seemed important to her. The psychiatrist who treated Dorman at Maine Central is convinced that she suffers from multiple personality disorder."

Jacobs shoved her hands deep into her jacket pockets. "I read about a case like that. Can't say I buy into that shit."

"There's a personal connection here, too," I added. "I knew Katrina Martin years ago."

"Was she sick then?"

I shrugged. "I don't know. She did a lot of drugs, so she always seemed strange."

Jacobs stood beside her cruiser. "Most men won't believe that a woman did all this killing," she said.

"Some women, too," I added, thinking about Karen Jasper.

Jacobs shook her head. "Anyone is capable of anything."

CHAPTER 30

I PARKED IN AN ALLEY ADJACENT TO THE DANFORTH Street apartment building. I estimated that I had a twenty-minute lead on the police, who would arrive prepared to arrest Amanda Squires.

I did not expect her to be at home.

The street door popped open without a problem. I listened at Squires's door, heard nothing, and went to work. The lock gave, and I stepped into a twenty-by-forty-foot room. There was an upright piano against the wall to my left, an archway to my right, a curtained archway directly across the room. An easel and canvas stood in the northwest corner of the room. A rolltop desk squatted immediately to my left, against the front wall.

"Someone just like me," I muttered, gazing at the desk's cluttered surface—a stack of unopened mail, grocery store coupons, an aspirin bottle, a dozen paperbacks, and a small basket filled with checks.

The checks, issued twice a month, were drawn on Maine Marine Bank and Trust, payable to Amanda Squires for five thousand dollars, and signed by Paul Crandall.

"She never cashed them," I said.

I opened a file folder that contained heavily marked

highway and topographical maps of the area immediately west of Portsmouth, New Hampshire. Somewhere in that maze of dirt roads and rutted logging trails, Stanley Markham had plunged a knife into Darcy Smith's chest. It was the same area where Lily Dorman had caught up with Markham and put a bullet in his head.

Everything comes full circle.

I pictured Gretchen Nash's caricature of Crandall, the short, rotund man she said was all tics and fidgets. Perhaps a middle-of-the-night visit to Stu Gilman was in order.

The only opened piece of mail was a letter to Amanda Squires bearing the ink-stamped return address of a California prison. I unfolded the single sheet of lined paper and read the childlike scrawl.

Dear Amanda,

Thanks for the stamps and the money put in my jail account. Yes I saw on TV about Stan M's escape. He stole my idea to get carried out with the dirty sheets. Just joking. We do all our wash here. I'm not sure how to answer your question. You're a good friend (the best!) so I won't lie to you. Please don't be mad. When I first got here I found out about post-conviction relief where you make a case for a shorter sentence. A few girls won theirs. That's why I said the things I did about my father. He was very strict and a real bastard but no sex stuff. I didn't want to be here for my whole life. Sometimes I hated my father like every girl does. But not to do what I did. I went animal and I'm paying for it. I never got the p.c. relief anyway. I pray you'll still talk to me. Please keep writing.

Your loving friend,
Sydny

Squires had fixated on the Clanton case, researched the story, recited details in class. She also had a personal relationship with the fifty-one-year-old multiple killer who admitted fabricating her victimization story to win the sympathy of the court, and an earlier parole-eligibility date.

"To quote a friend of mine, 'Sydny Clanton was dreaming the blue dream that never ends.' "

Was her friend inside her head?

As I pocketed the letter and several uncashed checks, a yellowed newspaper clipping pushpinned to a bulletin board caught my attention. The article from an Idaho newspaper was an early account of the murders of "a married couple in their ranch home near Moscow." The date was May 1, 1967.

On the day that Sydny Clanton savaged her parents, Lily Dorman was born.

I moved away from the desk. The apartment had the distinctive aroma of a pine forest, but I could not determine where the scent originated.

I walked through the archway to my right and examined a painting on Squires's easel. Oil pastels swept in broad strokes across the coarse paper. She had smudged and smeared the colors into a shimmering blue sphere streaked with red. It was so vivid that I imagined it pulsating, like a dream screen, the throbbing orb that conceals horrific reveries of night.

The sphere is a pulsating, living wall, a defense against horror.

"It's a talisman," I muttered.

It has magical properties—the power to ward off evil, the skill to elude whatever bubbles beneath consciousness.

I wondered about Lily Dorman's dreams. She would not want to know what shapes slithered and screamed beyond the grasp of consciousness. Keeping her beast locked in a closet carried a serious liability: she would receive no warning about what surged into the light of her days.

What most frightens you is what goes on inside your head.

I stared at her creation, studied its daubed blues, blended hues of sky and sea and cold blue eyes.

The odor of pine was strong again—through the curtained archway, I thought.

"She had an aura of fresh-cut pine. The screen turned blue. It made me sad, and I don't like to feel sad. So I got mad."

Sydny Clanton spoke those words. Clanton was not an "exception." Neither was Aileen Wuornos. Lily Dorman was a living reminder that the rules, based on our cultural myths of female innocence, do not always apply.

I stepped through the curtain and walked into a dimly lit room that contained ten aquarium tanks. Most wore pink heat lamps fitted to their tops; the remainder were covered with hardware cloth. All of them contained snakes.

Approach-avoidance, I thought. She was compelled to tease herself with what she most feared. The paired association seemed obvious. As a child, Lily Dorman stood in the swamp and conversed with her snakes, predators that she studied and understood. From where she stood on the dike, she heard her father's pickup drive into the yard, then heard his gun explode.

Harper Dorman killed the dog, then raped his daughter.

I pressed my fingers against the glass that prevented a copperhead from injecting me with its lethal venom.

You surround yourself with your horror, but keep it behind a curtain, a screen that offers you the illusion of control. You do not fear what you have held in your hand. You are at liberty to tease yourself with free-floating thoughts, sounds, tactile sensations, because you became what you feared.

The display was a herpetologist's dream and anyone else's nightmare. I felt certain that my rattling visitor had been in residence here until Lily Dorman deposited it in my study.

Squires sat in my house. Someone else drove the Volvo.

I wanted to spend more time in the apartment, to prowl through bookcases and drawers and file cabinets, to develop a feel for this person. Three quick blasts from the door's buzzer changed my mind.

Jacobs's people would not announce themselves, I thought, as I stepped into the hall and walked to the top of the stairwell overlooking the vestibule. A tall man with thinning hair, dressed casually in khakis and a blue jacket, pulled open the door and strode toward the stairs.

I retreated to the shadows at the rear of the building and watched as he approached Squires's door, keys in hand. "She isn't home," I said.

He turned and gazed disapprovingly in my direction. "Who are you?" he demanded.

Before I could answer, he slipped his key into the lock and said, "I'm calling the police."

I walked slowly toward the man. "No need," I said. "They're on the way."

He glared at me. "What's going on here?"

My mystery guest was taller than I, slender, in his forties. His gold Rolex told me that he was not a homeless person seeking shelter for the night.

"Where is Lily Dorman?" I asked.

"You're trespassing," he said.

I continued to move toward him. "The police are looking for her."

For a man his size, he was quick. He yanked his keys from the lock, clocked me with his forearm, and bolted to the stairs. I hauled myself off the floor and ran after him. As I reached the sidewalk, he climbed into a car and pulled away from the curb.

I figured that his identity would not be difficult to determine. The personalized license plate on his black Mercedes read "NORT."

"You've got one coming," I muttered, rubbing the side of my head and walking to my Jeep.

I drove down Danforth Street and passed three city police cruisers on their way to Squires's building.

STUART GILMAN LIVED IN A CUL-DE-SAC A HUNDRED yards from the Atlantic Ocean. I pulled into his driveway, powered down my window, and listened to the sea.

The few houses nestled among pines and low scrub growth were dark and silent. Lights glared from every window of Gilman's modern Cape Cod. I glanced at the dashboard clock: three-thirty A.M., long past my bedtime and long past Gilman's.

I walked to the small terrace in front of the house and peered through a window. Gilman sprawled over a hassock, with a yellow rubber duck in one hand and a nearly empty wine bottle in the other. *USA Today* lay open on the floor in front of him. His suit jacket was crumpled in a heap behind him.

The door was not locked, so I stepped inside and walked to the living room, which boasted a brick fireplace, puffed white and tan decor, polished hardwood floors with a plush, off-white carpet, copies of *Money, Business Week,* and *The Wall Street Journal.* The house and its transient library were about dollars.

Gilman looked up, his watery eyes streaked with red, his face baggy and sodden, his mouth in twitch mode. "You've got more hair on the bottom of your head than I have on the top," he said, his speech slurred. "What are you doing here?"

"I want to rent an apartment."

He nodded his head, as if apartment hunting in his living room in the middle of the night made perfectly good sense. "My wife took the kids. She pulled one of 'em right out of the tub."

Gilman held up the yellow bath toy. "She took them to a hotel."

"She must be angry."

He mumbled something that I could not understand, then thumped his bottle on the *USA Today* weather map. "I've been clipping these out of the papers. I intend to prove that these weather maps are more accurate than what those nitwits in Augusta and Boston predict. We have volatile weather here."

"Stu, how long have you been acting the part of Paul Crandall?" I asked.

At first, Gilman did not react. He continued to stare at his newspaper. Then his tics and twitches disappeared, and the color drained from his face. He dropped the rubber duck, released his grip on the wine bottle, and pushed himself from the hassock to a kneeling position. "What the fuck do you want?"

Gilman's voice had the same edge that I had heard when he caught me in the college's roomful of computers. I was determined not to be blindsided a second time in one night. I was also tired, hungry, and pissed off.

"For starters, an answer to my question," I said as I grabbed a magazine and rolled it into a tight tube.

"Get a cop and get a warrant," he said.

I gripped my copy of *Business Week* with my right hand and slapped it against my left. "You ready to post bail?"

"What the hell are you talking about? I haven't done anything."

"Creating a false identity, Paul Crandall, and conducting business under that name, is illegal. That's just for openers."

Gilman made the move I anticipated. He grasped the hassock, pulled himself to a half-standing position, and lurched toward me with the grace, coordination, and dexterity of Frankenstein's monster.

I stabbed forward with the rolled magazine and caught him on the bridge of his nose. He fell sideways onto the couch, covering his face with his hands. Blood seeped between his fingers.

"You broke my fuckin' nose," he howled as his blood stained the white sofa. "Shit. Clea's gonna kill me."

Still holding one hand over his nose, he pulled out a handkerchief and dabbed at the maroon marks on the fabric.

"No more stunts, Stu. You're too drunk to damage anyone but yourself."

I walked to the fireplace and glanced at the family photos arrayed on the mantel. "Nice kids," I said.

"You don't know what you're dealing with."

"Educate me."

Gilman sat upright, the handkerchief pressed to his face. I stared at his drunken eyes, now clouded by something more than an alcohol daze. Fear.

"Call the cops," he said.

"Who are you afraid of?"

He shook his head and stared at the floor.

"Okay, Stu. I'll talk. Harper Dorman was the superintendent of a Martin International building managed by Paul Crandall, a.k.a. Stuart Gilman. Thirty-six hours after somebody left Dorman in pieces, the same somebody killed three Harbor College students. MI owns the building where they were murdered, and you are MI's main squeeze on campus. One of the students, Jaycie Waylon, was an MI intern."

Gilman winced when I mentioned Waylon.

"You never bothered to tell me that. Then there's Steve Weld, college faculty member and federal agent investigating MI."

Gilman's head snapped up. "I didn't know that. Oh shit. I swear to Christ I didn't know he was a cop."

"Should I take that as an admission of guilt?"

"Take it that I didn't like the prick. I didn't kill anyone. Jesus."

"That's right. Your thing is prowling through backyards and peering in windows."

"Trespassing," he yelled. "I was taking a shortcut. It was a misunderstanding. How the fuck do you know about that?"

I ignored his question. "If you didn't kill anyone, you know who did."

"I don't know anything."

"Wendell Beckerman," I said. "Seconds before I found his body, you raced out of town in your Jag."

"You're going to get us both killed," Gilman yelped, his eyes darting around the room, his face a damp, full-fidget mess. "Clea wanted me home that night. I came home."

I waited until his breathing grew less ragged, then asked, "Why the payments to Amanda Squires?"

Gilman staggered to his feet and lumbered across the living room, one hand still over his nose, the other reaching into a desk drawer.

I leaned against the drawer, jammed his hand, then grabbed his wrist. Gilman shrieked.

"Ten thousand a month," I said, removing his hand from the drawer and retrieving the .32 caliber pistol he was after.

"Don't say another fuckin' word. I want a lawyer. I want the cops."

Gilman's red-streaked, vibrating face was a mask of terror. I was tempted to dump the drunk in Norma Jacobs's lap, but he had information that I wanted.

"What about Stanley Markham?"

He looked at me, rubbing his hand. "The killer? What about him?"

"He's dead, shot with the same gun that killed the others."

As comprehension dawned, Gilman's eyes shifted from useless to semifocused. His face resumed fluttering-mess status.

"Jesus Christ."

Compounding Gilman's fears had the desired effect, so I applied more pressure.

"I guess that proves your point, Stu," I said with a deep sigh. "If someone can find Markham and kill him, that person can certainly find us and do the same. We shouldn't discuss this any further."

I walked to the door.

"Where are you going?" Gilman asked.

"Back to my hotel. Then I'm going home."

"No cops?"

I shook my head, pocketed the cartridges from his revolver, and placed the gun on a table.

Gilman shot wild glances in a wide arc. "You can't leave me here."

"Stu, you live here," I said, stepping onto the porch.

Gilman stumbled after me. "Come back inside. Please."

"Why did your wife leave?"

Tears ran from Gilman's eyes down his bloodied cheeks. "I told her . . . some things."

"She was frightened?"

"Furious too. She said she wouldn't stay here another night, wouldn't let the kids stay here, and if I had any sense, I wouldn't stay here."

Gilman shivered in the cool night air. "I'm cold."

We stepped inside. Gilman secured the door, peeked out at the night, then led me into the kitchen where he fumbled with his Mr. Coffee. His hands trembled, and he could not separate the filters.

"I don't know where she put the fuckin' scoop. Clea usually does this."

"You sit down," I said. "I'll make the coffee."

"Wine always gives me a fucking headache," he complained.

My head throbbed where "Nort" had hammered me. I had no sympathy for Gilman.

I found the scoop inside the can. "What did you tell Clea?"

He shook his head. "What's going to happen?"

"When you've talked for a while, maybe I can tell you that."

Gilman gazed around the kitchen at walls decorated with his kids' drawings. Refrigerator magnets held school bus and soccer schedules, photos of two young girls modeling their Halloween costumes, a list of performances at a local theater, and a small message pad—"gal 2%, yogurt (*non-fat*), waxed mint d. floss."

"We tried to live on seventy-five thousand a year in Boston," he said. "Money was always tight. MI offered me one hundred and twenty thousand, the house, the car, the chance for my kids to grow up in a safe place with good schools. What would you have done?"

"Grabbed the opportunity," I said, giving Gilman the answer he sought.

"Damn right."

I joined Gilman at the kitchen table. "What went wrong?"

"Nothing is the way it appears," Gilman said bitterly. "Not a fucking thing."

I waited, listening to Mr. Coffee gag his way to the last drop.

"We needed the money," he said, rolling and unrolling a napkin. "I wanted to feel important. I didn't want to spend my life as a clerk for a fucking insurance company."

Gilman breathed deeply. "I went to a professional placement service in Boston. I filled out the forms, gave them my résumé, took some tests. Two weeks later, they called me with MI's offer."

He held up his hands, palms out, as if expecting a reprimand. "I know I should have suspected something. There weren't any interviews, no tour of the company, nothing. I drove up here on a Saturday and stopped at the office. It was like they expected me. I met Melanie Martin, had lunch with a couple of board members. They even had an office with my name on the door. God, I'm stupid. They knew how I thought, what my reactions would be. The tests I took in Boston told them everything they wanted to know."

MI's thoroughness and planning were like something out of *The X-Files*. I poured two mugs of coffee and returned to the table.

"My title is Vice President and Manager of Accounts. The job description includes the college, and all the Maine properties. The only account group that I manage is Mexico. I didn't know it, but all the companies are dummies, places to park money. Every cent that moved through those accounts came from Tijuana."

"Drug money," I said.

Gilman sipped his coffee. "That's what I finally decided. Well . . . Jaycie figured it out."

"She worked for you."

"Ten hours a week. She was a smart kid. I had her handling deposits, wire transfers, offshore accounts. Twice a month I flew to San Diego. She took care of things while I was gone."

"Who killed her?"

"I told you before. I don't know who killed anybody. I thought Markham killed Jaycie and her roommates. How many mass murderers are roaming around?"

Too many, I thought, but ignored Gilman's question.

I was convinced that Jaycie Waylon was Norma Jacobs's informant. The student did not break off her contact with the Portland police. She was dead.

"Tell me about Paul Crandall," I said.

"I didn't like that from the start. The explanation they gave me—"

"Who gave you?"

He shrugged. "It was in a memo."

"Melanie Martin?"

"God, no," Gilman said with a short, bitter laugh.

"I don't get it."

His eyes met mine. "She's seldom around. Clea's running joke is that I work for a ghost. Martin has a cottage on Monhegan Island. She developed the business and made herself a millionaire several times over. On paper, she holds the power, but she's never here."

"Who makes the decisions?"

"Norton Weatherly. That's where the Crandall thing originated. Doing business as Crandall Management didn't bother me. You can DBA anything you want to. As long as you pay the filing fee, it's perfectly legal. The memo packet included personal identification papers for Paul Crandall, but they had my photo and date of birth. I knew that wasn't right, so I went to see Weatherly. He minimized it, said the company had used that sort of arrangement dozens of times."

"You collected rent," I said.

Gilman stared at the backs of his hands and shook his head. "I can't do this. People are going to die."

"They're already dying faster than grave diggers can open holes for them."

He pushed himself from the table and struggled to his feet. "I have to find Clea and the kids."

"Amanda Squires shot at a friend of hers tonight," I said. "Squires wasn't at her place on Danforth. She's armed and wandering around out there. The cops are looking for her, but maybe you'll run into her before they do."

Gilman hesitated only a second before crumbling into his chair.

I refilled his coffee cup. "You were about to tell me about playing slumlord."

He looked at me. "You sonofabitch."

"I have to amend your appraisal, Stu. I am a pissed-off sonofabitch. It's been a long night. I've been shot at, hammered across the face, and I'm tired of fucking around with you."

He nodded, sighed, and sipped his coffee. "This is where things get unreal. I would deposit twenty thousand dollars in the Crandall account, and the slip would show a balance of half a million or more. The next month, there might be nothing in the account but the rents. Jaycie tracked transaction numbers. Somebody regularly made deposits in San Diego. That money flowed through here. I wired it to banks in the Bahamas."

"Why didn't the local bank get suspicious?"

"Crandall Management has two subsidiaries. Grand Bahama Real Estate Investment Group, and Crandall South in Miami. That's where the money ended up."

It made sense that money flowing from Portland, off-shore, then to Miami, would not attract attention in South Florida, where drug and money routes typically involved Central and South America. If the DEA did track the money, they would run into a legitimate real estate and investment business.

"How does Squires come into this?" I asked.

Gilman took a deep breath. "I handle all of MI's 'special projects.' That's what Weatherly called them. I was the new guy, so I got stuck with the job. He told me to write the checks and mail them to Squires. I asked him how I should record the expenditure. He said it didn't matter, that the checks would never be cashed."

For nearly two years, Gilman mailed the checks.

"It got so that I didn't think about it. Then Jaycie made her discovery. I got paranoid about everything to do with MI. I didn't feel that I could go to Weatherly. So I wrote Squires's check, but I didn't mail it. I drove to Danforth Street. It was like walking into a tomb. I'd been to all our properties except that one, and the units were always rented. The Danforth building was empty. Squires lived there alone."

"Did you talk with her?"

"She wasn't there. I slipped the check under the door and left. The place spooked me."

Gilman was a bit player in what impressed me as a grand theatrical production. As he had suggested, not much was real.

"If each department at MI moved only half the value of the Mexican accounts," he said, "three hundred million in profit would be a conservative estimate."

Gilman had grabbed a dream, achieved position and a modicum of wealth. The dream had soured.

"Steve Weld was a threat to the operation," I said.

"So was Beckerman, but I doubt that he knew it. His

mother was on the MI board of directors. She died a few months ago. Beckerman inherited everything, including a set of computer tapes. No one knew how she got them. They were duplicates of everything MI kept at Harbor College."

"All the illegal activity," I said.

"Weatherly called them 'off-book' transactions."

"Who is Edgar?" I asked.

"Jesus. Everything is falling apart. Edgar Heath. Weatherly said he hired Heath as a driver, but I think the guy is more than that. I met him only once, and he was armed. I think he's a bodyguard. Heath's another mystery. He gets paid to play nursemaid to Amanda Squires. I don't think there's any such person as Amanda Squires. I think they're all fuckin' fakes. I don't know who anybody is."

CHAPTER 31

JAWORSKI DRANK COFFEE AND STARED AT THE Weather Channel. "We've got a hell of a storm moving up the coast," he said. "Gale-force winds, heavy rain, tides three to five feet above normal."

He glanced at his Styrofoam cup. "Why is it that hotels make better coffee than I do?"

"You been up all night?" I asked.

"I napped. You?"

I knew that the sore muscles and muddy thinking of sleep deprivation would soon get me, but adrenaline held them at bay. "I'll catch up later. Jacobs call?"

"You ain't gonna like this," he said, climbing out of his chair. "I'd just gotten off the phone with Jacobs when Jasper called. Squires showed up at my P.D. after she left Mellen Street. Demanded to see Jasper and wouldn't talk to anyone else. The two of them talked and drank tea."

"Don't tell me that Jasper let her walk."

"She didn't have anything to hold her on," Jaworski said.

"What ever happened to attempted murder? Squires tried to blow away Gretchen Nash."

"News still travels slow around here," he said, "when it

moves at all. Jasper didn't know about the shooting. Squires said she'd stay at the Clear Skies and be available for further questioning. I called the motel. She isn't there. Never checked in."

"Of course she never checked in!" I roared. "What was Jasper thinking?"

"I ain't the psychiatrist," Jaworski said, "but I figure Jasper can't picture a woman committing these crimes. Some of it's the contradictions we've got in the evidence. Mostly I think she can't imagine doing something like this, so she can't imagine any woman doing it. Then you've got Ms. Amanda. Either she's damn convincing, or you're wrong about her."

Amanda Squires had appeared from nowhere, left her mark on Portland, then zipped up the highway and run her scam on a Quantico-educated state detective.

I collapsed into a chair. "I've been wrong," I said. "I went to Squires's Danforth Street apartment. She has a collection of snakes in aquarium tanks and a stack of uncashed checks signed by Paul Crandall. The whole thing is a prop. The rest of the building is empty."

"Jasper says it ain't Squires's voice on the tape log."

I rested my neck against the back of the chair. My eyes wanted to close and dissolve all thought into the deepest sleep. Perhaps adrenaline would lose this one.

"Squires isn't the only player," I said. "When I was at Danforth Street, a guy showed up. He knocked me on my ass and took off."

"I read through the notebook," Jaworski said, pointing to Lily Dorman's journal. "I'd wonder about anybody who didn't fall to pieces after growing up like that."

"We're fortunate that not everyone who lives through hell takes up murder," I said, struggling to fight off the urge to sleep. "I stuck Stu Gilman in a room. He is Paul Crandall."

"Lucas, Jasper and the feds want you in Ragged Harbor today. Hubble Saymes wants me there."

I forced myself to get up. I needed an extra charge to break from my inertia, and Jaworski had given it to me.

"Things are happening too fast, Herb. There's no time to get an army up to speed. We need to pay another visit to Martin International. This time we take our own vice president with us."

AS WE MADE THE SHORT DRIVE TO MI'S CORPORATE headquarters, Gilman dozed in the cruiser's backseat. His night of blood, sweat, and wine had taken a toll. He smelled bad. I was far from floral, but fairly certain I was not wearing eau de sleeping wino.

Jaworski radioed Portland P.D. for a records check on the licence plate NORT. It was a mystery that should not have been; the plate came back to Norton Weatherly.

"I could've told you that," Gilman mumbled.

"Why the fuck didn't you?" the chief snapped.

The first change at MI since our last visit was apparent when we drove into the parking lot. There were no cars.

"Ain't no holiday that I know about," Jaworski said, pulling and pushing his bulk out of the car and unwrapping a stick of gum.

I poked Gilman awake, and the three of us walked to the gate.

"Where are the dogs?" Jaworski asked.

I gazed along the fence. There was no sign of the menacing shepherds. I grabbed the chain-link barrier and shook it, creating a metallic din. Still no dogs.

"That's strange," Gilman said. "They're always on the grounds."

"How do people get in and out of the place?" I asked.

"The dogs wear electronic collars. These two, Mark

and Twain, don't respond to voice commands. They remain on alert until they receive a radio signal from inside."

Gilman slipped a plastic card through a black box on the gate. Nothing happened.

"Huh," Gilman grunted. "The signal lights aren't on either."

"Power's off," Jaworski said, gazing up at MI's flags snapping in the brisk wind. "Probably a tree blew down on some wires."

"We have our own generators," Gilman said. "They start automatically if there's an outage."

"No way I'm climbing over that sucker," Jaworski said, retreating to his cruiser and opening the trunk. "Does the V.P. authorize forced entry?"

Gilman shrugged. "I don't know if I can do that. I guess so."

In seconds, Jaworski returned with a crowbar. "You'd be amazed at the uses I've found for this thing," he said, and worked the gate lock. "Bought it at the local hardware for a buck-seventy-five, forty years ago. Best investment I ever made."

The gate popped open. "When those dogs get their collar buzz," Jaworski said, "do they restrain the intruder or shred him?"

"I don't know," Gilman answered helplessly.

Jaworski gave me the crowbar and slipped his gun from its holster. "Let's go," he said, pushing through the gate.

Bulbous black clouds rolled across the leaden sky. When we reached the main door, Jaworski watched for Mark and Twain, Gilman stood with his hands in his pockets, and I added to my résumé of authorized illicit entries.

"You're good at that," Jaworski said when the door squealed open.

"I watched you at the gate," I reminded the chief.

"Bullshit. You could be your own one-man crime wave if you ever set your mind to it."

He had no fucking idea.

We stepped into Martin International's entry hall, a vast cavern of exposed beams, slate floor, and a massive abstract marble sculpture. Skylights allowed shafts of the day's dim illumination to descend at angles into the room. The effect was similar to the sally ports in jails that I have visited, except that this foyer smelled considerably better.

"Which way?" Jaworski asked Gilman, his voice echoing through the halls.

"The place is empty," Gilman muttered, staggering ahead to a large, glass-walled room. "There should be a dozen clerks in there."

"Where are the executive offices?"

"Up there," Gilman said absently, pointing to a stairwell.

We climbed the stairs and stepped into another, smaller foyer. Gilman crossed the carpeted area and stared at a door.

"My nameplate is gone."

"Pry open that end door," Jaworski instructed.

Gilman wandered over. "That's Melanie Martin's office."

The door was not locked. I pushed it open and gazed into the vacant room.

Jaworski checked two more offices with the same results. "Nothing," he said.

"I was here two days ago," Gilman said. "It was business as usual. I don't believe this."

I stepped into the office and crossed the room to an open wall safe. It was empty except for two small, rectangular pieces of heavy paper jammed into a corner at the back.

"You find something?" Jaworski asked.

"Photographs," I muttered, staring at the image of a woman in her early twenties, dressed in jeans and a Portland State University sweatshirt.

"Know who she is?"

I shook my head and slipped the photograph into my jacket pocket. "But I know who this is," I said, handing Jaworski the second photo.

"It's a mug shot. Where have I seen this?"

"Stanley Markham."

"I don't get it."

"Stu, where does Norton Weatherly live?"

"South Portland, near the water. I can show you."

"Lucas, we've broken a lot of laws here," Jaworski said. "What the hell is going on?"

"These folks were reaping millions. Their operation was threatened. If we can catch up with Weatherly before *he* disappears, he'll answer your question more completely than I can."

WEATHERLY'S NEIGHBORHOOD RESEMBLED GILMAN'S. Half a dozen modern Cape Cod houses shared the left side of the road. Wind churned the Atlantic Ocean into a black froth opposite the houses.

I climbed from the car and stared at the sea.

"Storm's coming fast," Jaworski said. "By suppertime, maybe a little later, we'll get hit."

The salt spray stung my face.

"The last northeaster we had, I stood on the breakwater in Ragged Harbor and watched ten-foot waves snap mooring lines and flip motor launches and sailing yachts like they were toys. Rusty Haggard's forty-foot lobster boat smashed to kindling on the breakwater, fifty yards from where I stood. Some of the old-timers call a storm like that 'devil's breath.' "

As Jaworski talked, I remembered sitting in the sand on Nantasket Beach in Massachusetts as a teenager, watching a hurricane race toward land. Towers of black clouds rolled across the sky as ocean swells crested and broke and re-formed, then finally smacked down on the shoreline with a lingering roar. I remembered hearing the clacking of rocks tumbling over rocks as the tons of water retreated.

"I don't see Nort's car," Gilman said.

Jaworski's knock brought a woman in her forties to the door. She glanced quickly at Jaworski and me, then focused on Gilman. "Oh, hi, Stu," she said. "What are you doing here?"

"We're looking for Nort, Viv."

Viv and Nort were in dire need of name modification.

"He's at the office. Why aren't you there?"

"He's not at the office, ma'am," Jaworski said, and introduced himself.

"What do you want with Nort?"

I wanted to deck the bastard, but bit my tongue.

"I have a few questions to ask him," the chief continued. "When did you last see him?"

"This morning at breakfast. He took his briefcase and went to MI."

I watched Viv Weatherly's eyes and listened to her evenly modulated voice. Her tone lacked alarm, concern, even curiosity.

"Stu and I will wait in the car," I told Jaworski, grabbing Gilman by the arm and leading him back to the cruiser.

"You ever been in their backyard?" I asked.

"For barbecues. Sure."

"Could I get to the road through there?"

Gilman thought for a moment. "This street circles around. There's a hedge in back of their house. If you go through the hedge and cut across the neighbor's yard, I think you come out on this street at the other end."

"Stay in the car," I told him, and jogged down the road.

I slowed at the property abutting Weatherly's and watched the hedge. In seconds, I heard someone battling through the thick vegetation. Weatherly burst into the open, spotted me immediately, and said, "Oh fuck," then broke into a run directly at me.

I resolved not to get cuffed again, but debated whether to tackle him or step aside and trip him as he went by. My moment of deliberation cost me. Weatherly hammered me in the chest with his forearm, and I crashed down on my ass. He ran into the street, his legs pumping up and down like a lanky teenager who was awkward but fast.

I pushed myself to my feet and trotted after him. He was forty yards ahead of me and increasing the distance. I spotted his Mercedes parked on the right. I knew that I would not catch him before he got to the car, so I slowed to a walk, watching him and promising myself that I would teach this guy a few lessons at the first opportunity.

Weatherly slipped into the Mercedes. In an instant, the car's front end lifted off the ground. Flames flashed from the engine compartment, followed by black smoke and a roar. Fire engulfed the car. When the gas tank exploded, the Mercedes lifted again, shuddered, and returned to earth a shattered mass of twisted metal, melting in its own inferno.

Jaworski jogged up behind me. "What the hell?"

"Damn. I wanted to punch that prick," I said. "He should have let me catch him. I wouldn't have done that to him."

CHAPTER 32

I WAITED IN THE CRUISER WITH GILMAN WHILE JAWOR-
ski talked with the Portland police.

"What happened?" Gilman asked, watching police and
fire equipment pass.

"Someone planted a bomb in Weatherly's car."

"He's dead?"

I nodded.

"Oh God," he moaned, covering his face with his
hands.

Suddenly he dropped his hands. "Clea and the girls,"
he yelled, grabbing my shoulder.

"A Portland detective found them at the Radisson," I
said, prying away Gilman's hands. "They're safe, and they
have protection."

"I don't know what's happening here."

The operation that Weatherly ran at MI might bring
any crazy out of the woodwork, from a disgruntled client to
a street thug. I did not seriously think that either scenario
had played out on posh, residential Atlantic Way. I imagined something more sinister, connected to the other killings.

Jaworski stuck his head through the car window.

"They're going to need written statements from everybody," he said.

I shook my head. "There's no time, Herb. Have them start with Gilman. You and I can return later."

"What the hell is the rush?"

"MI disappeared. People are flocking to the cemetery by the busload in body bags. Squires walked in and out of your P.D. This is like Barnum and Bailey, three rings, and all the clowns are making their exit."

Jaworski relented. "I'll walk Gilman over. They aren't going to like this."

While I waited, I considered what I had and what I did not have. Weatherly was dead. Gilman probably knew more than he had told me, but he was distraught, sleep-deprived, hungover, and unaware of the significance of what he might know.

I studied the crumpled photograph of the young woman that I had found in Melanie Martin's safe. She stood beneath a tree on what appeared to be a college campus. A stack of books rested on the ground at her feet. There was something familiar about her, but I could not put my finger on it.

As Jaworski slipped into the cruiser, I asked, "Where's Portland State University?"

"Ain't one," he said. "Not here anyway. There's one in Portland, Oregon. Why?"

Perhaps collecting Portlands was not a fruitless hobby for a cop. I handed Jaworski the photo.

"This Squires?" he asked.

The hair color was different, but that did not mean much. "I can't be sure. It's old, and not a good picture."

He returned the photograph. "Where are you in such a hurry to get to?"

I gave him directions to Julia Westlake's office.

• • •

WESTLAKE WAS WITH A PATIENT, SO I SAT IN THE
waiting room, thumbed through a *New Yorker* to catch up
on the cartoons, and endured stares from the psychiatrist's
secretary, Jordan.

"I just figured out who you look like," Jordan said.

I gazed up from my magazine. I was alone in the waiting area, so it seemed safe to assume that she was address-
ing me. I was less than eager to hear what media-enhanced
person she thought I resembled.

"Blackbeard," she said. "You know, the pirate. He's all
hairy and grizzled like you. Same eyes, too."

"His name was Edward Teach," I said. "He was an
English buccaneer best known for his savagery."

"Isn't that neat?" she chirped. "Someone else must
have told you, too. How else would you know so much
about him?"

Westlake emerged from her office and rescued me.
"It's good to see you again, Lucas, but I have only about
ten minutes."

"This won't take any longer than that," I assured her,
following her into her office.

The room's informal decor reminded me of my Boston
office, a space that I occupied for twenty years. Westlake's
desk was a solid-core oak door sitting on two filing cabinets. Rough-hewn maple planks rested on bricks for bookcases. The shelves were filled with familiar titles, including
several issues of the *Journal of Psychiatry and the Law.*

"You've done forensic work," I observed.

"Custody cases, mostly. I don't do them anymore. Nobody wins, but the children always lose."

I handed her the photograph that I had found in Melanie Martin's safe.

"That's Lily Dorman," Westlake said. "God. I don't believe it."

"You said she left the hospital with a friend."

Westlake tapped the photo and looked at the ceiling. "Who was her friend on the ward?"

I waited, knowing that many facts float in the air above our heads until we remember them.

Westlake lowered her gaze. "Janine Baker," she said. "She was from up north somewhere. One of the border towns, I think. The main thing I remember about her is how angry she was. The ward staff had a horrible time with her. If she wasn't seducing the males, she was attacking the females. It had to be her idea to run. Lily would have followed along."

I thanked Westlake and went hunting for Jaworski. I found him double-parked on the next block, and ducked into the cruiser.

"Lily Dorman is all grins in the photograph," I told him.

"Why would Melanie Martin have pictures of this kid and a killer in her safe?"

"They were left for us," I said. "Let's make a quick run out to Bayberry Trailer Park. Then I may want to go sailing."

"You crazy? Couple more hours and we're gonna get whacked by that storm. The wind's already blowing like a sonofabitch."

"Any other way to get to Monhegan?"

"Lucas, why do I always feel like I'm a step or two behind you?"

"I don't know," I said, grinning. "There's a good shrink down the street if you want to check it out."

Jaworski glared at me, then pulled into traffic.

WIND WHIRLED THROUGH BAYBERRY'S COURTYARD. A rolling black sky gave the place an Alfred Hitchcock feel.

All the set needed was a hill, a Victorian manse, and the silhouette of an old woman rocking in her chair.

"Which one?" Jaworski asked.

"Three. I think it's best if you wait here."

He nodded and pulled out his pack of gum.

"Here's something to keep you busy," I said, handing him the scrap of paper with the phone number Lily Dorman had given her mother. "Find out who that is, and where it is."

"I'm also going to call a friend of mine, a detective in Portland, Orgeon. I met him on a trip out there."

"Dorman, Baker, Squires," I said.

"Got 'em."

"Excellent."

"Lucas, you know how city cops do that debriefing stuff after a big case?"

"My daughter's a New York City detective. She's mentioned it."

"When this is over, you and I are gonna do some serious debriefing."

"Whatever you like, Herb," I said, "provided that you're still chief and I'm not in jail."

It was shortly after one P.M., prime time for soaps, but this was one afternoon that Katrina Martin would have to tolerate an interruption. I knocked on the door, then glanced at the louvered window. The blue TV glow was absent. I raised my fist to knock a second time, and the door opened.

"I asked you not to come back," Katrina said.

"Lily thinks I'm her father."

She hesitated, then sighed deeply. "Of course," she said, backing away from the door. "Come in."

She stared at the floor like a child caught in a misdeed. "We needed a dream. I shared mine with Lily."

Katrina slowly met my gaze. "What harm did it do?"

I ignored the question and gave her the photographs.

"That's Lily. Where did you get this?"

"At Martin International."

She continued to stare at the picture. "I don't know what that is."

"Did Lily tell you where she worked?"

Katrina shook her head. "She's so young. I missed all those years. Where was this picture taken?"

"Possibly Portland, Oregon."

She shook her head and glanced at the second photo. "I don't know who this man is."

"Katrina, did Lily tell you anything about where she had been, or people she had met . . . anything at all?"

"Lucas, talk to her. She was just here. I told her you wanted to see her. She said that was fine, that she'd wait for your call."

I examined Katrina's eyes, wondering if I had lost her to one of the many worlds that occupied her mind. "Lily was here?"

"We had coffee," she said, pointing at two cups on the table. "She didn't stay long. She apologized, said she was going to be busy for a while, but would keep in touch."

Dazed, I nodded and backed out of the trailer.

"That's a cop," Katrina said, staring from the doorway at Jaworski's cruiser. "Is Lily in some kind of trouble?"

"We need to find her," I said, and could not say anything more.

"WE HAVE TO WAIT ON THAT PHONE NUMBER YOU GAVE me," Jaworski said as I slipped into the cruiser. "It's a cell phone. They take a little longer."

"You got one?"

"What? A cell phone? I just used it to call Reifer, my friend in Oregon."

Jaworski reached into his jacket pocket and gave me the small plastic device. "They're standard equipment these days, but I can't say that I use it much. The radio's usually all I need."

When I stared at the phone, Jaworski instructed me in its operation.

"What's the number on that slip of paper?" I asked, and punched the digits as he recited them.

I heard a click, then a woman's voice. "I expected to hear from you before now," she said. "You're slipping."

"Where are you?"

"You will find me. It's taking you longer than I expected, but I'll wait. I've waited for years."

She broke the connection.

I redialed the number and reached a recorded message. The party I was calling was out of area or had switched off their phone.

"So?" Jaworski asked.

The voice did not belong to the woman who had called my house, the same woman I had heard on the police tape log. The voice was familiar, but I could not place it.

"I don't know who that was," I told Jaworski. "Lily Dorman, but who the hell is she?"

She was confident that I would find her. I had only to follow my instincts, which told me that, whoever she was, she was familiar with my intuitive leaps.

"Lucas, I hate to tell you this, but Jasper and the feds have lost their patience. Jasper ordered the Markham patrols to continue, but now they're looking for you. We've got to go in."

"What the hell is she thinking?"

Jaworski stared at me. "I don't know what Jasper thinks. I do know that she's going by the book."

I shook my head. "We're close, Herb. We can't back

off now. We've been playing parts in a theatrical production, surrounded by actors and props. Gilman said, 'Nothing is as it appears.' Eloquent."

"Are you talking about the murders or this MI business?"

"It's a play within a play. Think about it. Why kill Weatherly?"

"He couldn't be trusted to keep his mouth shut. MI is cleaning house. They're liquidating, turning everything into cash, and vanishing."

"So, who killed him?"

"Who's left? It wasn't Gilman. One of Gilman's foreign contacts? The driver, Edgar Heath, sounds like muscle. Squires shot up Portland. Melanie Martin would be another guess."

"My benefactor," I muttered as Jaworski guided the car from Bayberry Park and drove to the interstate.

"MI supported Amanda Squires," I said. "Weatherly set up the arrangement. Gilman handled the money. Lily wanted to kill Harper Dorman. Jaycie Waylon was the target on Crescent Street. She was probably Norma Jacobs's money-laundering contact, but that isn't what got her killed. I had time for her but not for Lily. Her roommates had the misfortune of sleeping in the wrong place at the wrong time. Steve Weld brought heat to MI's operation. He must have been getting close to pay dirt."

"Luther Peterson saw a young guy walking on Crescent. You saw him tear out of there after killing Weld, and you said he'd been on your road."

"At night, or seated in a car, wearing a ball cap . . . a young woman could pass for a young male."

"What about Markham?"

"I'm saving him for last," I said. "Beckerman was more housecleaning. He could identify Squires. Same with

Gretchen Nash, but Nash was too quick on the draw. Beckerman's mother was on the MI board of directors. She had a set of computer tapes from the college, copies of all the illicit transactions. Her son had the misfortune of inheriting the tapes with the rest of her estate."

"And Lily Dorman wants you dead."

"She grew up thinking of me as her father. I failed to rescue her and her mother. I cared for hundreds of patients, but never took the time to drive here from Boston and make them safe. Lily learned about me from magazines. One of the articles she mentioned in her journal described my work on the Markham case, how I was able to determine his characteristics and help police find him. The daughter did her old man one better. She found the serial killer without any help, and she killed him."

"Smart and tough," Jaworski said. "There ain't much that scares her."

Jaworski's pocket squealed. He yanked out his cell phone and flipped it open.

"Hang on," he said to his caller as he pulled the cruiser to the side of the road and flipped open his narrow notebook.

I shifted my attention to the black sky. Scrawny pines heeled wildly in the wind from the approaching storm. I drifted with the arrhythmic snap of raindrops as they collided with the windshield, then dispersed in lingering smears.

Lily Dorman commanded my thoughts. Lines from a poem drifted aimlessly through my mind—lines about a phantom woman who caressed the world with a long blade.

she is not real
who strolls this night

through stone walls and dreams;
her insubstantial hands
slick with servants' blood,
she steals the air

"Tough," the chief had said.

Nothing scares her. I wondered why that bothered me.

"That was my friend Reifer," Jaworski said.

What am I missing?

"He made some calls, ran database searches on the names I gave him. Lily Dorman graduated from Portland State University. On her personal information sheet for the college, she listed Janine Baker, her roommate, as the person to contact in case of emergency. Reifer also ran a records check. Baker surfaced first. She'd just arrived in the San Francisco Bay Area when Oakland P.D. arrested her for solicitation. She posted her fifty bucks bail, then never appeared in court. Ten months later, Seattle P.D. caught her plying her wares on the Sea-Tac strip near the airport. A youth officer named Winston worked with the underage hookers on the strip, so Reifer called her. Winston's one of those cops who keeps everything. Said she kept her file on Baker because she'd never seen a kid so pissed off at the world. Baker's roommate, Dorman, washed dishes in a Chinese joint and spent the rest of her time in the library."

"Becoming brilliant," I muttered.

"Baker suddenly stopped showing on the strip. That bothered Winston for two reasons. One, they had the 'Green River Killer' dumping bodies all over the county."

"Most of them were working girls off the strip."

"You in on that one?"

I shook my head. "It has always bothered me that no one caught him."

Jaworski consulted his notes. "The second reason was that Baker's name came up in a murder investigation," he continued. "Victim was an off-duty cop, Robert Harper. He moonlighted as a doorman at one of the clubs on the strip. Baker had been hanging out there."

I looked at Jaworski. "Lily heard her father's name."

Harper the doorman.

I watched as he made the connection: "Oh, Jesus."

She kills people she knows, but don't forget the strangers.

"What else have you got?"

Jaworski flipped his hat into the backseat and stared out his window at the rain. He was unnerved. I had hammered him with the reality of just how volatile Lily Dorman was, that anything could trip her into killing mode.

After a moment, without a word, Jaworski returned to his notes. "Winston tracked down Dorman, who said she hadn't seen her roommate in a couple of weeks. That was it. Nobody saw Baker again, and she didn't show up in the computer after that. Winston checked with Dorman half a dozen times in the next two years, until Dorman disappeared."

"She went to Portland, Oregon?"

"Reifer says the timing is about right. Dorman was at the university for five years, and lived at the same address the entire time. She held a driver's license, never got so much as a traffic ticket, but there was no trace of Baker. The transcript office records show that when Dorman graduated, she paid for five certified copies of her grades. The college sent them to her address in Portland. There were no requests after that."

"I don't get it."

"I'm not finished. Reifer ran all the names through the

national databases. Nothing current on Janine Baker, Lily Dorman, or Amanda Squires."

"She's using another identity," I muttered.

"Jesus Christ," Jaworski grumbled. "When this is over, I may write my own book."

CHAPTER 33

JAWORSKI SLOWED THE CRUISER AS WE APPROACHED A state police checkpoint. He pulled to the right, switched on his strobe, and stopped.

"That you, Newman?" he called.

"Hey, Chief," the cop said, approaching the car. "Jasper ever catch up with you?"

"Talked to her on the phone."

"She and a couple of feds went through here an hour ago. They've got a search warrant for the Martin outfit in Portland."

"Norma Jacobs meeting them?"

"She's the lead at that end. Not too happy about having to work with Jasper."

I imagined the squat, acerbic detective hitching up her jeans and escorting Karen Jasper through the vacated MI building.

Jasper drove south as we drove north, a perfect highway choreography. I had no interest in sparring with our laptop-packing representative of the information generation. The detective possessed what Sergeant Joe Friday had sought weekly on *Dragnet*, "just the facts," but she did not have a hint about how to apply her data.

"You got the mad doctor in shackles?" Newman asked, peering into the cruiser, a broad grin creasing his face.

Jaworski snorted.

"Hi, Doc," the cop said.

I nodded.

"You two better get going. Jasper was close to putting a hold order on him."

"Thanks, Newman," Jaworski said, and guided the car slowly onto the highway.

"Are we the toast of police radio?" I asked.

"Ain't quite like the last *Seinfeld*," he said, "but it's close."

Fifteen minutes later, Jaworski pulled to the roadside at the intersection that led to the Ragged Harbor flats.

"Where are we going?" he asked.

"Monhegan Island," I said.

"You were serious."

"Melanie Martin has a cottage there. Gilman said that she seldom leaves the island."

"Don't mean she's there now."

"Indulge me, Herb."

"That's all I've been doing," he said as he considered my request. "We'll go to Pemaquid Point. My cousin keeps his boat there. This wind won't bother him. He'll take us to Monhegan."

On the drive east, Jaworski received another call, this one from his dispatcher. The cell phone number Katrina had given me to reach Lily Dorman was assigned to Martin International.

JAWORSKI'S COUSIN, AL LODGE, REFUSED PAYMENT FOR risking his forty-foot boat in the high seas.

"When it's a police matter, I think folks should do

what they can to help," he said, and spat a thick stream of tobacco juice into the Atlantic.

Jaworski stood beside Lodge at the helm. The cousins—a short, wide police chief and a tall, wizened lobsterman—engaged in an encrypted conversation that involved much pointing and gesturing. The men fell into a New England, seafaring argot that consisted of grunts, shouts, whistles, and occasional words.

The boat powered into the wind and the three-foot swells. I stood aft waiting for my stomach to erupt. When it never did, I realized that I had not eaten for nearly the same length of time that I had not slept.

As we approached the island, Jaworski joined me at the stern. "Al says the MI launch left Pemaquid a couple of hours ago. He didn't see it come back."

Lodge guided his boat to a dock at Lobster Point, which Jaworski assured me was within walking distance of Horns Hill Road, Melanie Martin's address on Monhegan. The MI launch rocked in an adjacent slip. Painted in gold on the stern panel was the boat's name, *Lily D.*

"Another coincidence, right?" Jaworski muttered, following my gaze.

We left Lodge to secure his boat, and climbed the ramp to the pier. A tall African-American man wearing a dark suit and topcoat strode toward us. Circuits in the dim recesses of my mind completed a clicking and snapping routine as the man veered toward the *Lily D.*

I remembered Gretchen Nash's words.

Shaved head. Lots of neck. White shirt, black pants. Maybe thirty-five. He wasn't interesting. You see guys like that all the time selling sneakers.

I appraised the man I believed was Edgar Heath, Lily's driver. He was powerfully built. The gray at his temples suggested that he was also past his basketball-playing prime.

"Edgar Heath?" I asked.

At first, he moved only his eyes, from the chief to me. Then his hands drifted toward his chest.

"Don't," Jaworski said, drawing his nine-millimeter.

"Hey, no need," Heath said.

He grasped his lapels and slowly opened his coat so that we could see his empty holster. "She took my gun," he said, holding his pose.

"Pat him down, Lucas."

I did as instructed and found no weapon.

"Where is Lily?" I asked.

He cocked his head to one side. "I escorted my passenger to the cottage. I don't know who she is now. I can't help her anymore. I did what I could, cared for her, saved her from her . . . indiscretions. It's gotten steadily worse for two years."

"You don't know who's at the cottage?" I asked.

"Can we sit on the bench?" he asked, pointing to the edge of the dock where a dauntless flounder fisherman packed his gear and walked quickly out of the frigid wind.

Heath sighed and seemed lost in his thoughts as he sat facing the Atlantic. "She told me to expect the cops. She said I should answer your questions, tell you the truth. When I was hired, I received a limo, a Glock semiautomatic, a pager with a set of codes, and a salary that allowed me to live comfortably. I have a condo in Portland with a view of the harbor. Not bad for a glorified cabbie, huh? I had one assignment, to respond immediately whenever summoned on the pager. At first, it was easy. I'd go out once or twice a week. Danforth Street, Commercial, High Street, whatever. My passengers were always female. It took me months to realize that they were the same person."

"Lily Dorman?"

"She answers to Lily," Heath said, extending his hands

in a gesture of helplessness. "She also calls herself Myra, Bobby, Angel, Molly. I don't know all of them. Most of the time she opened the car door and slipped into the back. Sometimes she waited for me to come around and open the door. One day she'd be dressed in jeans and a shirt. The next day she looked like a million bucks. I never knew which it would be, but it was always her."

He smiled ruefully and stared at his hands. "I remember when it clicked for me. She called late, said it was Lily, and gave me the address of a bar in the Old Port. I knew that she was in trouble. It wasn't the first time that I'd hauled her out of a shithole, but this time it was bad. Two guys were hitting pretty hard on her. They bought her drinks, pawed at her, wouldn't let her leave. Her eyes were big and watery, like a frightened child. She didn't know how to say no. I took her out of there. In the car on the way back to Danforth, she argued with . . . the people inside her head."

Heath crossed his long legs and ran his hand over his bald head. "They have different voices, different accents. When I stopped in front of the building, she got out and ran up the steps. I don't know why, but I looked in back. The seat was covered with blood . . . blood on the carpet, blood smeared on the door. I followed her. She was curled on the floor in the hallway, crying. She had puncture wounds on her arms. I held her until she fell asleep."

"You left her there?"

"I took her to my place. She was gone in the morning." Heath looked at me. "Please don't hurt her."

"Did you ever drive Lily, or any of them, to Ragged Harbor?"

"I know where the town is. I've never been in the village. I took her as far as the flats a couple of times, to a souvenir shop, I think. I didn't go inside."

"Loudermilk's," I said.

"I don't know. Could be."

"What about Portsmouth, New Hampshire? Did you take any of them there?"

He shook his head.

"The night that Harper Dorman was murdered . . ."

"I picked her up on Mellen and drove her to Danforth."

"Did you see any blood that night?"

"The only time I saw blood was what I told you."

"Who paid you?" I asked.

"Norton Weatherly. Tall, lanky man. He hired me. Once a month he showed up at my place, gave me an envelope with three thousand dollars in it. After the first six months, it went up to four each month. After a year, five. 'For loyalty,' he said. I knew that meant silence, and I knew that he and I had different notions of loyalty."

Heath shivered and jammed his hands into his coat pockets. "Weatherly considered Lily a liability," he said with a bitter laugh.

"Weatherly's dead," Jaworski said.

Heath looked at the chief. "Murdered? I'm not surprised. Weatherly thought he could do business with street scum the same as he did with bankers. He traded only in money, so he thought he was exempt from the stink of drugs, the violence."

"Did you ever drive Lily to Martin International?" I asked.

"Not Lily. I don't know who that one was. I picked her up there two or three times. Took her to the jetport. She always waited for me to open the door for her."

"Her appearance was that different from Lily's?" I said.

"Don't you get it? They are different people. They're locked inside one body, but they wear different clothes, talk different, walk different. They don't understand that if

the body dies, they all die. They think that each of them
has a body. They can describe each other."

"Is she at Melanie Martin's cottage?"

He nodded. "There's some connection there. Weatherly was a boss at Martin International."

"Why did she want your gun?"

"I don't know. Look, I've got to go."

Heath stood and buttoned his coat against the wind.

"No," I said.

"No, what?"

"Your devotion to Lily is apparent. I think you know
that she is dangerous."

"To herself, maybe," he said.

"She's a killer."

Heath shook his head. "I don't believe it."

I waited.

"I think we have an accessory here, Lucas," Jaworski
said.

"Oh, Jesus," Heath said, and looked at the clouds skid-
ding by. "She broke into pieces for a reason. Do you understand that? The pieces . . . the *people* keep her whole,
allow her to live."

I said nothing.

"One of them is anger. That's all she is. Rage. She
terrifies the others. They try to keep her locked up inside,
but sometimes . . ."

"She gets out," I prompted.

"At the cottage, she said that everything was spinning
out of control."

"Who killed the students?"

"I don't know."

"What about Harper Dorman?"

"I read the paper. I could figure out what happened to
him. Damn it, you were supposed to save them all."

His eyes flashed with fury.

"How do you know who I am?"

"She's been waiting for you," he said, his eyes fixed on mine.

"I'm not her fucking father."

He backed away and stared. "She says you are."

JAWORSKI HANDCUFFED HEATH AND LEFT HIM IN AL Lodge's capable hands. We walked from the landing and headed north.

As far as it went, Edgar Heath's assessment was accurate. Lily Dorman's world consisted of compartments filled with secretive people who emerged, darted from one task to another, kept their earth spinning and all their planets in the proper orbits. The organism could kill at night and be at work in the morning.

Dorman survived the abuse, the pain, the terror of childhood. The fragments, or people, who were aware of each other, might bicker or even argue, but they would always look after each other, perform whatever tasks were necessary to maintain what passed for stasis.

They don't know that there is only one body to house them.

We made the turn onto Horns Hill Road.

"You going to be okay with this?" Jaworski asked.

Heath's assessment did not include the gestalt, the whole that was greater than the sum of its parts, the predator.

"When it's over," I said.

CHAPTER 34

A LOW PICKET FENCE SURROUNDED MELANIE MAR-
tin's 1930s-vintage fieldstone Victorian house with its gar-
dens and pond. The wind off the Atlantic sliced through
leafless lilac and honeysuckle, bothered the pond into
muddy agitation, and slapped a pair of French doors back
and forth.

"Something ain't right," Jaworski said, pulling his
semiautomatic from its hip holster. "Wait here."

Jaworski walked to the building's rear. I waited until
he was out of sight, then headed up the gravel drive.

As I approached the house, one of the French doors
slammed against the stone structure and shattered. I hesitated, then stepped over the scattering of wood slivers and
broken glass and walked into a music conservatory. A
grand piano dominated the west end of the room, a low
stage extended wall to wall on the east.

A woman with black hair, wearing jeans, and a flannel
shirt opened to display a Joan Osborne T-shirt, lay
sprawled on the platform. Eyes wide, she seemed to stare
at the ceiling, her face a mask of shock or disbelief.

Dark blood pooled beneath her right ear. A Glock
nine-millimeter handgun rested on her open right palm.

I kneeled beside her.

Jaworski, gun in hand, entered the room from the north. "Didn't expect you to stay put," he said. "The house is empty. Who is it?"

"Squires," I said as I examined the head wound.

"Jesus Christ," Jaworski muttered, as he crouched beside me. "She wanted Heath's gun to blow her brains out?"

"That's what someone wants us to believe," I said. "The entry wound is behind her right ear. No stippling. There's an exit wound lower and forward on the left side of her head. That's no self-inflicted wound."

"Heath?"

I considered the chauffeur, his devotion to Lily Dorman, his exquisite sense of her suffering. "I don't think so."

I imagined Amanda Squires mechanically playing Brahms in a music room at Harbor College, her slight hands gliding over the keys.

she is not real . . .
her insubstantial hands . . .
she steals the air

In the key of blue, she said.
"We're missing a player."

"Baker?"

I stared at Squires's face. "Lily Dorman said that I would find her. She planned to kill me."

"She got the first part right," he said, snapping open his cell phone. "You walk back to the pier and collect Heath. I'll call Ragged Harbor."

I nodded, thinking that blasts of ocean air laden with purifying rain might clear my head. My mind was like a drawer brimming with unmatched socks.

The silversmith, Loudermilk, embellished the scrimshaw to order.

Our missing player was the timber rattler, the viper that injects its venom.

I stepped over the shattered French door and into the storm. No cleansing rain greeted me. Gusts from the Atlantic launched me toward Lobster Point. I thought of the return walk into the gale's force and growled my discontent.

According to most studies, Amanda Squires said in the seminar, women prefer to kill with poison.

All serial killers, male and female, choose victims who are vulnerable. That includes anyone whose back is turned.

I glanced over my shoulder at the darkness that followed me. Scrub growth shuddered in the cutting wind, but no one pursued me wielding a giant syringe filled with succinylcholine.

I shook my head, shoved my hands deep into my pockets, hunched my shoulders against the chill, and quickened my pace to the harbor.

I FOUND LODGE AND HEATH SITTING NEAR THE WOOD-stove in the bait shop. I nodded as I stepped into the small, overheated room.

Heath's eyes locked on mine. "You killed her, didn't you," he said, then lunged at me headfirst, his hands still cuffed.

Lodge was quicker and stronger than the driver. He locked Heath in a judo hold and lowered him gently to the floor.

Outside the shop, the launch ramp's chains banged against pilings.

"There's a Glock nine in her right hand," I said. "Someone wants us to believe that she killed herself."

Heath shook his head. "She never said she wanted to die. None of them did. I wouldn't have given her the gun if I thought that."

"Who's left? You took her there. You gave her the weapon."

His face was miserably blank.

Lodge released his hold and stood erect. "Edgar ain't killed no one," he announced, and spat tobacco juice into a Styrofoam cup.

I nodded my agreement. "You took her to see her mother," I said to Heath, fishing for some scrap of information that would help me to understand and perhaps give me direction.

"She hadn't been home in years. Lily didn't tell me that. Katrina did."

"What else did she tell you?"

"Katrina has her own problems, but she knew that something wasn't right with her daughter. She asked me to take care of Lily."

Heath covered his face with his hands. "We drove to Eastern Promenade and fed the birds."

Heath was distraught, but I had no desire to hear about cracked corn and pigeons. A wave of exhaustion rolled through me. "Let's go to the house," I told Lodge.

He helped Edgar Heath to his feet, and the three of us walked into the wind, a chilled, solemn procession to Horns Hill Road.

JAWORSKI HAD COVERED THE BODY WITH A SHOWER curtain. I stared at the low stage and thought of the woman of many faces and more souls.

"The storm's center veered south of Cape Cod," Jaworski said. "We've had the worst of it. Jasper and the feds will be here in a couple of hours."

"Do they know anything that we don't?"

"Doesn't sound like it."

"I want to see her," Heath said.

I looked at Jaworski, who studied Heath's face. "Stay with him," the chief said. "Touch nothing but the curtain."

With Lodge behind him, Heath kneeled beside the body as I lifted the heavy plastic. I expected the driver to again go for my throat. Instead, he looked up, his face creased with confusion.

"I don't know this woman," he said. "I've never seen her before."

CHAPTER 35

I SLEPT FITFULLY FOR THREE HOURS, UNTIL THE ABsence of the wind's roar awakened me.

I stared at the pebbled white ceiling. If I wanted to move, I could not. The plush sofa that I had crashed on was a spinal trap designed for polite sitting, and excruciating low-back pain if you dared recline. I added "chiropractic visit" to my mental to-do list.

Amanda Squires was not Lily Dorman.

The thought illuminated my fogbound head like a distant beacon across rough seas.

Lily Dorman is the missing player.

"Where the hell is she?" I muttered.

In a wing chair across the room, Jaworski pulled himself from sleep. Al Lodge sat cross-legged on the floor, opposite Edgar Heath.

"You didn't sleep so good," Lodge said.

"Understatement," I muttered.

I rolled onto my side, placed my right hand on the floor, slid to my knees, and leaned on the sofa to push myself to a standing position. My neck and one knee cracked.

"You could be the percussionist in a band," Jaworski

said. "You sound like a wood block. Remember Spike Jones?"

"Are you always this witty when you first open your eyes? Remind me never to sleep with you again."

Jaworski snorted and opened a piece of gum.

"If a wood block's one of those things you beat with drumsticks," I said, "I feel like one."

As I stretched to loosen kinks and unravel knots, the Coast Guard delivered Karen Jasper and a small army of seasick federal agents. The state investigator huddled with Jaworski. Men and women in blue jackets imprinted with the initials BATF, FBI, or DEA fanned through the house with cameras, radios, measuring tapes, powders, sprays, and yellow plastic crime-scene ribbon.

Jasper turned from Jaworski, glared briefly at me, then walked to the stage and glanced at the corpse. She nodded to the chief, then fixed me with her burning eyes and strode in my direction. "I don't like you," she began.

"You had her and you let her go," I said.

"There was nothing to hold her on. We still require evidence. There is no evidence that this woman engaged in any illegal activity. You know that. You avoided us. If you came in and talked with me—"

"You made it clear that you had no interest in anything I had to say."

She looked at the ceiling, then snapped her gaze back to me. "I want to know everything that you know about this woman, about Martin International, and about the murders. We're going to hold you until you've answered every *factual* question that we have."

If Jasper's gut ever told her anything, she would mistake it for indigestion.

I grabbed my wallet, found my attorney's business card, and handed it to Jasper. "I have nothing to say."

She did not look at the card. "You're obstructing," she snapped.

"I'd call it exercising rights guaranteed to me by the United States Constitution. Bunch of old men thought they had some pretty good ideas, so they wrote them down. Some other old men amended it a few times, but it's held up pretty well."

She spun on her heels and stalked off to join her army.

"You didn't have to needle her," Jaworski said.

"Yes I did. I'm insufferable. Remember?"

I wandered onto the patio, where a small troop of agents had gathered. I stood in the stiff, chill breeze, listened to bits of conversation, and allowed my mind to drift.

"Looks like a suicide," one agent said.

"Probably is. We'll have to wait for the medical examiner."

An autopsy and report would take days. I did not have days.

"There is a confusion about what Lustmord *is,* Amanda Squires said.

I was convinced that everything Squires said contained an explicit message.

". . . the pure joy of killing, a sexual excitement unlike any other . . ."

She was not describing her own love of the rush, the excitation associated with the kill. She was Lily Dorman's surrogate.

"Some of us love to fuck. Some of us love to kill."

Squires, whoever she was, was searching for conscience.

"The Mexican connection blew up on them," an agent said.

"They had six countries wrapped up."

"Jasper estimates two hundred million dollars."

"Lustmord *is not the exclusive province of men.*"

"She doesn't care about the money," I muttered. "She's having a good time."

Jaworski approached behind me. "Jasper says you and Al can return to the mainland. She wants you at the P.D. until this crew catches up with you. There's a couch in my office. Grab some sleep."

"Jasper trusts me?"

The chief looked down and shuffled his feet in what had become a familiar dance. "I gave her my word that you'd stay put."

I nodded. "I don't have anywhere to go, Herb."

"You figure that's Janine Baker in there?"

"Makes sense," I said with a shrug. "I don't know."

Jaworski gazed into the conservatory. "Everything connects to MI. They gained respect as a legitimate outfit, then playacted their way to the top of the corruption heap. What went wrong?"

"One of their clients hit the tequila too hard and washed up on your beach," I said. "The feds handled the investigation, and Steve Weld showed up. Baker and Dorman would have operated on different agendas after that. Baker was in it for the money. Dorman is entertaining herself."

Jaworski shifted his gaze back to me. "So, where is Lily Dorman?"

THE BLACK SKY FADED TO SLATE GRAY AS AL LODGE and I trudged the road to the harbor.

"Don't know much about murder," Lodge said, talking around a walnut-sized chaw wedged in his cheek. "Except what I seen on TV. I heard you and Herb talking. This woman kills for the hell of it."

"I believe that."

"She's got more money than she can spend, but that don't matter to her."

I nodded. Lodge weighed his thoughts.

"She ain't practical. What she feels like doin' decides what she's gonna do. Ain't nothin' else matters to her."

Lodge's words echoed Sydny Clanton's as she confronted Charlie Manson. Whether the little guru's gofer got sliced hinged on Clanton's feelings.

I looked at the lanky lobsterman's back as he piloted his boat, and recalled his incisive observation about Edgar Heath.

"She ain't come full circle," Lodge said, and arced a stream of tobacco juice across the wind. "Best you don't stand right behind me."

I glanced at the years of brown stains splattered across the boat's stern.

Full circle.

Feelings dictate Lily Dorman's behavior. Anyone who hurt her in the past, or tries to stop her now, dies.

Intellect would tell her to take the money and run. The Bahamas or Costa Rica.

She can't run until she has killed me and confronted the birthplace of her nightmares.

I was not the source of her suffering, but I had failed to protect her. I was a child's dream of salvation, and I had become another nightmare.

Full circle.

You want me to find you.

She was not ready to be found on Monhegan.

Good and evil inhabit the same circle. The circle itself is complete, but Lily Dorman has not concluded her circuit.

You must finish the task of making yourself whole.

She said that I would eventually find her. "I'll wait," she said. "I've waited for years."

She had more confidence in my intuitive gymnastics than I.

The apartment on Danforth Street was furnished with props.

What about the trailer park?

Would she bring her performance to her mother's doorstep?

THE TRIP TO PEMAQUID WAS UNEVENTFUL. THE SEA remained choppy, but the wind had calmed considerably.

Lodge stood at the helm. I sat in the stern, away from Lodge's occasional blasts of black liquid, and thumbed Lily's journal, searching for something that would tell me where her circle began, and where it would end.

I flipped back through the pages. Lily's notes to Dr. Westlake would not help me. What drove Lily Dorman was primal, something in a horribly aching past.

I found an intriguing passage about her snakes in the swamp behind Bayberry Court, how they shed their skins and became new creatures of God. Then her handwriting changed from a child's neat script to a heavy scrawl.

We went to an amusement park today. Inside the beast's belly, a mirrored room showed me what I am. Mom was afraid. She waited outside. Harper took me inside, touched me inside, and laughed like the metal monster. Then I was no longer there.

Was this the beginning, the first time that Lily Dorman broke away from herself?

You must enter the beast again, look with confidence into the mirrors, see that you are whole, a new child of God.

She would go there before she vanished again, I thought, but I had no idea where "there" was.

CHAPTER 36

JAWORSKI'S DISPATCHER ESCORTED ME TO THE CHIEF'S office.

"He says that you're to make yourself at home," she said, and closed the door as she left.

The mute TV reflected the scene outside the police station. An underfed, black-haired woman in a fire-engine-red suit and matching lip gloss maintained a somber expression as she spoke into her microphone. The on-screen banner changed from LIVE IN RAGGED HARBOR, MAINE to TAPED EARLIER as the station cut to views of the college entrance, Crescent Street, footage from Jaworski's press conference, and yearbook photos of Susan Hamilton, Kelly Paquette, and Jaycie Waylon.

I turned away. The chief's vinyl sofa hulked against the wall. I would sleep later, either in my bed or in the jail cell that Karen Jasper had waiting for me. I did not intend to subject my back to a second round of pain. I paced, paged through an instruction manual on the proper use of Mace, paced more, then settled into a chair.

Jaworski's corporal, Dickie Stevens, pushed open the door. "Will it bother you if I watch some videotape?" he asked. "The chief's got the only VCR."

I told him to go ahead, then watched as he screened the memorial service videos. Solemn faces streamed past the camera in silence. In the background, in black, white, and gray, Jaworski and I engaged in soundless dialogue as we surveyed the mourners.

"He's here," I told the chief.

The killer was conflicted, I thought at the time, but I had not realized then that "he" was a "she." Now I understood the frenzy evident in Harper Dorman's apartment, the savage attack on Jaycie, then the patient efficiency with the Crescent Street scene. Lily Dorman would attend the memorial service not because of any psychic turbulence. As I had suspected, the killer was there to enjoy her sense of invulnerability.

Dawn Kramer drifted across the screen to the chapel. Then Amanda Squires clung to Wendell Beckerman's arm in a brief procession of the now dead. Squires snapped her head in the camera's direction; her eyes scanned to her right, then stopped.

"Someone called her," I muttered.

"What's that, Doc?"

Squires's eyes widened. She shook her head, turned away, and moved beyond the camera's reach.

"Can you back that up?" I asked Stevens.

"Sure."

Squires zipped backward across the screen.

"Right there," I said.

Again, Squires walked.

"Can you slow that?"

She seemed to freeze; her body, wrapped in a dark jacket and ankle-length skirt, moved in hesitating increments to the beat of the VCR's soft click. Squires's eyes shifted to the camera; her neck muscles tightened.

"Hold it."

The thin line of her mouth hardened as she glared into space beyond the camera. Stevens froze the image.

"Someone called her," I said again.

"Batson taped the same people from a different angle. Want me to try that?"

"Please."

This time, the view was from Beckerman's side.

Stevens slowed the tape as Squires reacted. The corporal pointed to the screen. "Just over my shoulder, on that little hill," he said.

I pushed myself from the chair, ignoring a twinge in my back. "She has a gun."

The blurred figure stood alone on the knoll behind Stevens. Her left hand gripped what appeared to be a handgun.

"Go slowly forward."

Squires jerkily shifted her attention to the chapel. The woman on the hill folded her arms across her chest; the object in profile in her hand was clearly a weapon.

"Yeah, she was conflicted," I said. "She couldn't decide whether to mourn or to kill."

"What?"

"Can you enhance that image?"

"We don't have equipment like that. Maybe if we sent it out, but I wouldn't know where."

As I stared at the two women—the startled Squires, the unrecognizable woman and her gun—Jaworski walked through the door. "Heath's in booking," he said. "Jasper's holding him as an accessory. They're running Squires's fingerprints. Janine Baker's prints should be in the computer."

I pointed at the TV screen. "Meet Lily Dorman."

Jaworski looked from me to Stevens, then crossed the room and examined the indistinct picture.

Before he could react, I asked, "Herb, does Portland have an amusement park?"

"You don't find us entertaining?"

Stevens chuckled and left the office. I gave Jaworski the journal and pointed to the paragraph about the mirrors.

"I don't know of anything in Portland like what she's written here, but it could be that little park up the street."

Jaworski gave me a brief history of the Screamin' Demon, the amusement center that I had seen opposite the entrance to Harbor College. "When you walk into the mouth, blue lights flash and the monster roars. I always thought it was hokey, but the kids like it."

He walked to the window. I watched the TV view of him from outside.

"The mirrors are in the old fun house," Jaworski said. "They changed it, but it's still there. There's a giant slide with a big bowl at the bottom. The kids grab a burlap sack and walk up three flights to get to the top. You go left to get to the slide, right to enter the distortion room. The floors don't meet the walls, the chairs and tables are oversized or undersized. That's where they have the mirrors that make you fat, skinny, headless, or all head with no body. They call it the 'House of Horrors' now. You can hear the canned laughter on Main Street all summer. MI bought the place when they bought half the town. The new manager put every imaginable electronic gizmo in there."

Distortion.

I felt as if my head suddenly filled with cotton candy. Thoughts tried to wade through the sticky pink cloud of spun sugar. I could not get a handle on any of them.

Reflection.

"Reporters are blocking the front again," Jaworski said. "They've got police radios."

The reporters positioned themselves to know all things from all angles, to reflect back to us their impressionistic renderings of our lives. Reality is subjective and malleable. The only reality they could offer was their own.

Lily Dorman asked for a new father, and her mother gave her one. Katrina rearranged reality that dark night when mother and daughter caught a bus to the hospital.

"I didn't want to go," Lily wrote in her journal.

"I don't like the smells . . . the nurses' mysterious sounds when they walk . . . the hallways where some noises echo and others do not."

My cotton candy cleared like tumbleweed in a brisk breeze. "Heath," I said.

"Reporters probably saw me bring him in."

I was out of Jaworski's loop, on a totally different wavelength. "I have to talk to Heath."

"Can't it wait until they process him?"

"No."

Jaworski sighed. "I swear you jump around like crabs in a pot of boiling water. Come on."

THE CHIEF LEFT ME ALONE WITH EDGAR HEATH.

The tall, muscular man sat with his head cradled in his arms on a table. I pulled up a chair opposite him as he sat erect and stretched, his sleep-deprived eyes swollen.

"I don't know where she is," he said.

"A month before Lily killed her father, you drove her to Mellen Street."

He wrinkled his forehead.

"She went inside the apartment building. You waited at the car."

"That never happened."

"She wore a black dress, pearls, sunglasses, a black scarf."

"Who is she supposed to have killed that day?"

"No one. She talked to a woman who was leaving the building, asked her where Harper Dorman lived, then walked out. You opened the car door for her."

Heath shook his head. "The ones I opened the door for never went to Mellen. When she was the one I drove to the jetport, she waited for me to come around the car."

His eyes betrayed no involuntary movement. "I haven't committed a crime," he said. "I answered the detectives' questions. I am answering yours. I'm also tired. I need a shower. I'm hungry."

I showed him the photograph from Portland State University.

"She was just a kid then," he said.

Heath looked at me. "The smile, the bright blue eyes . . . I never saw her like that."

THE HALL WAS EMPTY. I WALKED TO THE REAR OF THE building and found a stairwell. In seconds I was in the familiar corridor that led to the municipal parking area.

Loud voices carried from the street where the reporters gathered. I moved away between parked cars and found an alley that led to Main Street two blocks south of the police station.

One hundred yards ahead, silver fangs glimmered, poised thirty feet above the sidewalk.

CHAPTER 37

I STOOD AT THE PLYWOOD FACADE THAT PROTECTED the amusement park from winter storms and local delinquents. A padlock on the temporary structure's makeshift door was shattered, the door splintered. I crouched to examine wood slivers so recent that the lingering wind had not moved them.

You killed Amanda Squires, then you came here from Monhegan.

The serpent's silver fangs glistened with blue pockmarks, as if sea spray had probed the teeth with tiny, piercing blades. I yanked open the door and slipped into summer's screaming demon. Blue strobes ignited in cluster-bomb bursts, sapphire clouds that hovered like a hologram in the air. The park was powered up, as if vendors expected a crowd of children to charge, squealing, through the fractured gate.

Rasping laughter exploded from speakers that surrounded the entrance to the House of Horrors. The metallic din startled me, the jarring blasts a blend of sadistic gaiety and guttural syncopation.

A child's trip to the ocean and this amusement park became her touchstone for terror, for the nightmares she would know and the shadowed images that lurked behind her mind screen.

Lily Dorman had been here. Perhaps she remained inside, waiting for the man she knew as father to leapfrog logic and find her. Then she would kill him.

The door to the House of Horrors dangled on a single hinge. I stepped into the dimly lit foyer where, in summer, a ticket seller sat in a booth and triggered gusts of air from the floor when the hapless thrill-seekers paid their admission.

I slipped over the turnstile, my feet landing on two planks that immediately slid back and forth in oppositional rhythm. I stepped to my right and remained against the wall. Tinny laughter resonated through the cavernous room that resembled a gym divided neatly in half by the three-story slide, its bowl at the bottom.

Did Harper extend the invitation? Or was your curiosity piqued by the aura of the fun house?

One of you said, "Let's go inside."

I moved along the wall to the stairs. The sweet aroma of hemp wafted from burlap sacks piled beside the steps for kids to grab on their way to the slide.

Bags to carry snakes.

A quick scan of the catwalks revealed no movement above, so I climbed.

You played on the slide for a while. Any kid would. Then did you go to the rolling barrel? Or was Harper impatient to enter the mirrored room?

Sparrows wintering in the rafters fluttered in awkward, stuttering loops beneath the ceiling. Water dripped from the porous roof, leaving small pools and filling the air with the dank stench of moldering wood.

As I climbed, the laughter grew louder, bleating from metal speakers pitched high in the corners and slathered white with bird shit.

I turned right on the catwalk, away from the slide, and walked the twenty yards to the room where a message scrawled on the door announced, LIVE BACKWARD IS EVIL. I pushed the steel door and stepped into the room. The door slammed. A sign informed me that the metal entry was not an exit.

The floor slanted into the room. Slabs of brightly colored wall, metallic blues and electric yellows, met the floor at freakish angles in impossible juxtapositions of matter and space. Four legs of different lengths supported a neon-red table; green chairs were too small or too tall.

I stepped forward, and light vanished, leaving me in blackness.

Pressure plates in the floor.

Brief explosions of light offered glimpses of shifting black structures, large rectangular blocks adorned with rotating mirrors that reflected fleeting images of me, a graybeard with wide, startled eyes.

I stared back at me, studied my eyes. I was immersed in the experience, and I was an observer.

At the center of the riotous whirling and flashing, a single, pulsing strobe illuminated a revolving mirror that spit out a headless reflection.

The programmed, maniacal laughter abruptly stopped. What had been an auditory assault suddenly became a suffocating silence punctuated by throbbing light and the gentle aroma of burning sandalwood. Incense, I thought, as my mind flitted through scenes and sensations from the 1960s, random associations triggered by a scent.

I struggled to cling to the moment, to the room that jarred my senses, skewed time, and sent the years tumbling over one another like stones in an ocean storm.

I was frozen in place, caught on a downward slope in a maze designed, I was certain, by a woman who wanted me dead.

Lily Dorman, like every human predator, was a student of behavior. People are seldom unpredictable. We like to think that we are inscrutable, but a moment's or a month's study reveals our habits, the patterns of behavior we become aware of only if we pause and take a long look inside. In the frenetic world that we've created, we've left little time for the luxury of self-examination.

You made yourself whole. You pulled together fragments, shaped an entity that fueled itself on rage at a father who had the power to set you free and refused.

Mirrors continued to spin, the lights to erupt in splashes of color like flakes of broken glass blasted from a cannon. My eyes accustomed themselves to the pulsating lights and allowed me to identify fragments of reality—a gray mop and bucket in a black corner of the twisted room, a snarl of black cables against an orange wall. I shifted my weight and slipped six inches to my right.

The aroma of pine replaced sandalwood.

The mirrors pivoted with an audible click, the explosions of light hesitated, then resumed, and I heard the unmistakable snap of a gun's steel hammer readied for firing.

I dove to my right as the weapon exploded, smashed a mirror to fragments, echoed thunderously through the room, and filled the air with the smell of cordite.

I crawled until I collided with the wall. The gun fired a second time and shattered another mirror.

"Shit," I muttered as I scrambled forward, again hitting a concealed pressure plate.

The large-caliber weapon blasted a mirror behind me, showering my legs with glass shards.

Convinced that technology, not Lily Dorman, held me captive, I slithered forward on my stomach until I reached the corner.

I found the mop, removed it from the bucket, and

wedged it behind the power cables. I threw my weight against the mop handle and felt the cables yield. White light arced and buzzed in a crazed, frightening dance as the electrical connection severed at its U-bolt.

In seconds, the room was black and silent. I lay on my back.

After a moment, I stood, and felt my way along the wall until I found a door and shoved it open. Afternoon's light and a cool ocean breeze greeted me. I breathed deeply, surveyed Main Street and the ocean from my sixty-foot perch, then turned and gazed into the room.

A black curtain covered the largest rectangular shape in the room. I shoved aside the drape to reveal a computer console—the source of the light show, the images, the fireworks.

"Fuckin' computer nearly got me," I grumbled, and headed for the fire escape.

AS I STUMBLED THROUGH THE PLYWOOD DEBRIS AT THE park entrance, Jaworski drove to the curb and climbed from his cruiser. "Figured I'd find you here," he said. "She in the park?"

"Not anymore."

"You look like you've been crawling around on the floor."

"You're a perceptive sonofabitch, Herb," I said, brushing grime from my shirt and pants.

I gazed up at the metal jaws. "I made a mistake. She knew that I'd find this place. She rigged the mirrored room for me. It's activated by pressure plates in the floor. Lights and mirrors with Magnum firepower accompaniment."

"She doesn't sound so fragile anymore."

"She isn't."

When Lily Dorman escaped from the hospital, she

headed west with her friend Janine. Dorman was shattered, bits and pieces of a soul cast like pulverized crystal into a gale. I imagined her clinging to the streetwise Janine Baker's sleeve. She had no choice; a bubbling stew of feeling and thought beneath consciousness determined her behavior.

"When they were on the West Coast," I said, "Lily modeled herself on Janine Baker, mimicked her friend, learned a sociopathic lifestyle. Think of what she was imitating. Baker was trouble. Lily assumed her personality, then escalated."

Jaworski unwrapped a stick of gum and shifted his weight from one foot to the other. "That journal has the ring of truth," he said.

"Her evolution didn't stop with what's in the diary," I said. "When Janine worked the streets, Lily waited tables and read books. What was she reading?"

"Probably get Ken Starr to find out," Jaworski cracked.

"You're spending too much time around me, Herb," I said. "Lily knew that she didn't want to live her life as a victim. When she was her father's toy, she had to split herself away to survive. Feelings overwhelmed her, threatened to destroy her. In the world, she needed to be whole. To her, that meant that she had to have no emotions, that she had to become the aggressor."

"What about Harper Dorman?" Jaworski asked. "Baker was a street con. As far as we know, she didn't spill blood."

Lily Dorman evolved from the dissociative extreme to a determined, focused, emotionless predator. She knew that she was a hybrid.

"She educated Baker," I said, "seduced and controlled her with money, the promise of limitless wealth, and fear. Dorman so believed in her own invulnerability that she planned to kill Beckerman at the memorial service in front of an audience of cops. Dorman studied Baker, but

Dorman already possessed the raw, primitive material that she needed."

"Lucas, is she one person now or a crowd? We've got one weapon, but the crime scenes look like the work of different killers."

"It's possible that Baker committed some of the murders," I told Jaworski, "but I doubt it. I think that Baker's appraisal of the world coming down around their ears was more pragmatic than Dorman's."

Years after serial killer Sydny Clanton's psychiatrist had written to me about her client, I met Dr. Susan Paynter at a conference in Las Vegas. "Sydny adapted," Paynter said, when I inquired about her former client. "She did what she had to do to survive in prison."

Clanton had operated at a primitive level when she had killed her parents. The murders she committed between Idaho and California, however, were the work of a deliberate, focused killer. Paynter believed that Clanton's slaughter of the Gleid family was a regression to the feral condition she had exhibited at home.

"Six months after they locked her up," Paynter said, "she had herself and her world under control. She was the most together woman on her wing. She wrote legal appeals for other inmates, counseled them on their personal problems."

Crazy or sane, there are few stagnant pools. We continue to evolve and to adapt.

Again, I gazed at the park entrance. "My mistake was to think of Lily Dorman as the same product of her unconscious that she was as a child. She acts roles in a well-scripted play, Herb. She doesn't slip from one personality to another."

"So where is she?"

"She wants me to think that she created these distractions, then disappeared. I'm not dead yet, so she's still here. We'll find her where I would least expect her to go. It's ironic. The amusement park represented the terror she experienced as a child, but the House of Horrors doesn't complete the circle."

"The trailer park?"

I wondered if she would carry the performance home.

"Maybe a final visit with her mother before she disappears again."

I shrugged. "I don't have anything else to suggest."

CHAPTER 38

AS WE DROVE SOUTH THROUGH A THICKENING FOG, JA-
worski called Norma Jacobs and arranged for her to meet
us at the entrance to the trailer park.

I slumped in my seat and dozed fitfully. Blurred video
images of Lily Dorman fluttered through my mind as I
struggled to make sense of the strange and lethal being
that she was.

"Trees down from the storm," Jaworski said, stopping
the cruiser fifty yards from the Bayberry entrance. "A place
like this will be the last the crews get to."

Jacobs drove in behind us.

"Fuckin' mess," the Portland detective said as she approached and surveyed the blocked road. "Looks like cruisers on the other side of Bayberry."

Jaworski and I pulled ourselves from the car and
looked where Jacobs pointed.

"Ain't Portland P.D.," Jacobs said. "I just left there,
and there wasn't anything on the radio. Must be Jasper
and the feds."

"Why are they down here?" Jaworski asked.

We stepped over a fallen tree and wound our way

through brush and limb wood to a barricade of three un-marked sedans and a state police cruiser. Jaworski's friend, Trooper Newman, flashed his halogen light at our racket.

"You ain't sneakin' up on no one," Newman said with a laugh. "Jacobs, they drag you along, too?"

"I figure to come back and pick up a cord of firewood when the highway department cuts this stuff," she said. "What've you got, Newman?"

"Jasper and three other suits went into the park to make an arrest."

"How long they been inside?"

"Ten minutes."

Jacobs looked at us. "Jasper gets the collar. Maybe I'll be home in time for *Wheel of Fortune*."

"What brought them down here?" Jaworski asked.

"Someone phoned in a tip, said Lily Dorman was in there."

Newman's clip-on radio crackled. "They made contact with a female subject," the trooper said, angling his head downward to listen to the transmission, his hand adjusting the squelch and volume controls. "Dorman's in Ellie McLean's trailer."

"Any point in hanging around?" Jaworski asked. "They won't let us near her until they finish with her."

Jacobs glanced at her watch. "I'm gonna hang around a few minutes."

I gazed into the courtyard. Visibility was near zero in the fog. The indistinct light from a lantern glowed deep in the park, and the muffled sound of voices drifted through the thick, damp air.

"Sounds like Dorman flipped her shit," Newman said. "She's sitting in the dark at McLean's kitchen table draw-ing pictures."

All that remained was for Lily to kill me and run. In-stead, she returned to the trailer park.

"Where's Katrina Martin?" I asked.

Newman's radio continued to fill the night with static and distorted voices. "Dorman's not responding," Newman said. "She put her face in what she's drawing and covered her head with her arms. Jasper wants Mental Health out here."

The trooper looked up from his radio. "Martin's not in the park," he said. "When I arrived, they'd gotten the residents out of there. Feds are putting 'em up at the Breakwater Motel. No way to know how long this will go on. That lantern you see in there is in front of McLean's trailer."

"Is Dorman armed?"

"There's a gun on the table, but they didn't ask for an assault team."

When Lily was young, Ellie's home was a refuge, a place to retreat from horror. She'd been functioning for years, albeit psychopathically. What terror could trip her now?

The answer to my question sent a chill from the base of my neck across my shoulders. Lily Dorman feared nothing. She had wealth, cunning, and power. She had ripped the doors from her closets and throttled the gnarled, green-eyed trolls that terrified all children in the night.

I turned to Jaworski. "You're right, Herb. We won't get near her. Let's head back."

"Yo, Doc," Jacobs said. "What's with the Nash broad? She don't like heads? I thought Squires was weird. Nash has all these fucking mirrors to help with her cheese flow."

"Chi," I said.

"Whatever. We still haven't found the slugs from Squires's gun."

"The shattered mirror at the foot of her bed," I said.

Jacobs shook her head. "That one was Nash's forty-four. Same as we found in the hall from when she tried to blow you away. We'll keep looking."

The squat cop turned her attention to Newman. Jaworski and I retraced our path to the cruiser. I tried to focus my attention on Nash's broken mirror. I could not concentrate.

We were twenty yards from where Jacobs and Newman continued their banter, punctuated by the crackle and static from the trooper's radio. Leaves rustled to my left. A small animal, I thought, gazing through the trees, watching the lantern flicker in front of Ellie's trailer. Then a shadow passed between me and the light.

"Herb, somebody's out there," I said.

He glanced into the woods. "Probably one of the officers."

No, I thought. The cops were in the courtyard—not concealed in the forest.

A twig snapped and I gazed again into the darkness. Fog licked around my ankles, the same heavy mist that drifted among the pines. All sound was muffled except the cracks and snaps of someone walking slowly through the woods.

The unsettling feeling that I was being watched washed over me. "Can you check on private flights out of the jetport?" I asked as we slipped into the car.

"The manager won't be there this time of night," he said. "I can check with air traffic control. What are you thinking?"

"Curiosity," I said. "I wonder if Dorman planned to leave tonight."

Jaworski flipped open his cell phone, called information, then punched in a new set of numbers. He explained who he was and offered his law enforcement identification number.

I continued to stare into the foggy night, through the trees, at the lantern's dim glow. Again, a shadow passed between me and the light.

"MI has two private jets out there," Jaworski said. "One is scheduled for a two A.M. departure. The pilot filed a flight plan for Miami."

I sighed deeply. "Might be best if airport security put a hold on the plane and the pilots."

Jaworski talked as I drifted into the place between consciousness and sleep. I heard the engine start, felt the cruiser's motion, and watched the crazy collection of images that caromed through my mind.

Spinning mirrors, oscillating lights, a soundtrack of manic, metallic laughter, and explosions from a computer-controlled Magnum handgun.

Lily planned to run tonight.

Layers of time slipped away and I smelled the fragrance of rugosa roses drifting on summer air.

In the late sixties, beyond the Provincetown dunes, Katrina Martin danced to the ocean's edge and stared at the dark sky as water washed over her feet. From high on the dunes, the scent of the wild roses carried on the breeze. As if struck with a sudden insight, Katrina ran to where I sat.

"I want to be an actress."

She was stoned—a laughing, frightening dervish who inhabited a chemically enhanced universe, and who wanted to occupy a permanent place in my life.

I patted the sand and asked her to sit.

The training I had gained on long weekends spent as an aide in a Boston mental hospital emergency room had taught me the patience that was necessary to work with drug cases. Most of the E.R. walk-ins were bad trips; they bought LSD laced with amphetamines, they ingested too much of their drug of choice, or they were so unstable that they should not have eaten anything stronger than a Fenway Park hot dog. Katrina's pharmaceutical travels

were alive with an ebullience and a feverish imbalance
that were both seductive and startling.

"There's no point in praying to an empty sky," she said.

*She curled into the fetal position and wrapped her arms
around my waist. Her voice faded to a whisper and she slept.*

I looked down at her long blond hair, matted from an
earlier swim, gleaming with grains of sand that sparkled in
the starlight. I brushed away sand from her eyebrows, her
forehead, her ear, my fingers lingering on the soft skin of
her neck. She was the most beautiful woman I'd known,
the most fragile and, I felt, the most dangerous.

*"Later, when I don't know you anymore, I will rewrite
your lines," she said.*

She rewrote all the players' lines, altered her daughter's reality, cast me as the father of her child.

*"There really isn't anything real," Katrina said, her
mouth a tight, serious line, her eyes luminous with mischief.*

Lily Dorman was left to define her own reality.

As we approached the turn onto the causeway to Ragged Harbor, Jaworski responded to a radio call. I listened
as his dispatcher told him that Detective Jasper and the
federal agents had Lily Dorman in custody and would
transport her to the P.D. for processing.

"She making any sense?" Jaworski asked.

"Negative, Chief. Jasper doesn't seem to know
whether Dorman can't talk or won't talk, but she hasn't
said a word."

Jaworski replaced the microphone. "What do you
think?"

"Something about this is fucked up," I said.

CHAPTER 39

JAWORSKI AND I WAITED IN HIS OFFICE. DICKIE STE-
vens brought a pot of coffee and joined us.

"That ain't Maxwell House," the chief said.

Stevens glanced at me. "It's some stuff the doc gave
me."

Jaworski grimaced. "Jesus."

"No, Chief. Honest. This stuff is good."

"Looks like something Public Works uses to pave the
streets. Probably tastes like it, too."

"We've been drinking it downstairs," Stevens protested.

"That's why you're downstairs."

"Herb, you drink it black, right?" I said.

"Yeah, black, but light passes through it. I've been
happy with my coffee for fifty years. Never got heartburn
from it. Not once. Now you want to feed me that shit."

As Stevens argued with his chief, I drifted.

*"Why do I sense heartburn in my immediate future?" I
asked.*

*Kai Lin reached into the bag. "Hot," she said, holding
up one jar, then lifting a second. "Mild."*

"There are some Tums in there, too," Sara said. "Amanda bought them, but I'm sure she'll share."

"Thinkers are prone to acid indigestion," I muttered, echoing the group's description of Amanda.

"You stay out of this," Jaworski snapped, and continued arguing coffee with his corporal.

"This is for you," Amanda said, handing me a narrow white box.

A carved ivory letter opener.

Scrimshaw, Jaycie said. Then she asked Amanda to explain the etching on it.

Jaycie rubbed her wet hair with a bath towel. "We nearly got wrecked driving up here. Some idiot coming down the hill wanted the whole road."

Lily Dorman.

Jaworski's phone rang. He grabbed it, listened, muttered a few words, and hung up.

"Jasper's got Dorman in interrogation. Sounds like a waste of time; she ain't talking. Want to take a look?"

I followed the chief through the corridor to the observation room. Two federal agents stood at the glass and watched as Jasper asked questions, and a silent Lily Dorman stared at the ceiling.

"Is your name Lily Dorman?" Jasper asked.

There was no response.

"Is Katrina Martin your mother?"

Dorman was motionless.

"She had no ID," one of the agents volunteered. "Nothing on her at all."

"Weapons?" I asked.

The agent nodded. "She never made a move for it."

I looked at her blond hair, her slender hands, the metal cuffs that gave her wrists a fragile appearance. "This is a waste of time," I told Jaworski. "Jasper won't get anything out of her."

"There's an emergency mental health counselor on the way," he said.

I stared at Lily Dorman, struggling to find a resemblance to Katrina—something in the eyes or the shape of her face.

"Could you get her to talk?" Jaworski asked.

"All I have to do is walk through that door."

"Detective Jasper doesn't want to be disturbed," the agent said. "No interruptions."

"Right," I said. "She's got momentum going in there."

The agent glared.

"I'd like to see your face, Lily," Jasper said.

Slowly, Dorman lowered her gaze and stared at the mirror. Her hair was in disarray, her makeup smeared. She smiled and said, "I have my father's good mind."

"Talk about weird," Jaworski said. "It's like she knows you're out here."

"Fuck it. I'm going home."

"Lucas, at least it's over."

He was right, of course. Eventually I would talk to Lily, in one institution or another. Perhaps then I would learn how her demons drove her to slaughter.

"Night, Herb," I said, found my way out through the back hall, and stepped into the cold night air.

CHAPTER 40

A BLACK HALO, LIKE A GARLAND OF COAL DUST IN THE mist, surrounded the illuminated sign.

Breakwater Motel.

I stood in the walkway's shadows and stared into the brightly lit office, where the clerk watched TV and a police officer read a newspaper. I looked in the other direction and counted the units.

Ten.

I don't like long odds, so I placed my shark persuader—a three-foot length of oak used by fisherman to stun large fish thrashing and snapping on the deck—between two vending machines, walked to the office, and stepped inside. The cop glanced up, then quickly returned his attention to the sports section. The clerk was reluctant to pull away from the news account of Lily Dorman's capture.

"Right with you," he said.

"Not good enough," I said, removing the gun from my coat pocket.

"Huh?" he grunted, turning slowly and offering me a clean shot at his chest.

I squeezed off a single round that slammed him from his stool to the floor.

The cop's newspaper flew into the air, his feet lifted from the floor, and he fumbled with his holstered gun. He was a cartoon character, startled, helplessly flailing. I fired the gun and watched him settle back in the chair.

I circled the desk, stepped over the clerk, typed my mother's name into the computer, and hit Enter. The screen blinked, then offered the information I wanted: Katrina Martin, Unit 7.

The odds had shifted.

CHAPTER 41

I DROVE THROUGH TOWN UNABLE TO GET LILY Dorman out of my thoughts.

"It's like she knows you're out here," Jaworski had said.

Did she, I wondered. Is that what her smile communicated?

"Harper crashed through the door," Lily wrote, "his shoulders hunched forward, elbows jutted out, and feet wide apart."

She avoided looking at his face, his eyes.

Karen Jasper questioned her. Lily stared at the ceiling.

"Lily was watching TV," Katrina said, "but she turned to see how Harper moved, how he held his shoulders, whether his hands were open or closed. That's how she knew what was coming. She read his body."

Katrina Martin wanted to be an actress. She would play history's greatest roles on the world's most fabulous stages.

"I won't lose her again," Katrina said of her daughter.

Her flat tone conveyed determination. Katrina's statement was not emotion-fueled flailing. She meant what she said.

What would she do to make sure that she did not lose Lily? What could she do?

Katrina betrayed Lily. Daughter forgave mother.

Lily Dorman fueled herself with vengeance. I could not imagine her forgiving anyone.

I have my father's good mind.

I pulled the car into my driveway, glanced at the dashboard clock—nine-thirty P.M.—and stared at the darkened house.

I climbed out of the car and into the cold, dry evening air. An hour's drive from Portland and a few hundred feet of elevation made all the difference in the world. The sky was wide, clear, and spattered with stars. I gazed at the heavens and listened to the sea.

Then I heard the phone ring inside the house. The answering gizmo could do its job. I could think of nothing that required my attention before morning.

Years earlier, Katrina asked me, "Are you a spiritual person?"

She wore black pants and a white sweater, and decorated a table with split walnut shells, each one fitted with a tiny paper sail on a toothpick, as if in anticipation of a breath that would carry them out to sea. There were no owls or pussycats, no pea-green boats, nothing runcible.

"I don't know if I'm a spiritual person," I told her. "What are you on?"

Her question was rhetorical. "Mescaline. Don't interrupt. Listen."

"I don't think 'spiritual' means tripping on dope," I said.

Katrina smiled. "It doesn't matter how you get there, Lucas."

I frowned my displeasure.

"Are you listening to me?" she asked.

I wanted only to leave, to sit alone on the beach and stare into black night.

"You're supposed to play your part," she complained. "Loving you is hard work. You make it that way. You're like the tall, dark, self-contained stranger, so . . . alien."

Katrina crowded me, and she frightened me.

"I've decided that I won't love you," she announced, spinning away, "but I do love the idea of being in love. Later, when I don't know you anymore, I will rewrite your lines."

She abruptly stopped twirling through the room and said, "There really isn't anything real. Our lives are illusory, reflections in a distortion mirror."

Katrina had foretold the story of Lily.

I pushed my hands through my hair, shivered in the chilly air, and walked into the house. I did not bother to search for a light switch. I crumpled newspaper and spread kindling on the fireplace grate. Flames quickly licked through the paper and lapped at the birch strips. I placed beech and maple limb wood on the fire, then held out my hands to the quick, intense heat.

The answering machine's red eye winked at me. Later, I thought.

When Lily Dorman saw multiple reflections of herself in the spinning mirrors at the House of Horrors, she knew what she was.

Dozens of children, all her, and at center, an image without a head.

None of the people in Gretchen Nash's paintings and sketches had heads. "Heads are the least attractive part of the anatomy," she said.

"You have an honest body. People always say 'honest face.' I don't read faces. I read bodies and their movement. You're a Leo, aren't you?"

"She talked to a woman who was leaving the building," I told Edgar Heath. "You opened the car door for her."

Heath shook his head. "That never happened."

Lily Dorman sliced her hand with her father's knife, and her mother crawled from the kitchen floor to wrap the cut with a piece of torn bedsheet. They would go to out-patient, mother told daughter.

"I didn't want to go," Dorman wrote. *"I don't like the smells, or the nurses' swishing sounds when they walk, or muffled voices, or hallways where some noises echo and others do not."*

Nash wanted to wait outside the emergency room. It was not just the smells, she said.

Sound is so muted. I feel like I say something and the walls suck it up.

I grabbed the poker, jabbed once at the logs, and placed the iron rod beside me as I sat on the hearth. I sipped a Shipyard, listened to the fire's crack and snap, and felt the warmth on my back. The last time I indulged myself with a brew and a blaze, a Volvo slowed in front of the house.

The flames illuminated the space immediately around me and cast dancing light shafts and shifting shadows the length of the room. As my eyes adjusted to the play of light and dark, I remembered the timered light. Before I could wonder why it had not switched on, I saw the woman's form on the sofa at the far end of the room.

"It must be someday," she said.

The bottle dropped from my hand and rolled in an arc, spewing amber foam across the floor.

"What do I call you?" she asked, her voice deeper than I remembered. " 'Father' seems so formal. How about 'Dad'?"

I studied the dark shape on the sofa surrounded by darts of light and moving shadows. I wanted to see her face, but I could not.

"You seem surprised."

Her voice had a lilting cadence, as if she suppressed laughter.

"You had plenty of opportunity to kill me. You waited until now. What do you want?"

She hesitated. "To talk, to fill in the years."

"I read your diary. Is there more?"

Seconds passed as Lily sat in silence. Finally she said, "You are going to die."

"We're all going to die. Whether I'm alive or dead, you get arrested."

Was I a witness to craziness or cunning? I wondered. I decided on the latter. She would be armed, confident that she held the advantage. My task was to tip her into madness. My only weapon was my ability to crawl inside her mind.

"I want you to listen—"

"Not interested," I said.

"You're playing a head game. It won't work."

"I wouldn't attempt to screw with your mind," I lied. "I know that it would be a waste of time."

She sat forward on the sofa, her forearms resting on her knees. Now I saw the outline of the gun in her left hand.

"I waited years," she said.

"Terrible waste of time," I said, testing to see how far I had to shove before I got a reaction. "Killing me kills you. The reason for you to be whole, to make your millions, to enjoy the hunt and the kill . . . dies with me."

I crossed my legs, using that movement as an excuse to slide a few inches to my left. The firelight careened erratically through the room.

At random intervals, Dorman's eyes glowed like embers across the black space, narrow mirrors of yellow-orange light. The room's altered luminescence allowed glimpses of her expression, a study in sculpted facial lines devoid of feeling. She was not the woman I had seen in Jaworski's interrogation room. Lily Dorman was the woman I knew as Gretchen Nash.

"Katrina said you were a kind man," she said, her voice low-pitched and hard, with a barely noticeable tremor.

"She knew me before I chased killers like you."

"Not like me."

"That's the one trait that all of you have in common. You think you're unique. Markham thought he was the only one. Someone should get a bunch of you together in a room and make you listen to one another."

"You are an insufferable, odious man."

"I've been in Maine less than two weeks, and that's the second time a woman has called me insufferable. I'll yield on that one, but I might quibble about odious."

To liberate the unreasoning rage deep within Lily Dorman, I had to represent a threat to her. When she was young, she was trapped. There was no escape from her father, the man who terrorized and tortured her. She retreated into her mind and found solace and power there. The police who arrived at the trailer when she burned her father, cornered her. I wanted Lily Dorman to feel trapped and taunted. I wanted pure rage.

"If you expected me to sit around and reminisce with you, you were wrong."

"You don't know what you're dealing with."

"Stuart Gilman told me the same thing. This trip has been one long déjà vu. Everything happens twice, or not at all."

I noted her quick, involuntary eye movement to the right, the first hint of disorientation that I'd seen, the only indication I had that she was vulnerable. The non sequitur was a distraction technique that I often used in hypnotic work.

"I have to admit," I said, "I am curious about Squires and Baker. Squires was obviously expendable."

She stood unsteadily, the gun at her side.

I needed her standing within five feet of me before she raised the gun. Driving a person to flail, and not tripping them into an act of directed aggression, required precision. It was time to allow her some slack, before I snapped the line taut.

She shrugged. One knee bent slightly, so that her body weight was no longer evenly distributed. "Amanda was a reasonably good actor, but weak."

"Where did you find her?"

"It doesn't matter."

"Her death won't be ruled a suicide," I said.

"The police will charge Edgar Heath. They won't know what else to do. It was his gun."

"They have Baker," I reminded her.

"For now," she said. "Janine is . . . devoted."

"All the years that you were in Oregon, there wasn't any trace of Janine . . . no traffic tickets, no charge accounts, nothing."

A slight smile creased her mouth. "Her name is Melanie Martin."

She took a step forward, the growing fireglow illuminating her face.

"How did you survive the House of Horrors?"

"I like to think that I got out of there alive because of my determination to avoid defeat by a machine, but you didn't intend that I die there."

"Astute."

"Not terribly. You had the perfect opportunity to kill me two nights ago. Will you tell me about Markham?"

Dorman shifted her weight and moved a step forward. "I made a compartment for him, welcomed him in, and gazed into his mind's eye. You remember his mind's eye, don't you?"

I did not care what she talked about; I wanted only that she talk.

"I never doubted that I could find him," she said. "He was on the run, frightened, not wanting to die, not wanting to be caught. His sister was all he had left. I knew that he wouldn't take a direct route. He never went anywhere in a straight line. I used a computer map program to track him. I plotted the least-direct roads, figured a range of driving times, and isolated one twelve-hour period and a ten-mile radius near Portsmouth. Then I used topographical maps to locate the campsites and vacation cottages in that area."

Her tone remained flat. She was not a proud daughter reporting her accomplishments to Dad. I had seen psychopathic indifference hundreds of times, but always in men.

"Markham never drove at night, so I did. From the time I arrived in Portsmouth, it was two hours until I walked up the rutted driveway to a hunting camp and saw the Pennsylvania license plate on the stolen truck. Perhaps the daughter is more skilled than the father."

"You took a great risk," I said.

"I don't think so," she said, moving a step closer. "I told him the story of his escape, how he found a car with keys in the ignition and money in the glove box. He never looked at the registration."

"You registered the car in his name," I said.

"He didn't believe me," she said. "The sound of the gun was loud and satisfying in the small cabin."

She gazed around my living room. "Probably like it will be in here," she said, her eyes settling again on mine. "He disappointed me. I expected more blood."

"Blood used to sicken you."

"People change," she said. "I feared and hated violence, and pain, and blood. I don't anymore."

I spread my palms on the brick hearth as if I were supporting myself, and grasped the fireplace poker. It was time to yank her hard and fast.

"A smart psychopath wouldn't have your perverse need to be present for the kill," I said. "She wouldn't take the unnecessary risks that you have. She'd hire someone, or she'd make sure that I didn't walk out of the amusement park. I'd be dead. She'd be pleased as punch. This way, everything blows up in your face."

"No one knows who I am," she said. "By the time they figure it out, it won't matter."

I focused intently on Dorman's eyes.

"The perfect psychopath doesn't feel anything. Unwieldy, ugly emotion doesn't enter into the homicide equation. You're carrying emotional baggage that you can't dump. The obsession that has driven you is based on an erroneous belief."

Again, her eyes flicked to the right.

"You have your justification, I guess. Your father fucked you."

Dorman winced.

"Others with your pathology have their rationales."

"You are my father."

"When I'm dead, I can't acknowledge that, can I? Shit. I'm not going to acknowledge it now. That's your erroneous belief. Katrina pitied you, so she lied. Harper was your father."

She hesitated. "Katrina is dead. Tell me that you are my father."

I shook my head. "Lily, I could hug you and comfort you and pat you on the head and tell you to call me Pop. I won't. You're not my daughter. You're just another fucking killer."

As her left foot moved forward and she raised the gun, I pushed myself from the hearth and swung the poker.

The cast iron hit her upper arm with a bone-shattering crunch. Her gun discharged into the floor, then clattered across the wide pine boards to the wall.

I intended the blow to cripple her, to drop her. Dorman did not go down.

She emitted a deep, guttural, rumbling growl. Lily Dorman's beast had freed itself.

Her left arm, useless, dangled at her side, but she charged. I swung again, cracking her across the face. Twisting from the blow's force, she fell headlong into the fire.

I dropped the poker and grabbed the back of her pants, yanking her out of the fireplace and onto the floor. Flames shot from her hair. The room filled with the acrid, curdled-milk smell of burned flesh. I whipped off my sweatshirt and smothered the flames, careful to avoid her singed skin. The facial burns were not life-threatening, but had to be horribly painful.

As I pushed myself up, Dorman's right hand shot out and grabbed my neck. Her eyes were closed, but the body continued to operate.

Her nails dug into my neck. When I could not disengage her grip, I punched her hard in the face. Dorman's arm fell to her side.

Breathing heavily, my heart booming, I collapsed onto my back. After a moment, I rolled over, pressed my hand to the floor to push myself to a standing position, and flinched in pain. I'd broken bones in my hand when I hit her. I used my left hand, and twisted to push myself up.

The poker slammed the side of my head, and I crashed down. Blood slithered from below my ear and dripped onto the floor. The room spun like a merry-go-round run wild. I had to get up, at least to roll over, but I could not coordinate arms and legs.

I heard her move, listened as she inched across the floor. Then I felt her hand on my leg as she pulled herself over me on her way to the wall. She wanted the gun.

I grabbed her leg and tried to hold her. She kicked free from my grasp.

The spinning slowed, and I focused on Dorman. Her eyes were still closed. She was like a wolf caught in a leghold trap, using every bit of its remaining strength to survive, even if that meant gnawing off its leg.

Pain knifed from my shoulder to my side. My head and jaw throbbed. I hurled my weight in the direction that Dorman crawled and landed beside her, inches from her seared face. She groped forward, her right hand sweeping in arcs ahead of her, feeling for the gun. I extended my arm, gripped the pistol, and rolled away.

Dorman gave up her search and lay still.

I sat with my back against the hearth and stared at her motionless form.

"I won't lose her again," Katrina had said.

"She never came home," I muttered as the door exploded open.

Jaworski aimed his gun at Dorman, then looked at me. "Jesus Christ. She alive?"

"Cuff her," I told him. "Then call an ambulance."

CHAPTER 42

DICKIE STEVENS LEANED BACK IN HIS CHAIR OUTSIDE Room 42 at the regional hospital. As I approached, he lowered his copy of the *Ragged Harbor Review* and said, "How come they never get this shit right? You tell 'em stuff, you give it to 'em printed out, and they still get it wrong."

"Comics are good," I told him. "Horoscopes aren't bad."

He smiled. "The docs get you fixed up?"

"Nothing that a few Band-Aids and ten pounds of adhesive couldn't repair. The chief around?"

"He and Jasper are with Dorman's doc at the nursing station."

I glanced into a darkened Room 42.

"I've been sitting here since they put her in there last night," Stevens said. "She ain't said a word or made a sound. She ain't even moved. From what I hear, the docs got her stabilized. She's in fair condition."

I nodded and walked down the hall.

Two federal officers huddled with a doctor. Jasper scribbled ferociously on her notepad. Jaworski sat with his hands clasped on his ample stomach and chewed gum.

"That tape holding you together?" the chief asked.

"Pretty much," I said, bending painfully into a fiber-glass chair beside Jasper.

"Three Boston lawyers showed up this morning," Jaworski said. "Whenever Dorman decides to talk, we won't hear what she has to say."

"Who called the lawyers?"

Jaworski shrugged. "She has players all over the country. Who knows? We leaned on Edgar Heath again last night after we brought you here. I'm convinced he's told us what he knows."

Jaworski nodded at the two feds. "Their buddies are tracking money and not having much success. They've located a couple of million in local accounts, and they're in court now to freeze all of MI's real estate holdings, but that's it."

"The bottom line, Dr. Frank," Jasper said, looking up from her notepad, "is that we have a case against Dorman for attempted murder. Her attorneys will point a finger at Janine Baker for the killings, Baker and Norton Weatherly for MI's money-laundering activities and the missing millions, and probably have a good shot at an insanity defense on the attempted-murder charge."

"What about her mother?"

"Lucas, she shot and killed a cop and a motel clerk, then beat her mother to death," Jaworski said. "We have no witnesses, no weapons."

"She beat Katrina to death," I repeated dumbly, imagining Lily's rage and her mother's terror.

"A heavy, blunt instrument."

"What about the Magnum she had last night?"

"Different weapon."

"There is no physical evidence," I said.

"Nothing," Jasper said. "We tore apart the Monhegan house, her mother's trailer, Eleanor McLean's trailer, the

Mellen and Danforth properties, and the MI facility. When we have secured the remainder of the company's property holdings, we'll go through them. The IRS might have some interest, but that's about it."

"Let me guess. She programmed the amusement park setup to erase itself."

Jasper nodded. "The hard drive was blank."

I ran my good hand through my hair, marveling at Lily Dorman's throughness. Had she anticipated every possible pitfall?

"None of these assholes is perfect," I said. "You're not looking in the right place."

"Dr. Frank, I'm doing my best to have a civil conversation with you. The FBI's experts in Quantico have been on this since yesterday. Dorman does not fit any of the profiles of killers who keep souvenirs, trophies, or other records of their exploits."

"So, if she goes down for attempted murder, with good time she walks in five to seven, disappears with her millions, and doesn't surface until she decides it's time to kill again. A good attorney won't let her go the insanity route. A successful diminished-capacity defense and she walks out of court."

"We have no evidence," Jasper said.

I looked at Jaworski. "Give me your nine," I said.

He sat up in his chair. "What for?"

"I'm gonna go blow Dorman's brains out. Jasper just told me that's the only way to close this case."

"Dr. Frank—"

"Your experts are wrong," I interrupted. "This was a kid who kept detailed, daily records on her fucking swamp snakes."

Jasper talked, but I did not hear her. I heard Ellie McLean describe Lily Dorman as a child, emerging from the tidal wetland behind the trailer park.

Vanessa Stripe needs help taking care of the babies. Billy Brown-spot is overweight.

Most students of criminal behavior focus on the violent act, its behavioral precursors, and the offender's subsequent actions. The organization of personality—the traits, quirks, and idiosyncracies—is ignored because it is considered irrelevant to the act.

"The swamp is where she buried Spike," Ellie said. *"That was her dog. She dragged him down there in a burlap sack, dug the hole all by herself."*

Personality traits transcend behavior. Whether Lily Dorman was in killing mode, painting-a-picture mode, or millionaire mode, she would always be meticulous. Crazy or sane, writing was her self-expression.

"At first I was afraid to walk on the dike," Lily wrote in her journal, *"so I sat in my favorite dry spot, listened to the breeze creep through the bayberry bushes, and wondered why my father, a doctor, after all, did not arrive, fix my mother, and send Harper away."*

When I had walked onto the dike, I had seen the small, weathered cross, fashioned by a child from lattice slats and roofing nails and hammered into the ground to mark the spot where she had buried her dog.

I covered my face with my left hand.

"You okay?" Jaworski asked.

"Herb, do you have to hang around here?"

"I was waiting for you."

"Let's take a ride," I said.

Jasper stood. "Dr. Frank, the special agents asked that you not leave until they've spoken with you."

I held up my hand. "I know. They have file folders to fill. You people chased after Markham until he was dead. Now that you're finally looking at the real killer, you don't have a fucking case. They can wait while I finish their job for them."

• • •

AS WE DROVE TO THE HIGHWAY, JAWORSKI SAID, "YOU
plan to tell me where we're going?"

"Bayberry. Are the feds still there?"

"They cleared out this morning."

"Does that miracle trunk of yours with the shotgun
and crowbar also contain a shovel?"

"Couple of 'em."

"I know that you don't climb fences. What about digging holes?"

"How deep?"

"Not as deep as you'd bury a dog."

"I can handle that."

I gazed at the crisp, clear sky, the blue that artists can
only dream of achieving on canvas.

"She sat at this table and drew pictures," Ellie McLean
told me. *"Lily was good at drawing. She kind of wrapped her
arm around her pictures while she worked on them, like she
was protecting them."*

"You think she took souvenirs?" Jaworski asked.

"You read her journal . . . 'The Story of Lily.' "

Jaworski waited.

"She labeled it 'Part One.' Lily Dorman was a work in
progress."

"So, there's more parts."

"Illustrated," I said.

Road crews had cleared the fallen trees from the Bayberry Park entrance. Jaworski drove to the swamp's edge
and stopped the cruiser.

"You get out okay?"

I nodded, shoved open the door, grasped the overhead
handle, and pulled myself up. As Jaworski retrieved a
shovel, Ellie McLean emerged from her trailer.

"You don't look too good," she said.

"How are you doing?"

"The FBI people ain't been gone long. They brought me home this morning. Nice folks. They bought breakfast for me at Denny's. He ain't gonna dig up bodies, is he?"

"Nothing like that."

"What happened to Katrina? They wouldn't tell us anything."

"She's dead, Ellie."

"I'm all set," Jaworski said, walking to the dike.

"Lily killed her mother?"

I nodded.

"Jesus, Lord," she said, crossed herself, and gazed at the vacant trailer. "I'll keep her place tidy. I don't know why. I feel like I should."

I left Ellie standing in the courtyard and followed Jaworski.

"Where am I going?" he asked.

"Fifty yards, straight ahead," I said. "There's a small wooden cross."

"Feels like I'm in a friggin' horror movie."

"You are."

I SAT CROSS-LEGGED ON THE DIKE, HOLDING THE wooden cross. Jaworski stripped off his jacket.

"You said you've been wrong, Lucas."

"More times than I care to think about."

"I hope this ain't one of 'em," he said, his breathing labored as he shoveled dirt into a pile. "At least the ground's soft."

Minutes later, with sweat dripping down his neck, Jaworski stuck the shovel in the dirt pile and snapped on latex gloves. "It's a plastic garbage bag," he said, kneeling above the hole and brushing away dirt. "This ain't the dog, is it?"

"Pull it out."

He yanked at the bag, dragged it from the hole, and slit it open with his pocketknife. "Aren't you going to look?"

"Notebooks," I said.

"A dozen of them. They're damp and stink of mildew."

"Find the most recent."

Jaworski prowled through the bag, selected and discarded notebooks, and finally settled on one. He was silent as he slowly turned the pages.

"This is incredible," he said, holding up a sketch.

The pencil drawing of Harper Dorman was nearly as detailed as the photographs Norma Jacobs had shown us. Red-brown streaks sliced across the lead-shaded lines.

"I think you'll find that Harper Dorman supplied the pigment."

"It does look like blood. She didn't sit in front of the body and draw this, did she?"

I shrugged. "She has an artist's eye and an archivist's memory. She also has patience, determination, and an unfailing belief in her invulnerability."

Jaworski flipped pages. "Here's one of Markham."

I struggled to my feet. "You've got your evidence," I said.

CHAPTER 43

TWO DAYS LATER, I STOOD IN LILY DORMAN'S DOOR-way at the regional hospital. Dickie Stevens sat at his post reading *The Boston Globe*.

"Ragged Harbor make the big-city newspaper?" I asked.

"They call me Richard in here. I told 'em my name is Dickie."

"She talked at all?"

"When the lawyers go in there, they make me move across the hall. She ain't made a sound that I know of. I swear she ain't alive."

I stepped into the darkened room and brought Stevens up from his chair.

"You can't go in there, Doc," he whispered loudly behind me. "Those lawyers will shit concrete blocks."

"Fuck 'em," I muttered, watching Lily Dorman's wrists strain against the leather straps that held her down.

Gauze bandages concealed most of her face and extended to her neck and right shoulder. Except for the intermittent pressure she exerted on her restraints, she was motionless.

"Go sit down, Dickie," I said. "Let me know if any lawyers show up."

Stevens hesitated. "The chief will have my ass."

"The chief won't know."

After a moment, I heard Stevens return to his post. I stared at the woman who had grown up believing that I was her father, and that I had left her at the mercy of a madman who happened to live with her mother. Lily had nurtured her hatred of me, used it to drive herself to wealth, power, and an elaborate plan of vengeance.

I watched Dorman's mouth move and barely heard her raspy voice. "I can wait," she said.

I did not doubt her fortitude. Maybe I should have left her in the fireplace, I thought, as I turned and walked from the room.

JAWORSKI'S DISPATCHER DIRECTED ME TO THE CHIEF'S office. "He's still upstairs with Mr. Saymes," she said, "but he shouldn't be much longer."

Karen Jasper sat in her corner with her laptop and notebook, translating her copious scribblings into report form. She looked like Linus arched over his piano.

"I still don't like you," she said, glancing over her shoulder.

"It's hard to like insufferable old men," I said as I sat opposite the TV and watched a muted soap opera. "No more live coverage of the front door, huh?"

"Don't talk to me. I'm trying to concentrate."

"I've decided that I do like you, Detective Jasper."

She swiveled in her chair. "I don't want you to like me."

I grinned. "Didn't think so."

"What the hell does that mean?"

I leaned forward. "Conflicts in relationships, collegial

or personal, are most likely to occur when both parties are a bit insufferable."

She spun around to her laptop. "I have work to do."

I gazed at the silent TV. A black-haired man had a permanently raised eyebrow; his opposite eye was frozen half-closed. I thought that he might be trying to look skeptical or suspicious. A blond woman who shared the scene was taller than the man, busty and semi-exposed, with a coy smile suggesting that she controlled the encounter.

When curiosity got the best of me, I lunged out of my chair and turned up the volume.

Black-haired man said, "We can meet them at El Diablo."

Blond woman responded, "I love Mexican food."

"What the hell are you doing?" Jasper snapped.

"Misreading social situations," I said, and killed the volume.

"Jesus. You're as bad as . . ."

Jasper stopped and stared at me. I was certain that she waited to see whether I would complete her sentence. I did not know what her problem with her father was, and I had no interest in finding out.

Jaworski came through the door and relieved the awkwardness. "This just came in," he said, placing a lab report on Jasper's desk.

Jasper scanned the blood analysis form, tucked it at the back of her notebook, and returned to her typing.

"Saymes give you a raise?" I asked.

"Hah. I ain't had cost-of-living the last three years. He gave me this spiel about how we all have to be reasonable. We settled on two years. I had in mind getting out when I turned sixty-seven, so that works."

"You talk to your prosecutor?"

"She doesn't figure she'll do much on Heath. Gilman will walk with probation and a fine. Baker will do serious time. Dorman ain't even talking to her lawyers. It'll be six or eight weeks before they can ship her for a psychiatric evaluation."

"Feds having any success with the money?"

"They wouldn't tell me."

Jasper remained silent.

"When does your class start up again?" Jaworski asked. "A lot of students are already back on the hill."

"No seminar," I said.

"What are you going to do?"

"I'm headed for Boston to spend a few days with my friend Ray Bolton, then I'll be back here to close things off with however many of my students return. After that, Lake Albert."

"When do I get my debriefing?" he asked, in what I now recognized as Jaworski's droll tone of voice.

I laughed. "First thing when I get back."

As I walked to the door, I reached for the lab report that Jasper had stuck in the back of her notebook. She slammed down her hand on the spiral-bound pad.

"Disappointed?" I asked.

She said nothing.

"You ran a comparison on my blood and Lily Dorman's. You were certain that I was her father. You followed your gut, Jasper, and you were thorough. That's admirable. If you were right, you would have shifted some fraction of the guilt from her to me, and felt justified in relegating me to your scrap heap of insufferable old men."

I waited. Jasper remained silent.

"Get over it," I said, and walked out the door.

ABOUT THE AUTHOR

JOHN PHILPIN is a retired forensic psychologist—an internationally renowned profiler. His advice and opinions on violence and its aftermath have been sought by police, newspaper writers, TV producers, mental health professionals, private investigators, attorneys, and polygraph experts throughout the country. He is the author of *Beyond Murder*, the story of the Gainesville student killings, published by NAL/Dutton in 1994, and *Stalemate*, which tells the true-crime story of a series of child abductions, sexual assaults, and murders in the San Francisco Bay Area. Along with Patricia Sierra, he is the author of *The Prettiest Feathers* and *Tunnel of Night*. He lives in New England.